EVERYWHERE SHE TURNS

"*Everywhere She Turns* is romantic suspense at its best."
                                    —Erica Spindler, *New York Times*
                                    bestselling author of *Breakneck*

TRACELESS
A *Cosmopolitan* "Red Hot Read" of the Month

"Skillfully managing a big cast, Webb keeps the suspense teasingly taut, dropping clues and red herrings one after another on her way to a chilling conclusion."   —*Publishers Weekly*

"A steamy, provocative novel with deep, deadly secrets guaranteed to be worthy of your time."   —*Fresh Fiction*

"*Traceless* is a riveting entanglement of intrigue, secrets, and passions that had me racing to its breathless end. I loved this book!"   —Karen Rose, author of *Die for Me*

"*Traceless* is a well-crafted and engrossing thriller. Debra Webb has crafted a fine, twisting thriller to be savored and enjoyed."
                                    —Heather Graham, *New York Times*
                                    bestselling author of *The Dead Room*

"The talented Webb has built a wide fan base that should be thrilled with her vengeful and chilling new tale."
                                    —*Romantic Times BOOKreviews*

"Betrayal, secrets, lies and passion lead to murder in a small town . . . *Traceless* is a breathtaking romantic suspense that grabs the reader from the beginning and doesn't let up. Riveting."
            —*New York Times* bestselling author Allison Brennan

MORE . . .

NAMELESS

"A complex plot and an eerily compelling villain make this fast-paced chiller outstanding reading. Take a deep breath and enjoy!"
—Romantic Times BOOKreviews (4.5 stars)

FACELESS

"Webb's tale reeks of corruption and deadly manipulation—an impressive brew!"
—Romantic Times BOOKreviews

"*Faceless* teased and taunted me until I stayed up all night reading, only to be stunned by the astounding ending. This is a blockbuster thriller screaming to be told in the movie theater, and I'd be the first person in line for a ticket. A perfect 10 you're sure to enjoy!"
—Romance Reviews Today

EVERYWHERE
SHE TURNS

Debra Webb

St. Martin's Paperbacks

EVERYWHERE SHE TURNS

Copyright © 2009 by Debra Webb.
Excerpt from *Anywhere She Runs* copyright © 2009 by Debra Webb.

Cover photographs:
Woman © Shirley Green
Background © Niall McDiarmid/Millennium Images

For information address St. Martin's Press, 175 Fifth Avenue, New York, NY 10010.

ISBN: 0-312-53296-2
EAN: 978-0-312-53296-3

Printed in the United States of America

St. Martin's Paperbacks edition / July 2009

St. Martin's Paperbacks are published by St. Martin's Press, 175 Fifth Avenue, New York, NY 10010.

10 9 8 7 6 5 4 3 2 1

This book was a joy to write, mainly because of three characters in particular, CJ Patterson, Suzanne Parker, and Candice Dobbins.

The character CJ Patterson was inspired by CJ Lyons, a dear friend of mine. The real CJ is not only a medical doctor but a fabulous author of medical thrillers. Be sure to look for her latest release—you will be wowed! Thank you, CJ, for loads and loads of awesome inspiration! And many hours of moral support!

Suzanne Parker and Candice Dobbins—you know who you are. These two characters leapt onto the pages of this story just as two wonderful friends did the same in my life. You give my world that extra spark. Endless fountains of encouragement and tireless cheerleaders. You are the best!

Ladies, this one is for you!

ACKNOWLEDGMENTS

Huntsville, Alabama, is my home. I love living here—loved visiting as a child when I lived on a farm outside Scottsboro. In my opinion, Huntsville is one of the best places to live in the entire South! When I considered making Huntsville the setting of this story, it was an easy decision to go for it. However, in any work of suspense there must be bad guys and sometimes those bad guys must be in positions of power—particularly law enforcement. So please know that all such characters in this story are absolutely fictional. The Huntsville Police Department and Madison County Sheriff's Department serve this community in an outstanding manner. The men and women wearing those uniforms have my utmost respect as do those in political positions and those who are a part of our medical community.

The mill village represented in this story was inspired by the very neighborhood where I live, but bear in mind that I have taken some creative liberties. My family and I are new to the village, but we feel at home already. This village was erected shortly after two of Huntsville's first textile mills were built in 1898. The homes in the village housed the mill workers and their families. A school, medical clinic, general store, and community center were also built for this village. Unfortunately the mill was torn down in the 1980s, and things didn't go so well for the village after that. Many of the lovely old homes fell into disrepair. The medical clinic and school closed. Crime rose dramatically in the area, and things were just plain bad. But a few years ago, families started to purchase the homes and move into the village with the intent of revitalization. My family and I are proud to be a part of that renewal. We are slowly but surely restoring a one-hundred-and-ten-year-old home and doing our part for the community. The work is hard but immensely satisfying. While on the subject of restoration, I must mention that I have discovered a new community jewel—the Habitat Store! And priceless new friends and neighbors, Lisa and Greg Day.

As always, I must acknowledge my truly awesome partner in crime, my husband. He is my rock, my heart . . . my world. He is the reason my dreams continue to come true.

So, read on and enjoy! And don't forget to visit my website, *www.debrawebb.com*

CHAPTER ONE

Huntsville, Alabama
Saturday, July 31, 3:30 AM

Women.

Bitches. Most every fucking one of them.

The world was about to be rid of one more stupid bitch.

All he had to do was catch her.

Mirth burst from his chest as she darted from the alley, plunging into the dark cover of the woods in a last-ditch effort to save herself.

Did she really think she could escape him that easily?

Stupid, stupid bitch.

Not in this life.

In this life, he was the killer. And she . . . well, she was the victim.

The only decision that remained was the manner of death.

Slice open her silky white throat?

No. Too clichéd.

The memorable mark of a truly magnificent killer was at its core quite simple: *originality.*

He allowed her a few precious seconds. Just enough to provide a fleeting glimmer of hope. Then he charged into the dark, dense woods, using the trampled underbrush she'd left in her wake as his path.

She should just face the one undeniable fact close enough for her to feel its hot brush on the nape of her fragile neck.

She was dead.

Within the hour her heart would slow to a complete stop. Heat would begin to seep from her flesh, and the final image captured on her retinas would fade to black.

His face would be that last image.

At that trauma-filled moment, when her brain released the massive dump of endorphins that gifted the dying with an eerie calm as their entire pathetic lives flashed like a bad movie trailer through their impotent minds, she would recognize her one fatal mistake.

She shouldn't have gotten in the way.

Bravado, curiosity . . . whatever it was that had made her dare to step out of her place, it had been just another bad choice in a long line of bad choices littering an insignificant existence mere minutes from being over.

Even now, as he grew nearer and nearer, so shockingly near he could hear the humid air raging in and out of her desperate lungs . . . could feel the sheer terror throttling through her veins . . . she still couldn't help herself.

She had to glance back. To see the truth that had been right in front of her for the duration of her short life.

He smiled.

This was going to be most satisfying.

CHAPTER TWO

Johns Hopkins Hospital
Baltimore, Maryland
10:30 PM

Dr. CJ Patterson fished in her purse for her keys as she neared her ancient Civic. In twenty-three minutes she would be home; five minutes after that she would be out of these scrubs and soaking in a tub full of hot, steamy water with an open bottle of chilled Saracco uncorked and parked within reach.

Forty-two patients in fourteen hours.

A twelve-car pileup on Interstate 695 had kept the ER buzzing for the final three hours of her too-long shift. Half a dozen cops were still attempting to interview the victims capable of answering questions.

"Just another Saturday night in Charm City." She reached for the door, but something she saw out of the corner of her eye snagged her attention. "Oh, damn."

Flat tire.

The second one this week. CJ heaved a disgusted breath. She had to get new tires.

Another reality hit on the heels of that one. She slapped her forehead with the heel of her hand. "Double damn."

Who'd had time to get the other flat tire repaired? Certainly not a third-year resident who worked ten or more hours most days and who spent the rest of her time studying for boards.

Damn. Damn. Damn. Plowing her fingers through her hair,

she pulled her ponytail free, glanced around the gloomy parking garage, and considered her options. Getting someone here to repair one or both tires would take hours on a Saturday night.

"Forget it." She did an about-face and headed for the nearest exit. There was always a cab or two waiting within hailing distance of the ER entrance on East Monument Street. She'd get a ride home and deal with this in the morning when she'd had some sleep. Tomorrow was her first day off in two weeks. Too bad it was Sunday, because she had a million things to take care of and the business world of nine-to-fivers had no appreciation for her frenzied schedule.

She pushed through the north exit of the staff parking garage into the muggy night air. Someday, when she had money, she might actually have a decent ride. One with good tires. And reliable air-conditioning.

Such was the life of a medical resident—every aspect of one's personal life was about the future.

Sweat had dampened her skin by the time she reached East Monument. At the ER's street entrance she stopped and stepped back from the curb before an arriving ambulance mowed her down. Lights and sirens, not good. Hard as she tried not to linger, her efforts were futile. Two of her colleagues rushed out to connect with the emerging paramedics and the patient strapped to the gurney.

CJ forced her attention back to the taxi a block or so beyond the ER's drop-off point. The arriving patient was in good hands. CJ's shift was over.

She had to learn that even the most committed physician needed boundaries. She couldn't save the world alone. Especially without sleep.

At the passenger side of the taxi, CJ opened the rear door and gave her home address to the driver. She collapsed into the seat, tossed her purse aside, and snapped her safety belt into place. Blessed relief hissed past her lips.

Finally.

"Tough night?" The driver lowered the volume of the jazz radiating from the taxi's speakers as he rolled out onto the deserted street.

"Long, long night," CJ explained. But that was the reality of choosing a career in emergency medicine. The ER was not the place for those who preferred banking hours and neatly scheduled appointments. Strange. Maybe the reason she loved the adrenaline-charged life of an ER physician was related to her drama-filled childhood. Wasn't all that one did connected to the environment of the formative years?

Obviously she'd been lunching with the psych residents way too much.

The driver had his own theories about tonight's chaos. He offered a lengthy discourse of how the full moon always made the crazies come out. CJ didn't bother telling him just how right he was.

The full moon—

Tires squealed. Metal crashed. CJ's head jerked, then banged the window as the taxi absorbed the momentum of an oncoming car crossing the intersection against the light.

For an endless, paralyzing moment there was no movement, no sound, other than the murmur of the jazz still whispering from the speakers.

"Son of a bitch!" The driver whacked his fist against the dash.

CJ shook off the shock, released the safety belt and rubbed at the dull ache in her right temple. The other car had broadsided the taxi. Both vehicles now sat in the middle of the intersection, steam rising from the hood of the offending vehicle.

Swearing profusely, the driver scrambled across the seat and out the passenger-side door.

CJ shoved that hot bath out of her mind for the moment and flung her door open. She caught up with the furious taxi driver as he confronted the driver of the other car.

"You didn't see the light? What are you? Blind?"

CJ looked from the dazed driver climbing from behind the steering wheel to the passenger emerging from the backseat. "You two okay?" Both occupants were male. Caucasian. Young, twenty, twenty-one.

"We gotta get to the hospital," the passenger shouted at no one in particular. He turned all the way around, staggering drunkenly, as if he needed to get his bearings.

An instant mental inventory of causes for his imbalance, from illegal substances to head injuries, quickened CJ's pulse. "Call nine-one-one," she instructed the taxi driver, who was still cursing and stomping his feet.

"Is either of you having difficulty breathing? In pain? Lightheaded? Nauseous?" Moving toward the passenger, CJ visually assessed the car's driver, who looked a little dazed and confused, as if he wasn't sure if this was real or just a bad dream. No apparent injuries. "Any head or neck pain?"

The passenger wore a black Bob Marley T-shirt. Now that she was closer, CJ could see that the T-shirt and his hands were as bloody as hell. Her pulse quickened. His inability to regain his equilibrium persisted.

"Is he calling the cops?"

CJ ignored the driver's question. "Where'd the blood come from?" she asked the Bob Marley fan, who appeared focused on her blue scrubs. No visible signs of injury. Eyes were glassy. His long dark hair was stringy but not wet or sticky. Where the hell had the blood come from?

"My brother." He grabbed her arm, tugged her around the open passenger door. "He needs help."

There was another passenger?

CJ pushed the guy aside and maneuvered her way into the backseat.

Damn.

Blood. Lots of blood.

Third passenger was a kid, not more than nine or ten. His pajama top was saturated in crimson. She tugged the top up and out of the way to get a look at his torso. He didn't flinch. Didn't moan.

Penetrating chest wound.

Shit.

She needed more light. Bracing her hand on the seat, she leaned closer. Something wet oozed up between her fingers. Blood. *Shit. Shit. Shit.* The seat . . . She checked the knees of her scrubs, the damned floorboard—blood was everywhere.

Instinct kicked in and training overrode emotion.

Patient had no other visible injuries.

Not breathing.

Oh, hell.

No pulse.

Adrenaline detonated in CJ's veins, sharpening her senses. "Help me get him out of here!"

The older brother stuck his upper body into the car. "What?"

"You and your friend," CJ commanded, "help me get him out of the car and on the ground. Hurry!"

The two men scrambled into unsteady action. CJ cradled the boy's head and neck as the brother and his friend lifted him out of the backseat.

"Put him down over there." She jerked her head toward the front of the taxi. The headlights would help her see what she was doing. Streetlights weren't enough.

"You! Taxi guy!" CJ shouted at the man still on his cell phone. He stopped explaining their circumstances and stared at her in question. "Tell them I need an ALS unit. We have full trauma arrest." She turned back to the boy. The battle was very nearly over. "Tell them to hurry!"

"You can help him, right?" The older brother dropped to his knees on the pavement next to her.

"We have to control the bleeding." CJ needed this guy focused on his little brother, not distracting her.

"You know what this means?" his friend yelled as he paced back and forth in the middle of the street. "The cops are coming. We gotta get outta here."

"Shut up!" the brother screamed.

"Give me your hand." CJ reached out to him. His eyes were wild with fear and whatever had him buzzed. His hand shook as she gripped his wrist and covered the wound with his palm. "Keep pressure there. It slows the bleeding."

Not that this kid had much left to leak.

CJ started chest compressions.

"They'll take us to fucking jail," the friend railed. "I ain't going to jail. This is your fault, not mine!"

"I said," the brother warned, "shut the fuck up."

CJ tuned out the heated exchange. Focused on keeping the

boy's heart pumping. She had no idea how long he'd been in full arrest, but he didn't have a chance in hell of surviving if—

Blood seeped from beneath the kid's left shoulder, spreading ominously over the pavement.

Shit.

She stopped the compressions.

"What're you doing?" the brother demanded. "Keep . . ." He motioned with his free hand. "Doing whatever. That's what you're supposed to do, right?"

CJ didn't answer. She carefully rolled her patient onto his right side. Her breath fisted in her throat, refused to fill her lungs.

Exit wound: left scapula. Major blood vessels, the heart . . . all lay smack in the middle of the path the bullet had taken. The puddle of blood on the pavement indicated that every chest compression she'd executed had sent more of what little blood remained in his slim body out that exit wound.

"Do something!" the brother wailed.

Where the hell was that ambulance? "Did you tell them to hurry?" CJ shouted to the taxi driver.

He nodded frantically. "They're coming! They're coming!"

"Help him, goddammit!" the brother shouted in her face.

CJ flinched but kept her focus on the kid. She lowered him onto his back. "We need pressure on that wound!"

The brother obeyed the order and she resumed chest compressions. The kid would likely die anyway, but he would damned sure die if she didn't try.

Just hang in there, kid.

"Don't you get it?" the brother's paranoid friend yelled. "The kid's dead. Nobody loses that much blood and lives. She's only doing that"—he waved wildly at CJ with both hands—"to keep you from freaking out. The kid's fucking dead, man."

Big brother shot to his feet. "If you don't shut—"

"Gun!" the taxi driver screamed. "He's got a gun!"

Don't listen. Don't look. Focus.

The distant shrill of sirens accompanied the screaming between the three men.

"Tell him," the friend shrieked at CJ, "that you can't save the kid!"

"Is that true?"

She ignored the brother's demand. Mentally marked the necessary rhythm.

He stuck his face close to hers. *"Is that true?"* he screamed in her ear.

"I'm doing all I can," CJ admitted without looking up. She braced for his reaction but didn't stop the only option she had available to help the patient.

"If he dies," the brother warned, "you die." He jammed the gun in her face.

Fear bumped against her sternum.

Ignore the fucking gun! Pump, pump, pump.

The sirens grew louder and louder. *Nearly here. Thank God.* Her shoulders and wrists were tired, aching. *Keep pumping!*

The friend started backing away. "I'm out of here. I'm not going to jail."

A police cruiser skidded to a stop on the other side of the taxi and the low-life driver took off.

"He's running!" the taxi guy bellowed to anyone listening. "The driver is running. Stop him!"

Pump, pump, pump.

"Drop your weapon!" *Cop.*

The unloading paramedics were shouting questions at CJ. "Full arrest," she called back. "Deep penetrating entrance wound midtorso. Exit wound left scapula. Massive blood loss." *Get that advanced life support unit over here!*

"Drop your weapon!" the cop repeated.

"He's only nine years old," the brother pleaded, his words directed at CJ and barely audible amid all the shouting. "You can't let him die."

CJ couldn't help herself. She lifted her gaze to his. No matter that the gun was still pointed at her, there was nothing reassuring she could say. The resignation that claimed the brother's posture and his eyes warned of his intent a split second before he acted.

There was no time to react.

The explosion from the gun shattered the night.

CHAPTER THREE

CJ swiped at her damp cheeks with the backs of her hands. She stared at her fingers . . . her palms. Blood. So much blood. Her hands trembled.

The man had turned the gun on himself and fired.

Right in front of her.

She pushed away from the closed bathroom door and dared to look in the mirror hanging over the sink.

Dark circles underscored her eyes. Her hair was a wreck. Probably full of tissue fragments. Blood splatter from the older brother had trickled and soaked into her scrub top, leaving a trail of crimson tears to join the swath of the younger brother's blood across the hem of her top.

She ripped off the top, flung it to the floor. The legs of her scrub pants . . . her knees . . . she was covered in blood.

Desperation rising in her throat, she rinsed her hands, pumped frantically at the soap dispenser, then scrubbed and scrubbed and scrubbed.

Over and over she washed her face, hands, and arms until her skin felt raw.

She stared at her reflection in the mirror.

Her lips quivered. "Hold it together." Her body shuddered as if to defy her command.

The image of the boy lying on the pavement, his older brother crumpled in a motionless heap next to him, would not be erased. She squeezed her eyes shut again and again. The picture just kept reappearing.

The runaway driver had been captured scarcely a block away. He'd spilled his guts. He and his deceased friend had been drinking heavily all evening when they were supposed to be babysitting. A beer run had left the older brother's new toy, a Beretta 9 millimeter, unattended at the house with the kid, who was supposed to be asleep.

Now the mother had two dead sons.

She didn't even know yet. The cops hadn't been able to track down her place of employment.

CJ swayed, sagged against the wall, and slowly slid down to the floor.

Closing her eyes, she let the sobs erupt.

It wasn't like she hadn't lost patients before, patients she'd been fighting to save with every ounce of knowledge and skill she possessed. The kid had pretty much bled out before he got to her. It wasn't her fault.

The older brother couldn't live with the guilt.

A no-win situation for all involved.

The cell phone on CJ's hip vibrated.

She ignored it.

Calls at this time of night were either work, and she was at work, or Shelley.

She couldn't deal with her sister's problems right now.

Maybe that was selfish, but CJ had spent the better part of her life picking up the pieces for Shelley and, before that, for their mother. These days, on the rare occasions when CJ bothered to go home for a visit, she stumbled over her sister's self-inflicted misfortunes and the resulting disasters everywhere she turned.

Right now CJ didn't care what her sister needed. She didn't possess the energy to care. There was nothing left inside her except utter exhaustion and regret.

The insistent tremor against her waist warned that the caller wasn't giving up.

I am not answering.

She'd ignored Shelley's call the night before. It hadn't been easy. Definitely out of character for CJ. But she'd done it. Shelley had obviously conveniently forgotten that their last conversation had resulted in their worst argument to date. Shelley had told CJ in no uncertain terms to stay out of her life. CJ had done just that. Her sister couldn't have it both ways.

When her cell shook with a third attempt to get her attention, CJ couldn't hold out any longer.

"Dammit, Shelley." CJ snatched the phone from its holster. She read the number on the screen. Huntsville area code and prefix. Not her sister's number.

CJ opened her phone and tucked it against her ear. "Patter—" She cleared her throat. "Patterson."

"CJ?"

A frown tugged at her throbbing forehead, then recognition flared. "Braddock?" Why the hell would he be calling her? CJ was reasonably sure she'd made herself very clear the last time she and the detective had spoken. If Shelley was in trouble again, CJ didn't want to hear about it. And she damned sure didn't want to hear from him under any circumstances.

"I hate like hell to have to make this call."

What was he talking about? Where was the cocky tone he typically used with her? The slow-motion replay of the anguished older brother firing that weapon, sending a significant portion of his scalp, skull, and brain spraying through the night air, reeled before her eyes even as realization unfolded in her weary mind. Dread kinked into a thousand screaming knots in her gut.

Taking her silence for the shock and uncertainty it was, Braddock went on, "CJ, I am so sorry to have to inform you . . . Shelley's dead."

CHAPTER FOUR

Huntsville
2:00 PM

CJ shoved the gearshift into park, turned off the ignition, and stared at the two-story house she'd called home for most of her life.

The entire structure leaned to one side as if it were weary of standing this last hundred or so years. What little cheap green paint that remained on the century-old wood siding was faded and peeling. The numerous patch jobs on the once-white roof were so old they had blended into a dirty variation of grays and blacks. Gutters sagged, their downspouts dented and dangling precariously. The grass stood high enough that passersby likely thought the place was deserted.

And it was . . . now.

Her sister was dead.

Emotion abruptly resurrected and churned deep inside CJ. She lifted her chin in defiance and, just as suddenly, it settled back into that numbness that had consumed her since receiving Braddock's call.

In half an hour she would identify the body.

The body.

Not just a body . . . her sister. The only family CJ had left.

The connecting flight from Atlanta had arrived in Huntsville a few minutes early. So she'd come here as if doing so would change the outcome of what surely was a bad dream. She'd get out of her rented car, go inside, and discover the call had been a terrible mistake.

Shelley couldn't be dead.

Climbing out of the rental, CJ remembered to grab her purse and lock the doors. In this neighborhood she'd be lucky if the hubcaps were still on the wheels ten minutes from now.

Oppressive humidity immediately closed in around her.

Home sweet home.

What had once been a white picket fence surrounded the overgrown yard. The rickety, lopsided gate creaked when she opened it. She'd meant to do something about that the last time she was here. But she hadn't stayed long enough to tackle anything on the ever-growing "big sister" list she mentally maintained.

Just go away, CJ! I don't need you interfering in my life!

You never change, Shelley. It's the same stupid mistakes every time I come back here. You're hopeless.

CJ closed her eyes and banished the voices. She took a deep breath and forced back the tears. Blinked and focused on the house that had never felt like home. That hadn't once provided the safe haven most people associated with their childhoods. Other voices, from that dysfunctional time in her life, attempted to strong-arm their way into her head, but she exiled those as well.

A dog barked somewhere down the block. Otherwise the mill village was uncharacteristically quiet for a Sunday afternoon. Too hot to get out and move around, forget about working up the energy to make noise. But that would change come dark. All sorts of activities would go on then . . . few pleasant and even fewer legal.

Basically nothing had changed.

It never did. Not around here.

At the door CJ reached for the knob; her hand shook.

No more rushing to Huntsville to get her sister out of one jam or another.

No more sending money.

No more screaming at each other.

No more tearful hugs and promises to do better.

Shelley was dead.

Deep breath. *Get it over with.* CJ twisted the knob. The door opened. God, why didn't that girl ever lock the door? Anyone could just walk in.

The too-familiar smell tugged at her senses as she stepped inside. Stale cigarettes and cheap perfume. Her sister's signature scent.

Memories whispered, tugged at her emotions. Her father coming home drunk and slamming the door, then kicking anything that got in his way. Her mother passed out on the kitchen floor, while the dinner she'd started burned on the stove. And Shelley hiding behind the door of their room upstairs, playing with her favorite doll.

Come play with me, CJ. Mommy's sick again.

CJ pushed aside the memories and reached for the switch next to the door. The single working bulb in the overhead fixture made a pathetic attempt at chasing away the darkness. The windows were covered with shades that had once been white, but years of nicotine-infused air had stained them an ugly shade of yellow.

Stunning, uncharacteristic silence echoed the emptiness.

It felt weird being in this house without the television blaring. Her whole life that had been the one constant. Some insignificant channel advertising products they couldn't afford to buy or broadcasting a life they would never live. An open portal to the fantasy that would never be.

CJ pushed a couple of empty beer cans aside and sat down on the battered coffee table. She stared at the tired sofa with its faded flowers and broken-down frame. The cushion where Shelley always curled up had a permanent indentation that marked her spot. CJ reached out, smoothed her hand over the tattered upholstery.

How had she let this happen?

She should have answered her sister's call night before last. Two AM the call had come. CJ had just gotten to sleep after a twelve-hour shift. Absolute mental and physical exhaustion had rendered the decision easy to make.

She'd known how it would go if she had answered. Shelley would be drunk or high. She'd cry about her wretched life with its endless cycle of failed attempts at change. Then she would beg CJ to help her, big sis would electronically transfer money, and all would be right in Shelley's world once more.

But CJ hadn't reacted the way she usually did this time.

She pulled out her cell phone and played the voice mail she hadn't bothered to listen to until after Braddock's call.

"CJ! Oh, God, you're not going to believe this! Okay, wait . . . don't worry! It's not like you think. I know it's two in the morning, but I'm clean. Six weeks and counting. No drugs. No bullshit." She squealed! "You need to call me. I have something really, really important to tell you." She sighed, the sound steeped in happiness. "I know I've never been good at anything. I've been nothing but trouble. But I promise it's gonna be different now. You'll see. Call me! Hey . . ." There was an extended pause, then, "I don't say it enough, but . . . I love you."

CJ had made a terrible, terrible mistake. Her eyes closed to contain the brimming emotion. She'd thought standing firm was the right thing to do. For years her one trusted confidant had been telling CJ that she had to stop enabling her sister's destructive behavior.

Now her sister was dead. *Murdered.*

CJ greatly appreciated the overwhelming numbness that allowed only intermittent bouts of the emotional storm she knew was coming. It wouldn't last. Reality would sink in and she would have to deal with the ramifications of her decision not to answer that call. She recognized the aura of denial. She'd seen it on hundreds of faces in the ER.

But maybe the numbness would get her through the next couple of hours.

Right now, she pushed to her feet; she had to identify her sister's body. And face the fact that she'd failed the one person who'd counted on her to always be there.

CJ walked out the door, closed and locked it behind her.

She stalled on the porch, surveyed the run-down neighborhood. Her whole life she couldn't wait to get away from this dead-end place. She had dreamed of escaping to something better . . . to something that mattered. Now there was no reason for her to ever come back.

Funny. While dreaming of and planning that grand escape, she'd never once considered the price.

Now she knew.

CHAPTER FIVE

"She's here."

He'd expected her sooner. Must've been hell getting a flight out of Baltimore on short notice.

His gaze cut from the foot soldier who'd reported the arrival to the window overlooking all that belonged to him. He reached up, traced the scar on his right cheek. Winced as if the knife blade had only just now sliced open his flesh. Fury roared inside him.

He had a news flash for that snobby doctor bitch. She'd better watch her step. He hadn't forgotten what she'd done to him. Thirteen years or thirty, she would get what was coming to her if she got in his way.

"What you want me to do?"

"Watch her." He braced his hands on either side of the window and leaned closer to scan the rows of streets that made up the mill village. *His* village. "I want to know where that bitch goes and who she talks to. She might think she's coming back here and gonna do some superhero shit, but she better think twice."

"What about the cops? You know she'll talk to Braddock."

Fuck the po-po. And fuck Braddock. He shoulda learned his lesson already. "Course she'll talk to the cops." He knew what

Braddock was up to. Maybe the law round here thought he was born yesterday and got this big today, but they were bad wrong. "They don't know nothing. Ain't a one of 'em can find his dick with both hands."

"Be hard to get close with the cops watching her."

He laughed. Was that fear he heard? "That's right." He faced his loyal foot soldier. Bent his head so he could look at the fool over his Locs. "But the cops ain't your problem." He bumped his chest with his fist. "The *King* is your problem. I'm the only one you need to be worried about."

The fool rocked his head up and down like he was having some kinda fit. Probably shit hisself.

"Now go on and do what I told you."

The man he called his "eyes" didn't waste no time. He got the hell out.

That was the only way to maintain loyalty.

Demand it.

He turned back to his favorite view. This shit was over.

Braddock had a hard-on for the King. Maybe he wanted to be chief or something. Whatever. That motherfucker had picked the wrong war.

And that doctor bitch, she'd be tits up with her fucking sister if she didn't watch herself.

Maybe she would anyway. She'd had it coming for a long time.

Too long.

CHAPTER SIX

2:30 PM

CJ made the right turn off Arcadia Circle into the parking lot of the Forensic Sciences building. The new two-story redbrick structure stood in the center of the divided parking area with only the few contractor-planted trees surrounded by ornamental grass as landscaping. When CJ had lived here the autopsies had been done in Birmingham or Montgomery. Some things, it seemed, had changed.

As promised, Braddock was waiting. With his neatly pressed khakis, navy polo, and expensive, hand-crafted leather shoes, he could have just left the golf course after a few holes with his buddies. Or gotten out of the informal service at the big Methodist Church on Whitesburg where the thirtysomethings gathered to see and be seen. But Braddock didn't play golf or go to church. No. The well-educated and highly polished major-crimes detective spent all his time making sure justice was served.

On his terms.

Regardless of the cost to others.

A burst of outrage tightened the muscles of her face. She should appreciate that any member of Huntsville's Police Department had shown up at all . . . but she didn't. She didn't trust the motive or the man. He wasn't here because he cared. There had to be something in it for him or his reputation.

CJ shut off the engine and pushed away the anger. She exhaled a weary sound. All she had to do was get through the next few minutes.

Then she never had to see Braddock again.

She got out of the rental. Braddock pushed away from his snazzy sports car and strode in her direction. His eyes were shielded by designer sunglasses. She couldn't recall offhand the brand, but she'd seen the hotshot surgeons around the hospital sporting similar ones. Nothing was too good for the self-important detective.

"CJ." He paused a solid eighteen inches of asphalt away. She'd ordered him out of her personal space enough times that he'd apparently finally gotten the message.

Still, the subtle scent of his familiar cologne and the masculine strength of his tall frame seeped into her senses. Reminded her of those few evenings they'd shared. Dinner and conversation. He'd said all the right things . . . made her yearn for more. Made her actually rethink the prospect of a real relationship in her life.

Good thing she'd gotten that painful wake-up call in the nick of time.

She stared at him now, too numb to feel the anger the mere mention of his name usually generated. That he didn't bother removing his eyewear was irrelevant. She knew how brown his eyes were. Intensely dark, completely unreadable, and entirely too observant.

And completely capable of deceit.

She adjusted the strap of the bag dragging at her shoulder. "Braddock."

His hands slid into his trouser pockets as if to ensure he didn't make the mistake of reaching out to her. "I know this is difficult. Like I said on the phone, you don't have to do this part—"

"I'm a doctor, Braddock." She shoved the car door closed and squared her shoulders. "Bodies are an integral element of what I do every day. I've seen my share of mutilation, assault, and more degrees of decomposition than I care to list. So let's just get this done." Her lips compressed into a hard but shaky line. She didn't want Braddock or anyone else identifying her sister. CJ needed to do this herself. *Be strong. Go through the steps. Don't think.*

Braddock studied her a moment. Did he think she should be crying on his shoulder? He just didn't know. She had been through this before with her mom. She'd always done what she had to do; she would do it now. Taking care of Shelley was her responsibility.

Too bad she'd failed so miserably.

Don't think. Just do it.

"All right, then." Braddock gestured to the side entrance. "The ME is waiting. I had to pull some major strings to make this happen."

Though she couldn't care less what hoops he'd had to jump through, she nodded. Followed as he led the way. She quickened her pace to keep up with his long strides. He wasn't carrying a weapon today. Maybe even he conceded to the Lord's Day on some level. His badge and cell phone were clipped to his belt. No matter that she wanted nothing to do with him; he was her only link to what had happened to her sister. There were questions she wanted to ask, details she needed to understand, but those could wait a few minutes.

Right now, she wanted this over.

She'd managed to pull off the whole I'm-a-professional-I-can-take-it attitude so far, but with the way her insides were quaking, that wasn't going to last long.

The heat index had to be well over a hundred, turning the city's miles and miles of concrete and asphalt into a highly efficient oven. Her blouse and slacks were stuck to her skin. Her hair was plastered to the back of her neck.

God, she hated this place.

Inside the lobby, the climate-controlled air chilled her sweat-dampened skin, making her shiver. Braddock acknowledged the security guard at the reception desk with a nod, then pointed to the double doors marked PERSONNEL ONLY. The guard responded with a two-fingered salute and the doors started their slow swing inward.

The fact that CJ had known for a long time that this moment was a strong probability considering her sister's lifestyle failed to diminish how much it hurt. How badly she wanted this to be a misunderstanding. Why couldn't it be like in the movies? She would stare down at the body and find that it wasn't Shelley.

But that wouldn't happen. Braddock was here.

Beyond those double doors a long white center corridor led to what CJ presumed were laboratories, autopsy rooms, and cold storage units. The too-familiar smells assaulted her. No matter how new or high-tech the facility, there was no perfected method to disguise the overpowering scent of preservative chemicals and refrigerated flesh.

A lump rose in her throat.

Her sister was in there . . . in one of those poly bags inside a deep metal drawer.

Focus on the steps.

A woman, blond hair, tall, buxom, stepped into the corridor. "Detective Braddock," she said with a smile, then turned her attention to CJ. "Ms. Patterson."

"Dr. Patterson," Braddock said, circuitously correcting the woman, "this is Medical Examiner Candice Dobbins."

"Dr. Dobbins." CJ extended her hand.

"*Dr.* Patterson." Dobbins cast a self-conscious glance at CJ, then gestured to the door across the hall. "This way."

Dobbins entered storage unit two. She paused long enough to pull on latex gloves, offered a pair to CJ. "We don't generally allow family members back here, but Detective Braddock insisted."

"Thank you." As she tugged the latex into place, CJ's heart started that desperate pounding despite her best efforts to keep the rate measured and steady. She consciously adjusted her respiration to a slower, deeper pattern in hopes of heading off another adrenaline dump.

Wasn't working.

Dobbins pulled a chart, then selected drawer nine. The glide of metal on metal hissed as she hauled open the long shelf.

Pulse thumping, CJ moved to one side of the extended drawer unit. She stared at the white body bag as if this was her first time seeing one, as if she were watching herself do this rather than actually doing it.

"She's scheduled for autopsy the end of the week," Dobbins explained. "If I can get to her sooner, I will. Preliminary tox screen showed no suspicious compounds or illegal substances."

Startled from the surrealism, CJ's gaze met the ME's. "No drugs?" Shelley had said she was clean in her voice mail, but CJ had assumed that she had lied yet again.

Dobbins shook her head. "No drugs." She flipped through the chart and continued. "At Detective Braddock's request I performed a priority tox screen and a brief visual assessment as soon as she arrived."

Shelley had told her the truth. For once.

The bottom fell out of CJ's stomach. Her head started to spin with emotions she couldn't afford to feel right now.

"There is," Dobbins said as she prepared to open the bag, "evidence of past physical trauma, bruises from several days to more than a week old, as well as abrasions, scratches, and bruising as recent as a few hours before death."

CJ managed a nod. "Her ex-boyfriend beat her up pretty badly just over a month ago." The bastard. CJ would bet anything he had done this. She turned to Braddock. "Have you arrested Ricky Banks?" If Braddock hadn't taken that step already, he was a bigger fool than she'd thought. "You know what he did to her on a regular basis." Banks's mistreatment of Shelley went back more than a decade. "It's a miracle this didn't happen before now."

"I'm well aware of Shelley's relationship with Banks," Braddock confirmed. "He's at the top of our suspect list."

He'd removed the sunglasses. She tried to read what she saw in his eyes, couldn't. That he shifted his attention away from her scrutiny too quickly suggested there was more he had no intention of sharing.

The outrage that always accompanied any time she spent in his presence stirred. "I want all the details, Braddock."

He shared a look with Dobbins. CJ's anxiety level skyrocketed. Why didn't he just give her the facts he had? On the flight here, she'd compiled a mental list of questions she needed to ask. Between arranging that flight and clearing her schedule at the hospital, she'd had her hands full until she'd collapsed into the seat on the plane.

"You're aware," he began, choosing his words so carefully that she couldn't possibly miss the tactic, "that there's a lot we won't know until the autopsy is complete."

That part she got. The outrage shifted into all-out fury. "But there are things you do know, like who found her? Where was she? What were the circumstances?" *Breathe.* Her mind kept telling her to look down, to just look at Shelley, but she couldn't. Not and hold it together.

"There are things we don't fully understand just yet," he confessed. "It's complicated. In the best interest of the investigation, we're not prepared to release certain details at this time."

"Are you refusing to tell me anything at all?" Could he do that? More of that anxiety and outrage coiled inside her. She needed to know, to understand how this had happened.

"I'll give you what I can." Reluctance and frustration presented itself in his posture, on his face. "She was found in the woods on the west side of the intersection of Triana and Johnson. A couple of kids stumbled upon the scene just before dark on Saturday evening. A nylon rope had been used to hang her . . . by the neck. There was drug paraphernalia. But as Dr. Dobbins said, none in her blood."

The image of Shelley hanging from a tree in those woods invaded CJ's mind.

Well before becoming a doctor, CJ had been intimately familiar with murder. She'd grown up in a neighborhood where the occasional murder and the frequent robberies and assaults were more often than not a part of the norm. Her own father had been murdered. But this wasn't the guy down the street . . . or the bastard of a father who'd slapped their mother around and terrorized his own children.

This was Shelley. Her *baby sister.*

CJ didn't wait for Dobbins. She reached down, carefully opened the bag. Her heart sank.

She stared at her sister's ashen skin. Long honey-blond hair lay behind her head like a silk sheet. Her blue eyes, the same deep, deep blue both she and CJ had inherited from their mother, were closed in death. Her slender throat was bruised and bore angry ligature marks. There was an abrasion on her left cheek. Bruising on her upper arms as if someone had grabbed her and maybe shaken her. CJ's chest tightened in agony. She should have been here . . . shouldn't have let this happen.

She lifted her gaze to the ME's. "Did you find anything else?"

"Minor scrapes and tiny tissue tears along her shins and thighs, possibly indicating that she may have been running through the underbrush in the wooded area where her body was discovered."

Running. Fury bolted through CJ. "Have you even questioned Banks yet?" She glared at Braddock, wanted him to see the accusation in her eyes. He'd said Banks was on his suspect list, but that told her nothing. "You have to know he did this."

"We're still working on tracking him down."

Was he kidding? That he remained totally calm and utterly rational made her want to scream. He wouldn't be so damned unfazed if the victim had been a resident of the Twickenham District or the Ledges.

"Until we've confirmed cause of death, reviewed any evidence—"

"Banks has always been a bully." Who did Braddock think he was talking to? CJ had known Banks since he was a snot-nosed kid. "I can't even tell you the number of times he's roughed her up. Long before you showed interest in her life," she added pointedly. "I can see him chasing her down like an animal and then humiliating her by leaving the drug paraphernalia." Sick bastard.

"CJ"—Braddock used that tone, the one a parent uses when gently scolding a child—"there are certain ordered steps in any investigation. Rest assured—"

"That bastard killed her." CJ peeled off the gloves. "His arrest is the only step I care about." With a final, aching look at Shelley, CJ promised to make sure Banks paid.

She was finished here. "Thank you, Dr. Dobbins." CJ headed for the exit, tossing her gloves in the receptacle near the door. She would find Banks and she would make him tell the truth. He'd lived in the mill village his whole life. Finding him shouldn't be that difficult.

"CJ," Braddock called after her.

She didn't turn around or slow her departure. She had nothing else to say to him. Unfortunately, she understood all too well how this investigation would go—the same way it had gone when her father was shot dead on the sidewalk in front of their house. The same way it went when her mother died of what was labeled an accidental overdose. No one would really investigate the case. Just another dead lowlife from the village.

Good riddance.

Braddock caught up with her in the corridor and fell into step beside her. "I will find and arrest the person responsible for this. But to do that, I need the autopsy results and evidence. Right now we don't have either."

CJ stopped and turned to glare at him. "There's no evidence? What about fingerprints? Hairs? Fibers? You haven't found anything?"

The resignation on his face gave her the answer even before he spoke. "Unless the body gives us something, we have nothing. No prints, no trace evidence from the scene at all. We're in the process of a third sweep. We could get lucky. But I've never relied on luck to close a case."

This was insane! "Wait." CJ should have thought to ask this already. "How long had she . . . been there before she was found?"

"It's been hot as hell. That escalates things. And, like I said, it rained before her body was discovered."

CJ held up both hands for him to stop overexplaining. "Just give me the preliminary estimate."

"Ten to twelve hours, possibly longer."

CJ had gotten the call from Shelley around two Saturday morning. That meant her sister had been murdered later that morning—well before noon if the preliminary estimate of time of death was accurate.

She should have taken that call. Should have called Shelley back.

Those mental walls she had used to keep her emotions in check shrank around her now, making it impossible to breathe.

CJ couldn't talk about this anymore. Braddock was saying something to her, but she couldn't listen.

Not right now.

Right now full-on reality was throttling through her.

Her sister was dead.

The bastard responsible was out there . . . getting away with it.

CHAPTER SEVEN

3:30 PM

Braddock guided his Pontiac G6 onto the shoulder of the road. The strip of Triana Boulevard that ran between Johnson Road and Redstone Arsenal was deserted except for the white forensics van.

He sat there, his hands braced on the steering wheel, his gaze focused on the woods. Images from another wooded area . . . the river . . . another murder flashed one after the other through his mind. Female . . . only nineteen years old.

His fingers tightened on the wheel and his palms started to sweat.

No one fucks with me.

He closed his eyes, exiled the painful visions.

Don't look back . . . focus on the case. His jaw tightened. Shelley deserved his undivided attention. He had to do this right for her and for CJ—no matter that she hated him now.

With one last glance at the street, he emerged from his vehicle. *Don't let the emotions get in the way.*

All he needed was one piece of evidence to connect this homicide to the bastard he wanted more than he wanted to wake up tomorrow.

He wasn't stopping until he nailed that low-life son of a bitch.

Where the hell was Cooper? Lines of frustration furrowed on his brow. His partner was supposed to be here with the techs performing the third sweep.

"Braddock!"

Speak of the devil.

Cooper materialized from the trees where the warning signs and yellow tape marked the area as officially off-limits to pedestrian traffic. She tramped from the underbrush and double-timed it across the ditch to meet him.

A tight-fitting blue tee was tucked into her equally tight jeans. She didn't look a whole lot like a cop, much less a homicide detective. With long blond hair tucked into one of those ponytails that poked through the back of her baseball cap, she looked like a teenager who'd been up to no good.

Adeline Cooper liked to brag that she could shoot a flea off a dog's ass from a hundred yards. Braddock couldn't say she was quite that good, but she was tough as nails and never even flinched while cutting a perp off at the knees . . . or busting his balls.

He was going to need her to get through this. Would she have made the same decisions as he? He'd kept way too much to himself for far too long. If he'd been smart, hadn't been so damned focused on his own selfish need for vengeance, he would have allowed her in all the way. Now things had gone to shit and she wasn't going to be happy that he'd kept her in the dark to some degree.

"You find something?" If she had, Braddock would gladly wash her big-ass truck for the rest of the summer. His partner drove a two-decade-old Ford Bronco, four-by-four, lifts and seriously large tires included. She washed it once a week, by hand. She swore it was the closest thing to a baby she would ever have. She'd hit thirty this year. He was beginning to believe her.

"Damn straight I found something." She jerked her head toward the woods. "Follow me, Little Red Riding Hood, and I'll show you to Grandma's house and why I'm a detective and those dudes back there are just evidence techs."

"That's what I wanted to hear." Anticipation lit, searing

away some of the anxiety ripping through his gut as he slogged through the overgrown path behind his partner.

The uniform posted to protect the immediate scene gave Braddock a nod. The central search area was under guard and cordoned off until this final sweep was completed. Before crossing that cautionary yellow line, Cooper stopped and turned back to him. She liked setting the stage for her reveals. Over the past two-plus years, he'd gotten used to her need to dramatize her revelations.

"Since it hadn't rained in forever before Saturday evening," she began, "we didn't find any tire tracks on the roadside. We couldn't determine what route had been used by our perp when he brought the victim to this location or when he split." She rolled her eyes. "In part because those kids and their friends trampled the area like a herd of elephants before the uniforms got here."

"Yeah, yeah," he reminded her, "I know that part."

"Anyway," Cooper said with a pointed look, "so we have no tire impressions. No shoe imprints, not even the vic's. Except," she qualified, "for the sneaker treads of adolescent boys. The perp left no trace evidence behind—at least nothing we've found so far." She gave a little shrug. "To the less experienced, less dogged detective, it might seem that this investigation was a wash."

He motioned for her to get on with it. "You are aware that I was here for the first and second evidence sweeps. Or did you sleep through those?"

"Just bear with me, partner." A twinkle of you'll-see in her eyes, she turned to the yellow tape boundary. "But what our killer did leave was all the needles and crap we understand was relevant to the vic in some way. As if he was showing us a snapshot of how she lived her life."

Braddock's fingers tightened into fists as those snapshots flashed across his retinas, one stark view at a time. Shelley Patterson with dozens of hypodermic syringes dangling from her skin. And that wasn't the worst of it. The idea of just how far the piece of shit had gone with his this-is-your-life theme made Braddock's gut clench even now.

Self-disgust expanded in his chest.

That young woman was dead because of him.

That was true only in part. Shelley Patterson was dead, he reminded himself, because of her association with a total scumbag.

That scumbag was going to pay . . . for at least two of his crimes. Braddock wouldn't stop until he'd gotten the job done.

"He was staging," Cooper offered, her whole face gleaming with that I-think-I'm-on-to-something glow.

"Staging, huh?" Braddock surveyed the scene. The two techs were almost finished with the third sweep. It wasn't routine, but he'd pushed for this, called in a number of markers. An initial sweep had been done when the body was discovered. A second one early this morning just to make sure they hadn't missed anything in the rain. Now, a third and final recheck by different techs for a fresh perspective.

Braddock turned to his partner. He'd been thinking along the same lines about the perp's heinous presentation. "To send a message?" He knew all about the messages this bastard liked to send. Sounded like his partner was on the same track.

Cooper nodded, her pleased-with-herself smile stretching into a full-fledged grin. "He even signed his work."

"Are you serious?" How had the techs missed something like that? His partner had to be speaking in figurative terms.

Cooper shoved a pair of shoe covers and gloves at him. "Hurry, I can't wait for you to see."

Protective wear in place, he lifted the tape for his partner, then ducked under it himself. The nylon rope that had been secured to a limb more than ten feet off the ground had been removed and taken to the lab with the body. The perp had apparently used lower limbs to climb high enough to hoist up the vic, then secured the rope since there were no markings to indicate a ladder had been used. Shelley Patterson wouldn't have been able to climb into that tree without a ladder, even if Braddock had had any notions of labeling this a suicide. The plastic garbage can placed on its side a few inches from where her feet had dangled wouldn't have provided the needed height. It was just another part of the staging.

Then again, the ground had been hard as a rock after the long weeks without rain. A ladder might not have left indentations. That was a hell of a lot of gear to haul to a scene. Had the bastard been completely unafraid of being caught?

Of course he had. He owned this territory.

For now.

Even more remarkably, Shelley's wrists and ankles showed no ligature marks. Had she stood by and allowed her killer to prepare the noose for her own neck?

The tox screen had revealed no drugs in her system.

The other choice was that she'd been dead already. Braddock leaned toward that scenario. The bastard had killed her and then he'd staged this scene to send the cops—to send Braddock—a message.

Until the autopsy was completed they wouldn't know which one of the two was the most viable possibility. But considering the details he'd opted not to release to Shelley's sister, Braddock hoped like hell the vic had been dead when this sick bastard did his dirty work.

Her death was already on Braddock's conscience. The idea that she may have endured immeasurable suffering . . . well, he hoped that wasn't the case.

Focus, pal. "Let's see this amazing find," he said to his partner.

She motioned for him to come closer to the tree. "Right up there." Cooper adapted a Vanna White pose, directing his attention to the tree.

Braddock removed his sunglasses and tried to see what the hell she was talking about. It was the perfect hanging tree, that was true. Lots of nice, sturdy branches accessed reasonably easily from the ground without the aid of a ladder by someone tall enough and with enough upper-body strength.

"You can't see it like that," Cooper huffed. "You have to climb up there."

Braddock shot her a look. "You climbed up there?"

She made an impatient sound. "Absolutely. I needed to see what the killer saw while he worked. You know, touch all the places he touched."

That was another thing about his partner. She was a freak. "Okay. Okay. I gotcha."

He tossed his sunglasses to Cooper, grabbed a branch, and prepared to propel his body up onto the lowest limb.

"Don't wrinkle those khakis."

He didn't appreciate the humor in her comment, but apparently both techs did.

"All the way up to the branch he used to secure the rope," she prompted.

Since he wasn't vertically challenged like his partner, it wasn't necessary for him to climb onto that final branch. He could see what she'd discovered by standing on the one just below it.

Letters had been carved into the bark. He frowned, considered what the combination spelled. "How do you know this hasn't been here for weeks or months?" Anyone, some kid or whatever, could have done this.

"Arborist."

Braddock sent his partner a look. "An arborist? You had an arborist out here? Today?"

She nodded. "He says the work is fresh. The last forty-eight hours for sure."

Braddock didn't even want to know how she'd gotten an arborist out here on such short notice. On Sunday at that.

"Remember the guy I told you about with the shoe fetish?"

Jesus Christ. "I remember." He definitely didn't need to hear that story again. "Enough said."

"He was more than happy to come take a look," Cooper said with a wicked smile.

"It's nice to have friends," Braddock commented, distracted now by the carefully shaped letters. Whoever had done this hadn't rushed. The work was too meticulous. Perfectly straight. Precisely spaced. Took major balls to spend this much time at the scene of a crime, before or after.

The bastard thought he was untouchable.

The idea that he or one of his minions might have staged the scene first and then come back with the body was gaining ground in Braddock's opinion.

"I checked with information," Cooper advised. "There are six listings with that last name. But none whose first name begins with an *E*."

Interesting. He doubted it would be a name. A clue to puzzle over, probably. The killer wanted to show Braddock who was boss. This was a game to him. Didn't matter about the collateral damage.

"Could be something." Braddock moved down one branch, then jumped to the ground. *Could be nothing.* He dusted off his khakis. "Whatever it is, you know it won't be this easy."

"It never is." She cocked her head, narrowed her gaze thoughtfully. "I figure it's an anagram."

"That makes the most sense." He reached for his Wayfarers, then slid them into place. "But you'll have to knock on doors just the same." They'd spent most of the morning tracking down and interviewing everyone close to Shelley. They still hadn't located Banks, the ex-boyfriend. But Braddock had a plan in place for that hurdle. They'd have him before this day was over.

He wanted Ricky Banks. Though he didn't believe for a second Banks was the killer, with the right incentive Banks just might decide he was far more afraid of losing his freedom than he was of the repercussions of seeking immunity.

"Yep," she agreed. "Gotta follow all leads, no matter how unlikely." Stripping off her gloves, Cooper started back in the direction of the street. "Thanks, guys," she called to the techs as she ducked under the tape. "Gimme a ring when you finish up here."

Once beyond the tape, Braddock shed his gloves and shoe covers.

"So, what'd the sister have to say?"

Braddock trailed after his partner, ducked to avoid a limb that went right over her head. "Not much."

"You think she knows anything that might be useful? Maybe she heard from the vic recently."

"She doesn't know anything," he assured Cooper. "I've got Jenkins watching her just in case she makes contact with Banks." If he knew CJ, she would be pounding the pavement looking for the scumbag. Having Jenkins keep an eye on her was as much for her own protection as it was to observe any contact.

"Good idea. About the other . . . did you tell her?"

"No."

"That's going to come back to bite you in the ass, partner. She already doesn't like you. She finds out you're keeping something like that from her, she's going to be out for blood."

Yeah, well, he was used to CJ going for his jugular. That was his fault, too. Just something else to regret.

He paused at the street. "I'll just have to deal with whatever she tosses my way." He glanced around even though he knew Cooper's truck wasn't here. It wasn't like it could be overlooked. "Where's the monster?" She didn't like that he called her vehicle that, but she'd given up trying to win him over to the joys of owning something fully capable of climbing over small buildings.

"I was running a little behind after lunch." She hunched her shoulders in one of those careless shrugs she was famous for. "I got dropped off."

"Uh-huh." Which meant lunch wasn't about dining.

"About the carving." She paused before opening the door of his G6. "Could be the first move in a game."

Braddock opened the driver's-side door. "Could be an invitation to play."

"Or a riddle." She dropped into the passenger seat and propped a sneakered foot on the dash. Braddock grimaced.

"It might"—he started the engine and pulled out onto the street—"be a reference to a place or an event."

"True," she agreed. "I'll run it through the system and make some calls."

As unnecessary as he knew it would prove, ruling out *E. Noon* as a name was step one.

CHAPTER EIGHT

Mill Village
3:48 PM

CJ shoved her three-quarter sleeves higher up her arms. Sweat slid down between her shoulder blades. She raised her fist and banged on the next door.

She'd been knocking on doors for the last hour. This house had been her initial stop, but no one had been home. She hoped against hope that was no longer the case. Frances Jennings never missed a Sunday in church. Surely by now church was over.

If the cops couldn't find Ricky Banks, it was because they didn't know the right places to look. Or simply didn't care, like Braddock. CJ had grown up in this neighborhood. She knew where to look.

The door opened a tiny crack.

Thank God.

"Mrs. Jennings?" CJ couldn't see a damned thing through that narrow opening, but, according to the neighbors, Frances Jennings still lived at this address.

"You Cecilia Patterson's girl? The doctor?"

"Yes, ma'am." Anticipation fired in CJ's veins. It was definitely Frances Jennings, one and only aunt to Ricky Banks. "Is it okay if I come in, Mrs. Jennings?"

"I heard about your sister." Frances opened the door a little wider, eyed CJ suspiciously over her bifocals. "It's a shame, that's what it is."

CJ nodded, pushing aside the images that immediately tried to invade her thoughts. "I was hoping to talk to Ricky." Just saying his name made CJ want to tear something apart. A year younger than CJ, Ricky had been in and out of Shelley's life since middle school. One of the mistakes her sister hadn't been able to stop repeating.

"He ain't here, but you can come on in." Frances Jennings shuffled back, opening the door wider and staying slightly behind it as if she feared she might need it as a shield. Life in the village would do that to a person.

"Thank you." CJ stepped across the threshold, flashbacks from all the times she'd been here before, usually complaining about Ricky, tumbled one over the other.

Francis closed the door and set the lock. "The two of 'em never could seem to stay away from each other. I always thought they'd end up married."

Yeah, right. Ricky loved whoring Shelley out too much to marry her. She was his meal ticket. "I know what you mean," CJ lied.

Frances smoothed the skirt of her Sunday-go-to-meeting dress and lowered her hefty bulk into her rocker-recliner. She set the chair in motion. "Neither one of 'em could ever stay out of trouble, either."

Moving to a chair, CJ tried as inconspicuously as possible to survey the living room and what she could see of the kitchen beyond. "It's harder for some than others." *Careful. Don't say the wrong thing. Don't let her see your hatred.*

Frantic scratching somewhere deeper in the house had CJ leaning forward in her chair before she could stop herself.

"Don't pay no mind to that," Frances said. "It's that big old dog of Ricky's. I make him keep that beast shut up in his room when he ain't here."

CJ nodded, relaxed marginally. Ricky had a brute of a mutt. A pit bull or Rottweiler or something like that. A savage pet for a savage man.

"The police were here looking for him last night." Frances folded her hands together in her lap.

Another shot of adrenaline pierced CJ's chest. "I guess they just want to talk to him about Shelley." She tamped down the outrage that mounted, threatened to climb into her throat and out of her mouth in violent screams. "Surely they can't believe Ricky would hurt Shelley like that. He likes to push folks around when he gets fired up, but he wouldn't kill anybody." The words left a bitter taste in her mouth.

Frances nodded, her saggy double chin wobbling with her stern conviction.

CJ held her breath.

"That's what he said. He didn't kill nobody. The police just want somebody to blame. Why, that boy has gone to church with me every Sunday for the past twenty years. 'Cept for today. Wears that crucifix I gave him every day of his life. He ain't guilty of a thing but trying to survive."

CJ made a concerted effort not to roll her eyes. If dear old Aunt Frances only knew.

The naive old lady harrumphed. "That's why I told 'em I didn't know where in the world that boy was."

"The problem is"—CJ had to tread cautiously here—"if he doesn't answer their questions, the police are going to presume he's guilty."

Frances stopped her rocking.

"He really should tell them what he knows so they can start looking at other possibilities." CJ moistened her lips. "You . . . you know as well as I do how the police are about folks in this neighborhood. They probably figure nailing Ricky for her murder would kill two birds with one stone. They're not going to bother looking for the real killer if they've got someone they can blame."

The old woman's eyes narrowed behind her corrective lenses. "You mean like putting Ricky in jail takes him off the streets and then they don't have to worry about him causing no more trouble?"

"Yes, ma'am, that's exactly what I mean. Shelley's dead."

Emotion pounded against CJ's sternum. "They figure she didn't deserve any better than she got, so why not rid the city of another one like her?" She leaned forward, pressed the older woman with the certainty in her eyes. "They don't care about us. They'd have torn this village down years ago when they demolished the mill if some hoity-toity historian hadn't insisted the historic value had to be preserved. And all those promises of new jobs for all the laid-off mill workers were over and forgotten as soon as the new mayor was elected."

The rocking resumed. "Politicians always make promises and then they do nothing. Without the mill, some folks felt they had no choice but to turn to crime to survive. And not one thing was done to stop it."

CJ nodded, the movement stiff. "We can't let the police get away with accusing an innocent man just so the mayor's views on keeping the streets clean look good." Her lips tightened with the lie. "I'll go to the police with Ricky. My sister would want me to."

Frances stilled once more, her gaze engaging fully with CJ's, searching for the sincerity in her eyes that she heard in her voice.

Think! What now? "Maybe if I could talk to Ricky, I could make him understand that the only way he's going to get through this without serious trouble is if he lets the police know he didn't have anything to do with what happened to Shelley. I feel certain he has an alibi. But it won't do him any good if he doesn't give it to the police. Running or hiding just makes him look guilty." CJ reached out, patted the old lady's hand. "You have my word I'll go with him." Damn straight she would. "I want the truth just as much as he does."

The silence boomed in CJ's ears.

Just tell me where he is!

Frances Jennings tapped her fingertips together. "Those homeless folks still sleep under that Governor's Drive overpass, you know. No matter how often the police shoo them away, they just come right back. The police don't pay no real attention. The president himself could be right in the middle of that horde and nobody would notice."

CJ's respiration came in tiny, fragmented bursts. "But they don't usually come out until after dark." *Where would he be now?* She needed to find him *now*.

The old woman nodded again. "Yes'm. In the daytime they like to mill around in the park. With all the hippies and those no-account kids in black skulking about, the homeless just sort of blend in."

Of course. CJ should have thought of that.

"I should be going. I have a lot to take care of." She pushed to her feet, tried not to appear in too big a rush. "It was nice to see you again, Mrs. Jennings."

"You know when the funeral'll be yet?"

Pain radiated deep, squeezed CJ's heart. "No, ma'am. Not yet. But I'll be sure to let you know as soon as . . . the arrangements are made." On second thought, she reached into her bag, scrounged up a piece of paper and pen. "I'll give you my cell phone number. If you need me, just call." She jotted down the number, then passed the paper to the older woman.

Frances Jennings stared at the number. "I might just do that. You know my bursitis has been acting up lately."

"Call me and I'll see what I can do."

Mrs. Jennings walked her to the door. The impulse to run across the porch and down the steps throbbed in CJ's muscles, made keeping her stride steady and even next to impossible.

The park. Of course he'd go to the park. Big Spring Park was always littered with the homeless. No one paid the slightest attention.

What better way to hide than in plain sight?

The five minutes required to reach the downtown area had CJ ready to hyperventilate. By the time she parked and headed along the sidewalk, she felt on the verge of exploding. She wrapped her fingers around the cell phone in her pocket. The second she laid eyes on that son of a bitch Banks, she was dialing 911.

Ricky had always used his elderly aunt when he needed help. Like Shelley and CJ, he'd had no other family.

Now CJ had none.

Her lips compressed as fury pounded inside her.

She methodically checked the most frequented hangouts around the park. Near the bridge, the waterfall, and the picnic tables. Nothing. She walked faster, hurrying from one side of the public green space to the other, weaving and scanning.

Big Spring Park was slap in the middle of downtown Huntsville. The expanse of green space sprawled around and between the office buildings. The manmade lake created for the park covered a large portion of the area. Ducks meandered around the water's edge, picking at the litter left by the human visitors, hoping for food.

Finally, CJ grew desperate and started to ask anyone she encountered if they knew Banks or had seen him.

Heads shook. Gazes narrowed with suspicion. But no one admitted to knowing him, much less having seen him. The exercise proved a waste of time.

A swell of exhaustion washed over her as she neared the distinguished building that housed the city's Museum of Art. She should just stop. She was no cop. What the hell was she even doing out here shaking down rebellious teenagers and the homeless?

Shelley was dead. Nothing CJ did was going to change that. The police would pretend to investigate, but if they didn't nail her killer, what difference did it make?

It wouldn't raise her from the dead.

It wouldn't give CJ a second chance to do a better job being a big sister.

To the powers that be, Shelley was insignificant. Just another impoverished young woman who'd been arrested on drug possession charges twice and prostitution charges once that CJ knew of.

Who around here was going to miss her?

The cell phone clasped in her hand vibrated. CJ jumped. Her nerves were beyond rattled. She hoped it wasn't Edward again. He was worried sick about her. She should have called him as soon as she'd arrived, but he wouldn't have understood her need to do this. Edward Abbott was a bit overprotective, but he was her dearest friend.

Taking a steadying breath, she peered at the screen. Not Edward. Or Braddock. She didn't recognize the number, but the prefix indicated a local caller.

Tension slid through her. *Please, please let it be him.* She'd given the aunt the number in hopes she would call and pass it on to her no-good nephew. CJ slid the phone open and pressed it to her ear. "Patterson."

"What the fuck are you trying to do?"

Ricky Banks.

A moment of triumph was instantly replaced with rage, seizing CJ's entire being with the urge to act. Her pulse quickened. "Ricky, I have to talk—"

"Are you trying to get me killed?" he demanded.

Images of Shelley's body lying cold and still on that slab swam before CJ's eyes. "If you're innocent," she said with a far steadier, calmer voice than she had a right to muster, "you should tell the police. They're not going to look for anyone else as long as they're focused on you." Even an idiot should understand that. If he was innocent, his actions were obstructing the investigation.

But he wasn't innocent. He was a low-life piece of wasted DNA who loved brutalizing women.

"You don't know shit." He launched into a tirade about just how stupid CJ was and how she'd been gone for seven years and didn't get how things were now.

"Ricky!" she tried to interrupt, but he kept screaming in her ear. *"Ricky!"* she screamed right back even as she cautioned herself to stay cool. "Just shut up and listen to me."

Incredibly, he shut up.

"Braddock is the one investigating Shelley's murder. All you have to do is tell him where you were and who you were with when Shelley was murdered. Then you're off the hook. If you didn't do it, you have nothing to worry about." No response. CJ checked to ensure the call was still connected. "Hiding out is only making you look guilty." She took a breath, grappled for the composure that had fled the instant she heard his voice. Prayed she had convinced him that she wasn't the enemy. If she could get him to come out of hiding, the cops would get the truth out of him. He wasn't nearly as badass as he wanted everyone to think.

"Is that what you think? That all I have to do is explain myself and I'm off the hook? What the hell you been smoking?"

"Don't be stupid." *Keep your cool just a little bit longer.* "Just . . . tell me where you are."

"Right behind you."

Before CJ could whip around, a strong forearm clamped around her throat. A sweaty palm slapped over her mouth. Her phone hit the ground. She kicked, twisted, tried to jerk free.

"Be still," he growled between gritted teeth.

Like hell! Her shoe heel connected with a shin.

"Goddammit!"

He slammed her against a brick wall. She kicked him again. Got her head banged against the wall for her trouble.

"Be fucking still!" he growled, bracing his forearm against her throat.

Since the gun in his hand wasn't pointed at her, she stopped moving. *See what he has to say.* Air sawed in and out of her lungs, propelling the racing blood already roaring in her ears.

"I did not kill her," he said, his nose no more than an inch from CJ's. "I can't go to the police because he'll kill me if I open—"

"Who'll kill you?" she challenged. If Shelley's murder involved more than him, she wanted to know.

"I ain't getting dead for nobody." He pressed his arm harder against her throat. She couldn't breathe. "If you know what's good for you—"

"Hands up, Banks!"

The pressure on her throat eased enough for her to drag in a lungful of air.

"Drop the weapon and put your hands in the air."

In an effort to see who'd shouted the orders, CJ craned her neck as far as Ricky's hold would allow.

Banks twisted to get a look as well.

Tall guy. Civilian clothes. Big gun.

The idea crossed her mind that she'd obviously pissed off Lady Luck, since guns were suddenly everywhere she turned.

She saw them in the ER now and then, but the last twenty-four hours had been a little over the top.

The instant the big-ass gun aimed at his head registered in Ricky's brain, his arm fell away and his gun dropped to the grass.

"Ricky Banks"—the man stepped forward, gun still leveled on its target—"you're wanted for questioning in the death of Shelley Patterson. Back away from the woman and let's do this the easy way."

Another man, this one dressed in jeans and a T-shirt, too, moved in, grabbed one of Ricky's raised arms, and twisted it behind his back.

Before CJ could ask, the first man who'd spoken flashed his badge. Huntsville PD. "Are you all right, ma'am?"

CJ nodded. Took her first decent breath since her cell had vibrated with Ricky's call.

"You set me up," he snarled.

Her gaze collided with Ricky's. She'd set him up all right, but not with the police. He'd grabbed her before she had a chance. But if that was what he thought, she couldn't care less. "Maybe I did," she tossed back.

"You'll be sorry," he warned. "You don't even fucking know how sorry."

CHAPTER NINE

CJ paced the interview room where Braddock had insisted she wait. The coffee one of his colleagues had delivered sat untouched on the table. She'd asked to observe the questioning. Back when she'd had time to watch television, they did it on *Law & Order* all the time. But Braddock had let her know in no uncertain terms that her request was out of the question.

That had been more than an hour ago.

What was taking so long?

Ricky Banks wasn't that complicated. CJ had been going head-to-head with him for more than two decades. Shelley had been three months away from her fifteenth birthday and the scumbag had finagled his way into her pants. Another popped cherry to add to his scorecard. Afterward, poor Shelley had just kept crying and saying the same thing over and over.

I don't want to be like Mom.

So CJ had plotted the perfect revenge to boost her sister's spirits. With a pair of old Widow Daniels's late husband's golf clubs in hand, CJ and Shelley had released years of pent-up frustration and anger on Ricky's piece-of-shit Camaro.

Ricky had been pissed. He'd growled and threatened for a couple of weeks, but he'd finally let go of his grudge against the

Patterson sisters and moved on to badgering some other poor souls.

But he'd never let go of his hold on Shelley.

No matter how many times he hurt her, she always got involved with him again.

And every time she hit bottom, CJ had been the one to pick up the pieces.

Just like with their mother.

The door behind her opened and CJ turned, hoping this was Braddock with news.

Closing the door behind him, Braddock glanced at the untouched Styrofoam cup. "You didn't like the coffee?"

"Did he kill my sister?" She had no desire to make small talk with this man.

He pulled out a chair and took a seat. Gestured to the one across the table.

CJ shook her head. She couldn't sit. Her nerves were raw and still vibrating with too many emotions.

"Considering the evidence we have now—"

"Which is none," she said for him.

"Which is none," he agreed. "Our only avenue was to verify his alibi and to look for signs of a recent physical altercation. Considering some of the bruising—"

CJ flinched, couldn't help herself.

"We can assume Shelley struggled against her attacker." That said, he heaved a frustrated breath.

This was going to be bad.

"Banks shows no indication whatsoever of a recent struggle. But he could have been wearing gloves and long sleeves. We're executing a search warrant of his home before we make a final decision. If nothing else, we're hoping to find some leverage to get him talking about anything he knows that might prove useful to the investigation."

"What's the bottom line, Braddock?" She knew; she just wanted to hear him say it out loud.

His gaze settled heavily onto hers. "In light of the fact that my partner confirmed his alibi, unless we find that leverage I mentioned . . . we have no choice but to release him."

Hearing him say it didn't give her the victorious feeling she'd thought it would. She expected the police to fail her sister. Wanted Braddock to have to admit out loud his incompetence. Yet, all hearing the words did was hurt. CJ rubbed her tired eyes, threaded her fingers through her hair. She'd been sure it was Ricky. Sure enough to hunt him down when the police had insisted they couldn't find him.

CJ had found him.

Looking back at the risk she'd taken, she was damned lucky the cops had shown up when they did.

Wait. That can't have been coincidence.

The cops had been watching her.

Her gaze locked with Braddock's once more. "You used me to find him." The end result was the same, whether law enforcement had found him or she had, but there was something innately wrong with the way Braddock had gone about this tactic. Outrage burned away the fog of fatigue. Once again, he had fully lived up to her expectations.

"Yes," he admitted. "I did put surveillance on you. You grew up in the village. The people there see you as one of them. I knew they would talk to you when they wouldn't talk to us. But," he qualified, "the surveillance was also for your protection."

He had an answer for everything, except who had killed her sister. "Is this the way you conduct a homicide investigation? Prompting private citizens to put themselves in danger?" She didn't know why Shelley had trusted him. Always wanted to call Braddock whenever she felt the need to reach out to law enforcement. *I help him out with what's going on around here and he helps me out*, she'd once told CJ.

He hadn't helped Shelley; he'd used her.

Just like he'd used CJ.

"I didn't put you in danger, CJ. You did that all by yourself. But I won't lie to you. Sometimes"—Braddock stood, pushed in his chair—"we have to take advantage of whatever opportunities are in front of us. The first forty-eight hours after a crime are crucial. You do want to know what happened to your sister, don't you?"

"Of course." The son of a bitch. He was turning this around

on her. "Like you said, I know the people in the village. I grew up there. And the other thing I know for certain is that the police never go out of their way to investigate anything that happens to those people."

Braddock braced his hands on the table and leaned forward, pressing her with those dark eyes of his. "This is what you obviously don't know. You don't know *me*."

CJ grabbed her bag, slung it over her shoulder. "Maybe I don't know you as well as Shelley did. But look where that got her."

She walked out the door.

Someone in the village had to know something.

All she had to do was find that someone.

CHAPTER TEN

"Who's the old guy?" Ever-present Pepsi in hand, Cooper hopped onto Braddock's desk and studied the screen monitoring the goings and comings in the lobby. "I thought she didn't have any family."

"She doesn't." Braddock stared at the monitor. "That was Edward Abbott. Professor over at the university. Retired last year." CJ's last words kept echoing in his brain. *Maybe I don't know you as well as Shelley did. But look where that got her.*

Cooper knocked back a slug of her preferred beverage. "Kind of old for a boyfriend."

Braddock shoved aside the words—the reality—haunting him. "According to Shelley, he's a family friend. A father figure, I guess." Not that Shelley had liked Abbott that much. He'd been a part of their lives since she and CJ were kids.

"Abbott lives around here?"

"Williams Street. Old money. His family was one of the original settlers in Huntsville. He's the last of the line. Never been married. No kids. My guess is he's the reason Dr. CJ Patterson rose so high above her humble beginnings."

Cynthia Jayne Patterson owed a lot to the man, according to her sister. Abbott had taken care of the burial expenses for their mother. Ensured the future Dr. Patterson had gotten whatever she needed. Braddock wondered if there had been more to Abbott's relationship with the mother. Maybe one or both daughters were his biological offspring. That would explain his long-term involvement in their lives. Unless, of course, he was simply a guy who exemplified the term *Good Samaritan*. A few of those still existed.

"Father figure?" Cooper arched a speculative eyebrow. "Or perv? Maybe he's got a thing for the sister."

"That's possible," Braddock allowed. CJ didn't confide in him. But then, she had her reasons. And those reasons were going to make this investigation a whole lot more complicated. He had no one to blame for that but himself.

"Maybe," Cooper put forward, "little sister was jealous of how much attention big sister got from pseudo-daddy or sugar daddy, whatever the case might be."

Maybe. Braddock had picked up on just a hint of envy, but in all the ways that counted, Shelley had idolized her sister. "I don't think this is about Abbott," he countered. "What would he have to gain by murdering Shelley? Let's face it, he'd have a hell of a lot to lose. He's a very wealthy man. Offing an on-again-off-again prostitute seems a little out of character for a man in his position."

"Banks isn't our man," Cooper said, moving on from the subject of Abbott. "You know it and I know it. He's a bully, not a killer. His alibi checked out. And his aunt swears he came in about two that morning and she started trying to get him up at noon. He was dead to the world for those hours in between."

She held up her hands before Braddock could say what was on his mind. "I know. I know. The aunt could've lied. She's family. Might be protecting him. But I believe her. My instincts are usually right on the money when it comes to reading people."

Braddock could vouch for that. He was hoping like hell she didn't turn that high-powered perception too keenly on him. They'd been partners for nearly three years. She'd seen him through a hell of a lot. But this crossed the line.

If he went down, he wasn't taking Cooper with him. This wasn't her mess; it was his.

"Banks might not have killed her," Braddock admitted, "but he knows who did. And, by his own admission, he was one of the last people to see her alive."

Cooper pulled the open case file to her side of the desk. "Banks was in and out of the Patterson home that night. So were two other men the neighbor, Mr. O'Neal, couldn't identify."

O'Neal lived next door to Shelley. The argument between Banks and Shelley had awakened him, which was the reason he'd been up at one-thirty or so in the morning. He had seen at least two other males come and go between two and three that morning but he hadn't gotten a good look at either one. A stroke had sentenced him to a wheelchair, limiting his views to those from his first-floor windows. O'Neal hadn't been concerned about the late-night visitors. Men were in and out of Shelley's place at all hours, most any given night of the week.

"Shelley used to be one of the King's foot soldiers," Cooper went on as she perused the interview notes she'd taken.

The King. Tyrone Nash. The self-professed ruler of the village. A true scumbag. Braddock's jaw tightened. The piece of shit even had business cards flaunting his self-ordained status. He had deemed the prostitutes he operated his "foot soldiers." Others who worked for him were his "eyes" and his "ears." Nash had himself quite an imagination to go with that inflated ego.

"Shelley wasn't turning tricks for him anymore," Braddock reminded his partner.

"True, but since Nash keeps tabs on every-damned-body living in the village, he probably knows exactly what happened whether he killed her or not."

"Probably?" Braddock shot her an are-you-kidding look. Frustration tightened in his gut. "You know damned well he ordered her death. There is no way in hell it happened without his approval."

"I have a theory on the E. Noon thing," his partner offered.

"Oh, yeah?" Braddock hadn't spent much time on that. He'd been too focused on CJ. Just another indication he was way over the line here.

Cooper nodded. "It's *no one* spelled backward."

No one fucks with me.

The words, written in blood—in his niece's blood—loomed ominously in Braddock's head. Nash had sent him that note. Nash had killed her. Just like he killed Shelley. Braddock didn't need any evidence. He knew it in his gut.

All of this, every damned step, was a waste of time. A game that bastard had set in motion. He wasn't afraid of being caught. He was too careful. They would search for evidence and interview dozens of folks, and it would all boil down to one thing: no way to legally prove Nash was the one.

But he was. This time Braddock was going to get him.

Cooper closed the file. "Look," she said quietly, "we both know how badly you want Nash."

Braddock blinked. He'd been lost in his own misery. "It's him. We both know where the *no one* comes from. Nash is making sure I understand it's him."

"I totally agree," Cooper went on. "He's a piece of shit. Nobody"—she pressed Braddock with her gaze—"wants that bastard to go down more than I do. But we have to do this right, partner. No mistakes. No jumping the gun. By the book."

"By the book," he agreed, mainly to keep her happy. He would make this stick. One way or another he would find what he needed to nail that blood-sucking lowlife.

Whatever it cost him.

"You're a good partner."

Braddock looked up, surprised at her statement. "I'd say thanks, but I'm not sure you meant it as a compliment."

She shook her head at him. "I just wanted you to know that I like what we have." She searched his eyes a couple of seconds too long. "I don't want to see that change."

Too late.

Everything had changed.

Shelley Patterson was dead.

And he was the reason.

CHAPTER ELEVEN

CJ sat on the front steps of her childhood home and absorbed the sounds of the village. Two houses down a couple were having it out, their angry voices carrying in the darkness. Across the street stray cats yowled and hissed in a territorial battle that likely involved the resident's freshly discarded trash. Beyond that, the constant ebb and flow of traffic and sirens, underscored by the distant, lonesome wail of the ten o'clock train, provided a familiar urban melody that had lulled her to sleep every night for most of her life.

As on so many of those nights, Edward sat next to her on the steps, his presence comforting, familiar. She never would have escaped this world without his help and boundless encouragement.

His quiet strength proved more heartening than he could possibly know. Yet inside, where no one else could see, she trembled. CJ didn't want to feel alone, but tonight she felt entirely alone even with Edward's patient vigil.

Her sister had been CJ's only family. Her responsibility.

Now Shelley was gone. CJ had failed her.

"I wish you would reconsider," Edward prompted, unwilling to concede on the issue.

CJ appreciated his concern. He didn't want her staying here

alone. But she needed to be here. Close to her sister's things. Close to *her*.

"I'll be fine." She patted his arm, allowed her hand to linger there in hopes of reassuring him of her fortitude. "I'll call you before I go to bed and the first thing when I wake up in the morning." Again that surreal feeling washed over her, as if this were a dream or theater production playing out beneath the struggling spotlight of the feeble porch light.

"You haven't eaten, have you?" Kind gray eyes searched hers. "I'm certain you're utterly exhausted."

His diagnosis was accurate on both observations. She felt emotionally and physically drained, completely spent. "I couldn't eat. Not tonight. I'll get some sleep and perhaps we can have one of your splendid brunches in the morning."

With a surrendering sigh, he settled his hand on hers. "I'll stop badgering you, then. You mustn't worry about the arrangements. I'll take care of everything."

He'd done the same thing when her mother died. CJ appreciated his kindness, but she needed to do this for her sister. Later they would have that conversation. She couldn't do it tonight.

"Thank you . . ." She stopped, drew in a deep, steadying breath. "For always being . . . you, Edward." A heartfelt smile quivered across her lips. "I don't know what I'd do without you." A tear slipped past her firm hold; she swiped it away. Couldn't do that right now, either.

He squeezed her hand ever so gently. "As much as I enjoy your company," he said, standing up, "I should go and let you get settled."

CJ pushed to her feet. Her limbs felt weak, unsteady.

He hugged her chastely, gave her a smile, and said goodnight. CJ watched him go, wondering why such a good, kind man was still alone. He'd turned fifty-two this year. He'd never been married, hadn't even come close. He was tall and extremely fit for his age, and even the gray hair lent a distinguished quality to an undeniably attractive and wealthy gentleman. Any woman would be lucky to have Edward in her life.

Maybe he'd been so busy taking care of the Patterson sisters he hadn't taken time for himself. That burden settled heavily onto her shoulders alongside the too-numerous others. CJ closed her eyes and cleared her mind.

She didn't need to try sorting any of this out tonight.

Tomorrow would be soon enough.

Grabbing her bag, she climbed the final step up onto the porch and hauled her weary body to the door. She dug in her bag for the key. Tomorrow she would go through the house to get an idea of where to start with the packing up. Maybe, if she was really lucky, she would find something that would give her some degree of insight into Shelley's final days. To CJ's knowledge, her sister hadn't kept a journal, but there could be other clues: notes to herself, a calendar . . . something.

CJ shoved the key into the lock and gave it a twist. She might even attempt to talk to Ricky one-on-one. Maybe he would open up to her if it was just the two of them. Alibi or not, she was nowhere near convinced of his innocence. Anything she could get out of him might help focus the investigation in the proper direction.

Inside, the house was dark, stuffy. CJ closed the door and dropped her bag on the sofa. She reached for the light switch. A loud thwack followed by shattering glass stopped her cold.

Lifting her gaze to the ceiling, she stared at the cracked plaster.

For two beats she tried to convince herself she'd imagined the sound. Maybe a squirrel had gotten in somehow.

The scuff of hard soles on bare wood jolted her out of denial.

Fear rammed her heart against her sternum.

Cell phone. Pepper spray. She probed in her bag for both, her gaze never leaving the staircase across the room.

Her respiration echoed in the silence.

Someone was up there . . . not her imagination.

Another creak.

She froze.

Shelley's bedroom.

He was in Shelley's room!

Blind fury lashed through her, propelled her across the room and up the stairs.

"Don't you touch my sister's things!"

The words exploded in the air startling her with the realization that she'd voiced the thought.

She hit the upstairs landing without slowing and lunged into the darkness of the hall toward her sister's room.

A body plowed into her.

Knocked her backward.

She hit the floor.

The breath whooshed out of her lungs.

The pepper spray slid across the floor. Her death grip on the phone was all that kept it in her hand.

A foot came down right next to her head as the intruder scrambled over her.

The boom of footsteps on the stairs catapulted her upright.

She raced after him.

Definitely a him. Big. Strong. Hard-muscled.

Stumbling down the last two steps in her haste, she landed on all fours on the living room floor.

The back door banged against the wall.

He was getting away!

She staggered up. Ran.

She burst through the door he'd left open. Stumbled around in a circle, searching the darkness.

Where the hell was he?

Peering across the moonlit yard, she got a glimpse of a dark figure as he ducked into the alley.

"Bastard," she snapped. She fought to catch her breath. If she'd turned the upstairs light on, maybe she would have gotten a glimpse of his face.

Dammit.

Her body started to shake. She was cold. And it was hot as hell, sticky, muggy out here.

The adrenaline was draining away.

She took a deep breath, then another.

Calm down.

It was over.

He wouldn't be back.

The scumbag had likely heard about Shelley's death and

decided to see if there was anything in the house worth taking.

"Piece of shit."

Catching hold of the railing for support, she climbed the back steps and went inside. She'd see if anything was missing and what had gotten broken, then she would call the police.

For all the good it would do.

Turning on lights as she went, she moved through the kitchen to the living room and up the stairs. At the landing, she switched on the hall light this time.

The consuming quiet pressed in around her, felt creepy.

Call the police now.

As she eased cautiously toward Shelley's room, the little voice that had been screaming at her, which in her emotional outburst she had ignored, prompted her to slide her phone open and do what she should have done in the first place.

At the bedroom door, she slid her hand along the wall until she hit the switch. Light flooded the room.

CJ poised her thumb to enter the three digits, then froze.

The window was broken. Glass had spewed across the floor. Shelley's things were tossed all around the room. But none of that was what held her transfixed, unable to move or even to scream.

On the wall above the bed was a message written in bold crimson swipes: STAY AND THERE'LL BE TWO DEAD BITCHES.

The phone slipped from her icy fingers and bounced on the floor.

CJ blinked.

Her lips parted with the sound that burst from her lungs.

She whirled and ran for the stairs.

Plunged downward, barely staying vertical.

She rushed for the door . . . and rammed into a hard chest before she could stop her forward momentum.

The scream died in her throat as her reactions scrambled to catch up with the message her brain was sending.

"CJ, what's going on?"

Braddock.

All the hurt, disappointment, regret, anger, and fear folded in on her. She crumpled into his arms.

He was whispering to her. She couldn't make out the words over her sobs. Strong arms lifted her. He carried her across the room and settled on the sofa with her in his lap, cradled in his arms.

Once the tears started, they wouldn't stop. She clung to his strength, to the warmth of his body. She was so cold. So tired. The misery was so overwhelming.

And no matter how vehemently she'd denied it, she'd missed him. It felt good to be in his arms. All those nights they'd talked, just being close to him had warmed her . . . made her want things she'd never dared to want. Made her want to give herself to him and to take all he'd had to offer. Even now he had the power to make her tremble with that same need when she shouldn't.

She didn't want to think anymore . . . didn't want to feel this agony. She wanted to lose herself. Her lips found his. She kissed him with all the emotions churning madly inside her. Wanted to learn every part of him the way she'd dreamed of so many times before.

"Slow down," he murmured as he tried to draw away.

"Can't." She pulled his mouth back to hers, kissed him harder. Her fingers knotted in his shirt, tugged at it until she found naked skin. Hot . . . smooth. She wanted to touch more of him. Wanted him to touch her. She tore at the buttons of her blouse. Her breasts strained against the satin of her bra, begging for attention.

She guided his hand to her breast. He squeezed. She gasped, squirmed in his lap.

Years of frustration and restraint exploded inside her. Watching her drunken mother's male friends paw at her mother. Holding her sister while she sobbed because some bastard had taken advantage of her when she was wasted. CJ was always the good girl, the one who cleaned up the mess—who did the right thing.

She didn't want to do the right thing anymore. She wanted to go to that mind-numbing place. To forget everything else.

She wanted Braddock to take her there. She'd dreamed of being with him for months even as she'd tried every tactic she knew to forget him.

Jesus Christ, why didn't he do something? "What're you waiting for?" Her voice was thick with need.

Those dark, dark eyes clashed with hers. She saw the desire there. He wanted her . . . no matter that he hesitated.

"You don't want to do this," he murmured.

A blast of fury ignited in her belly. "You don't know a damned thing about what I want." She tugged his polo up and off. Just looking at all that bare skin and toned muscles made her want to taste him. To lick him all over just to prove she was every bit the woman her sister had been.

She had needs, too. Plunging her fingers into his hair, she pulled his face close to hers. "Now fuck me, Braddock. Maybe I'll find out why my sister thought you were so goddamned amazing."

The words prodded the reaction she'd wanted.

He threw her down on the sofa, tore open her slacks, and stripped them from her legs. Looming above her, he stared at her panties a long moment, clearly surprised by the frilly, sexy underwear beneath all those conservative clothes she wore.

What the hell had he expected? She was a woman, too. Just because she didn't screw every man she met, like her sister, didn't make her less of a woman.

Then he ripped those lacy panties from her body. Anticipation roared inside her.

He kneed his way between her thighs. Wrenched open his trousers . . . and hesitated. "Changed your mind yet?"

"Shut up and do it." She shoved his trousers and boxers down his hips. Her pulse skipped as his fully aroused penis nudged her belly.

He grabbed her hips, lifted her, then pushed fully inside with one determined thrust.

She cried out with the pleasure of it. Forgot all else as she wrapped her legs around his and instinctively ground her pelvis against his. She'd waited so long for this . . .

He moved, the slightest retreat before plunging in again. Her muscles clamped around him. He growled. She took that as her cue and began that rhythmic flexing that was as primal and instinctive as breathing.

Felt good.

She traced his muscled chest with her hungry fingers. Smoothed her hands over his back while he thrust over and over . . . stretching her . . . filling her . . . and driving her closer and closer to the edge.

That spiraling sensation started, sweeping her up into a whirlwind of pure pleasure. She dug her nails into his back, screamed with the ecstasy of her first orgasm in so damned long. So, so damned long.

He stopped, his penis deep inside her as every inch of her body pulsed with the remnants of the bliss coursing through her.

She moaned as the fight drained out of her along with the sensations . . . fading . . . fading . . .

His hand slid between their bodies. She tensed. He touched her. A gasp escaped her lips. The pad of his thumb pressed hard against her clitoris. Her eyes flew open and she braced to push him away.

"Not yet," he muttered thickly. "You haven't seen amazing yet."

His cock throbbed inside her, but it was his fingers that were driving her out of her mind. Slow, steady circles, right there on that place where millions of nerve endings were concentrated. Then he started to move again. Slowly at first, then faster. His hands moved beneath her hips, lifted her into him so he could drive move deeply.

Her muscles clenched with the beginnings of another climax.

He thrust harder, faster.

She curled her knees forward, wanting more of him . . . wanting all he had to give. This time she didn't close her eyes. She wanted to see his face, the face that had haunted her dreams so many times.

And then she started to come again. Her eyes drifted shut as her body reacted to the building climax. The sensations burst inside her, the waves stronger this time, washing over her entire body. Again and again.

He came, too.

Three . . . four final, deep thrusts. His lips found hers. The kiss went on and on.

When he stopped, he lifted his mouth from hers to look into her eyes.

She saw the regret in his and everything inside her went cold.

Reality crashed around her.

What the hell had she done?

He pulled out, righted his trousers, and stumbled off the sofa.

She snatched up her slacks, jerked them on. Tried to pull her blouse back together to cover herself. *Dear God. What have I done?*

His gaze collided with hers and she recognized that she'd said the words aloud.

She turned away, couldn't look at him. Her face burned with embarrassment.

And she had no one to blame but herself.

"What . . ." He cleared his throat. "What had you running down the stairs?"

That he could back away and move on to business as if they hadn't just done *it* sent renewed fury firing through her veins.

The blood . . . the words . . . Shelley's things . . .

Oh, God. CJ grappled for her composure. "Upstairs. There . . ." *Pull it together, think rationally.* "Someone broke in. Left a message on the bedroom wall."

"Stay here. I'll check it out."

While he was upstairs, she grabbed her ripped panties from the floor. Half the buttons were missing from her blouse. She had to be losing her mind.

What the hell had she been thinking?

She hadn't. That was the point. Months ago, when she'd thought he was so charming and trustworthy, she'd been certain that they would begin a real relationship. The idea of making love with him had teased her dreams, made her yearn for that moment. She'd been drawn to him on every level—ones she hadn't even known existed before being kissed by him. Then she'd discovered that he was no different from all the rest. She'd tried to forget him completely, but Shelley just kept bringing him up.

Even now, with Shelley dead, Braddock was still an integral part of what was left.

Maybe that was the reason CJ had lost total control tonight. She'd needed a mindless outlet, but mostly she'd needed him. He'd just happened to walk through the door before she regained her senses.

CJ's fingers stilled in their efforts to tidy her hair. She hadn't heard him knock; she'd just rushed down the stairs and found him in her living room.

She walked over to the door, turned the knob. Unlocked. His car was parked on the street.

Had she left it unlocked when she came in?

Did he have a habit of just walking in uninvited?

Maybe Shelley allowed him that privilege, but CJ—

The sound of him coming down the stairs had her turning to face him.

"What're you doing here?" she demanded, her body still hot and quivery from the sex. Ensuring the panties were wadded in her fist, she folded her arms over her chest to hide the missing buttons.

He looked uncharacteristically tousled and too damned good-looking. She hated, hated, hated that she couldn't not notice that about him.

"I was on my way home and I wanted to check on the house. I figured you would be at Abbott's." He gestured to the door. "When I stepped up onto the porch"—he shrugged those incredibly broad shoulders—"I heard you scream. I tried the door and it was unlocked, so I came in. You plowed into me."

This was all too overwhelming. "What about the . . . ?" She pointed upstairs. "Is that blood? I didn't get close enough to inspect it."

"Definitely blood. I called for a forensics tech. He's on the way."

She worked at not looking at the sofa. Or at him.

"How long had you been home when you noticed the vandalism?"

"I just got here. The intruder was still inside." Good grief. She'd gone upstairs without calling the police. Like a crazy woman. The thought of someone touching her sister's things had pushed her over the edge.

Where was her brain?

"Did you get a look at the intruder?"

Somehow Braddock was closer and she hadn't realized he'd moved. "What?"

"Did you get a look at the intruder?"

She shook her head. "It was dark upstairs. He knocked me down trying to escape. By the time I got back down here and outside, he was long gone. I barely got a glimpse of a dark figure running into the alley."

"Jesus." Braddock pulled out his cell and entered a number. "I'm putting surveillance on your house for the night. You shouldn't be here alone. And you damned sure shouldn't be chasing intruders around." He sent a frustrated glare at her. "Did you even consider calling the police?"

The cold hard facts of what she'd just done—barging up the stairs after an intruder, sex on that sofa, the words she'd said to Braddock in the throes of her temporary insanity—lined up in a taunting row in her head.

She couldn't be in this room with him.

"I . . . I have to take a bath." Even as she said the words, she felt his semen slipping down her thighs. "I can't do this."

She rushed up the stairs and closed herself in the bathroom. Sagged against the door.

"Oh, my God. Oh, my God."

How had she gone so incredibly stupid in a matter of minutes? Unprotected sex! She had to be out of her mind.

Her sister was dead. *Murdered*.

Of course she was out of her mind.

She pushed away from the door, knelt by the tub, and turned the hot water to full blast. She reached up and snagged a clean towel. Her hands shook. She cursed herself over and over until the tub had filled with steaming water.

Stripping off her clothes, she vowed to burn them.

Then she sank into the hot water and let it wash away his touch . . . his scent.

But the images . . . the sensations he'd invoked would not be banished so easily.

Another regret she would have to learn to live with.

If Shelley were here, she would laugh and say that the good girl had finally fallen off her high-and-mighty pedestal.

CJ closed her eyes. She didn't want to be here, didn't want any of this to be real.

The sound of Braddock's voice downstairs reminded her that it was real, all right.

Shelley was dead.

And CJ had totally lost control.

CHAPTER TWELVE

Ricky sat stone still.

Satan raised his head. Listened. Then looked to his master.

He smelled it, too.

Someone was here.

Ricky didn't have to wonder who it was; he knew.

He'd been expecting this visit all evening.

His aunt had gone to her niece's house in Scottsboro. She would stay there until this was over. It was best. Things were going to get ugly around here. No place for an old woman.

This was his trouble. He would deal with it.

He was prepared. Satan was at his feet and his Glock .40 cal lay on the table next to him.

Let the motherfucker come.

The knob on the front door turned with a creak. Ricky sat back in his aunt's ragged old rocker and waited.

No fear. That was the way to handle this shit.

If the son of a bitch smelled fear, it would all be over.

The door flew open, banged against the wall.

The King stormed in, his bodyguards right behind him like a trio of shadows, falling into place around him as he stopped in the middle of the room. The King never went anywhere without his unholy trinity—his three most trusted men.

Ricky knew better than to stand or even move. "What's up, Ty?" Satan trembled with the tension of holding back his primal instincts. "Still," Ricky cautioned. He had a series of one-word commands for Satan. The animal obeyed him faithfully. He knew if he didn't, he wouldn't be eating for a day or two. That was the key with these beasts. Keep them half starved and they did whatever you wanted.

Tyrone sent a disgusted look at the dog, then rammed Ricky with a piercing glare. "You skating on thin ice, Ricky boy. I am not playing with you no more."

"I didn't start this, Tyrone." Ricky's fingers itched to reach for the gun, but that would be a bad mistake. If he showed the slightest indication of aggression, even twitched, he was a dead man.

"That's the truth." Tyrone stepped closer, settled his tall frame into a chair. "But you going to end it."

Tyrone Nash was three years older than Ricky's twenty-eight. He'd started out running drugs for anyone who needed a fast pair of legs. He'd cheated and killed his way to the top. One dead nigger at a time.

He called himself the King. Dressed like a rap star, with all the bling to prove either claim. He'd earned or stolen the respect or fear of every single human being living in the village. Most of the cops in the west precinct were scared shitless of him. He ran all the prostitutes this side of the parkway, owned some portion of the drug business in the whole city. And nobody, nobody dared to cross him.

Old Tyrone was slick as shit and as hard and cold as pure ice. He didn't care about nobody but himself. He'd just as soon kill you as to look at you.

And he was looking at Ricky right now.

"Whatever you say, Ty. I got no beef with you. I know my place, man."

Tyrone smiled, his teeth a brilliant white contrast to that black-as-night skin. "But Ricky, my man, I got a beef with you. I got a dead bitch in my territory and another smart-ass bitch digging around in my business. I can't get it right in my head why you let this shit happen."

Fuck. Ricky swallowed back the fear clawing its way up the back of his throat. "I tried to keep that crazy bitch under control, but Braddock was putting ideas in her head." Ricky laughed, the sound as pathetic as a scared little girl's. "I'm pretty sure she thought she was gonna help take you down or something."

Ricky didn't blink, didn't even breathe for the next few seconds. Old Ty stared long and hard at him. Like he was trying to see the lie. Ricky wasn't stupid. No way was he gonna lie to the guy . . . not to his face, anyway.

"That's why she's dead," Ty said at last.

Ricky nodded. "That's why she's dead." Shelley should've known better than to fuck with the King.

"What did you tell Braddock?"

Ricky had been prepared for Ty to demand a full report. The King had moles all up in HPD, but none who could get close to Braddock. Tyrone hated Braddock. That dude was living on borrowed time.

"I told him I went over there that night," Ricky admitted. "That me and Shelley had a big-ass fight and then I left. That's all there was to tell." Ricky shrugged. "That's what he got."

Tyrone propped his elbows on the chair arms and steepled his fingers like he was going to pray or something. "What did you tell him about me?"

Shit.

"Why would I tell him anything about you?"

Tyrone shot to his feet.

Satan growled.

Pistols leveled around the room.

Ricky froze . . . didn't even breathe.

"You fucking with me, boy?"

Ricky shook his head. "No way, Ty."

Hearing his master's distress, Satan issued another low warning growl.

"That fat mother fucker growls at me again I'll put one right between his fucking bug eyes."

Ricky pulled back on Satan's leash, drawing the animal closer to his leg. "Silence." The animal instantly went quiet.

One of Ty's bodyguards racked his pistol.

A twinge of fear sliced through Ricky. "He asked me about you, of course. But I didn't tell him shit. I just kept saying I didn't know nothing about no King."

Sweat beaded on Ricky's forehead. If he'd been a praying man, this would've been the time to do it. The silver crucifix he wore burned his skin as if reminding him that it was never too late to start a convo with his Maker.

"Braddock didn't believe you. He forced the issue, didn't he?" Ty braced one hand on his wiry hip; with the other he reached up and stroked the long thin scar on his cheek. No one knew where the scar had come from. No one had the balls to ask.

"I . . ." Ricky held on to that I-dunno expression. "He didn't exactly say he didn't believe me."

Tyrone narrowed his gaze at Ricky. "But he asked you specific questions, didn't he?"

What the fuck? Did the guy have someone on Braddock now? Or maybe Ty had finally gotten to that tight-ass partner of Braddock's.

"Sure." Ricky nodded like a fucking bobblehead doll. "He asked all kinds of questions. What was the deal between you and Shelley? Did you order a hit on her? Had I ever witnessed you ordering a murder or conducting any other business?"

He couldn't tell him about the other question. Definitely not that one. If Tyrone found out Braddock had offered Ricky immunity to give up what he knew, he was fucked. Tyrone wouldn't care about the answer Ricky had given; he'd kill him on principle just to cover his ass.

"And what, pray tell, did you say to all those prying questions?"

"I told him I didn't know jack shit about you or what you do. I told him I got my own business to take care of."

Tyrone moved his head side to side. "You think Braddock's a fool?"

Sweat slid down Ricky's jaw. Every answer, right or wrong, dug the hole a little deeper. "No. I . . . I mean, yeah. He's a fool if he thinks he can come over here messing with the King."

Please let that be the answer Ty wants to hear.

"Braddock," Tyrone said, his jaw throbbing with tension, "has a reason for getting in my business."

Ricky nodded, though he didn't have a fucking clue where this was headed.

"It's personal. Between me and him. But it don't matter. He's been trying to get in my shit for three years and he don't seem to get the message I'm sending him. Now you gonna make sure he gets the message. Loud and clear."

Holy fuck.

"How . . ." Ricky cleared his throat. Felt his balls draw up into his belly. "How do you want me to do that?"

"You play his game until I tell you different."

"But . . ." What the hell was he talking about? He couldn't know Braddock wanted him to roll over. "What game?"

"That, Ricky boy, is for you to find out. And, while you're at it, you'll keep that doctor bitch off my ass. Make sure she gets the message I'm sending her way."

Just like that, Tyrone turned and walked out. His bodyguards glared at Ricky before doing the same.

When the door banged shut, Ricky sucked in a ragged breath.

He was so fucked.

If he got into the middle of this war between Braddock and Tyrone, he would end up just like Shelley.

If her smart-ass sister didn't know it already, she'd better figure it out in a hurry.

Shelley was a casualty of war.

CHAPTER THIRTEEN

3021 Appleton Street, 12:30 AM

Braddock was still reeling from the events of the past two and a half hours.

Had he lost his fucking grip on reality?

Apparently.

He damned sure had lost all semblance of self-control.

The forensics tech was almost finished upstairs. The perp had entered the house through the unlocked window in the bedroom. All the windows in the house were unlocked. It seemed that before the perp had finished his task, the worn-out window sash had dropped unexpectedly and shattered the glass. Braddock couldn't say whether the perp had been too rattled to simply kick through the wooden sash and climb back out the window or if he'd intentionally mowed CJ down to frighten her.

Whatever the case, if they were lucky, some of the prints lifted would give them a match. But they'd have to be damned lucky. Shelley had entertained lots of guests in her bedroom. Even with eliminating the prints they'd collected immediately after her murder, they could be interviewing matches for weeks. And if the perp had worn gloves, as Braddock imagined he had, the whole exercise would be a colossal waste of time and manpower.

CJ had refused to make eye contact with him when she'd finally emerged from the bathroom wearing a big, fluffy white
robe he recognized as one of Shelley's. She'd stayed in the
kitchen since. He'd smelled the coffee brewing but didn't dare
invade her space. As much as he would have loved a cup of coffee, it wasn't worth the backlash that was surely coming.

She already despised him. He doubted she liked him any
better now, no matter how amazing the sex.

He took a breath. He could still smell her scent on his
skin . . . on his clothes.

No matter what he wanted to feel, he recognized what had
just happened for what it was: big-ass mistake.

"All done," Greg Day, the evidence tech, announced as he
descended the stairs. "I'll try to have something for you on the
blood by noon. The prints"—he shot Braddock one of those
looks—"will take some time."

"I appreciate the priority status." If that blood was human,
Braddock wanted to know ASAP. "If the blood turns out to be
human, compare it to Shelley Patterson's."

No one fucks with me.

This had to be Nash's work. Bastard.

Day gave him a salute and headed for the door.

"You'll call me when you get the lab results?"

"Definitely," Day called over his shoulder as he exited.
Braddock turned to find CJ lingering in the doorway leading
into the kitchen. A rap on the front door waylaid what he
needed to say. He held up a hand for CJ to hold on.

He'd called in back up. Braddock wanted to make the necessary introductions and get the hell out of here before he said or
did something else stupid. "Sorry to drag you out of bed," he
said to the newest detective on his team. Jenkins was a good
man. A little young, fresh off the beat, but a damned quick
study and ambitious as hell. Braddock was reasonably sure CJ
wouldn't want him hanging around here tonight.

"Dr. Patterson"—he kept the introductions formal—"this is
Detective Wesley Jenkins. He'll be right outside the rest of the
night if you need him."

"Detective Braddock gave me your cell number, ma'am,"

Jenkins offered. "I put through a call to your cell so my number would be handy. Don't hesitate to contact me if you have any questions or if you hear or see anything you feel isn't right."

"Thank you, Detective Jenkins," she said.

A *but* was coming. Braddock could feel it.

"I'm sure I'll be fine now." She lifted her chin in defiance of what she likely knew Braddock was thinking. "The doors and windows will be locked. I can slide the bureau in front of the broken window."

No, he wasn't the one out of his mind. She was.

"Thank you, Jenkins," Braddock said, dismissing the detective. "I'll check in with you on my way out."

Jenkins gave CJ a nod and made his exit before the shit hit the fan.

"You listen to me," Braddock said before she could hurl whatever explanation she'd concocted at him. "This is no game." He pointed to the stairs. "Just because the guy who did this didn't gut you or slice your throat doesn't mean he wasn't dangerous. That writing on the wall"—he stabbed his finger toward the stairs again—"is a warning. Tyrone Nash knows you're here and he's watching you."

CJ looked him straight in the eye. "Just because I fell apart and let you inside me doesn't mean you know me."

The words were so cold, so emotionless, he flinched.

"I can take care of myself. I've been doing that for a very long time. So don't go all martial law on me." She pointed at the door, mimicking his gesture. "You can leave now. I'm finished with you."

The rational argument he'd planned to throw at her, the hard-ass cop attitude he'd been prepared to exhibit, fled for parts unknown.

He'd expected her to be pissed. To yell, maybe stomp her feet. But he hadn't expected a total stone-cold lack of emotion.

Months of frustration and anger mounted. No matter how many times he'd tried, no amount of apologies got through to her. He was wasting his time.

"Well, all right, then." He strode to the door, that anger

building with each step. He hesitated, turned back to her. "Jenkins will be right outside. You can throw me out, but the street is public domain. He isn't going anywhere."

He didn't wait for her comeback. He walked out. The door slammed behind him. He listened for her to engage the lock before walking away.

She wasn't going to make any of this easy. And he was going above and beyond the call to fuck it up even further.

He gave Jenkins strict orders not to move unless she did. As he walked to his G6, his cell vibrated, and he almost hated to check it. Knowing CJ, she could very well have called the chief already to report his indiscretion and his overbearing tactics.

Thankfully, it was his partner. "Braddock."

"Our boy got a late-night visitor," Cooper reported.

When Braddock and Cooper had parted ways, he was to check on the Patterson house and CJ while his partner tailed Banks.

"Nash paid him a visit, did he?" No surprise there. The question was, how had old Ricky boy held up under the interrogation?

"He did," Cooper confirmed. "Nash must've pissed him off good. Banks roared off in that shitty Charger as soon as Nash was out of there. I followed him to that shack they call a cantina on Drake. Maybe if he gets drunk enough I can extract a little information."

Braddock knew full well that Cooper could take care of herself, but some of those joints in what was fondly referred to as Little Mexico were damned dangerous for a woman. "I could use a beer myself." That was a hell of an understatement.

"No way, man. He won't talk to me if you're around. Go home, get some sleep. I've got this covered."

He could argue, but it wouldn't do any good. Cooper was as hardheaded as she was smart.

"All right, but don't take any unnecessary risks. I kind of like what we have, too."

Cooper laughed before disconnecting.

Braddock exhaled a lungful of frustration. Sleep would be impossible. But a shower was absolutely essential. He had to wash CJ off his skin. He couldn't let anything, not even her, distract him from getting the job done.

And he damned sure didn't want to be responsible for any more pain in her life.

He'd already caused more than enough.

CHAPTER FOURTEEN

3021 Appleton Street
1:40 PM

CJ swiped the strands of hair that had fallen free of her ponytail from her damp face, then plunked her hands on her hips. Her T-shirt clung to her sweaty skin. She'd been at this for hours. First thing when she'd gotten up that morning, she'd taken Jenkins a cup of coffee and asked him if it would be okay to clean up Shelley's room.

Jenkins had checked with Braddock, who'd given his okay. The forensics guy likely wouldn't be back.

CJ had begged off breakfast with Edward. He'd been disappointed, but she had needed to do this. And, truthfully, she hadn't been able to face him after last night. He'd always believed in her, trusted her to be smart and do the right thing.

Last night had been more than a mistake. It had been wrong on so many levels, she couldn't begin to label them.

She had made the mistake of trusting Braddock once. That wasn't happening again. Last night had been some kind of mental meltdown. Otherwise she would never have allowed him to touch her, not in a million years.

Focus, CJ. Clues. She needed clues. Where was her sister's cell phone? Braddock had said that Shelley's cell hadn't been found at the scene. Where the hell was it? Shelley never went anywhere without it.

She blew out a disgusted breath.

First thing, she had opened every window to air the place out and get some relief from the heat, then she'd gone through the entire house. Every shelf, every drawer, every hiding place they had used as kids. She'd basically turned the house upside down, then slowly put things back in a slightly more organized manner. Gloves and about a gallon of bleach had cleaned up the biggest part of the mess on the wall in Shelley's room. CJ shuddered. It would take stain blocker and paint to finish the job.

If Banks and Nash thought they could scare her off that easily, they could think again. She wasn't going to be run out of her own house.

So far her work had proven futile. The cell phone was nowhere in the house. She'd found no notes, no *anything* relevant to what had been going on in her sister's life the past few days or weeks. All she'd discovered was the obvious indication that her sister was eating better than she had in the past. There had even been empty milk containers in the trash. Shelley never drank milk.

Had someone else been staying here? There were no clothes or toiletries that would point to that being so.

Frustration wound CJ a little tighter.

Why hadn't Shelley talked to her about this change?

Regret and guilt tied big knots in CJ's stomach. Because her sister knew that she wouldn't believe her. She'd promised to get clean too many times.

Dammit. There had to be something here. This was Shelley's home. Her haven. A scribbled note, anything, indicating what had turned her around. Made her want to give up the drugs and pull her act together. She'd been trying to get clean for years. What had suddenly made it happen? Even if only for a few days.

CJ turned to leave her sister's bedroom, but stalled at the door.

Wait. Wait. Wait.

The bathroom.

CJ hurried down the hall to the only bathroom in the house.

She stared a moment at the antiquated medicine cabinet that hung over the wall-mounted sink. How had they done this?

Open the door first or don't open it? She couldn't recall.

Screw it.

CJ grabbed hold of the glass door, a hand on either side, and pulled. She pulled so hard she stumbled back and hit the wall when the cabinet pulled free so easily. The contents jangled around inside the cabinet.

"Damn." Using her foot, she closed the toilet lid and placed the metal and glass cabinet on top of it. She'd already gone through the contents of the cabinet. Aspirin and miscellaneous store-bought pharmaceuticals. Nothing CJ didn't know about already. Her sister kept an array of over-the-counter pain killers and sleep aids on hand at all times.

Holding her breath, CJ tiptoed, leaned over the sink and peered into the wall cavity. A smile stretched across her lips. "Ah ha!"

When she and Shelley were kids, they had discovered quite by accident that the crosspiece that was supposed to support the worn-out medicine cabinet was actually six inches too low. They'd been fighting over who got the last pink Flintstone vitamin and had ripped the medicine cabinet right out of the wall. Evidently there had been a longer cabinet there at one time or another. Either that or the carpenter who'd installed it hadn't bothered with proper brace work. He certainly hadn't secured it properly.

Anything they didn't want their mother or any of her "friends" to find, they'd hidden in that cavity.

Holding her breath, CJ reached in. Three items sat on the aged two-by-four crosspiece: a bottle, what appeared to be a business card, and a folded piece of paper.

Anticipation sent her pulse into a faster rhythm. As a doctor, she couldn't help herself. She looked at the bottle first. Large. Vitamins? Then she read the label and the attached prescription sticker.

Prenatal vitamins.

CJ's chest tightened.

Did this mean . . . ?

The business card wasn't a business card. It was an appointment card. Shelley had had a doctor's appointment at the village clinic at the end of next week. CJ dropped the vitamins and the card onto the counter and focused on the paper. Hands shaking, she carefully unfolded it. Standard clinic visit form. Shelley had seen the doctor at two o'clock on July thirtieth.

Friday.

The day before she was murdered.

Diagnostic code . . . Adrenaline pumping through her veins, CJ scanned the form until she found the entry she sought.

Positive pregnancy.

Shelley was pregnant?

That ferocious pounding that accompanied her treatment of every trauma victim rushed into the ER erupted in CJ's chest now.

Her sister had been pregnant.

CJ sagged against the doorjamb.

No wonder she'd been so excited when she called and left that voice mail. She wanted to share the news with CJ.

So . . . who was the father?

Ricky Banks?

Did he even know about this?

Oh, God.

The form fluttered to the floor. CJ shoved the medicine cabinet off the toilet and yanked up the lid.

She heaved again and again though she'd eaten nothing but toast this morning.

CJ collapsed onto the floor, flinching when her knee hit the corner of the medicine cabinet. Medicine bottles were scattered over the battered linoleum. Dust and grime had collected on the baseboards and in the corners. The wallpaper that had been there for as long as CJ remembered had faded and wrinkled, peeling away from the wall here and there.

All those insignificant details inventoried in her stunned mind as she grappled with this new truth.

Shelley had been pregnant.

It didn't matter at the moment who the father was.

It only mattered that the killer had murdered two people.

CJ staggered to her feet, washed her hands, and threw cold water on her face in an effort to snap out of the daze this news had induced. She stuck her face under the stream of water and rinsed her mouth.

When she'd pulled herself back together she reached down and picked up the form and the appointment card.

These were evidence. Sort of. Of course the autopsy would reveal that Shelley had been pregnant. But the fact that she had known before she was murdered could be significant. Especially since she'd obviously felt the need to hide the evidence of her pregnancy.

Why would she have done that unless she'd feared repercussions?

CJ had been wrong. It did matter who the father was. If he was a married man or just a jerk who didn't want children with—CJ swallowed hard—a known prostitute and drug addict, he may have taken matters into his own hands.

She should call Braddock.

CJ hesitated before reaching for her cell phone. The thought of talking to him . . .

No. First she should go to the clinic and see if anyone there knew who the father was. Shelley had been excited. She very well could have gone on and on to whoever delivered the news to her.

CJ made it as far as the living room before her knees gave out on her and she dropped into the closest chair.

She closed her eyes and fought the overwhelming ache twisting in her chest. This was so unfair. Shelley had talked about wanting a kid. On one of those rare occasions when she and CJ weren't fighting, she'd enthused wildly about how she would never be like their mother. She would stay clean and be a good mother. Her baby would never do without the most important element of childhood—loving attention from his or her parents.

That was the deal. Their childhoods hadn't been so screwed up because they were poor or lived in a less-than-desirable part of town. Their childhoods had been unstable and scary and miserable a good portion of the time because no one had been there to see after them.

CJ had done her best to be both mother and father, starting at age ten. But it hadn't been enough.

Agony throbbed inside her.

Everything Shelley had ever set out to accomplish had blown up in her face. A lot of her choices had been bad ones, leaving no one to blame but herself. But sometimes fate just cheated her.

Like this time.

Anger propelled CJ to her feet. She could sit here feeling sorry for her sister's misfortunes and guilty for not being better at taking care of her, or she could find out who killed her.

By the time CJ had snagged her bag, grabbed her keys, and stormed out to the car, she was damned pissed off.

Other than a decent burial, this was the one thing CJ could do for her sister.

Keep looking until she found Shelley's killer.

Mill Village Medical Clinic

The clinic was closed.

CJ stared in disbelief at the opening hours. Since when was the clinic open only two days per week?

Wednesdays and Fridays only?

What were sick people supposed to do the other five days of the week?

CJ knew the answer: wait until they were sick enough to go to the ER. It cost everyone four times as much and the hospital ended up unable to collect.

Bad business all the way around.

Dammit.

Frustrated, she started back to her car. Detective Jenkins had parked across the street. She refused to be intimidated by his presence. He could follow her around twenty-four/seven and she wasn't going to do anything differently. Braddock could kiss her—

A Camry turned into the parking lot. CJ hesitated before opening her car door. Someone else who didn't realize the clinic wouldn't be open. The vehicle was a little upscale for any of the village residents. Well, except maybe for the crime lords and slumlords. They generally drove nicer vehicles.

Maybe she could at least get the name of whoever was running the clinic. The physician's signature on the patient visit form was impossible to make out. Big surprise there. If she had to track down the doctor in charge at home or at another clinic, she would.

A woman emerged from the Camry. "The clinic's closed," she announced without preamble.

Hello to you, too. CJ was in no mood to take any crap. The lady would just have to deal with it. "Yeah, I see that." She took a couple of steps toward the Camry. "Can you tell me the name of the doctor who runs the clinic?"

The woman stared at CJ across the top of her car. Her gaze narrowed. "CJ Patterson?"

CJ tried to place the woman's face. There was something vaguely familiar about her. Long brown hair, round face. Boxy frame, not exactly fat, just square. Medium height. "Yes. I'm CJ Patterson."

She was just about to ask the woman's name when the woman spoke up again. "You don't remember me, do you?"

The fact that her expression had grown colder with the statement didn't bode well for getting information.

"I'm sorry." CJ shook her head. "I'm really bad with names." That wasn't generally the case, but the other woman didn't have to know that.

As if the woman had decided the conversation wasn't worth pursuing, she reached back into her Camry and withdrew with a large shoulder bag and an armful of files. She bumped the car door closed with her hip.

"Like I said"—she sent CJ a pointed look—"the clinic is closed." She tossed her head, sending her hair flying over her shoulder, and marched toward the clinic's entrance.

Wait. There was something familiar about that move—the whole tossing-her-head thing, as if she'd just dismissed CJ. "Juanita." CJ recognized her now. "Juanita Lusk."

Key halfway to the door's lock, the woman's hand stilled. "I guess you're better with names than you thought." She shoved the key into the lock without a backward glance.

It was all coming back to CJ now. Juanita had been a junior when CJ was a freshman at Huntsville's University of Alabama. Juanita had been in pre-med, too.

Carter Cost.

Yeah, CJ remembered. He'd dumped Juanita for a brief fling with CJ. Her first and only mistake with men—until Braddock.

Evidently Juanita still held a grudge.

CJ bolted into action, catching the door before it closed behind Lusk. She parked herself in the threshold and didn't budge.

"I already told you," Juanita snapped, "we're closed."

"I'll only take a minute of your time. Please," CJ urged, "it's really important."

An indifferent huff previewed the lack of compassion that claimed Lusk's face. "Get out of the way and let me lock the door before the whole fucking village shows up."

CJ stepped around her and waited while she locked the door. Lusk didn't switch on the lights, just turned and headed through the lobby. CJ stayed right on her heels.

The clinic looked exactly as it had when she was a kid. Same scuffed tile floors and worn-out waiting room seating. The TV and VCR were new to the clinic but far from newly purchased. Beyond the lobby there appeared to have been a halfhearted face-lift in the last decade. Still three exam rooms to the right, a toilet, lab/supply room, and office on the left. Straight back at the end of the corridor that divided the rear section of the clinic in half was an emergency exit, the one the staff generally used to come and go.

Inside the cramped office Juanita dumped the load of files on the already cluttered metal desk and dropped her bag on the floor. "What do you want?" She plopped unceremoniously into the chair behind the desk. "When I get finished here I have catching up to do at the Downtown Clinic too."

CJ didn't sit. Mainly because the only other chair was stacked full of files. She could do this better standing, anyway. "My sister, Shelley, was a patient here. I'm sure you've heard that she was murdered over the weekend."

Lusk's indifferent expression didn't alter in the slightest. "Yeah, I saw the two-liner buried in this morning's paper."

Anger unfurled in CJ's belly. "You know, college was a long time ago and I'm really sorry you haven't gotten past it, but my sister is dead and I really don't give a shit if you didn't get the guy."

Lusk's face softened just the tiniest bit. "The way I remember it, you didn't either."

CJ's shoulders sagged as the fight drained out of her. "True."

"Look, Patterson." Lusk waved a hand around the tiny office. "I have a lot of work to do. I'm sorry as hell about your sister, but that's the way it goes around here. What is it that you want from me?"

"She had an appointment with you next Friday."

Lusk flipped through the dog-eared appointment book on the desk, stopped on the appropriate page, and scanned the names. "Yep. Two o'clock." She grabbed a pen and scratched out Shelley's name.

CJ flinched. Tears stung her eyes, but she wouldn't let this grudge-carrying witch see it.

"According to the clinic form I found at the house," CJ continued when Lusk didn't offer any information, "Shelley was pregnant."

"If that's what the form says, then that's the case."

"How far along was she?"

Lusk twisted the pen in her fingers and appeared to consider the question. "I believe I estimated six weeks, probably based on the date of her last period. She was supposed to come back for the vaginal exam. I could look up her file, but, as you can see"—she waved her hands over her desk—"I'm little overwhelmed at the moment."

CJ shook her head. That wasn't really her concern. "Did she mention to you or any of the other staff who the father was?"

Lusk cocked her head. "Are you seriously asking *that* question?"

CJ blinked. "Yes. There's a murder investigation, and—"

"Maybe you're in denial," Lusk interrupted, "but your sister spent most of her nights working the streets as a prostitute." She held up a hand when CJ would have blasted her. "Fortunately, she'd started cleaning up her act. She'd been drug-free for nearly two months. And she was clean, no STDs. She was a work in progress. I'm not judging; I'm simply making an honest statement."

CJ moistened her lips, tamped down the emotion swelling in her throat. Emotion aside, she recognized that Lusk had a point.

"The father could have been any one of a number of men." Lusk lifted her linebacker shoulders and let them fall. "She didn't tell me and I didn't ask. Most of the young women who come in here are working girls. I test them, treat what ails them, and don't ask questions. They don't talk."

"Could she . . ." CJ worked at steadying her voice. "Could she have talked to anyone else here?"

Lusk opened her arms wide. "I'm it, Patterson. The clinic staff begins and ends with me right now. Both the nurse and the receptionist quit a week ago. I shouldn't even be operating this clinic without one or both, but then the folks here go without medical attention." She braced her elbows atop the stack of files. "Maybe you've forgotten how it is around here since you landed that prestigious residency at Hopkins."

Now the real issue surfaced. Lusk was jealous. Did she have nothing better to do than to keep up with a former classmate's career? What was wrong with this woman? CJ's sister was dead!

"I'm sure you won't mind if I see her chart."

A guard went up as visibly as if Lusk had pushed CJ out of her office and slammed the door. "What does her chart have to do with her murder?"

CJ shook her head. "Nothing. I just wanted some insight—"

"Whatever. I'll dig it up. Obviously I have nothing better to do." She pushed to her feet. "Just give me a minute. I don't think I filed Friday's charts."

"Thank you."

CJ rubbed at her forehead. A long-overdue headache was

brewing. No sleep, no decent food, way too much caffeine. And Braddock. A recipe for trouble.

While she waited, CJ surveyed the office. Lusk was right. She was way behind on paperwork. If she was running this clinic alone even for one week, she had to be overwhelmed. CJ moved closer to the wall where Lusk's credentials hung. University of Alabama in Birmingham. Surprise flared at what she didn't see.

"That's right," Lusk said from the door.

Feeling like she'd just been caught with her hand in the cookie jar, CJ turned to face her.

"I didn't get *MD* behind my name." Lusk shoved the chart at CJ. "I had to settle for being a nurse practitioner. Which means I do twice the work you do and get paid half as much."

CJ wanted to ask what had happened, but she was pretty sure Lusk wouldn't want to discuss it with her. What could she say: *I'm sorry* or *Sucks for you*?

"I have a son," Lusk explained as if she'd read CJ's mind. "He needed me. Try surviving your residency with a baby on your hip."

Wow. Even surviving nursing school with a kid had to be tough. Tack on the additional requirements for practitioner and that was saying something. "How old is your son?"

Lusk hesitated, then said, "Nine."

"Pictures?" CJ knew the interest on her face looked fake, but it was the best she could do.

"I don't think you seriously want to see a picture of my kid." Lusk settled behind her desk once more. "Look at the chart. I have work to do."

CJ skimmed Shelley's medical chart. Nothing she hadn't expected. Shelley had been in several times for STDs. Tests to ensure she did or didn't have one or more on different occasions. A follow-up to the concussion and fracture she'd gotten from that worthless asshole Banks just over a month ago. Same old Shelley. Lab results from last week. CJ didn't know what she'd expected to find, but she hadn't found it.

She passed the chart back to Lusk. "Thank you."

"Yeah." Lusk tossed it onto the pile of others.

CJ hesitated a moment, felt like there was something more she should say. Take a step toward mending that bridge, maybe. After all, this woman had taken care of Shelley's medical needs.

"Use the back door." Lusk didn't bother looking up again.

CJ didn't bother taking that step she'd considered. Instead, she walked out.

How was it that she'd been gone for seven years and no one or nothing that mattered around here had changed?

Absolutely nothing.

Except her sister was dead.

CJ would know the reason her sister had been murdered.

She glanced back at the run-down clinic.

Maybe she already did.

That was exactly why she was going to visit the one person who knew Shelley almost as well as CJ did: Ricky Banks. This time the police weren't coming between them.

CJ wanted him all alone.

Ricky and his scumbag cronies weren't the only ones who could play games.

She was about to show him she hadn't forgotten the lessons she'd learned as a kid.

CJ Patterson could lie, cheat, and steal . . . if it meant finding her sister's killer.

CHAPTER FIFTEEN

Juanita Lusk didn't move for a long time after Patterson left. She stared at the mound of files on the desk, her mind frozen yet somehow spinning wildly.

She had work. A ton of work.

She should get started.

"Oh, God."

Shelley Patterson was dead.

A tremor of uncertainty quaked through Juanita, shattering the quivering mass of stalled thoughts.

Fuck. Fuck. Fuck.

She glanced around her office. Tried to think what to do.

This really had nothing to do with her. Nothing at all.

Shelley was dead because she didn't know how to stay out of trouble. She was always . . .

Fuck.

Who was she kidding?

Juanita needed a cigarette. Grabbing her bag, she plopped it on top of the mountain of work. Fished around inside until she found her Marlboro Lights. Lighter. Where was that damned lighter? Her hands shook.

"Shit!" She turned her bag upside down, let her stuff tumble over the desk, onto the floor. The lighter fell into her lap. Hand still shaking, she snatched it up and lit the Marlboro.

She didn't care that it was a smoke-free environment.

She had far bigger problems.

Juanita dragged in a lungful of smoke, savored it for as long as she could before allowing it to escape.

She'd promised her son she would quit.

Maybe when this was over.

Fear wrapped around and around her heart, tightened like a threatening serpent.

What had she done?

Christ. She'd made the mother of all mistakes.

How was she supposed to know the son of a bitch would go this far? Yeah, he dabbled in drugs. Had himself a regular little habit going on. But with all he had going for him, who would have imagined he would do *this*?

Shelley was dead.

Juanita clasped a hand over her mouth to hold back the desperation rising in her throat.

This couldn't be happening.

Okay, okay. Don't panic. She shoved the half-smoked cigarette into the abandoned Coke can on her desk.

No one knew. It was her secret.

"You're okay." She pulled in a deep breath. "Just do your job, Juanita." She braced her hands on the desk and let the air seep slowly into her lungs. "No need to panic."

Nobody would ever know.

She shook her head.

No way.

This murder had nothing to do with her.

She hadn't killed anybody.

She had nothing to worry about.

A stillness crept over her, narrowed her view until one vivid truth filled her consciousness.

No, she had nothing to worry about except . . .

CJ Patterson.

CHAPTER SIXTEEN

Braddock reclined in the uncomfortable metal chair and propped his feet on the table as two uniforms delivered Banks to the interview room.

Banks, looking exactly like a man with a hellacious hangover, stared in bewilderment as the door closed. He'd still been in bed when the cops arrived.

"What the fuck?" He turned around, stumbled back a step as his gaze landed on Braddock. He held up his hands. "I done told you everything I know."

"I wish that were true," Braddock said as he dropped his feet to the floor and stood. "But, you see, I know you're lying." He walked around the table and pulled out the other chair. "Have a seat."

Banks glared at him for about ten seconds, then swaggered to the chair and plopped down in it. "What the fuck do you want?"

Braddock had waited until Banks was in the room to do this part. He picked up the small roll of blue painter's tape from the table, pulled the chair he'd vacated across the room, and stepped up onto it. After tearing off a strip of tape, he plastered it across the camera lens and stepped down from the chair.

"What the fuck?" Banks mumbled.

Braddock pulled his chair back to the table and took a seat. He shoved the roll of tape back into the table's only drawer, then reached beneath the desk to turn off the microphone. "Now. I understand you had a few beers with my partner last night."

Cooper had called Braddock at three-thirty this morning to say she'd delivered Banks to his house since he was shit-faced. She'd learned a couple of interesting tidbits, nothing case-breaking, but enough to give Braddock some leverage.

"Your fucking partner," Banks said, his speech still slightly slurred, "set me up. That's called entrapment."

Braddock turned his palms up. "Prove it."

Banks puffed out a breath. "Fuck you."

"The problem is . . ." Braddock sat back, studied the scumbag. "You're the one who's fucked."

The other man's gaze narrowed. "How do you figure that?"

"Considering two uniforms picked you up at your house this morning and hauled you in—not to mention my partner took you home in the wee hours of the morning—I would say Nash has concluded that you're cooperating with the police."

Banks laughed. "I ain't doing shit with the police."

"You know that," Braddock allowed, "and I know that, but Nash doesn't."

Fear made its first appearance in the scumbag's eyes.

"Detective Cooper reported that you kept talking about Nash having a plan to have his revenge with me. Why don't you start with telling me about that?"

"I was drunk. I don't even remember what I said. But I don't know nothing about what Nash does. I told you that."

Nothing Braddock hadn't expected. Shelley had warned him that Banks wouldn't talk without some major motivation. Braddock stood, sending his chair scraping across the tiled floor. "You see, Ricky"—he leaned forward, braced his hands on the table, and put his face in the other man's—"that's just not acceptable to me."

"Ain't shit you can do about it," the bastard had the balls to say.

Braddock smiled. "That's where you're wrong." His smile vanished. "I will watch every move you make. Have you hauled in every single day until you wish you were anybody but Ricky Banks. I'll put the word out on the street that you're a snitch. You won't have a customer left in this county or the next who'll do business with you. And you'll be so sick of seeing my face that you'll want to take that unlicensed Glock of yours and put yourself out of your misery before someone else does it for you."

"You want me to help you," Banks scoffed, "the way Shelley helped you? Yeah, right. I don't wanna get dead like her."

Self-disgust cramped Braddock's insides. "I guess it all depends upon who scares you the most, Banks. Nash or me."

The stare-off lasted long enough for sweat to break out on the other man's forehead.

"I can help you." Banks swallowed hard. "You just have to give me time to set things in motion. Ty is careful." He blinked for the first time. His hands shook as he shoved the hair back from his face. "You won't be able to connect him to any of his past activities. It'll have to be something new."

Now they were getting somewhere. "Seventy-two hours." Braddock let that sink in a moment. "That's all the time I can give you. Can you make that happen?"

Banks nodded eagerly. "I'll make it happen."

"You get what I need on Nash and I'll make sure you're taken care of."

"Can I leave now?"

Braddock dragged his chair back to the wall and removed the tape from the camera lens. "Absolutely. I'll have someone take you to your car."

Braddock left the room. Jenkins waited in the corridor. "Take that piece of shit to his car. It's parked at that cantina on Drake."

"Did he give you anything useful?" the junior detective asked, anticipation gleaming in his eyes. He wanted deeper into this case so bad it hurt. He followed Braddock around like a groupie. Told everyone he wanted to be just like him.

Braddock grinned. "He'll get us what we need."

Jenkins nodded as if he hadn't expected anything less. "Of course. I don't know why I asked. He didn't have a chance against you."

"Get some sleep. You'll need it," he told Jenkins before heading to his office. He needed to touch base with Greg Day at the lab. If that turned out to be Shelley's blood . . . It wouldn't be enough to nail Nash legally, but it would confirm a connection between the note he had received after his niece's murder and the message to CJ. His cell vibrated. He checked the screen. Cooper. She'd relieved Jenkins an hour ago. The chief had allotted only three detectives on this case. They would have to do the best they could with minimal manpower.

"Braddock."

"She's waiting outside Banks's house," Cooper reported.

A frown furrowed across his forehead. "Jenkins is taking Banks to his car now. Keep an eye on her until I get there."

After last night's break-in, he would have thought CJ would be more careful. He should have known better. She'd spent her whole life taking care of her sister. To CJ's way of thinking, finding her killer would be necessary to finish the job.

If it didn't get her killed first.

4:05 PM

Braddock watched the house on Clopton where Banks resided with his aunt. CJ sat on the steps waiting for his arrival. According to Jenkins, Banks had made a stop at the liquor store on the corner of Drake and the Parkway.

CJ couldn't get past the idea that Banks was the one who'd killed her sister. Banks would insist when she asked that it hadn't been him. It had been the King.

The King. Braddock's jaw tightened with the hatred that exploded inside him each time he thought of that bastard. He was a king, all right. King of a run-down village filled with desperate people eking out the same desperate lives their parents and their grandparents before them had eked out.

It was way past time the cycle was stopped.

The only way to end it was to neutralize its core. The hub that held all the spokes together, spinning in that vicious circle.

Change wasn't about to come to this neighborhood as long as scumbags like Nash ran things.

Cooper didn't see this case the way he did. Whoever had killed Shelley, Nash was responsible. He would have given the order. Just as he had two years ago when he'd murdered Braddock's niece.

Fury whipped through him, slicing his heart into quivering pieces.

Sweet. Beautiful. And only nineteen.

Braddock had promised his brother when he left for Iraq that he would keep his family safe. His wife, daughter, and son would be well taken care of until his tour was over. Six months later, his brother had been shipped back home in a wooden box. Barely two months after that, Kimberly had disappeared. She had gotten into a fight with her mother. Declared that she was going to live with her uncle.

Braddock had given her a firm talking-to when she'd showed up at his door. He'd told her how much her mother needed her. How much her brother needed her. Then he'd made the mistake of telling Kimberly that her mother was on her way to Huntsville to pick her up. The next time he'd turned his back, the kid was out the door.

Her body hadn't been discovered for nearly a month.

But Braddock had gotten the message mere days after her disappearance. A note, handwritten in blood.

No one fucks with me.

Analysis had immediately shown that the type was the same as Kimberly's. By the time the DNA analysis came back confirming that it was his niece's blood, her body had washed up on a Decatur riverbank.

That dull ache that lived inside Braddock roared. He'd gotten his niece killed. His determination to take Nash down for his crimes had prompted a reaction.

Nash had let him know that his interference would not be tolerated.

Braddock's fingers tightened into fists. God, he wanted to kill that son of a bitch.

For more than a year and a half he had been working every case that could even remotely be connected to Nash. Missing prostitutes. Two homicides. Numerous assaults and robberies.

Anything in the village or any other part of Nash's territory, Braddock got involved. He worked day and night, seven days a week if necessary.

Whatever it took to legally bring that son of a bitch to his knees.

Then, eleven months ago, Shelley Patterson had stumbled into his life. After he'd finished the investigation into the break-in at her house, Braddock had kept the friendship going with her. He'd noted how connected she was to both Banks and Nash. He'd seen her connections as an opportunity. Then he'd developed protective feelings for her. He'd wanted to help her. Not long after that he'd met CJ, and he'd been hooked on the Patterson sisters.

CJ had trusted him at first, even liked him on a personal level. The physical attraction had been off the charts. God, he'd wanted her and, he was pretty damned certain, she had wanted him too—for a lot more than a stress-relief fuck.

Until he'd screwed it up.

But Kevin Braddock was determined when it came to the job. He hadn't let his failure with CJ stop him from pursuing his quest to get Nash. Three months ago Shelley had come to him with a plan to end the King's rule once and for all.

Now she was dead.

Braddock had allowed that to happen. The same way he had allowed his niece to become a target.

Maybe it was time to stop playing by the rules.

Tyrone Nash was going down.

A black Charger rolled up the street, drawing Braddock's attention back to the present.

His pulse quickened. Banks knew he was being watched. CJ was in no danger from him as long as that was the case.

But she was making herself a major target with Nash. And that was damned dangerous.

CHAPTER SEVENTEEN

2204 Clopton Street, 4:15 PM

Finally.

CJ heard Ricky's Charger roar into the driveway at the back of his aunt's house. Inside, the dog barked even louder in response to his master's return.

She touched her back pocket and the cold metal cylinder there. Pepper spray was her only means of defense. She didn't know if it would put a big dog down, but it would definitely slow Ricky down if he gave her any trouble.

Cell phone was in her front pocket. She was good to go.

The car that had been following her had disappeared. She'd been annoyed by the cop's presence at the clinic, but now she kind of wished he were still around.

She climbed the steps and stood at the door a moment before knocking.

Deep breath.

Be strong.

She raised her fist and banged on the front door.

The dog roared into action. Deep, throaty bark. Frightening growl.

CJ hooked her thumb in her back pocket, ready to snatch that pepper spray if necessary.

Heavy footsteps approached the door. There was no security

peep hole. Since Ricky didn't open the door right away she had to assume he had another way to identify his visitor. One of the windows, maybe.

He said something to his dog. The growling stopped instantly. The door opened.

"What do you want?"

CJ lifted her chin and glared at the hulk of a guy. Images of him chasing Shelley through those woods sent pain spreading out from her chest. "I have to talk to you." She had to stay calm. If she wanted him to talk to her, she couldn't go in there ranting and screaming. No accusing . . . just talking.

Ricky glanced at the street, right then left. "I told you to stay away from me. I don't know nothing about what happened. Stop nagging my ass. I'm getting enough shit from the cops."

She put her body in the threshold before he could shut the door in her face. "I do know something about it and we need to talk."

"Whatever." He gave her his back but left the door open.

His dog followed him, glancing back repeatedly at CJ.

She stepped fully inside and closed the door. Her heart hammered wildly but she couldn't let him see just how scared she was. So she sucked it up and headed in the direction he'd already gone.

In the kitchen, he was in the middle of preparing a sandwich. His dog sat at his feet, his tongue lapping at his jowls hungrily.

"Spit it out," Ricky said as he slapped mayo on two slices of bread. "I got things to do."

She could just imagine what kind of things he had to do. "Shelley was pregnant."

His gaze shot to hers. "What?" He made one of those faces that said he thought she was full of crap.

"I verified it at the clinic today. She was about six weeks pregnant." CJ met his condescending glare with determination in hers. "Was it you?"

"Six weeks, you say?"

She nodded.

He braced his hands on the counter and appeared to pull up a mental calendar. Then he shook his head. "No way."

"Are you certain? The two of you hadn't been intimate in the past two months?"

He plopped bologna on the bread, rolled his eyes. "We were never *intimate*, Dr. Patterson. We fucked. You ever tried it?"

Equal parts fury and frustration burned her cheeks. He couldn't know about last night. "Answer the question, Ricky. I'm not interested in discussing my sex life with you."

After tearing off a big bite of his sandwich with his teeth, he laughed as he chewed. "You have to have one before you can talk about it. Is that it?"

"Did you and Shelley—"

"Yeah, yeah." He took a slug of Maker's Mark bourbon straight from the bottle. "No. Shelley and I hadn't fucked in about three months. All we did when we ran into each other was fight."

That couldn't be right. "But you gave her a concussion and broke her wrist just a little over a month ago. What did she do? Blow you off?" Anger stung through CJ at the thought of this brute hurting her sister. He outweighed her by seventy-five or eighty pounds, stood eight or ten inches taller. Scumbag. Maybe he hadn't killed Shelley, but he'd been abusing her for years.

Ricky shook his head. "I took the fall for that, but I didn't lay a hand on her." He took another slug of bourbon. "Here's the thing." He wiped his mouth with the back of his hand. "Shelley's dead and she's still busting my balls. What the fuck's up with that? I didn't lay a hand on her a month ago and I still got harassed about it. I didn't do nothing but yell at her the other night, and the cops are all up my ass."

Of course he would say that. "I was told that you were the one who beat her." Mr. O'Neal, the neighbor, had seen Ricky at Shelley's that night. Had heard the yelling.

"Did Shelley say it was me?" He crammed another hunk of sandwich into his mouth.

CJ had to think about that a moment. She and Shelley had spent the whole time arguing when CJ was here last. But now that she thought about it, Shelley didn't say it was Ricky. CJ had taken O'Neal's word for it.

"I didn't think so." Ricky swallowed. "I'm the one she called for a ride to the ER. But I didn't lay a hand on her. The next day the cops questioned me about it just because I was the one who took her to the hospital."

CJ rubbed at her right temple. That dull ache just wouldn't go away. "Did she tell you who did it?"

"You have to ask?"

A frown furrowed. "Are you saying Tyrone beat her up?" Was it possible Tyrone had killed Shelley? CJ needed to take a big step back and look at this without all those emotions getting in the way.

Ricky laughed. "Are you serious? He don't get his hands dirty like that. But I guarantee you one of his people took care of it for him."

"But why?" CJ couldn't fit all the pieces together. "Shelley worked for you, right? Why would Nash get involved?"

"She used to work for me. Two and a half, three months ago she started working directly for Tyrone kind of under the table, if you know what I mean. I raised hell with her about it, but I know the food chain around here. Tyrone's the top and I'm somewhere in the middle. So I shut the fuck up and recruited some fresh meat to take her place."

CJ gritted her teeth. *Don't let him see your disgust. Keep him talking.* "Is it possible Nash was the father?" CJ had butted heads with Nash a few times years ago when he'd been a fledgling tyrant. He'd had a thing for her, sort of. She'd kept telling him no when he would ask her out, until her name was shifted to his mortal-enemy list. And then he'd tried to take what she wouldn't give him. She'd left her mark for him to remember that he couldn't always have what he wanted.

"I doubt it." Ricky reached into the fridge and pulled out what appeared to be a small chunk of raw steak. He tossed it to the dog. The big animal devoured it. "The King don't touch the whores. Like you," Ricky pressed with a haughty look, "he keeps his sex life private."

CJ let the ugly reference to Shelley being a whore slide. It hurt her to think it, but it was true.

"Could one of her johns have gotten her pregnant?" Surely there was a way to narrow down the possibilities.

"I don't think she was working the streets for Tyrone. I think she was working on something else for him. Like I said, under the table."

God. What did that mean? "Was she muling drugs?" She'd done it before.

Ricky shook his head. "Don't think so."

This was going in circles. "Was there a guy in her life? Somebody new?"

"Yeah." Ricky leveled his gaze on hers. "She got off on letting me know she was moving on to bigger and better things. Apparently, she misjudged her worth."

Again, CJ let the comment slide. She didn't want to argue with him. She wanted answers. "Do you know who the guy was?"

"Matter of fact, I do." He smirked. "She had herself a cop."

Tension prodded CJ's instincts. "Was she dating this cop?" The only cop she was aware her sister ever talked to was Braddock. Dread welled inside CJ. Images from last night elbowed their way into her head, turning the sickening dread into something far more painful.

Ricky shrugged. "Maybe. Mostly she was playing him. Or he was playing her."

"Can you spell that out, please?" Jesus Christ. Couldn't he just give her a straight answer? But then, maybe she already knew the answer. God, if she found out Braddock had . . .

He wouldn't do that—not again. Shelley wouldn't have . . . surely she wouldn't have.

"I don't know. But they were up to something. You should ask him if he knocked her up."

"Do you know this cop's name?" she asked, just in case it was someone else. It had to be someone else.

"Sure. You've met him already. It's Braddock. Asshole," Ricky muttered, then downed another slug of bourbon. "He'll get his. Soon, at the rate he's going."

"If you . . ." She had to get out of here. She had to think. Then she was going to find Braddock and demand some answers. Or maybe she would kick the shit out of him just on principle. Report him to his chief. Something! "If you think of anything else, will you let me know?"

Ricky plopped the bottle of bourbon on the counter. "I know she was your sister and all, but she's dead. You can't bring her back. Why you doing this? You gotta know you're stumbling around in hazardous territory."

"I have to do this. I'm not letting her killer evade justice the way my father's killer did." CJ looked him square in the eye, tried to read his reaction.

Ricky moved his head side to side, heaved a big breath. The smell of bourbon had her holding her breath.

"You did something most around here couldn't manage." Resignation cluttered his expression. "You got out. Escaped. What the hell you doing taking this risk? Go back to Baltimore, CJ. You don't belong here no more. That's the other side of the coin, girl. Most of these people"—he gestured magnanimously— "spend their whole lives trying to get out but can't. You got out. But you can't come back. You ain't one of us no more."

CJ should have thanked him for answering her questions. But she couldn't. She had to get out of there. His words kept echoing around her.

You don't belong here no more.

CHAPTER EIGHTEEN

3021 Appleton Street, 5:05 PM

The door opened after his first knock. Braddock sized up CJ's state of mind in one glance. Outraged.

Whatever Banks had said to her, she was not happy. She'd called Braddock's cell phone the instant she walked away from the meeting with the scumbag. Obviously the discussion had included Braddock, and whatever the result, it wasn't good.

"Come in, Detective." She left him at the door and took a seat on the sofa.

Detective, not *Braddock*. Oh yeah, she was not happy. He stepped inside, closed the door. "You said you had new information." He doubted anything Banks had told her would be earth-shattering. Just more bullshit.

"Please"—she indicated a chair—"sit."

He sat in the chair closest to her position on the sofa, then waited. After all, she'd called him.

As much as he wanted to pretend he wasn't mentally braced on the edge of his chair, he was. After last night, he wasn't sure about anything except to expect the unexpected.

He blocked the memories that immediately tried to fracture his concentration. That she sat on that sofa—right where he'd made his last mistake with her—disturbed him.

No, that was wrong. It tugged at him. Made him want to repeat the same mistake again. But she would never let that happen. Not in this lifetime.

CJ crossed her jean-clad legs, then folded her hands in her lap. "First, have you discovered anything new in your investigation? Any word back from the lab on the evidence collected last night?" She glared at him with enough frost to chill an iceberg. "Anything at all?"

That she didn't want to get straight to the point of her meeting with Banks surprised him. "The blood on your wall was not human." He'd gotten the news on the way here. "Feline." That the blood hadn't been Shelley's changed nothing for Braddock. This kind of warning was Nash's MO. He was a freak who got off on instilling fear and torturing all manner of life-forms.

CJ shuddered visibly but quickly resumed deep-freeze mode. "Is that all?"

"We also discovered an additional piece of what may or may not be evidence at the scene." He'd give her this one thing. She still wouldn't like or respect him, particularly after last night. Maybe she'd at least see that he and his partner were actually attempting to solve this case. "What appears to be a name was carved into the tree branch used to secure the rope."

Her eyes widened. "What name?"

"E. Noon. Ring any bells?"

She thought about that a moment, then shook her head. "You're saying someone climbed into that tree and carved their name on the same branch my sister was . . ."

He nodded, then briefly explained his partner's discovery and the arborist's assessment. The Noons who lived locally had been questioned. Following that lead had been a waste of time but necessary for covering all the bases. They were banking on the "no one" theory. That assumption played into the staging. The victim was "no one." Insignificant.

No one fucks with me.

And it tied to his niece's murder.

At this point, he couldn't share any of that with CJ.

"I can't recall ever knowing anyone with that name." CJ

fixed her gaze on his, set his instincts on point. "But I'm well aware that Shelley had a number of *intimate* acquaintances I didn't know about."

The statement hung in the air for a pulse-pounding second.

"Such as yourself, *Detective* Braddock." Her voice grew more agitated with every word. "Just how intimate was your relationship with my sister?"

How the hell could she ask that? They had been over this issue before. "There was nothing intimate about my relationship with Shelley. You know that." That she refused to give him even one iota of credit made his blood boil.

"The two of you first got acquainted after that break-in when the photographs were stolen."

"That's right. The photos of you and Shelley as kids." Something else she knew as well as he did.

"I met you not long after that," CJ said pointedly.

"Okay." This had gone far enough. "Is there a reason we're going over this?"

She kept going as if he hadn't said a word. "I found you charming and intelligent. Seemingly trustworthy. A refreshing change from most of the cops I've known around here."

He looked away. Resisted the urge to walk out the door. CJ was too pivotal to this case.

And too damned important to him, whether or not she ever trusted him again.

"Shelley adored you," she said, twisting the knife she'd already buried deep in his back. "You were all she talked about whenever I called or visited."

He swung his gaze back to hers, fury clawing at his ability to remain calm. "It was a mistake, CJ. One that I put the brakes on before it went too far. But you refuse to believe that."

"That's what she said." Anger flared in her eyes. "I guess I'll never know for sure."

"You do know," he reminded her, unable to keep his own anger from his tone. "Think about it. The same thing happened to you last night. Only I didn't stop, because it was *you*." He stood. Couldn't sit there and pretend this was a civilized conversation. Goddammit.

She came off the sofa, went toe-to-toe with him. "Last night was . . ." She blinked. Sucked in a breath. "My sister is dead. Someone broke in." She flung her hand toward the stairs. "I was angry and . . . scared."

He wanted to reach out to her so badly it hurt, but he didn't dare. "So was Shelley. Plenty of times." Pain shimmered in CJ's eyes, and seeing that was like a sucker punch to his gut. "That particular night two guys roughed her up pretty bad. She was too wasted to pick herself up off the street where they'd dumped her, so she called me." Braddock had patched her busted lip and iced her black eye. She'd clung to him and wept like a child. Then she'd kissed him, and for an instant . . . one fucking instant . . . he'd kissed her back. Then he'd pushed her away and fought her drunken advances until she passed out. She'd been sorry the next day. They'd both been sorry. But sorry hadn't been enough for CJ.

CJ had refused to talk about it since. To talk to him at all. The only good to come of that night was Shelley's decision to stop hooking.

The truth was he couldn't change what he'd done. Maybe if he were in CJ's shoes he would feel the same way. Maybe forgiveness was too much to ask for. CJ didn't see any aspect of sex as casual. Each step in a relationship, every kiss, was an important decision. That was the reason last night had completely blown him away. He still couldn't believe it had happened.

"That night Shelley was scared," he said, the anger gone from his voice. "Scared and alone. I'm sorry as hell you can't deal with it, but it's done. I can't change what happened."

"Did she tell you she was pregnant?"

Surprise flared in his gut. "Are you certain about that?" Shelley hadn't mentioned being pregnant. She'd sworn she wasn't in the business anymore. He'd gotten the impression once or twice that she was seeing someone. But when he'd asked, she'd insisted it was nothing. Just friends having fun.

"That's right, Braddock." CJ hugged her arms around herself, managed to summon some more of that anger. "She was pregnant. Ricky says you were the only man he ever saw her with."

So that was what this was all about. Maybe it was time CJ

knew the rest of the story. It wouldn't make things any easier between them. In fact, she'd probably hate him even more. But he couldn't keep this from her any longer. "We were friends, CJ. That's all. I was there for her when she needed me. Kind of like Abbott is there for you," he threw in, mainly because he was jealous as hell of how CJ idolized the older man. Abbott was perfect. Never hurt her. Never screwed up!

When she would have launched a rebuttal, he cut her off. "About three months ago Shelley brought up the idea of trying to bring down Tyrone Nash. She was sick of seeing the folks in this village preyed upon. She wanted things to change. She wanted free of his influence and control."

Realization dawned in those blue eyes. CJ could see where he was going. But he knew she wasn't going to understand.

"So you took her up on it?" she accused. "Used her?" She shook her head. "I knew it."

"I recognize my responsibility in her death." No point in pretending otherwise. It haunted him every minute of every day, right alongside his responsibility in his niece's death. The fight suddenly drained out of him. He dropped back into the chair. "If I hadn't agreed to allow her participation, she might still be alive."

CJ stood there without saying anything.

Braddock wished there was something he could say or do, but there was nothing . . . other than making the man responsible for Shelley's murder pay. "The goal was noble," he went on when she said nothing, asked nothing. "Shelley let me know in no uncertain terms that if I didn't help her, she would attempt her goal alone. I couldn't let her do that."

"She didn't tell me what the two of you were doing," CJ finally said absently, as if her full attention was somewhere else—anywhere but here with him.

"Did she tell *you* she was pregnant?" he ventured, knowing that couldn't be the case since CJ hadn't mentioned it when she'd ID'd the body.

"No." Pain cracked in her voice and he wanted to take back the question but it was too late.

"I found prenatal vitamins from her last visit to the clinic."

She chewed her bottom lip a moment before continuing. "She just got the lab results on Friday. But that leaves plenty of time for her to have informed the father, who likely found the idea more than a little inconvenient."

"Shelley didn't talk to me about being involved with anyone. When I specifically asked that question, she insisted the only thing she did was hang out with friends." He was as surprised to hear Shelley had been pregnant as CJ must have been. "Our every conversation and meeting was focused on Nash. She wanted to initiate change, I wanted to help her. That's all there was between us. Ever."

CJ blinked as if coming out of a trance. A kaleidoscope of emotions played out across her face, finally landing on that too-familiar rage at him. "I guess that makes you a hero, Braddock. What was she doing? Passing along Nash's movements, his schedule, to you? Playing the part of undercover operative for your investigation? You helped her, all right." CJ backed a step away from him, distancing herself physically and emotionally. "Helped her get murdered."

The band of guilt tightened around his chest. He wasn't trying to dodge the bullet here. He knew exactly what he'd done.

"And the baby," CJ added as if she'd only just thought of it herself. "The baby was murdered, too. Seems like she gave up a hell of a lot to let you help her. I hope you're doing the same to find her killer."

She turned away from him, walked to the door, opened it wide. "Goodbye, *Detective* Braddock."

He couldn't argue with her anymore. At the door, he hesitated. "Think very carefully about how you proceed from here, CJ," he cautioned. "Nash will be watching you. That warning he left said it all. No matter the good you think you're doing, the wrong kind of interference could get you hurt, and it could adversely affect this investigation."

"Is that a threat?"

What the hell? "No, it's not a threat. It's a statement of fact. I'm on top of this investigation. I won't stop until it's done."

Anger tightened her lips. "Consider yourself warned, Detective. *I* won't stop until it's done."

* * *

CJ marched down the steps and watched Braddock drive away. Her body shook with the fury twisting through her. Why hadn't Shelley told her about this? That one was simple: Shelley had known CJ would attempt to talk her out of the idea.

Why hadn't Braddock told her? Another easy answer: They hadn't been on speaking terms. And he had known she wouldn't agree with the decision. Even now, he knew more than he was sharing. Every time they discussed the investigation, she got that feeling that he was leaving something out.

And Jesus Christ, she had been right.

This was her sister, dammit!

She had a right to know what really happened. She had a right to see Shelley's killer brought to justice.

She had a right . . .

Tears spilled past her lashes. CJ scrubbed them away. No more crying. She damned well wasn't going to be vulnerable. She was going to see this through.

She braced her arms over her chest and surveyed the street, the homes. Most of the residents she could name, had known them her entire life. This was where she'd grown up, where she'd learned the hard way that life was what you made it.

Her sister, these people, deserved justice the same as anyone else in this damned city.

Like she'd told Braddock, she wasn't going anywhere until this was done.

An approaching car slowed, rolled to the curb in front of her house.

Edward.

As if to defy her decision, he emerged, his gaze seeking and unerringly finding hers.

He was not going to be happy about her plans.

"I was worried." He closed the car door and made his way to the rickety gate. "I hadn't heard from you since this morning. Are you all right?"

No, she wasn't all right.

"I'm sorry." She raked her fingers through her hair. "I should have called." She motioned for him to come in. "I'm glad you're here. We need to talk."

He didn't ask any questions. But he didn't have to. She could already see the disappointment on his face.

Inside, he waited until she'd settled on the sofa before taking a seat. Always the perfect gentleman.

"Have you eaten?"

And always concerned for her well-being.

"At some point today." She would, she just hadn't taken the time yet. But he would worry if she told him the truth. She couldn't tell him about last night's break-in, either. He would insist she stay at his home. She needed to be here. He wouldn't understand, given the circumstances.

Having Edward here made her feel even guiltier about what had happened between her and Braddock. She was a grown woman and Edward wasn't her father, but she had worked hard her entire life not to disappoint him.

"Have you made a decision about when you're returning to Baltimore?"

She pushed aside the unsettling thoughts of last night. Her decision. It hadn't been an easy one to make, but it was the right one. "I went to the clinic today."

"I'm surprised the village clinic is still in operation."

She was too. "Wednesdays and Fridays only."

"But today is Monday."

"The nurse practitioner was there catching up on paperwork. Juanita Lusk. We actually attended the university together."

"Was there a reason you visited the clinic? You're not feeling ill, are you?"

CJ leaned forward, braced her elbows on her knees. "Edward, I learned that Shelley was pregnant. About six weeks."

Sadness settled in his features. "I'm certain that news makes this all the more difficult for you."

She tamped down the emotions that threatened. "Very much so. But," she went on, bracing for his disapproval, "this news only reinforces my feelings. I can't leave until the police have done their job." She held up a hand when he would have spoken.

"If I leave now, Shelley's case will get pushed to the back burner. She'll be forgotten and nothing will ever get done. I can't let that happen."

Edward nodded thoughtfully. "And what about your residency? You must not forget your own future, CJ. I understand what you feel you need to do for your sister, but you can't rationalize yourself out of the equation."

"You're absolutely right." She'd thought long and hard on how to go about this without damaging her future. "I called my attending this morning. I discussed my options with him and he agreed that my plan is a viable one. Since I'm a third-year resident, I have a number of elective hours remaining. I'm going to stay here and ensure Braddock does his job. While I'm here, whether for a few weeks or a couple of months, I can help out at the clinic to fulfill my elective hours. My attending was quite impressed with the idea. He believes the experience will serve me well in the future, both personally and professionally."

CJ took a breath. She'd gotten it out without falling apart or stumbling. There was no reason for Edward not to see the brilliance in her plan.

He considered her announcement for a time. "Your proposal is sound. And your attending is quite right. Service in a disadvantaged area such as this will show compassion and selflessness."

There was a *but* coming. She steeled for it.

"I understand that you feel you must do this. My only reservation would be about allowing yourself to get caught up in the people and problems here. This is your hometown and it's very easy to permit a sense of obligation to stand in the way of better things. The misery in this village will drain your determination and ambition if you are not very careful."

He presented a rational, practical case. That was true. But Shelley hadn't been his sister. As hard as he tried, he couldn't possibly know how she felt. Not deep inside, where this horrific act had left a hole so deep CJ worried she might just fall in and disappear.

Before she could restate her case, he went on, "Let me hire a private investigator to find the truth. Waiting for the police to come through will be frustrating and perhaps pointless."

There was an option she hadn't considered. "I appreciate the offer, Edward." She clasped her hands, struggled to find the right words to explain what she felt. "You've always been there when I needed you. But this is something I have to do personally."

"Do the police have anything at all in the way of evidence or suspects? What about that Banks fellow? He was the one who hurt Shelley a few weeks ago, was he not?"

"He says not." CJ understood perfectly that, like Braddock, he wasn't telling her the whole story. "He also swears he's not the father of Shelley's child. But I'm not so sure. Shelley had been tangled up with him for most of her life. My work at the clinic will give me the opportunity to talk to the people who come in. Maybe find the answer to this awful puzzle."

"Do you have a theory as to why Banks resorted to murder? There has to be a motive even for an unsavory character such as him."

That was the part she didn't quite understand yet. "Banks claims he's innocent. He says Shelley was involved with Tyrone Nash. But so is he. I don't know if he's just trying to shift guilt. But . . ." CJ shook her head. "I can't get past the idea that he is most likely the father of the baby she was carrying. I have no choice but to wait for the answer to that question. A DNA test can determine paternity. But that takes time."

"We could offer a reward for credible information," he suggested. "Money talks, as they say."

He was so sweet. To be honest, the idea was tempting. "That's a very kind gesture, Edward. But I'm afraid we'd be inundated with false leads and misinformation. I really believe the only way to do this is by using the back-door strategy. Anything we do that tips off the person responsible is going to blow up in our faces."

Edward stood. "Let me take you out for an early dinner. I'm sure you're exhausted. And tonight you'll stay in my home. A good night's sleep will do wonders."

CJ willed her body to rise. He was right. She was exhausted. "I thought I'd continue to stay here." Other than last night, she hadn't stayed here in months . . . not since learning about Shelley and Braddock. She'd stayed with Edward whenever she visited, which had only been twice since late February. "I need to be here." She didn't know any other way to explain the urge to be near Shelley's things.

"I'd like to be able to convince you otherwise, but . . ." He bowed his head in acquiescence. "If you feel staying here is necessary, so be it."

Relief left her already weary body weak. That had gone far more easily than she'd expected. Edward was a good friend. He wanted the best for her. But he didn't understand that no matter how Shelley had hurt CJ and taken advantage of her, she was still CJ's little sister.

She walked him to the door. "Thank you, Edward." She drew in a satisfying breath, the first in several days. "I can always count on you."

"Call me if you need me."

He gave her a hug. She inhaled deeply. The subtle scent of his crisp sandalwood cologne reminded her that there were some things she could depend on.

Standing in the door, she watched him drive away. Then she closed the door and sagged against it.

Alone again.

She looked around the sparsely furnished room. Inhaled the familiar pungent scents.

Alone with the ghosts of her past.

She shuddered when she thought of the message she'd washed off the bedroom wall: *Stay and there'll be two dead bitches.*

Neither Tyrone Nash nor Ricky Banks was going to scare her off. She would find some boards or something to nail over that broken window. And until this was over, she would keep every one of them locked no matter how damned hot it got in the house. Motivated by the thought, she checked the windows to ensure they were locked.

She was going to finish this.

As if her determination had somehow summoned him, she recognized the sedan across the street and halfway down the block. Jenkins was back on duty.

Braddock wasn't backing off the surveillance.

She closed her eyes. Wished she could put him out of her mind for good.

Last night had done nothing to facilitate that end.

That could never happen again. She had to protect herself from a number of dangers . . . and Braddock was definitely one of them.

CHAPTER NINETEEN

Downtown Free Clinic
Tuesday, August 3, 10:30 AM

The waiting room was packed. Standing room only. CJ weaved her way through the crowd and waited until the receptionist was free.

"Good morning, I'm Dr. Patterson. I understand Juanita Lusk is here today." Actually CJ was hoping Lusk was here. She'd mentioned working at this clinic, too.

The harried receptionist glanced from the line to CJ. "We're a little busy right now. Are you here about the referrals?"

CJ hesitated, then said, "Yes."

The gentleman next in line abruptly bent forward and puked.

"Jesus!" The receptionist jumped up, shook her head, then said to CJ, "Go on back. She'll be in one of the exam rooms. She's expecting you."

"Thank you." CJ slipped through the tangle of people and entered the double doors marked PERSONNEL ONLY. She wasn't in the habit of lying, but she was definitely getting in some practice here.

Whatever it took. Like the old days.

The first three exam rooms she passed housed waiting patients but no doctor. Six other patients waited in chairs along the wall. A nurse entered the fourth room. CJ peeked inside—no

Lusk. The final room on the left was the one she was looking for. CJ waited outside the door since Lusk was with a patient.

"I won't have the money to get the prescription filled before Friday."

"Ms. Tyler," Lusk said as she made her final notations in the chart, "Nikki needs the antibiotic now."

The patient was a girl, seven or eight years old. Pale, skinny. The mother looked pretty much the same.

"I know," the mother said, her face worried, "but I don't have the money."

"Okay." Lusk heaved a big breath. "I think we have a few samples around here somewhere. Just wait here and I'll find them."

"Thank you, Doctor. Thank you so much."

Lusk nodded and turned to the door. She missed a step when she saw CJ watching from the corridor.

"I don't know how you got back here," Lusk said as she moved past her, "but I don't have time for any more of your questions."

CJ lengthened her step to keep up with the woman. "This isn't about the murder." It was, but Lusk didn't need to be made aware of that.

"Talk fast, Patterson." Lusk stopped at the lab station and started going through cabinets.

"I'm going to be in town for a while."

"Great." Lusk slammed one door and opened another.

"Anyway, I checked with my attending and he authorized me to volunteer here in Huntsville to fulfill the requirements of some of my elective hours."

Lusk glanced at her before diving into the row of drawers.

"So, if you don't have any objections, I'd like to help you out at the village clinic."

Lusk grabbed a handful of samples, then stared at her. "What're you up to, Patterson?"

"I need to stay," she admitted. "Make sure the cops do their job. But I don't want to put my position in Baltimore at risk, so I'm working the only option available to me."

Lusk shoved the drawer shut. "And you want me to help you?"

"Actually," CJ said, following her back down the corridor, "I would be helping you. I can work the same day as you, so the clinic can see twice as many patients, or I can work a different day. Give you a day off. I would be helping you and the village residents."

Lusk breezed into the exam room, gave the patient's mother the samples. "Bring her back in two weeks if she isn't greatly improved."

The mother thanked Lusk over and over as she ushered her little girl out of the room.

Lusk placed the patient's chart on the growing stack on the table in the corridor. "I've a good mind to say no," Lusk warned, her gaze narrow with suspicion. "But I could use the help. There's not enough time in the day to see everyone who needs medical attention. And I could get my preceptor to rush the paperwork through . . . if I was convinced of your sincerity."

CJ knew where this was going. "This isn't about the past, Juanita. This is about doing the right thing. I have to see this through. You don't have to worry about me stepping on your toes. You'll be the one in charge. I'm not planning to usurp your authority."

The stare-off lasted another ten or twelve seconds. "You're on." She allowed CJ to see in her eyes just how serious she was. "But you fuck with me and you're out. Do we understand each other?"

"Absolutely."

Lusk grabbed the chart at the next exam room. "In fact, you can start right now. You'll find what you need in my office." She pushed her lips into a fake smile. "One good deed deserves another, right?" Lusk entered the exam room. "Good morning, Mr. Rodriguez. What seems to be the problem?"

CJ located the office, left her bag, and donned a stethoscope. Getting on Lusk's good side wasn't a bad idea. Who knew? Maybe the woman would remember something Shelley had said that would make a difference.

Meanwhile, CJ would be doing what she loved most: taking care of people.

5:30 PM

CJ dropped the final chart on the mountain of others.

The last patient was out the door.

She stretched her back, rotated her neck.

"This is what I do every day," Lusk said as she placed her final chart on top of CJ's. "Not that different from what you do."

The hint of a smile tilted one corner of CJ's mouth. Maybe they would get along after all. "Just a little less blood." Images from Saturday night . . . the kid . . . invaded her thoughts. A lot less blood.

Lusk glanced at the mountain of charts. "Thanks, Patterson." She gestured to the pile. "I'll be here for a while."

"About the village clinic—"

"Tomorrow too soon for you?" Lusk grabbed an armful of charts. "Wednesdays would be a good day off for me. I'll make sure the paperwork gets done ASAP."

"Tomorrow's great." The sooner the better for CJ's purposes.

Lusk jerked her head toward her office. "I'll give you my keys. I'll get duplicates made by Friday."

Anticipation chased away CJ's exhaustion. "That works."

The keys were on a chain with several others. Juanita unhooked and handed three to CJ, stating which door each unlocked as she did. "I've annotated as many of the charts as possible as to the patients who shouldn't be given barbiturates, opiate derivatives, stuff like that." She gave CJ a knowing look. "You're new; they'll try to play on your sympathy."

"I'll stick with your notes." CJ backed toward the double doors. "Just so you know, Baltimore hasn't made me soft. I'm tougher than you think."

"Go on. I'll lock the door after you're gone." Lusk shook her head and shuffled into her office.

The receptionist had left already. The waiting room looked

like a tornado had come through. The few magazines provided for the patients' entertainment were scattered about, along with coffee cups, soda cans, and various other discarded food wrappers and containers.

CJ pushed through the entrance and took a deep breath. As tired as she should feel, she didn't. She felt exhilarated. She'd taken the first step toward putting her strategy into action.

"CJ Patterson, is that really you?"

She turned to face the man who'd called out to her. Dark hair . . . tall. Blue eyes.

A mixture of anticipation and irritation detonated in little consecutive bursts. *Carter Cost.*

Dr. Carter Cost.

The rich, gets-whatever-he-wants, womanizing shit.

Irritation won the battle.

"Carter." Her tone sounded as icy as she'd intended it.

He noticed. "It's been a long time."

Not long enough. "It has. Well. I was on my way—"

Cost glanced at the clinic, then at her. "I was on my way in there." He hitched a thumb toward the clinic. "I'm the preceptor here and for the clinic in the mill village. When Juanita called around noon and asked me to push through an authorization for you, I thought she was kidding me."

CJ suddenly felt very sorry for Lusk. Not only had she missed out on completing the requirements to have an MD after her name, which she obviously deserved, but she had to work under the oversight of this guy. No wonder she had such a foul disposition.

Crap. That meant CJ would be stuck dealing with him.

"How long will you be in town?"

CJ snapped back to attention. "A few weeks, probably. My sister—"

"Oh, God." Sympathy flashed in those big eyes, which at one time had tugged on her heartstrings. "I'm sorry. Shelley . . ." He shook his head. "It's just terrible."

"It is, terrible. Yes." CJ really did not want to do this with him.

"Look." He wrapped those long fingers around her forearm,

squeezed gently. "Let me sign off on a couple things in here and we'll have dinner."

No was on the tip of her tongue.

"You can't say no," he insisted with that charming smile that had probably broken many a heart. "I won't have it. That's an order. Give me five minutes."

Before she could argue, he disappeared into the clinic.

She supposed he was why Lusk hadn't bothered locking the door directly behind CJ. She was expecting Cost.

Maybe CJ had judged too quickly, feeling sorry for Lusk. She might still be carrying a torch for her old flame.

She had nothing to worry about where CJ was concerned.

She wasn't about to try the same poison twice.

But she would have dinner with him. As preceptor of the village clinic, he would have some knowledge of the patients and the neighborhood. Not to mention he could ensure she was approved for working at the clinic as long as necessary.

Follow all leads—that was going to be her motto.

Someone somewhere knew something.

She had to find that someone.

CHAPTER TWENTY

Huntsville Public Library
7:20 PM

Edward set his book aside and observed the soiree in the lobby below. A local artist had created another masterpiece. This one he'd donated to the library. The proceeds of a silent auction would benefit literacy. The artist stood in the center of it all, eating up the compliments and puffing with pride for his latest masterpiece.

How grand.

In Edward's opinion, the true treasures in this building were the books. He picked up his book to resume his reading.

This was where he felt most at home.

Always had.

The world had become obsessed with television and the Internet, when books had been in front of them all along. Any subject could be researched in depth right here in the library. Any skill could be learned. All that was required were patience and persistence.

Quite frankly, losing oneself in a well-crafted story was so very easy.

But lately, he'd found losing himself, even in the best story, to be impossible. His concern for CJ would not allow true escape of any measure. Particularly after last evening's disturbing announcement.

Even in death, Shelley had wielded one last injustice upon her sister.

CJ, poor, poor CJ, was left to grieve and struggle with the results.

Edward had scarcely slept last night. Today he'd tried to distract himself, but nothing he attempted had relieved the ache deep in his soul. Hardly twenty-four hours after her return, CJ had allowed the past to draw her back in. Did she not realize that it would swallow her up? Destroy her future?

He simply did not understand the compulsion. Shelley was dead. Risking her own future would not change that sad fate. CJ should return to Baltimore and focus on that future. There was nothing more she could do here. This was assuredly that maddening Detective Braddock's doing. He would attempt to use CJ, as he'd used Shelley, for his own purposes. Edward had worked so diligently to keep CJ away from the path her sister had chosen. Now she seemed determined to walk that path, even if her motives were noble.

Edward desperately needed a plan of immediate action. CJ believed the man responsible for her sister's murder was one Ricky Banks, an associate of Shelley's. Quite an unsavory human being. Banks's personal security was a rather large, quite nasty dog. He used that animal to inspire fear in those he employed. Edward used the word *employ* for lack of a more fitting term. Drugs, prostitution, all manner of crime against others filled the disgusting man's resume. That he also possessed a penchant for abusing women further disturbed Edward.

If Braddock were worth his salt, this ghastly business would have been settled by this point. Unfortunately, his attempts had proved utterly inadequate.

Now Edward was forced to watch CJ punish herself as this fiasco of an investigation played out. In due time, surely, the matter would be closed.

Unfortunately, time was often the bane of one's existence. There was either far too much or not nearly enough. At its core, one's life was all about timing.

Time worked against CJ in this tragedy. Her quest to find

justice for her sister could keep her here and perhaps even distract her permanently from the future she deserved.

Somberness settled over Edward once more. He did not want her to throw away the unparalleled opportunity before her. Not when she was so very close. That choice could change everything. Could jeopardize all he'd worked so hard to accomplish.

Guilt plagued him for doubting her at all. CJ had never let him down before. Since she was a little girl, her insights and grasp of reality had been astonishing when one measured them against her life experiences. But this was a monumental obstacle even for one so brilliant and courageous.

CJ would need him more than ever now.

Coming here this evening to soothe his soul was like coming full circle. His journey with CJ had begun here.

A smile tugged at his lips. He remembered well the first time he'd noticed her at the library. Thirteen years old and fearless when it came to protecting her younger sister. Long, silky blond hair hanging down her back. Tattered dungarees and T-shirt. The equally shabby sandals she'd worn had scarcely met the criterion of "shoes required."

As usual, Shelley had been giving her sister difficulty. She wanted to go to the park and play, while CJ, like Edward, wanted to lose herself in the aisles and aisles of books at the public library.

Those big blue eyes had filled with suspicion when he'd approached and suggested they go next door for ice cream. Eventually he'd persuaded her to trust him.

From the moment she'd smiled at him for the first time, he had known CJ was special.

He had guided and groomed her unrelentingly for the brilliant future she deserved.

Now, sixteen years later, that future was threatened.

He would not allow her to fall.

The village and the people there would only drag her down and swallow her up. Her emotional attachment to the past prevented her from seeing the imminent danger.

He must protect her.

No one else was going to do the job properly.

Stronger measures were necessary now. One often was forced to step several degrees outside one's comfort zone to ensure the greater good.

The cell phone in his pocket vibrated. He frowned. Usually he turned the nuisance off before stepping through the library's hollowed doors. But with the tragedy that had befallen CJ, he didn't dare cut off that communication link.

He didn't recognize the number.

Worry trickled. Perhaps he should see to this. She could be calling from most anywhere. The hospital. The police department.

The worry hurdled toward panic.

He rose from his chair, cast a glance at the mingling crowd below, then surveyed the mezzanine. Deserted. Still, a little too open for a private conversation. He climbed the stairs to the second floor and found it mostly deserted as well. The woman behind the help desk of the reference section glanced up, smiled at him. Edward returned the smile and journeyed to a corner of the second floor that was rarely visited. The city's historical records.

With the push of a button, he returned the missed call.

"Good evening, Mr. Abbott."

Edward frowned. The voice was male but certainly not one he recognized. There was a surliness about the tone. Quite distasteful.

"Who is this?" Edward inquired. Few people knew his cell phone number.

"This is your worst nightmare, Edward old boy," the voice taunted. "I'm starting a new game. Are you ready to play?"

"I'm certain you have the wrong number." The man had used his name, but Edward clearly did not know him. The very idea was ludicrous.

"Oh, no, Eddy boy. I have the right number. Now . . ." He paused for effect. "You ready to play?"

A new kind of uneasiness took root deep in Edward's stomach. "Who is this?" he repeated.

"I already answered that question. Try to keep up."

Enough of this folly. "What is it you want?"

"Now we're getting somewhere," the overbearing voice said. "What I want . . . well, I haven't made up my mind. This call isn't about what I want. It's about making the first move."

"I believe I'll hang up now." Edward didn't play games. He made it a point not to involve himself with those who did. This man was obviously some sort of con artist.

"I don't think you want to hang up, *Professor* Abbott."

"Make your point, sir." Edward doubted the caller deserved such a designation.

"Sir." He laughed. "I like that."

Fury ignited, burning away a little of the uneasiness.

"My point is, Edward Abbott, that I know what you did *that* night."

The fury vanished, giving the unease a new boost. "What are you talking about?"

"I'm talking about that poor bitch Shelley Patterson. I know all about you and what you did. The tragic ending to the sick story is right there on video. I bet you didn't know that ho was recording your ass."

"Whatever you think you know," Edward challenged, "you are very wrong. If you harass me again—"

"You'll what?" the man interrupted. "Go to the police? I don't think so. Here's the lowdown, old man, I want something from you. As soon as I make up my mind what, I'll let you know. Until then, you think about what you did. What you said. You think it all over. I'll call again in a few days and give you my decision. Until then, you just need to remember one thing."

Edward didn't bother with a response.

"I own your ass, motherfucker. And it's for sale. You be prepared to pay the price and life will be good again."

Dead air rang in Edward's ear. He stared at the phone. He didn't have to wonder who the caller was.

He knew.

As an educated professor of mathematics, he knew something else: that for every equation there was a solution. Sometimes the equations were complicated, sometimes simple. But always utterly solvable.

CHAPTER TWENTY-ONE

Carter Cost sat in the darkness of his BMW. He'd been watching CJ since they left Applebee's. She'd driven straight to the shack her crazy sister had called home. Once inside, she had turned on all the lights. Then she'd walked to the neighbors and borrowed what appeared to be a hammer. After that, she'd lurked around in the garage using a flashlight. Eventually she'd emerged with an armload of boards or something along those lines and gone back into the house.

For the next half hour he'd heard banging.

What the hell was she doing?

His fingers tightened on the steering wheel.

The better question was, what was he going to do?

She knew.

Fear crept up his spine, took root at the base of his skull.

With Shelley dead, he'd thought this was over.

Why didn't CJ go back to Baltimore? What resident in her right mind would risk such a prestigious position? She'd gotten her attending on board with the idea of filling elective hours. Carter couldn't exactly deny the request. That would look suspicious. But this ridiculous plan could very well backfire on her. A residency position at Johns Hopkins came with certain expectations, complete focus being first and foremost.

He shook his head. Some people just didn't appreciate the gifts life gave them. His residency at the Mayo Clinic had been such a gift. His grandfather had reminded him of that every day since Carter had returned to join the family practice.

Carter wasn't allowed to deviate from the plan that had been in place well before his birth. When he finally married, that too would be part of the plan, the nuptials a well-thought-out business negotiation. Just another reason Carter was in no hurry. He enjoyed his freedom far too much.

What little he had.

His family couldn't control what he did between the hours of 11:00 PM and 6:00 AM, but only by virtue of the fact that every single one of them insisted that seven hours' sleep each night was not only beneficial but essential.

If his family learned of his latest indiscretion, he would be eviscerated. Disowned. Left in the cold to survive on his own.

That was unacceptable.

He liked his life. Huntsville's medical community had no choice but to look up to him; he was, after all, a Cost.

Fury tightened his jaw. He had worked hard to rise to the family's endless list of standards. His reputation in the cardiovascular field was growing. His personal client list had exceeded expectations for the length of time in practice.

He couldn't let this happen.

The police couldn't care less about another prostitute ending up dead. Particularly one from the west side. That she was pregnant would be considered a consequence of the job.

Except that CJ was presenting the pregnancy as motive. Insisting the pregnancy made the murder a homicide with special circumstances.

A capital offense in the state of Alabama.

He understood full well how this, like all else in life, worked. The squeaky wheel got the grease. If she cried foul long and loudly enough, someone would pay attention just to shut her up.

Then he would be screwed.

He had to find a way to stop this.

Any one of Shelley's sleazy associates from the village could serve as suspect or perpetrator. There wasn't a single one of them above killing out of necessity or for sheer sport. And every one of them was expendable.

Yes, he decided. That would be the quickest, most painless way out of this mess. All he needed was a dead body and evidence that pointed to the victim's guilt in Shelley's murder.

He would never get so lucky.

Sometimes a person had to make his own luck.

Sweat dampened his palms. A shudder quaked through him. The stress sharpened his needs. A call to his supplier might be in order a little early.

Just as he reached for his cell, it chirped. If it was his father again, Carter was going to ignore the call. His father was suspicious of Carter's late-night activities. He'd started calling each night and morning to ensure his only son was following the rules. He, of course, didn't say as much, but Carter knew what the calls were about.

He wouldn't put it past his father to have him watched.

Carter longed for a call from his mother saying his father had suffered a sudden heart attack or stroke. He didn't wish his father dead, just out of commission on some level.

Maybe then he could live his life rather than the family plan.

A third chirp nudged Carter to check the screen. A local number, but not one he recognized.

He started to ignore it but at the last moment answered. "Cost."

"It's not nice to stalk the pretty doctor."

Carter twisted in his seat, scanned the darkness for whoever was watching him. "Who is this?"

"The better question is, who do you think you are? You don't belong here, boy. You shoulda realized that a couple months ago and maybe your balls wouldn't be in a vise right now."

Shit. Carter swallowed back the bile that rose in his throat. "What do you want?"

"Why don't you name the price, Dr. Cost? You'd have a better idea what your future is worth than I would."

Fear ignited in his gut. "I don't know what you're talking about."

"I got you on video, pretty boy. Pushing that bitch around. Telling her she better get rid of that fucking baby. Threatening her if she didn't. Yeah, I got it all."

Carter went numb. "You're . . ." He tried to swallow but his throat had gone bone dry. "You're bluffing." Those words—*his words*—echoed in his brain.

The bastard laughed. "You need to wake up, cracker. I don't fucking bluff nobody. Your ass is punked, motherfucker. Now, you think on it awhile. I'll get back to you."

Carter couldn't move, couldn't breathe while his entire life flashed before his eyes.

For the first time he realized he had underestimated the importance of a plan.

He needed one.

Fast.

His hands shook. He reached into his console, popped a couple of pills.

A sense of calm rushed over him.

He could figure this out.

He knew people . . . people who could make things go away.

CHAPTER TWENTY-TWO

CJ scanned the chart of her next patient. Follow-up. She'd had a series of STD tests on Friday. The same day as Shelley.

Pushing open the door to the lobby, CJ called the patient's name. "Celeste Martin." Eight patients still waited and she'd seen twenty already. No wonder Lusk was overwhelmed.

A young white woman, twenty according to her chart, pushed out of the molded plastic chair and slinked toward CJ. Fiery red hair, a color nature hadn't intended. Puffy blue eyes accentuated with far too much eyeliner and mascara. Judging by her acute thinness and her too-pale skin, she didn't eat right and rarely stepped out in the daylight.

"Good morning, Ms. Martin."

Celeste gave CJ a long, cautious look. "Where's Lusk?"

"She'll be back on Friday. I'm Dr. CJ Patterson." CJ held the door open for her patient. "Room two."

The woman walked with a bit of a hitch in her stride. CJ wasn't sure if that was her usual gait or if she was reacting to pain. Judging by the stilettos she wore, she could have twisted her ankle. If so, she'd climbed right back into the saddle again, so to speak.

Celeste slouched against the exam table. "How'd my tests come out?"

"They were all negative." CJ flashed a smile. "Nothing to worry about there."

Celeste grimaced as she straightened away from the table. "I'll just come back Friday to see Lusk 'bout the rest."

"Come on." CJ patted the table. "Scoot up here and let me have a quick look and listen." When the woman didn't oblige her, CJ added, "You're here. Might as well."

Celeste hesitated, doubt lingering in her eyes. "Lusk knows me. I like talking to her."

Chalk one up for Lusk. She'd built quite a patient-physician relationship. This wasn't the first patient today who wanted to come back on Friday.

"I understand." CJ closed the chart. "But I couldn't help noticing you're in pain. I can help you now; why suffer until Friday?"

The woman's hand went to her right side. "It hurts bad." Her face scrunched with the pain she'd obviously been trying to hide. "I got real scared last night. I couldn't sleep, it hurt so bad."

"Why don't you take off your blouse and let me have that look?" The spaghetti-strap camisole and mini miniskirt didn't cover that much, anyway.

Celeste hesitated another moment but then grabbed the hem of her cami and peeled it over her head. CJ clamped her mouth shut to prevent the gasp.

Angry red marks, recent, and purple and yellow bruising, several days old, colored her torso. Her bare breasts were covered in the same.

"Come on." CJ patted the exam table. "Ease up here and lie back, please."

Celeste grunted with the effort. She tugged her short skirt which had slid upward, back over her hips. No panties. Not surprising. The bruising extended to her hips as well.

Not wanting to put her off until she'd completed her exam, CJ kept the questions related to any symptoms the patient had experienced. Grimaces and soft groans came whenever she touched the fresher injuries.

"Let's get an X-ray. Make sure this is all soft tissue damage. Then maybe an ultrasound."

"I could use some Vicodin."

"We'll talk about that after we see what's going on."

Since there was no nurse or medical assistant, CJ searched for a gown, got the patient into it, and escorted her to the last exam room on the right. It was the largest, and that was where the X-ray machine was. She'd volunteered in enough free clinics to know her way around an X-ray machine.

As CJ prepared the patient for the images, she did what she'd been doing all morning. "You grow up around here?"

"Nah, I'm from Mobile. I came up here last year. Got a place over on Beacon a couple months ago."

"Okay, I'm going to step behind the screen." CJ headed that way. "Don't move."

CJ selected the appropriate settings. "Here we go." A couple of clicks and she moved back to the patient's side to position her for a second view. A third view and CJ was ready to have a look. "Just stay put while I process these."

As she went through the steps, she continued her questioning through the open door between the exam room and cramped developing room that had surely once been a closet. "You like it here?"

"It's okay."

"I hear Ricky can be a tough guy to work for." CJ held her breath. She'd skipped several questions and gone straight to the ones that might rouse suspicion.

"I don't work for him no more. Tyrone wanted me working for him."

CJ's heart thumped. "You must be a hard worker." It was the best she could come up with.

"Have to. I don't do my part, he'll kick my ass."

CJ paused before pulling the films. "Did he do this to you?"

"Hell no. Uh-uh. No way. He ain't gonna damage the merchandise." She made a face and put a hand to her side. "Shit happens, you know?"

Yeah, CJ knew all right. "I guess you heard about the woman who was murdered last weekend." An ache speared CJ. It still didn't seem real. "You can sit up now." She clipped the films onto the viewing box. She had to do this as nonchalantly as possible.

"Yeah." Celeste rolled to her side and pushed up. She'd been through this before. "I partied with her a couple of times before she gave up the life. She was cool. She let me stay at her place once when Tyrone was punishing me."

Anticipation pounding in her veins, CJ barely restrained the need to dive into a long list of questions. "Good news. No fractures." She helped the woman off the table.

"That's good." She turned to CJ at the door. "Do I still get the Vicodin?"

"Does Lusk usually give you medication for your pain?" Bruising this bad warranted something for pain, but CJ didn't want to step on Lusk's toes. She saw none of the notes Lusk had mentioned in Celeste's chart. And she'd like to do an ultrasound as well.

"Yeah. She knows being a foot soldier is hard sometimes."

"I'm not sure I understand the whole foot soldier concept."

Celeste shrugged. "He's the King, we his army in the streets."

Talk about an ego. "You were saying that he punished you."

"Like he did Shelley, you know. And anybody else who don't do as they told."

CJ tensed. "I'm sorry. I don't understand."

"The first time you fuck up, he tells you what for. Makes you feel bad for screwing up."

Back in the exam room, Celeste shouldered out of the gown and reached for her cami. "The next time you get shunned. Can't work. You get pretty hungry. That happened to me not too long after I got here. Shelley helped me out. Gave me a place to stay. Something to eat."

CJ's heart squeezed. Shelley had liked helping others. "That treatment sounds a little harsh." This girl, like the others she'd seen today, didn't look as if she could afford to miss even one meal. Most were living on drugs. She got that. But still, this was abuse clear and simple.

Truly sick bastard.

"If you stupid enough to piss him off the third time, then you in big trouble. That could get you dead."

More of that tension stiffened CJ's muscles. "Dead? Tyrone kills people who make mistakes?"

CJ snapped her mouth shut. She hadn't meant to ask that question. She'd gone too far.

The deer-caught-in-the-headlights look in Celeste's eyes signaled that she recognized she had said too much.

That frightened gaze suddenly narrowed. "Your name is Patterson, too. You're her sister."

"Yes."

"That's why you asking all these questions." She shook her head. "Goddammit." She glared at CJ. "Bitch, you'll get me killed if you go mouthing off to Tyrone."

"No." CJ gave her head an adamant shake. "I told you, I won't tell anyone."

"Yeah. Uh-huh. You gonna give me them Vicodins or not?"

"I'd like to do an ultrasound." Celeste shook her head. The simmering fury on the woman's face said that CJ wouldn't be getting anything else from her. Truth was, CJ couldn't blame her. "Okay." Getting her some relief was the least CJ could do. "Let me see what we have on hand. But if the pain persists, I'd like you to come back on Friday for that ultrasound.

"Whatever." Celeste didn't look at her.

There were more patients in the lobby. CJ would just keep asking questions until she got the answers she needed.

Or until Tyrone found out what she was up to and stopped her.

He, of all people, should know that stopping her would be easier said than done.

6:35 PM

CJ didn't lock up until she'd seen the last patient, even if they'd showed after closing time.

She collapsed into one of the ugly molded plastic chairs and rested her head in her hands.

The quality of life in the village was unspeakable. She'd known it. She'd grown up here. But seven years away . . . she'd banished the worst parts from her mind. On the rare occasions when she'd come home, Shelley had made it a point to conceal as much of her life from CJ as possible.

Instead of complaining to Shelley, why hadn't she asked real questions?

Instead of making demands, why hadn't she listened?

A rap on the door jerked her from the troubling thoughts.

CJ was exhausted. She pushed to her feet. But if there was someone else who needed medical care, that was why she was here. And maybe, just maybe, she would learn something more.

She dragged to the window and split the blinds to see who was out there before unlocking the door. Some old habits were instinctive.

A man, ragged clothes, disheveled hair, waited at the door. He turned slightly as she watched. Blood stained the front of his shirt. Her pulse thumped. She surveyed the parking lot and didn't see anyone else, which indicated the blood had likely come from him. No vehicle. He'd apparently walked from one of the village streets. Muggings and fights, usually over women or drugs, were an everyday affair.

She rushed to the door, unlocked it, and pulled it open. "You're injured?" The idea that he could have left someone injured and had come here for assistance flashed through her mind.

"It hurts bad." He pressed a hand to his chest, grimaced.

"Come on." She ushered him inside and down the corridor to one of the examining rooms. "Take off your shirt." She washed her hands and grabbed a pair of gloves. The usual adrenaline dump seared through her veins.

A hand clamped over her mouth. She reached up. A cold blade pressed against her throat. Fear bloomed in her chest even as his overwhelming body odor filled her lungs.

"All I want is the drugs," he growled against her ear. "Don't give me no trouble and there won't be none."

His breath was rancid. She nodded her understanding. Told herself to stay calm.

Slowly she sidled toward the door with him in tow. The knife blade burned her skin as they moved, piercing the outer layer of epidermis. As they shuffled awkwardly along the corridor toward the supply room, her thoughts raced.

Should she go for the pepper spray? She'd tucked it into the pocket of her lab coat this morning. Just in case. But she'd dropped her guard as the day progressed without incident.

She should never have allowed complacency to slip in.

Nothing she could do about that now. She had to think. Make a new plan.

Her hands were free. She could go for it.

As if he'd read her mind, the pressure on the knife blade increased.

At the supply room door she stalled.

"Open the door," he ordered.

"Locked," she mumbled into his hand. She'd kept it locked all day since she'd been the only staff on site.

"Where's the key?"

Now was her chance. "Pocket." Her heart hammered against her sternum.

She waited to see if he would reach into her pocket for the key, but he didn't.

"Unlock it," he snarled, "but don't do nothing stupid or I'll slice your throat wide open."

CJ reached into her pocket. Her fingers brushed the canister. What did she do? Take the risk? Or play along?

"Hurry up!" he roared.

Her fingers latched on to the key ring and she pulled it from her pocket. She couldn't get a deep enough breath . . . couldn't keep her hands from shaking as she sorted through the keys.

She unlocked the door, pushed it open. He ushered her inside. The cabinets were locked as well. Different key. She picked through the keys and selected the right one, jammed it into the cabinet's lock, and opened the door.

Sample boxes and small plastic bottles of various medications waited on the shelves.

She didn't ask him what he wanted. She dropped the key ring back into her pocket and waited for his instructions.

The blade came away from her throat. He pushed her away. "Stay over there!"

Could she make it past him to the door before he grabbed her? Maybe. He was busy sorting through the boxes and bottles.

Her hand went into her pocket. Fingers curled around the pepper spray. She flipped up the safety catch.

When he started to stuff the drugs into his shirt, she braced to make her move.

One, two, three . . .

She lunged for the door.

He twisted. Reached for her.

She aimed the pepper spray at him, pressed the trigger.

He screamed. One hand went to his face, the other groped for her.

She darted out of his reach and through the door.

Pulling the door shut, she fished for the ring of keys. Held her breath until the pepper spray around her dissipated. Her hand trembling violently, she managed to single out the proper key and ram it into the lock.

"You fucking cunt!" he screamed through the door.

The knob twisted in her hand. She held on with all her might.

"Open the fucking door!"

She turned the key. Didn't work. The knob was twisted in the wrong position. She pulled, gave it a twist in the other direction. Turned the key.

The lock engaged.

He kicked the door. Banged on it with his fists. All the while screaming profanities at her.

She backed away.

Call the police.

She reached into her other pocket for her cell.

"CJ?"

She whipped around.

"What's going on back here?"

Braddock.

Thank God. "He . . ." She pointed to the supply room. "He came for the drugs."

Braddock charged forward, grabbed her by the shoulders, and looked her over. He winced when he touched her throat where the knife had marred her skin. "You should take care of that." He took the keys from her hand and moved toward the door.

CJ collapsed against the nearest wall. Her eyes and nose stung from the spray.

"He's got a knife," she remembered to tell Braddock as he unlocked the door. She supposed he'd realized that from the nick on her throat. Braddock had already drawn his weapon.

She heard him tell the man to put his hands up. Heard the ensuing argument and the brief scuffle.

She pushed away from the wall and checked to see that Braddock had everything under control. He was cuffing the guy. The knife lay on the floor. Blood stained its sharp blade. Her blood. She shuddered. Her skin burned where he'd pressed it to her throat.

She moved to the exam room and took a look in the mirror over the sink.

Only a minor nick. She cleansed the wound. Applied some antibiotic cream and a small bandage. While she patched her wound she heard Braddock on the phone ordering Jenkins to come get the guy and haul him in.

She washed her hands and face, then braced herself on the sink. Maybe Edward was right. She was taking far too many liberties with her future . . . with her life.

For what?

Shelley was dead.

Nothing CJ did was going to bring her back.

But what about all these people?

The abuse they suffered, particularly the women, at Tyrone's hands was incomprehensible. Could she just walk away and pretend she didn't see this?

The way the rest of this city had been doing for years?

You don't belong here no more.

Ricky was right. She didn't belong here anymore. But what kind of person would she be if she just walked away and didn't try to stop this madness?

The conversation between Braddock and Jenkins was hushed. She stayed put. Didn't want to deal with that. She dabbed her eyes again with a wet paper towel.

Bone-tired, she cleaned up the mess she'd made and tidied

the exam room while Braddock finished up with the would-be thief. She'd already taken care of the others after her final patients were out the door.

Right now she wanted to go home and collapse.

Home?

You don't belong here no more.

This wasn't home. Did she even really have a home? Her apartment in Baltimore wasn't home. It was just a place where she slept and showered.

"You okay?"

She looked up. Braddock waited at the door.

"Yeah. I'm okay." She gestured to her throat. "It's just a scratch."

"But it could have been a hell of a lot worse," he suggested.

She took a breath. He was right. "Why are you here, Braddock? Do you have news on the investigation?" His man Jenkins had been parked outside the clinic all day. Fat lot of good it had done her. But then, that wasn't his fault; she was supposed to call if she needed help. Unsavory-looking characters had been coming in and out of the clinic all day. There was no reason for the guy who'd showed up at the door last to have been viewed any differently.

Unless Braddock had news, they had nothing else to talk about. She didn't want to deal with him anymore, either.

"I heard a disturbing rumor."

"What rumor?" That his broad shoulders filled the doorway so completely unsettled her somehow. Made her want to lean against that strength. No way. That wasn't ever happening again. She was just feeling vulnerable after the incident with the addict.

Those dark eyes probed hers. She didn't like him looking at her that way. "Say whatever you have to say, Braddock. I have to fill out an incident report and then I'm out of here." She was tired. Tired and disgusted. Mostly with herself.

"I don't know what you think you're doing, but you're making yourself an easy target." He took a step into the room, planted his hands on his hips, and leveled a you'd-better-listen-up gaze on her. "You cannot come back here and start interrogating Nash's people. Do you want to get yourself killed?"

Oh, so that was what this was about. Word had gotten to him that she was asking questions. Well, he could get over himself. Like she'd told him, she wasn't going to stop until Shelley's killer was brought to justice.

"What am I doing?" She flung her arms wide, stared up at him in challenge. "Asking the questions you haven't asked."

Actually she had no idea what he was doing at this point, because he hadn't told her anything about his goals or strategy for the investigation. Well, except that he would get the job done. She'd heard that from cops before. He was the last cop she would trust.

"Look, *Dr. Patterson*." He moved in closer, putting his face right in hers. "The people you questioned today will go straight to Nash and tell him what you're up to. They get brownie points for that sort of thing. What part of this don't you understand? Nash is a bad guy. A pimp. A major drug dealer. I've watched bodies loaded into the meat wagon with missing tongues. Eyes. Hearts."

She flinched. Every word prompted images of how Nash might mutilate the women she'd questioned today.

Braddock went on, "That's how he sets an example to the rest. I don't want to watch your body get stuffed into a bag and then heaved onto a gurney."

Focus. Think logically. Not emotionally. "First . . ." She took a breath. "How do you know what I've discussed with my patients? Have you been sitting outside questioning them?" The idea made her want to slap his smug face. "Or did you order Jenkins to do it?" He was young, handsome. Jenkins could easily have charmed the ladies who'd been in and out of here today.

Braddock shook his head. "I didn't have to ask. I got more than one phone call filling me in on your interrogation tactics."

"You have informants here?" If that was the case, why didn't he know what had happened to Shelley? Someone here had to know. Oh, wait. Of course he had sources here. That was how he'd been using Shelley.

"That's right, CJ." He stepped back, took a breath. "I actually do my job. I've spent two years developing informants in the village."

"Then what's the holdup? One of them surely knows who killed my sister?"

"I wish it was that simple." He held up a hand when she would have launched her next tirade. "It's very possible that one or more knows exactly what happened. But they're afraid to talk. This is the kind of thing that could get them killed."

"You mean the way it got Shelley killed?"

Braddock turned away from her. He ran his fingers through his hair. She recognized what he was doing: working to temper his anger and come up with the right thing to say to get her off his back.

Not going to happen.

Finally he settled his gaze on hers once more. "What's it going to take to get you to trust me?"

She laughed. Couldn't help herself. "I'm never going to trust you again, Braddock. All I want from you is for you to find the person who murdered my sister."

His expression shifted from frustrated to grim. "What did you learn today?" He set that dark gaze on hers. "Quid pro quo, Doc."

She hated when he called her that. The last couple of times she'd come home—after their fledgling relationship was over—he'd called her that just to make her crazy. Mainly because she knew he meant it disrespectfully. "That Tyrone Nash mentally abuses the women who work for him, and when that doesn't work anymore, he kills them."

"That's right," Braddock agreed. "But we don't have any evidence linking him to a single murder. So we wait, we watch, we question, until we find the link we need."

She shook her head. "Tyrone is not that smart. There has to be something you're missing, *Detective*."

"Six," he said.

"Six what?" He wasn't making sense.

"That's how many bodies of young women have been found in the past two years. Each one died a brutal death, but their bodies weren't found for weeks or months after the murder. Three were found in water, two were burned, one was immersed in a fifty-gallon drum of diesel fuel. Whatever evidence might have been left on or in the body was long gone or too contaminated to utilize."

"But Shelley's body was found within hours of her murder," CJ countered. "And she wasn't burned or submerged in anything. She was right out in the open." How could Braddock not see this? "Killing someone and dumping the body in such a way that the evidence was destroyed is one thing. But Tyrone couldn't possibly have carried out such a flawless plan when he murdered Shelley, leaving her body . . . the entire crime scene right out in the open." CJ folded her arms over her chest. "You have to be missing something."

"That's right. He took extra precautions with her."

"You can't be sure it's him," she argued. Not that she didn't want to see Tyrone in prison, but focusing on him alone meant Braddock wasn't looking seriously at anyone else. Including Ricky Banks. "Excuse me." She pushed past him to get out the door and strode to the office.

CJ had no idea where the incident report forms would be. She'd just have to prowl around.

Braddock followed. Leaned against the door frame. "Evidence or no, there were other similarities to what we believe is Nash's MO."

A frown nagged at her forehead as she perused Lusk's files. He'd told her about the E. Noon thing, but was there more? "What similarities?"

Her fingers stilled on the folders. She turned to face Braddock. The air evacuated her lungs.

Then she knew.

Missing tongues. Eyes. Hearts.

"You didn't tell me everything about the circumstances of Shelley's death." Her knees tried to buckle; she locked them, told herself to breathe. She had known he was keeping some parts of Shelley's death from her. She'd had that feeling all along.

"There was no reason to tell you," he said quietly. He held

up a hand when she would have debated his statement. "We keep some elements quiet . . . for confirming leads or confessions. Telling anyone at all could interfere with the investigation."

Fury jolted through her. "Tell me all of it."

"There were dozens—forty, to be exact—hypodermic needles sticking in her body. As if the killer had been decorating her with her most well-known vice."

CJ sat down, almost missing the chair. The visuals his words prompted had bile burning at the back of her throat.

"The perp stitched . . ." He closed his eyes a moment before meeting hers once more. "He stitched up the opening to her vaginal canal. And removed her clitoris."

She wouldn't make it to the toilet. CJ lunged toward the trash can sitting next to the wall.

She heaved. She cried. Her body convulsed with the agony throttling through her.

Please, God, please let those horrific things have been done postmortem.

As a doctor, she was all too aware of how the human body reacted to fear . . . to pain. *Please, please, don't let Shelley have gone through that with her dying breath.*

Braddock thrust a damp paper towel in front of her. CJ accepted it. Wiped her eyes, then her mouth. She settled her bottom on the floor. "I need to know if those . . . things were done after she was . . . dead."

"I can't confirm the answer to that question until after the autopsy. I'm hoping that's the case."

She glared at him. "What was the fucking medical examiner's preliminary conclusion?" If he told her he didn't know, she was going to scream.

"Postmortem."

"Thank God." Sobs tore at CJ's chest.

Braddock joined her on the floor, leaned against the wall. "There are elements that point to Nash, but there's also a sophistication that almost rules him out. As you pointed out, this was a savvy set-up. Nothing left to chance. Not a single piece of evidence left behind except the carving on the tree limb."

Maybe it was the shock of hearing this news or just the fact that they were both sitting on the floor with the trash can she'd puked in standing between them, but CJ looked at the man, really looked, for the first time in months.

He'd turned thirty-five this year. Dark hair and eyes. Classic square jaw. Good nose. The kind that never needed to be touched with a scalpel. He was a well-dressed, good-looking man whose eyes were warm and compassionate.

Maybe he really was trying to find Shelley's killer. Maybe he really did care about the people here. And maybe she was a little crazy.

She didn't like noticing anything nice or good about him.

But then, she was in shock at the moment. Her brain was on autopilot. She felt numb and somehow drunk at the same time. She recognized the symptoms. If she stood up, she would likely pass out.

She would just sit here for a bit.

"I tell you what, CJ." He looked directly at her, let her see how serious he was. "If you promise to go home and stay out of trouble tonight, you, my partner, and I will have a conference tomorrow. We'll go over everything we've got. Check in with the ME and see if they've been able to move up the autopsy. We'll talk it all out."

She wasn't sure how to respond to the offer. Was he trying to get her to agree to something? It sounded exactly like the way oncologists delivered the prognosis to the patient right before they explained the treatment. Ultimately it meant the patient would live, but quality of life would suck.

"We'll keep you informed of every step of this investigation. You'll be sick of hearing from me before it's over."

Now came the *but*.

"All I ask in return is that you lay low for now. Stop asking questions and digging around. I don't think your sister would want you to get hurt . . . not even to bring her killer to justice."

Shelley had trusted Braddock. That may very well have been the primary contributing factor in her death, but the fact remained: She'd trusted this man.

At one time CJ had as well. Before he'd betrayed her trust on the most primal level.

Still, she had two choices.

She could get herself into the kind of trouble she might not be able to talk her way out of. *Her throat burned where the knife had ripped at her flesh.*

Or trust this man to do his job.

CHAPTER
TWENTY-THREE

1407 Dubose Street, 11:40 PM

Tyrone looked out over his village. It was quiet tonight. That was the way he liked it. His people doing their thing. No interference from the po-po. Something to be said for free enterprise.

Fury tightened in his gut when he thought of that doctor bitch having the nerve to move back into his village. Banks better get that taken care of fast or Tyrone was gonna end this shit. He did not tolerate disrespect. CJ Patterson was disrespecting him big-time, coming into his territory acting like she was all that. Like she was better than him.

Maybe he should remind her that she still had it coming for the last time she'd gotten in his way.

He touched the scar on his cheek, the one that reminded him just how fucking annoying that bitch could be. Yeah. They had a history. One he'd bet his sweet black ass she wouldn't want to repeat. She'd gotten in that one swipe, but he'd put the fear of God in her tight white ass.

A tap at his door hauled his attention from the window.

Excitement heated his skin, made his dick twitch.

It was nearly midnight.

Late . . . but worth the wait.

The door opened just enough for his number one to stick his head in. "Widow's here."

Tyrone nodded. "You know what to do."

The number one member of his unholy trinity hesitated like he had something else to say but didn't want to spit it out.

"What?" Tyrone demanded. He didn't want to hear no shit. He had plans for relaxing and enjoying the rest of this night.

Number one stepped into the room, closed the door behind him. "We got trouble."

Tyrone's survival instincts reared. "What trouble?"

"Celeste and a couple other foot soldiers said that doctor bitch was asking questions at the clinic today. Questions about you and what happened to Shelley. Some say Celeste spilled her fucking guts. She say that doctor just kept drilling her but she didn't say nothing important."

Rage pulsed in Tyrone's belly. He shook his head. That Patterson bitch just didn't know when to walk away.

"She was asking about Banks, too. Wanting to know if Banks worked for you. Lotta questions, Ty. Lotta questions. She been talking to Banks. She been over to his house. And I already told you about that cop bitch bringing him home. The dickhead was falling down drunk. Then the po-po picked him up again today. Somethin' going on with that motherfucker."

Tyrone digested all that his number one had said. "The Patterson bitch needs another lesson. You know what to do." He puffed out his chest. He'd tried to do this the easy way and CJ just didn't want to pay attention. Now she would be sorry. "This is on her."

Number one gave a nod of understanding, then left the room to do his duty.

That was all any of Tyrone's people had to do. And he took care of them. Roof over their head. Food in their bellies and clothes on their backs. Still, sometimes somebody fucked up.

Especially the bitches.

That was why women disgusted him. They didn't think with their heads. And they assumed that pussy was the road to riches and glory.

Fucking hos. All of 'em.

The door opened again and Tyrone felt the burden of his position lift.

His people called his visitor *Widow*. Long, sleek black dress. Black hat and veil. Like them fancy white fools over in Twickenham wore to a funeral. But the part he liked the best was the black stockings. Maybe he liked the garter that held those stockings up the best.

The door closed and Widow leaned against it. "I was held up, but I'm here now. You look tense."

Damn straight, he was tense. "That don't matter." Tyrone's heart started that *thump-thump-thump*ing. His cock got hard as a rock just looking. He licked his lips, moved nearer. Motherfucker, he wanted some of that. "We can talk about that later."

"Why don't you tell the Widow what's making you so tense?"

The veil lifted and Ty's gaze went directly to those full, glossy lips. "That bitch doctor," he said, his mouth watering to taste those sweet lips. "And that fuckup Ricky Banks."

Widow made a sound of understanding as Ty moved closer and closer. "I'm here now."

"That's right." Ty moved in the final step. Reached out, released the buttons that held the dress secured at Widow's waist. The dress fell open and Ty's hands moved over smooth, taut skin. He pushed the dress off Widow's shoulders. Let it fall to the floor.

No panties. Just the lacy garter belt that held up those sleek black stockings.

Slowly, releasing one button at a time, Ty opened his shirt. He shouldered out of it, tossed it to the floor. Widow's eyes traveled over his smooth, muscled chest. Ty kept every inch of his body sleek and smooth. He worked hard to pump up his muscles, big and strong.

He released his fly, shoved his jeans down his thighs. Heat roared through him as Widow's breath caught . . . those hungry eyes focused on Ty's throbbing cock.

He braced a hand on either side of the door, leaned in close, and tasted those cherry-flavored lips. He let his weight fall against hot, smooth skin. Kissed his way down that pale throat, sought out a flat little nipple and sucked hard. Widow shivered.

Ty drew back. "Turn around."

Widow obeyed.

Ty couldn't stop himself—for a moment he had to admire all that beautiful white flesh. Creamy and taut. And that ass. He loved that tight little ass and those long, toned legs.

Long as Widow took care of the King, the King would take care of Widow. That was the way the world worked.

Ty leaned in, snuggled his cock between those sweet, hot cheeks. Then he put his arms around Widow's hips and slid his hands down that lean pelvis until he found what he was looking for. Ty groaned as his fingers latched around Widow's hard dick. Widow's ass arched into him.

"Yes," Ty murmured.

This was what he loved—a hot, tight male body.

Wasn't no fucking pussy good enough for the King.

CHAPTER TWENTY-FOUR

2204 Clopton Street
Thursday, August 5, 1:05 AM

A low growl woke him.

Ricky rolled over in bed. The room spun.

What the hell?

He should've never drunk that tequila.

Fuck.

He licked his lips. Scowled at the shitty taste in his mouth.

"Satan!" He waited, listened. The dog didn't come. "Shit."
Ricky sat up. The taste of tequila and bile rushed up into his
throat. He had to hold his head. Felt like it was gonna roll off.

Wood flopped against wood, telling him Satan had lunged
out the dog door. He must've heard or smelled something outside.

Ricky gave it another minute in hopes that the room would
stop spinning. Then he staggered to his feet.

"Whoa. Fuck." He hadn't gotten this wasted in a long time.

It was her fault. That crazy bitch was asking questions. Two
of his hos had come to him tonight. They'd been scared to
death that the new doctor was trying to get in Ricky's shit by
using them. He'd bellowed. Pushed the hos around a little, just
to keep them scared and knowing who was boss. Then he'd
threatened to let Satan loose on 'em if they went to that clinic
again when CJ was there.

Wouldn't be no more of that shit.

Tomorrow he was going to show CJ Patterson what she got for fucking with his hos. He'd start with her rental car. He owed it to her, anyway. She and her sister had fucked up his Camaro that time. He never had gotten his payback for that.

Then maybe he'd burn her fucking house down with her in it.

She wouldn't give him no more trouble then.

Fucking bitch.

He dragged on his jeans, stumbled around getting them up. Satan was outside raising all kinds of hell. Ricky hadn't fed the dog in two days except that one piece of meat. Maybe he'd eat his fill of whoever was messing around outside. He grabbed the .40 cal from under his pillow and shoved it into his waistband.

People knew better than to come around his place.

If it was that bitch Patterson, he hoped Satan ripped out her holier-than-thou heart. Serve her right, coming back here acting like she was better. She'd cut her teeth in this hellhole just like him.

He didn't have no real beef with CJ. But she'd gone too far now. Asking questions, getting in his business.

He wasn't about to let her get him killed.

Tyrone would only stand for so much bullshit, then he would make them both sorry.

Hardheaded bitch. He'd warned her.

He padded barefoot down the hall and into the kitchen. Drawing back the shitty curtain his aunt had had for a hundred fucking years, he squinted to see what the hell Satan was after. The dog was jumping and barking at something in that big old Pecan tree.

What the hell was hanging from that branch?

Looked like . . .

A floorboard creaked behind him.

Ricky whirled around. Reached for his weapon.

He felt two tiny pings on his chest.

What the hell?

An electrical charge ripped through him. His muscles jerked, twitched.

He hit the floor.
He wanted to scream . . . couldn't.
Wanted to fight back . . . couldn't.
Electricity roared through his body.
Every part of him twitched and jerked.
He bit his tongue, tasted the blood.
Lights exploded behind his eyes.

Ricky roused. He licked his lips. Tasted metal.
Smelled something nasty . . . had he shit himself?
He told his eyes to open. Couldn't make it happen.
His body felt heavy. He wanted to move. Couldn't do it for
nothing.
He could hear Satan growling and snarling. He wanted to
call out to the dog . . . couldn't do that either.
Slowly, he managed to make his lids slide upward.
The stained ceiling confirmed that he was in his house.
On the floor. Kitchen. The battered linoleum felt cool be-
neath his back.
What the hell happened to him?
He tried to lift his right arm again.
Too heavy . . . and something held it down.
He concentrated hard on turning his head to the right. Finally it rolled in that direction. His arm was stretched out, his
palm up. What the hell was in his hand? He tried to lift it, pain
shot up his arm.
He worked at moving his other arm. Rolled his head that
way to see. His left arm was extended away from his body,
palm up, just like his right. Something in that hand too.
He lifted his head, stared at his legs. His legs were spread
apart. He was naked. There was something around his ankles,
pinning him to the floor. He couldn't move them; when he
tried, it hurt like hell.
Wait. He dragged his gaze back up to his hips. What was
that stuff all over his pelvis? Dark . . . reddish.
Blood?
Had he been bleeding?
Shit! Had someone cut off his dick?

He wiggled, tried to get free.

A scream echoed in the room.

Pain exploded in his hands and arms, his feet and legs. That was when he realized the screaming was coming from him.

He coughed. Almost choked on his own spit.

He raised his head again, tried to see. Was his dick still there?

There was something sticky on his chest. When he looked down, his chin touched his chest and he could feel it. He struggled to focus his blurry gaze. More blood.

Fuck!

He tried wiggling again. But his body was so heavy.

Drugs. Somebody had drugged him. Wait. He remembered his body convulsing, the shock . . . like electricity zapping him hard.

Taser. Somebody had Tasered him.

Motherfucker.

He tried to look around the room. Couldn't see anybody. The light over the stove was on . . . it was dim but he could see. Where was these motherfuckers?

"I will kill you!" he warned. "Nobody fucks with Ricky Banks."

Satan was scratching at the front door.

"That's right, boy," Ricky shouted to his dog, "come on in here. Satan will eat your ass up!" he told whoever was listening. "Yeah, you hide, motherfucker, you're dead anyway."

Ricky tried to look back toward the living room. He couldn't tilt his head back far enough to see.

"Come on, boy!"

Why didn't the stupid mutt come through the dog door? He'd gotten out that way. He knew how to get back in.

And where the hell were Tyrone's zombie fuckers? Ricky knew who had done this. Tyrone wanted to show him who was in control. Twisted motherfucker. Just wait. When Ricky got his hands on that—

The television suddenly blared to life, the volume loud.

"Hey!" Ricky shouted.

The front door opened.

Ricky stilled.

The screen door slammed, the wood-against-wood sound echoing above the television.

Then all the pieces fell into place for Ricky.

Satan bounded into the room, growling, snarling.

"Still!" Ricky shouted.

The dog didn't listen. He was in a frenzy.

"Still!" Ricky squeaked as the dog circled him.

He should've fed that fucking dog before he went to bed.

"Satan! Still!"

The dog sniffed the blood. Lapped at it.

Ricky's body started to quiver.

"Stop!" he shouted. "Still!"

The wide tongue lapped faster.

Ricky struggled. Tried to jerk his hands free. Pain speared through his palms.

"Still!"

Teeth sank into Ricky's skin. He screamed. The harder he fought, the more vicious the attack.

He turned his face away. Satan's huge mouth clamped down on Ricky's throat. He screamed; the sound was weak. He tried to get away. His skin ripped—blood spurted in the dog's face, across Ricky's chest.

Ricky went limp. He could feel the blood gushing from his body, Satan's teeth tearing out plugs of flesh.

The blackness closed in on him until all he could see was that stain on the kitchen ceiling.

His lips formed the word *still*.

But he never heard the sound.

CHAPTER TWENTY-FIVE

3021 Appleton Street, 7:15 AM

CJ's eyes opened, then slowly closed once more.

She needed to wake up, but she just couldn't bring herself to put forth the necessary effort.

She moistened her lips. Grimaced at the funky morning taste in her mouth.

Taking that sedative had been a mistake. But after what she'd learned from the women at the clinic, and then the confrontation with that drug addict, not to mention Braddock's visit, she'd been desperate for any kind of relief. She'd picked through Shelley's over-the-counter offerings—pill form, definitely no capsules—and gone for it.

Now she remembered why she never did that. She hated the sleep-aid hangover. An alcohol hangover would have been preferable.

Unfortunately, either way, she wasn't going to have the clear head she needed this morning. Braddock and his partner were going to bring her up to speed today.

She had to get up. Shower. Get dressed and find out what time the meeting with Braddock was scheduled.

The room was darker than usual. She'd nailed some old interior shutters she'd found in the garage over the broken window. With the meager light filtering in between the louvers, the stained wall wasn't even noticeable. She would take care of that eventually.

Maybe spruce up the whole place and put it on the market. Too much to think about right now.

A minute or so more and she would drag herself up.

Thankfully, a rare morning breeze drifted through the louvers along with the light. She'd been sweating when she fell asleep last night. Her skin still felt damp. It was hotter than blazes this time of year. The sheet was stuck to any skin not covered by her nightshirt. Yuk.

Her nose twitched. She drew in a breath, analyzed the smell. Something new overwhelmed the stale scent of cigarette smoke and cheap perfume.

Feeling too damned groggy, she mustered her determination and struggled onto her elbows to look around the room.

She blinked. Looked again.

"Jesus."

She clambered from the bed, stumbling because of the sheet tangled around her legs. CJ scrambled to her feet, flipped on the light. She looked down at herself. No injuries. No coagulated blood. Some amount of blood had soaked through the sheet and left a faint coating of dried blood on her shins and feet.

Where the hell had the blood come from?

Gingerly, she picked up the sheet. Lots of blood.

Heart pounding, she checked the bed. More blood had soaked into the fitted sheet. Probably the mattress, too.

Her senses locked into self-preservation mode.

Was someone in the house?

Apprehension knotted in her stomach.

She listened . . . silence.

The sheet slipped from her fingers as she cautiously moved around the bedroom. No blood on the floor. She eased into the hall, listening for sounds of an intruder and scanning for a blood trail.

The other two bedrooms were clear. No one in the bathroom. She started to turn away from the bathroom door, then hesitated. She stared at the closed shower curtain.

Where was her pepper spray? In the bedroom on the dresser next to the bed.

Just do it.

Pulse pounding, she inched toward the tub and stretched her arm until she reached the curtain. Big breath. She snatched it open.

The air rushed out of her. No dead body in the tub. That was good.

Her hand went to her face to push her hair back, but she hesitated. Not until she washed her hands.

She gathered her courage once more and headed down the stairs. A step creaked and she flinched. Careful. Someone could be down there.

The living room was empty. She moved to the kitchen. Nothing out of place. No one waiting to pounce on her. Back door was still locked.

How the hell had anyone gotten in?

All the windows were locked. She'd opened them last night for long enough to let some air in, then she'd closed and locked every single one before going to bed.

Her cell phone was still upstairs, charging by the bed. Still taking care just in case, she moved back to the living room to check the front door.

She turned the knob. No resistance.

The door opened.

That was impossible. She'd locked that door.

That knot of apprehension that had formed in her stomach expanded, rising up her esophagus and blocking off the ability to breathe.

Call Braddock.

She dared to poke her head outside and checked the street. The idea that someone had come into the house while she slept sent a shudder through her.

The usual nondescript sedan sat across the street. She'd totally forgotten about the surveillance on her house. She couldn't tell if it was Jenkins or not. How had anyone gotten past him?

Uncaring that she wore nothing but a blood-stained nightshirt, she rushed across the porch and down the steps. Apparently Jenkins noticed her coming and emerged from the car.

"What's wrong?" He headed across the street, met her at the rickety gate.

"Call Braddock." The words rushed from her mouth. She looked back at her house. "Someone was in there last night. There's blood all over my bed."

"Show me," Jenkins said as he pulled out his cell phone to make the call.

CJ showed him to the bedroom, stood in the corridor while he had a look.

While he was on the phone she escaped to the bathroom. Couldn't bear the smell any longer.

Maybe Edward was right. Maybe she shouldn't be staying here.

Where the hell had the blood come from?

Was it human?

She thought of the cats she'd heard squalling and hissing across the street the other night. Had another harmless animal been sacrificed to send her a message?

Was it Nash trying to scare her off?

Or was it Ricky?

Bastards.

She locked the bathroom door and turned the water in the shower to hot.

She stared at her hands . . . at her legs.

The list of bloodborne pathogens she might have been exposed to paraded through her brain.

Not to mention that if it was human blood, there could be a body around here somewhere.

She climbed into the shower and scrubbed and scrubbed and scrubbed until her skin was raw. Memories from that night on the street, of the boy who'd bled out, kept flashing in her head. Then images of Shelley . . .

CJ couldn't bear it—had to block the horror. Had to get the blood off!

When she'd thoroughly scrubbed her hair, her face, and every inch of her body, she braced her hands against the damp tile and fought a wave of nausea.

What was she doing here?

How was anything she attempted going to help solve her sister's murder?

She was no cop.

Maybe Edward was right about that, too. She was risking her future, her life . . .

For what?

To make up for letting her sister be murdered.

CHAPTER TWENTY-SIX

Braddock lowered to a crouch to inspect the body. "Looks like old Satan had himself a feast."

"To say the least." Cooper sat back on her haunches and surveyed the nude body. "I hope he was dead before the dog got to that part." Cooper heaved a sigh. "Such a waste. Banks was cute . . . before his dog decided to take a few bites out of crime."

Ricky Banks lay sprawled on his kitchen floor in a position that could only be labeled crucifixion style. His hands had been screwed to the floor with six 3-inch wood screws straight through each palm. What appeared to be a man's belt had been cut in half and used to secure his ankles to the floor with the same type screws. His pet, Satan, had ripped out, and apparently eaten, a good portion of his throat, some of the chest area, including a nipple, and most of his manhood. Blood had pooled and coagulated on the floor beneath him. Arterial spray had covered the mutt and splattered around the room. The smell of blood and excrement was thick in the air.

"Where's the dog?" Cooper glanced up at her partner.

Braddock had arrived on the scene five minutes or so before Cooper. Animal Control had just secured the animal and taken it away minutes before Cooper arrived. Chances were he would be put down, but for now he was evidence.

"Animal Control rounded him up."

"I'll bet that was a challenge." Cooper leaned down. "What's this?"

Braddock moved to her side of the body and got down on his hands and knees to get close enough to see the small marks in question. "Taser marks." He pushed back into a crouch. "Guess that's how the perp disabled him."

"But that wouldn't last more than a few minutes. This"—she gestured to the body's positioning—"took some time. I'll bet he was drugged at some point." She leaned close again to inspect the body. "Probably a needle mark around here somewhere."

"Braddock! Take a look at this."

One of the officers, Larry Metcalf, who'd responded to the neighbor's call about a disturbance, poked his head in the back door, motioning for Braddock to come out to the yard.

He and Cooper exchanged a look, stood simultaneously, and headed to the backyard. The second officer who'd responded to the call was interviewing the neighbors. The forensics folks were sweeping the house and the yard, which had already been cordoned off as a crime scene. The entire property was considered part of the scene for now.

Officer Metcalf led the way to a large tree in the center of the backyard. "What do you make of this?"

A piece of meat hung from one of the limbs.

"It's a pork shoulder," Cooper said as she walked around the dangling chunk. "Looks to be intact." She visually measured the distance from the ground. "Must've been just out of Satan's reach."

"Might be part of some sick training ritual." Braddock had seen these guys wrap massive log chains around a young Rottweiler's or pit bull's neck to build muscle mass.

"Might be," Cooper offered, "what kept Satan occupied while the perp prepared Banks for dinner."

Braddock shook his head. "That's a sick thought, Cooper."

"Well, yeah." She sniffed the meat, touched it with her gloved hands. "But this is pretty fresh. It hasn't been hanging here long."

As if on cue, the meat wagon rolled up to the curb. The street was already crowded with onlookers. Two additional officers had been called in to protect the perimeter.

"One of the neighbors said," Metcalf put in, "that Banks didn't feed that dog regularly. Helped keep him mean."

"It's hard to feel bad for a guy like that," Cooper commented as she stared back at the house.

Guess this was the end of Braddock's deal with the poor bastard.

He and Cooper walked back to the house. "You think this is Nash's work?"

Braddock shrugged. "He may have gotten wind that I was leaning on Banks for information."

"Were you?" She stopped at the door and looked him in the eye. "I mean, did you push that last interview too far?"

"Yeah." No point lying. "Maybe."

Cooper shook her head, then searched his eyes. "Did this interview include anything either of us might regret?"

"Just the usual carefully worded warnings."

Cooper didn't look convinced, but she let it go at that.

Back inside the house they went room by room, mindful of the evidence techs' work, looking for anything that might reveal any appointment Banks had had last night. Anything at all with possible relevance to his murder or that of Shelley Patterson.

In the front right pocket of the victim's jeans, Braddock found his little black book. It contained names of the girls working for him, their cell numbers, and their addresses. He bagged the black book. The .40 caliber they'd found on the kitchen floor would be tested. A number of unsolved robberies and homicides might just be cleared up with that one.

By the time Braddock had finished a walk-through of the house, Cooper was in the backyard again. In the tree, no less. He walked out to where Officer Metcalf stood by watching.

"Looking for anything in particular?" Braddock inquired. He had an idea.

"Looking for a signature."

E. Noon. He'd figured as much.

She slid down the branch to the trunk of the tree, then jumped down. "Nothing there."

"Did you check the pork shoulder?"

"Funny." She hitched her head toward the house. "I'm gonna have a look for that signature."

Braddock couldn't argue her logic. "There is some fairly complicated staging to the scene."

"That's what I was thinking," Cooper said, excitement building, playing out on her face. "The way he was laid out. Like he was being crucified or something. And the way his weapon was on the floor just out of reach."

"Braddock, Cooper, you might want to see this."

Candice Dobbins was on her knees next to the body. The vic's hands and feet had been freed and he'd been rolled onto his side. Dobbins was directing an evidence tech in the taking of additional photos.

"Take a look," Dobbins pointed a gloved finger to the vic's back, directly between his shoulder blades.

A silver cross had been secured there, the top of the cross pointing downward.

"Glued, I believe," Dobbins offered.

"More staging," Cooper muttered.

What the hell was Nash up to? Other than sending Braddock a big fat message.

"You estimated a time of death yet?" Braddock realized Dobbins had barely gotten to the scene, but knowing the time was crucial to diving into his investigation.

"Considering the body temp and progressive state of rig, the coagulation of the blood . . ." She shrugged. "I'd say he's been dead a good five or six hours."

Cooper moved around the kitchen, looking for the signature. Braddock joined her search. Tangible evidence right up front would be nice. Even the best killers made mistakes.

Braddock's cell vibrated. He checked the screen. Dispatch. He opened it. "Braddock." Dispatch passed along two urgent messages from Detective Jenkins. Braddock needed to call him as soon as possible.

Anticipation fired in his veins. Why the hell hadn't Jenkins called him directly? He checked the incoming call log, missed call from Jenkins. Braddock stepped out the back door and made the call. One ring and Jenkins answered. He didn't give Braddock a chance to speak. He should come to CJ's house. Now. The detective's final words kept replaying over and over even after the call ended.

Blood is all over the bed.

3021 Appleton Street

Five minutes after Braddock arrived at CJ's house, he called the Forensics techs to the scene.

He and Jenkins were at a standoff in the bedroom. CJ waited downstairs in the living room.

"I can't believe someone got in without you noticing a thing," Braddock repeated. Maybe if he kept going over that same detail, Jenkins would 'fess up. He'd either fallen asleep or had been AWOL. "What happened at the clinic yesterday was bad enough, but this is totally unacceptable."

Jenkins shook his head, his gaze downcast. "I was right here all night. I didn't hear or see anything. And that guy at the clinic was just like all the other people who came in and out." He met Braddock's gaze then. "Unless I'd followed him inside—and you told me to stay outside—I couldn't have known."

He could be telling the truth. The perp could have slipped through the back and left the front door unlocked just to make HPD look bad.

But Braddock wasn't convinced.

"Here's the deal." Braddock stepped into the other detective's personal space. "If I find out you're lying to me, your career at HPD is over. Period."

Jenkins nodded. "I understand."

Braddock glared at him one last time. "Now get back to your post."

He watched the humbled detective go. Jenkins had never given him any reason to doubt him. But this was one hell of a big reason. Giving him grace, they were all operating on adrenaline.

Not enough sleep. No time off. It would help if the chief would budge on the manpower cap. Wasn't going to happen. Three detectives were all Braddock was allotted for this case.

Fury still charging through him, he went back downstairs to talk to CJ. She was pretty shaken.

She stopped her pacing and stared at Braddock as he descended the final steps.

"I don't understand how someone got in without . . ." CJ shook her head in confusion, gestured vaguely. "They did this and I never even knew." She hugged her arms around herself. "I slept right through it."

She had told him about taking a sleeping aid. That was likely the reason she hadn't awakened. But the problem, as he saw it, was that whoever came in and left this warning had no idea she'd taken something to help her sleep.

The intruder hadn't cared.

Didn't care about the official surveillance sitting right in front of the house.

That would be just like Nash.

She could have been injured or killed if she had awakened while the intruder was still in the house.

Fear trickled. She had Nash's attention, all right.

"We need to talk." Braddock ushered her to the sofa. The first thing that needed to be clarified by the lab was whether or not the blood on her bed belonged to Banks.

CJ looked painfully young and vulnerable this morning. The bandage on her throat reminded him of the crazed addict from the clinic. That she could have been killed for a handful of pain pills made him sick to his stomach. Reminded him of another victim who hadn't been so lucky.

CJ's hair was tucked into a ponytail, and the jeans and tee were seriously tighter-fitting than the clothes she generally wore. Not at all like the highly educated, conservative doctor.

Evidently she noticed his preoccupation with the way the tee hugged her breasts.

"I ran out of clothes." She rubbed at her forehead. "When I was preparing to come here I just threw a couple of things in a bag." She hugged herself tighter. "These are Shelley's."

He'd thought as much.

"There's something you should know," he said to preface the news. Though he was certain she had no warm, fuzzy feelings for Banks, she had known him for years. And he was her number one suspect in her sister's murder.

Big blue eyes peered up at him. "Did you hear from the ME on Shelley's case?"

Braddock shook his head. "There was another murder last night."

Her face paled.

"Ricky Banks."

She stared at him for a long moment before she reacted. Her expression blanked of emotion and she seemed to have trouble gathering her thoughts. "How?" She shook her head. "I mean . . . yes. How was he . . . murdered?"

"He was secured to the floor in his home and his dog tore out a couple of essential arteries."

Her face pinched in horror. "Satan killed him?"

"We have reason to believe the animal was provoked into a frenzy." Between his owner's starvation tactics and the killer's bait, that was a damned solid conclusion. "Then let loose on Banks."

CJ dropped her head back on the sofa. "What does this do to Shelley's case?" She lifted her gaze to Braddock's once more. "I don't mean to be unsympathetic, but does this mean he didn't kill Shelley, or is this even relevant to her case?"

"I can't answer that question yet. There are elements that are similar, indicating we could be dealing with the same perp. But it's too early to say for sure."

"It has to be Tyrone." Fury compressed her lips into a thin line. "He's crazy like this." Her eyes widened with concern. "Do you think the blood was . . . ?"

"That the blood on your bed came from Banks?" He shrugged. "That's a possibility."

Her breath caught. "Oh, God." Her hand went over her mouth.

"What?" He moved to the coffee table, directly in front of her.

"That girl." She searched his eyes, hers filled with remorse.

"Celeste. She said more than any of the others. What if Tyrone—"

"Don't even think about it." He took her hands in his. "Listen to me, CJ. I know you grew up here, but you've never been a part of this life. Not really. You escaped—"

"That's what Ricky said." She looked away, bit down on her bottom lip.

The urge to reach out and soothe the flesh she tortured was nearly more than he could restrain. He tightened his grip on her hands. "These girls, like Celeste, Nash feeds off them. Uses them until he's finished and there's nothing left but a burned-out shell. Maybe your questions prompted his taking action against Celeste—"

Her face fell; pain glittered in her eyes.

"But the reality of it is, this kind of thing is inevitable when you're a part of Nash's world." That wouldn't make her feel better, any more than it did him.

"If he hurt her, it's my fault." She shook her head. "You didn't see her. Beaten and bruised. Too thin. All Tyrone's 'foot soldiers' are like that. It's sick. Just sick."

"That's Nash's standard operating procedure. Until he's stopped, that and more will continue."

"He has to be stopped."

"He does." He stared at their hands. Had forgotten he was holding hers. Evidently she'd only just noticed as well. She pulled her hands free of his. "But not by you. This"—he jerked his head toward her stairs—"was a second warning. You can't keep digging around in Nash's business."

She folded her arms over her chest, tucking her hands beneath her arms as if she needed to protect them. "I told you, I'm not going to stop until I'm done."

"No matter the cost?"

Fury lit in those blue eyes. "You're a fine one to ask that question."

He was the one looking away this time. She had him there. "Trust me." He leveled his gaze on hers. "You don't want to carry that burden."

The silence dragged on a full minute.

Okay, he had a homicide scene to get back to. "Let's have a look at your locks." He pushed to his feet, stepped from between the sofa and coffee table.

She stood. A couple of inches of flat belly were revealed by the short tee. His throat tightened. Flashes from the other night, when he'd been so deep inside her, slammed into his gut. God, he wanted to touch her.

"It wasn't locked when I got up," she told him, "but I'm certain I locked it before I went to bed."

Braddock shook off the forbidden thoughts. The techs had already dusted the door for prints. He squatted down to get a closer look. There were signs of forced entry but those marks appeared older. He twisted the knob.

"You need a new lock with a deadbolt today if you plan to continue staying here." He pushed upright. "Anyone could unlock that door with nothing more than a credit card."

"God. I should have thought of that. My apartment in Baltimore has three locks; two are deadbolts."

"You can't bully your way around in this neighborhood and then leave yourself open to attack." He hated to harp on what she surely recognized at this point, but he needed to be certain the message got through. "You're operating on emotion, and that can be hazardous to your health."

"I can see that." Her arms went around her torso again. "I won't make that mistake again."

"Consider yourself lucky that you're getting another chance. Not all of Nash's targets get that."

A sedan pulled to the curb in front of her house. Braddock recognized the driver emerging.

Edward Abbott.

Abbott glanced at the official vehicles, then at the house. A uniform delayed him at the gate.

CJ was out the door and down the steps before Braddock could utter one of his usual negative comments about the guy.

Edward Abbott embraced CJ as if he hadn't seen her in years. When he drew back he surveyed her from head to toe, then hugged her again.

Braddock moved across the porch and down the steps so he could hear the exchange.

"You're sure you're all right?"

She nodded. "Just a little shaken."

Abbott's head wagged. "I was afraid something like this would happen. You really shouldn't be staying here. It's not safe."

CJ sensed his presence and turned to Braddock. "Edward, I believe you know Detective Braddock. He's investigating Shelley's murder."

Abbott stepped forward, extended his hand. "We've met once before, I believe."

Braddock shook the man's hand. Firm, confident grip. "You would be correct." Abbott had come over to check on Shelley when Braddock investigated the break-in nearly a year ago.

"Is there anything new on Shelley's case?"

"We're waiting on the autopsy results." Sounded better than *no*.

"Ricky Banks is dead," CJ told her friend. "Someone murdered him last night. In his aunt's house."

Edward frowned. "Isn't he the man you suspected of . . . hurting Shelley?"

Hurting . . . yeah. Braddock resisted the impulse to roll his eyes. This guy was such a suck-up.

"Yes. But now I don't know." She glanced at Braddock. When he didn't stop her, she added, "He may have been murdered by the same person who killed Shelley."

"CJ, I must insist that for your own protection you stay at my home for the rest of your visit."

Braddock's cell phone vibrated. For once he was glad. This guy was about to make him gag. "Braddock."

"I found it."

Cooper.

"It?" Braddock's attention was still on Abbott, who was countering oh so eloquently and kindly each of CJ's protests.

"E. Noon. Get over here, Braddock. You're not going to believe this."

CHAPTER
TWENTY-SEVEN

Cooper waited at the front door.

Twenty or so neighbors still loitered just outside the crime scene perimeter. Hoping to get a glimpse of Banks carted away in a body bag, no doubt. Some would linger out of morbid curiosity; others, the ones who had been the deceased's employees in one capacity or another, more likely to ensure he was actually dead.

Braddock's partner motioned for him to hurry. He weaved his way through the crowd. When he'd double-timed it up the steps, Cooper shoved shoe covers and gloves at him and whispered, "You gotta see this, Braddock."

"You've pushed my expectations to the max." He hopped on one foot, then the other, to pull on the protective shoe covers. "This better be good."

She cut him one of those I-am-not-shitting-you looks as she ushered him through the door. "Trust me, our perp has a truly warped sense of poetic justice."

Braddock snapped the gloves into place as he went. "Nothing like a little originality." The organized chaos of the evidence techs continued to play out in the kitchen like a carefully choreographed theatre production.

The ME's assistants were bagging the body. Obviously the

perp hadn't left his John Hancock on the body. Before Braddock could ask just where the big surprise was, Dobbins said, "We found the penis. The dog didn't eat it."

"Show it to him," Cooper urged, that just-wait look still on her face.

Braddock's curiosity spiked. "Where'd you find it?"

His partner and the ME exchanged a look. "You tell him." Cooper smirked.

Dobbins picked up the plastic container next to her gear and turned back to Braddock. "The dog didn't consume all of the victim's genitals. The penis was severed and inserted . . ." Another of those glances at Cooper. "Into the victim's rectum."

His partner pressed her lips together, but there was no way to disguise the twinkle of amusement in her eyes. It wasn't actually funny, but when guys like Banks got theirs like this, it was hard not to be somewhat entertained.

Dobbins opened the container. "There's the signature."

Despite being smudged with blood and other *stuff* Braddock didn't really want to think about, the signature was visible. *E. Noon* was written in black, maybe with a Sharpie or other permanent felt-tip marker, along the flaccid length of the victim's penis.

The rub of metal against metal announced that the assistants were preparing the gurney for exiting the premises. "That's my cue." Dobbins closed the container and grabbed the bag that accommodated the tools of her trade. "Considering the connection between this homicide and Shelley Patterson's, I'll try to fit Banks in late tomorrow."

"That would be extremely helpful." Braddock held up a hand before she could get away. "One other thing. You're sure there was nothing like this"—he gestured to the container—"when you did your prelim exam on Patterson?"

Dobbins shook her head. "Not that I encountered. But, as you say, in light of this . . ." She glanced at the container. "I'll certainly be looking for her missing clitoris."

When the ME was out the door, Cooper said, "So far none of the neighbors saw or heard anything last night. Other than the dog barking, but he did that a lot, so it wasn't something that would have aroused suspicion. Not until he started howling."

"Of course no one heard anything." That was always the case in the village. Hear no evil, see no evil. What you didn't see and didn't hear couldn't get you killed. As far as the dog howling, Braddock had a theory on that. The poor animal had probably gotten confused and distressed after his frenzy ended.

"A couple of uniforms have Nash's residence under surveillance. Nothing's moving around over there." Cooper glanced around the room. "You want to poke around here a little more or go on over and question the King."

"Let's pay Nash a visit now. We can come back here later when the techs have finished up."

"So what happened over at the sister's?" Cooper asked as she picked her way through the living room.

Braddock waited until they were in his G6 and headed for Dubose Street before explaining. "She woke up with blood all over her sheets this morning." He met his partner's gaze as he slowed for an intersection. "Forensics is rushing the test to determine if the blood could have come from Banks or if we have another body waiting somewhere."

"Another one?" Cooper's brows lifted. "There was that much blood?"

"Enough to indicate someone had been seriously, maybe fatally injured."

"Damn." Cooper shook her head. "This is stacking up like a war."

Exactly. And Braddock had started it by using Shelley Patterson to get at Nash. He'd have to live with that one.

He'd let her down just like he'd let down his niece. What kind of cop allowed a nineteen-year-old girl to give him the slip?

Would CJ Patterson be the next victim of his failing ability to get the job done?

Nash's usual array of eyes and ears loitered on his porch. Reclining on chairs that the manufacturer hadn't intended to be utilized out of doors.

Braddock didn't wait for an invitation. He climbed the steps and flashed his badge for the first gorilla that sauntered his way. "We need to see Nash. Now."

The gorilla jerked his thumb toward the door. "Go on in. He's been expecting you."

Cooper rested her hand on the butt of the weapon clipped to her hip. Even though they'd been welcomed with open arms, that didn't mean things couldn't change once they crossed the threshold. Far too many folks here in Alabama considered anything that moved inside their house fair game when came to protecting one's self and property.

The King reclined on a red leather sofa, his black silk pajamas worth more than he was. The unholy trinity, as he called his personal bodyguards, stood close by, prepared to protect him at all costs.

"I'd ask you to sit," Nash said in greeting, "but you won't be here that long."

"Good morning to you, too, Tyrone." Braddock liked the way Nash's lips flattened into a frustrated line whenever he called the scumbag by his first name.

"Mr. Nash," Cooper announced, "you do have the right to have an attorney present before answering any of our questions. Would you like to call your attorney?"

Braddock suppressed a smile. *Way to go, partner.* She wanted the piece of shit to know they weren't fucking around.

Nash looked Cooper up and down, then curled his lips in disapproval. A scowl lined his face, made the scar on his cheek pucker slightly. "I don't need no lawyer. I don't know shit about what happened to Banks, so save yourself some breath. I was at home all night last night, ask anyone here."

"Is there anyone who doesn't work for you who can verify that you were here all night?" Cooper countered.

Nash flared his hands. "This is the village, policewoman. Everybody works for me." He motioned around the room. "These are my people. They all work for me."

Yadda, yadda, yadda. "Since that included Ricky Banks," Braddock offered, "we'll need a list of the people who worked with or for him." Braddock had the little black book, but he wasn't about to miss an opportunity to yank Nash's chain.

Nash settled a glare on Braddock. "You think someone in this village killed my man Banks?" Nash shook his head. "No way. Don't nobody do shit in this village without my authorization."

"I guess that leaves you, then," Braddock suggested. "Why don't we go over exactly what you were doing between the hours of midnight and three this morning?"

"Like I told you," Nash shot right back, "I was here. Watching reruns of *True Blood* and sipping Patrón."

Braddock claimed the few steps that stood between him and the red sofa. The threatening glares of all three tough guys followed his every move. Braddock ignored them, sat down on the coffee table in front of Nash. "I would think, seeing you're the king of the village and all, that you would be just a little"—he held his thumb and forefinger slightly apart—"ticked off that someone murdered your number-one go-to-boy right here in your own territory. There must be someone out there who isn't the slightest bit afraid of you or your reputation."

Nash stared at him a long moment. "I got my ways of dealing with these matters."

Braddock belted out a laugh before his face captured and reflected the sheer fury throttling through his veins. "I know you do." He reached into his jacket pocket; the trinity reacted by reaching for the weapons stashed in their waistbands. Braddock lifted an eyebrow at each before withdrawing a business card from his pocket. "Call me when you've got that list ready." He tossed the card at Nash. "*Today.*"

He stood. "I won't even ask if these thugs have licenses to carry weapons." One last look at the bastard on the sofa and Braddock turned his back and headed for the door. The only way he would get anything from Nash was if a gun was bored into his skull, and maybe not even then.

"You got people, Five-oh?"

Braddock froze. His gaze locked with his partner's. She gave her head the subtlest shake, warning him not to go there.

"We all got people," Nash went on nonchalantly. "Even my boy Ricky had people. I'm sure they'll be deeply pained by this tragedy. Sometimes you cross a line . . . make a mistake and somebody gets hurt. You know what I mean, don't you, Five-oh?"

Oh, he knew. The urge to kill this bastard with his bare hands roared like a hurricane.

Now was not the time.

And Nash was right. There was a line to be crossed here. Braddock wanted to lunge across it; he wanted it so bad he could taste it even as he walked away. But he had no choice but to wait. And when he had the evidence he needed, then he would cross that line so fucking hard this piece of shit wouldn't know what hit him.

Cooper followed Braddock out the door and to his car. She didn't say anything, though he knew she wanted to, until they eased away from the curb.

"You can't let him get to you like that."

"Easy for you to say." His fingers clenched and unclenched on the steering wheel. The rage pulsed beneath his sternum, ballooned in his chest.

"If the chief gets wind that you're letting Nash get to you, he'll take you off this case." She stared at his profile. "I know you don't want that to happen."

That was the thing his partner didn't understand: The only way Braddock would be off this case was if he stopped breathing.

CHAPTER
TWENTY-EIGHT

Village Medical Clinic, 7:18 PM

CJ paced the pavement between her rental car and the clinic's rear entrance. Where the hell was Cost?

She'd called him half an hour ago. How long did it take to get from Governor's Bend to here? Ten, fifteen minutes, tops.

The entire day had passed with her combing the city for Celeste Martin. CJ had started with a door-to-door search in the village. No one admitted to knowing the woman, much less having any idea where she might be.

Jenkins or one of his colleagues had followed her every step of the way. She'd gotten worried that no one would talk to her with him around, so she'd given him the slip.

It hadn't been easy. She'd had to park down a narrow little road that only longtime residents of the village knew about. It paralleled the train tracks off the west side of Holmes. She'd waited a good twenty minutes and then she'd taken a back way through Huntsville Park to get back to the village.

It infuriated CJ that no one would open up to her. Every damned one she asked pretended not to know Celeste. That was bull. The girl had been working the streets around here for months. Prostitutes were like actors or secretaries or any other group of professionals: they chatted amongst themselves about work.

She'd questioned folks at the Kroger parking lot. Then she'd moved to the Wal-Mart lot across the street. She hadn't bothered with the mall across the parkway—too much security for any of Celeste's friends to mark that territory.

How could the girl have simply disappeared?

It wasn't possible.

Unless . . .

Guilt congealed in CJ's gut.

That girl was missing or in trouble because of CJ's meddling.

Ricky Banks was dead. CJ had pushed him for answers about Shelley's murder. Celeste Martin was missing. CJ had questioned her extensively. The girl had been too trusting or naive or maybe just desperate for someone to care not to realize her mistake until well after she'd made it.

Dammit.

CJ folded her arms over her middle and fought to contain her emotions. Her sister was dead. The police had no idea who had killed her. CJ's efforts to solve the mystery were only causing more trouble.

Braddock had begged off the briefing he'd promised her. He and his partner were busy with this latest homicide. CJ understood. She'd decided to try to locate Celeste.

Celeste wouldn't be missing if it weren't for her . . . would Ricky be dead?

CJ had no idea what she was doing.

Edward's words echoed amid the whirling thoughts.

This is clearly further indication that you should go back to Baltimore. There's nothing more that would prove constructive you can do here.

He was right about one thing. This morning had been a warning. She hadn't told him about the cat's blood. It was bad enough she'd had to explain about the rabid addict at the clinic. He'd noticed the bandage on her throat.

But last night had been about her work at the clinic yesterday. She was certain. Tyrone wanted CJ to know that her digging around in this investigation was not appreciated.

Next time she might be the one to bleed.

Celeste had told her that the first transgression wasn't so bad, but the second was far worse, and the third time Tyrone was disobeyed . . . someone got dead.

Maybe she should just bury her sister and walk away.

Seeing that the killer was brought to justice wouldn't change the fact that Shelley was dead. Wouldn't resurrect Ricky—even if he deserved a second chance. And it wouldn't find Celeste.

CJ had almost convinced herself to get back into the rental and drive away when Cost's BMW rolled into the lot.

Renewed anticipation rallied her determination. She couldn't go back to her life in Baltimore and pretend none of this mattered.

That was the bottom line.

A realization hit CJ—an obvious fact she was more than aware of but one she hadn't seen in exactly that light before.

She and everyone in this village had been doing that for decades: pretending the things they thought they couldn't change didn't really matter, turning their heads and backs, walking away, moving on. It was all the same.

And it had to stop.

It might as well start with her.

"What's so important it wouldn't wait until the clinic opened tomorrow?" Carter asked as he emerged from his luxury automobile. The BMW's headlights flashed and a distinct tone confirmed that the security system had been activated.

"There's something I have to check on a patient I saw yesterday." No reason to tell him what she was really up to. Required too much explanation. She wouldn't have had to call him at all if Lusk had gotten that key back to her. She'd picked it up yesterday since she needed to get a duplicate made. CJ figured by now that if she got it back she'd have to come to the clinic tomorrow while Lusk was in and remind her.

Carter grinned as he fished through a ring of keys. "You always were dedicated."

A compliment? Maybe. Sometimes it was difficult to read what Carter Cost meant by his words or his actions. There was an arrogance about him. Probably seeded by his family's money and a lifetime of being the only son. Not to mention being the only male of his generation in the whole Cost family. His settling down and producing heirs, male ones in particular, was essential. It didn't take a lot of imagination to comprehend that he'd been given anything he ever wanted by all who entered his world, however briefly. Including any number of college girls like herself and Juanita Lusk, who'd been charmed by his handsome looks and fancy car.

"I appreciate you coming, Carter." He'd done her a favor. No matter that part of her understood perfectly what he was—a rich, self-centered playboy—she was grateful for his effort.

He opened the clinic's back door, reached inside, and flipped the switch. Fluorescent bulbs flickered, then glowed, lighting the corridor inside. "Not a problem." He flashed her that sexy grin that had lured many an innocent virgin to her deflowering. "Besides, I have an ulterior motive."

Of course he did. "Oh yeah?" Feigning surprise was better than telling him she'd expected as much. After all, she wasn't inside the clinic yet.

"Dinner?" He held the door open while she passed through.

"I'm sure your calendar has been booked for weeks." *Don't tell him no yet!* CJ hurried toward the office and the filing cabinets waiting there. "How could you possibly have time to fit me in?" She smiled sheepishly and waited for him to unlock the office door.

"CJ." He slid the key into the lock but hesitated before making the turn. "We haven't seen each other in years."

Ten, to be precise.

"I cleared my schedule just for you." He turned the key, opened the door.

She didn't wait for him to move aside; she slid sideways past him. "That was thoughtful of you."

She went straight to the stack of charts on the desk. Staying late last night to chart her notes had paid off. She'd stacked the charts in alphabetical order for Lusk's convenience. CJ would have filed them, but she'd been concerned Lusk or the preceptor, the kindly Dr. Cost, might need to review them first. Besides, the neat, alphabetized stack she'd left was a major step above the disorganized piles of paperwork lying about the office.

"P. F. Chang's is great." He settled a hip onto the edge of the desk. "Unless you'd prefer a more intimate setting without all the social expectations."

CJ pulled Celeste's chart from the stack, scanned for the patient's home address. Got it. She returned the chart to the proper place, then smiled at Cost. "You're too sweet, Carter. But I'll need a rain check." She posted a sad face. "Tomorrow's the autopsy and I'm not really feeling social. Is that okay?"

He sighed, adopted his own sad expression. "You're breaking my heart, Patterson."

She gave him a punch to the arm. "Come on. I'll bet you've got a whole list of hot babes lining up for their chance at dinner with you. You're one of the most eligible bachelors in Huntsville. Any young, single woman alive would jump at the chance to become Mrs. Carter Cost and mother to your heirs."

The faux sadness vanished with one downward sweep of his thick dark lashes. He stood. "A rain check is fine." He glanced around the untidy office. "If you're done here, I should get going."

The change was more than just his eyes. His face, his posture, all of it shifted. Gone was the flirtatious doctor of charm. Had she hit a sensitive spot?

It didn't matter. She had what she'd come here for. She should just go. Dr. Womanizer would be fine. It would take a lot more than CJ's snub or anything else she said to injure his massive ego.

At the door, she hesitated. "Seriously, Carter. Thanks for coming."

He suddenly noticed the healing cut on her throat. She'd ditched the bandage today. "What happened to you?" One corner of his mouth lifted in a halfhearted smile. "That looks like something I would do trying to shave with a massive hangover."

"Only I wasn't the one wielding the blade." She told him about the incident and how he would find a report in that pile of files.

He complained about how the lack of needed security at the free clinics continued to be ignored by the powers that be, then seemed to get distracted by the piles of files.

"Thanks again," she said, moving toward the door.

He gave a nod. "Goodnight, CJ."

She walked to her rental, got in. The clinic door closed with him still inside. Maybe since he was here he'd decided to do a little catching up. Judging by what CJ had seen so far, the clinic's paperwork was seriously behind.

Still, she couldn't shake the notion that she'd said something that hit a nerve.

Whatever. Keeping an eye out for her tail, she drove through the back alleys to 3805 Beacon Street—the village address Celeste had listed on her personal data form. CJ parked in front of the duplex. She'd been to that door already. The woman inside had insisted she had no idea who Celeste Martin was.

Either the woman had lied or Celeste had. It was remotely possible that Celeste had lived at the address and then moved since yesterday, but CJ didn't believe that to be the case. Not to mention the woman occupying the address would have had to move in today.

Not plausible.

CJ pounded on the door. Until now, she'd knocked quietly in deference to anyone who might be sleeping. Now she didn't care. Music blasted loud enough to wake the dead, anyway. A couple more hard pounds and the door opened.

"What?" The woman visibly stiffened when she realized it was CJ again. "I done told you they's nobody named Celeste living here."

"One of your neighbors says differently." CJ wasn't taking no for an answer. "She's not in trouble. I just need to speak to her."

The woman looked past CJ as if making sure there was no one else with her. "Look, you get on outta here. I don't need no trouble." This time she spoke quietly, her voice barely audible with the music so loud.

"Please." CJ eased a few inches closer. "I really need to find her."

The woman tortured her bottom lip, her face a study in uncertainty.

"I swear," CJ pleaded, "I won't tell anyone you helped me. All I need is a location where I can find her."

"Celeste didn't come home last night." The woman's lips trembled. "You wrong about her not being in trouble. She fucked up bad. If she ain't hiding, then she . . ." The woman caught herself. "She ain't here." Head shaking adamantly, she prepared to close the door.

"Did she get into trouble with Tyrone for talking to me?" CJ's abdomen tightened at the idea. She hadn't meant to get the girl in trouble. "She didn't really tell me anything. We were just chatting. I haven't lived here in a while and I was only catching up."

"I can't say no more."

The door started to close and CJ blocked it with her shoulder. "I know you're scared, but if Celeste needs help, I want to help her. Just tell me where she is."

"Don't you get it?" the woman hissed. "I don't know where she is. She ain't here. If she ain't working the street, and I know she ain't, then the only other place she could be is under the bridge."

"Under the bridge?" Where the hell was that?

"Governor's Street overpass. She might be hiding with the homeless."

Ricky's aunt had said he might be there. CJ should have remembered that. If Celeste was scared, she would do what Ricky had done—go into hiding in a place with people no one cared about.

"Thank you." CJ understood the risk the woman was taking even being seen speaking to her. And Tyrone seemed to have eyes everywhere she turned in this village. "I'll look for her there."

As CJ was about to walk away, the woman said, "If she ain't there, then you know she's probably being punished."

CJ's gaze meshed with hers.

The woman's dark eyes confirmed CJ's worst fears. "Some don't come back."

Corner of Governor's Drive and the Parkway

CJ parked in the lot on the west side of the Medical Plaza. East of the overpass where the homeless gathered at night, Governor's

Drive flourished with massive, prestigious medical clinics and plazas. The overpass served as a kind of border. To the west of the overpass it was like crossing into another country. Dive businesses. Rundown housing. Nothing pleasant or attractive.

When had the parkway become that dividing line? The wealthy and socially elite built enormous mansions on the east side, the ritziest of retail shops and restaurants were erected on that side.

Misery and poverty survived on the west. The landfill, most of the homeless missions . . . all on the west.

Wasn't anyone out there paying attention?

CJ checked her pockets. Keys and cell phone in the left, pepper spray in the right. The sun had dropped behind the mountains, leaving the city of Huntsville cloaked in dusk, and still the heat simmered from the concrete and asphalt. Sweat dampened her skin. Moments from childhood: running barefoot down the street, the sun baking the asphalt that in turn broiled her and Shelley's feet. But they didn't care. It was summer, no school, and all the kids in the neighborhood were outside from daylight until well after dark.

Her chest ached with the memories. Even in the clutches of poverty, life had been so simple then.

The future had been an open window of possibilities. They could be anything, could go anywhere.

Except Shelley was dead.

Murdered.

CJ's jaw tightened. She prayed her determination to avenge her sister's murder hadn't caused the death of another woman.

One who had already suffered far too much.

Tyrone Nash had to be stopped.

Another memory flashed across the screen of her retinas. Tyrone cornering her in her own house. Her mother passed out on the sofa. Shelley locked in her room crying with the music blaring because of something Tyrone had said to her at the bowling alley. CJ had confronted him. He'd backed her into her own living room and tried his best to rape her. Her mother hadn't heard a thing. Shelley hadn't heard a thing.

But unluckily for Tyrone, CJ's mother always kept a butcher

knife on the floor just beneath the skirt of the ratty old sofa. When he'd thrown CJ to the floor, ripped off her shirt and started dragging off her shorts, her fingers had sought and found that knife.

The slice across his cheek had been a mistake. She'd meant to cut the son of a bitch's throat. He'd let her go, grabbed at his face. She'd scrambled away from him and threatened to do more damage if he didn't get out. He had stomped out, cursing her and threatening to come back and finish what he'd started.

But he never had.

From that day forward he'd stayed clear of CJ and her sister.

Until a few years ago, after CJ had moved away.

She wondered now if Tyrone had lured Shelley in just to get back at her.

Nausea roiled in CJ's stomach at the idea. Leaving had been the best thing for her . . . and the worst for her sister.

Twenty-five, thirty women and men, mostly men, sat or stood around under the bridge. Some were eating the leftovers they had probably discovered in trash cans; others were drinking from bottles camouflaged in brown paper sacks. Conversations lulled as she walked past the huddles. No one said anything to her, just looked. The fingers of her right hand were tucked in her jeans pocket. The cool, metal cylinder was comforting.

The roar and bump of the traffic overhead was rhythmic, almost soothing. Was that why, other than the obvious shelter from rain, the homeless gathered here?

So far, she hadn't seen Celeste. CJ's pulse kicked into overdrive. This wasn't exactly the place to be at night, but she had to find that girl. Had to know she was okay.

A wild mane of red hair drew CJ's attention to a huddle on the opposite side of the underpass. Her heart rate picked up, urging her pulse to skip. Dodging traffic she darted to the other side. The girls in the huddle stopped talking and stared at CJ.

"Hey, ladies." CJ walked right up to the group as if she belonged. Her heart sank when she could see that the redhead was not Celeste. "I'm looking for a friend of mine."

"What the fuck you doing under this bridge, bitch?" one of the women demanded.

Was she deaf? "I'm looking for a friend."

Another swayed her shoulders side to side and made a sound of disbelief. "Do any of us look like we roll that way? I don't think so. You take your lesbian ass some place else."

Stay cool. "No, I'm not looking for sex," CJ explained. "I'm looking for Celeste Martin. She's a friend of mine and I need to give her back that twenty I borrowed from her the other day."

"Here, girl," the largest of the skinny group said as she held out her hand, "I'll give it to her."

The ladies stopped puffing their smokes long enough to laugh at their friend's joke.

"Seriously," CJ interrupted, maybe a little more firmly than she'd intended judging by the glares aimed in her direction, "I need to find Celeste."

Dead silence echoed beneath the bridge. The emptiness punctuated by the rhythmic flow of that endless traffic.

The big girl stepped forward, stuck her finger in CJ's face. "You listen up. I don't know why you out here slumming, or why you calling Celeste your friend, but you best mind your own fucking business or you be wishing you was back on Ledges or wherever the hell you came from."

"If you really knowed Celeste," one with a big 'fro hairdo accused, "you'd know she won't be coming back here."

"You got that right," one of the ladies confirmed.

"Hell no, she won't be back," another chimed in.

"She done shit in her nest good," the big girl added.

"Is she in trouble?" CJ was relatively certain she wouldn't get an answer, but nothing ventured, nothing gained.

All eyes settled on CJ. Some were filled with frustration and disbelief that she had to ask; others showed the same fear she'd seen in the eyes of the lady at the house on Beacon Street where Celeste lived.

"What she probably is," said Big Girl, who seemed to be the leader of the pack, "is dead."

"If she didn't get the hell outta here fast enough, she definitely is," 'Fro Girl agreed.

"Now get on outta here before you draw the po-po," Big Girl scolded. "They be thinking we done kidnapped your white ass."

"Thank you." CJ hesitated long enough to garner another collective glare from the group before cutting back across the street, her heart thumping so hard she couldn't catch her breath.

This was her fault. If Celeste was dead . . .

God, she didn't want to believe she'd caused this, but there was no other explanation.

CHAPTER TWENTY-NINE

If CJ hadn't been so caught up in obsessing about what she'd done, she might have paid more attention to the vehicle parked next to hers. Or the three big-ass guys hanging around her rental.

But she hadn't been paying attention.

She never even looked until she was almost there and then it was too late.

She stalled. The rear passenger door of the fancy black SUV opened and Tyrone Nash emerged.

Fear coiled around CJ's throat, squeezing off the ability to breathe.

She was in a public place, though it was closed. Traffic was steady just a few yards away.

Tall, thin, relatively handsome for a scumbag, Tyrone glared at her. The scar on his cheek stood out against his otherwise smooth skin. Clips from that night—his brute strength, her sheer desperation—whizzed through her head like a drunken bee.

"Dr. Patterson, I presume," he said in that silky voice that he'd refined over the years. He could talk the talk with the most sophisticated in the city when he chose. But most of the time he talked the same trash as those hoodlums serving as his body-guards.

CJ restrained any reaction. She stared at him, hoped he saw the hatred in her eyes. This pig was responsible for the suffering of so very many women, including her sister.

The silk shirt and trousers and gaudy leather shoes likely cost more than his girls earned in a month or maybe two. The expensive sunglasses he wore, even at night, reflected her vulnerable position.

She truly was a fool, running around out here in the dark.

Edward was right. Braddock was right. Damn, even Ricky had been right about her.

Maybe she shouldn't have given her official tail the slip.

Tyrone walked up to CJ, stood toe-to-toe, stared down as if assessing her under a microscope. "You just keep on." He shook his head. "Warning after warning. What's it gonna take to keep you out of my business?"

Maybe it was the fact that he was in her face. Or maybe she'd wanted to do this since her one lucid thought had formed after Shelley's death.

She slapped him. Slapped him as hard as she could for being the scumbag he was. For luring desperate young women into a life of misery and shame. The rush of adrenaline that fueled the move receded as quickly as it came. She shuddered with the force of its withdrawal . . . or maybe from touching this bastard barehanded.

His bodyguards closed in. Tyrone held up a hand to stop them.

"I got a score to settle with you already, Dr. Patterson. So I'm gonna give you that, but you listen to me closely." He leaned nearer still. "The next time you wake up with blood all over you . . . it'll be yours."

He turned and walked back to his fancy SUV. One of his goons opened the door. He took one last look at CJ, then climbed in. The goon sent her a look that said he knew something she didn't, then got into the backseat with his boss. The final two loaded up and the vehicle barreled out of the parking lot.

CJ stood frozen beneath the distant glow of the street lamps. She couldn't move. Couldn't speak. If she did, the emotions building inside her would burst free.

Tyrone had killed Celeste.

She didn't have to wonder anymore.

She knew.

A car roared across the parking lot. Adrenaline blasted through her veins. She lunged for her rental. The car skidded to a stop next to her, trapping her between it and the rental.

That was just like Tyrone. To send his other thugs to do his dirty work. Bastard!

She jammed her hand into her pocket after her keys.

The front passenger window of the other car powered down.

Hurry! She hit the unlock button. Reached for her door.

"We have to talk."

CJ whipped around to face the familiar deep voice.

Braddock.

Between the panic and the darkness she hadn't recognized his car.

The margin of relief that trickled through her was instantly replaced by suspicion. Where the hell had he come from?

He would be pissed that she'd lost the surveillance he had assigned to her. Apparently he knew her well enough to pick up her trail.

The charge of fear that had propelled her into escape mode vanished like the final blink of warning before her cell phone's battery died. Her body trembled. She couldn't restrain it.

"Don't just stand there, CJ. Let's go."

An argument was on the tip of her tongue. But he could have news.

She'd barely gotten the door closed when he hit the gas. Fumbling for her seatbelt, she asked, "Where are we going? Do you have news?"

He didn't answer immediately. During that lapse of silence they passed a row of streetlights, allowing her to see the tic in his clenched jaw. Definitely angry.

"We've had this conversation. Just a few hours ago, in fact."

"What conversation is that?" The idea that she hadn't re-locked her rental and that her purse was in there vyed for her attention. *Dammit.*

"You're going to get yourself killed if you don't stay out of Nash's way."

Oh, that conversation. "I didn't exactly go looking for him." That part was true. "He came to me."

"Because you were what?" Braddock braked for a light, shot her a dark glower. "Going around asking questions about one of his girls? After having given Jenkins the slip? The man is already skating on thin ice. Do you want to help him get fired?"

She hadn't thought about that. "None of the village residents would talk to me with him following me around. I was desper-ate to find Celeste." Besides, Braddock should be utilizing his time trying to find Shelley's killer, not keeping up with CJ's activities. She could take care of herself.

Flashes of blood scrawled on her wall and poured over her sheets had her backtracking on that one.

"I don't know how to get this through your head." The light turned green and he set the car back in motion. "You can't keep taking these risks."

"If I don't, who will?" That was the real question here. "Ev-eryone's afraid. No one will stand up to Tyrone."

Silence throbbed inside the car.

She was right and Braddock knew it.

Something Tyrone had said to her bobbed to the surface of her churning thoughts. "The blood." She chewed her lip to stop its quivering. "It wasn't Ricky's."

"I know. I got a call from the lab an hour ago. I drove over to the Appleton house to give you the news, but you weren't there. It took me a while to track you down."

"You have my cell number." She patted her pocket. "You didn't try to call me." He hadn't wanted to call. He'd wanted to see what she was doing. Probably had been following her around when he got the call from the lab. "If you were that worried, why didn't you call?"

"Because," he admitted, "unlike Jenkins, I knew where to look. I've been following you around since you left the meeting with Cost at the clinic."

CJ wanted to be mad. She wanted to yell at him. But she wasn't stupid. She was grateful. Tyrone could have dragged her into his SUV and killed her the same way he probably had Celeste.

"He killed her." The realization drained any remaining fight out of her. This was her responsibility. She'd gotten that girl murdered.

"You can't be certain of that." Another of those sidelong glances shot her way.

"It's true." CJ leaned against the headrest. She was tired. All of this was unbelievable. She'd stayed to help find her sister's killer and she'd gotten dragged into the muck and mire of this dirty underworld. How could she get herself out and still learn the truth about her sister's murder?

"Did Nash say that?"

"Of course he didn't." Why was Braddock patronizing her? "He said something like if I didn't stay out of his business, the next time I woke up and found blood on my sheets it would be mine. It isn't a confession, but I got the message."

Braddock's jaw started that rhythmic pulsing again, but he said nothing.

She'd just told him that Tyrone had committed a murder! What was wrong with him? "You have nothing to say? Shouldn't you go question Tyrone or something?"

He cut her another of those looks. "You know the answer to that. It's a little thing called lack of evidence."

More of that thick silence.

She frowned as he slowed for a turn off Whitesburg. "Where're we going?" She'd expected that he would just drive around, then take her back to the parking lot.

"Someplace where we won't be interrupted." He glanced at her. "While I try to get it through your head once and for all that you're making yourself an easy target."

"We have to go back to my rental car first. I didn't lock the door and my bag is in there."

He didn't argue or complain, just executed a U-turn and headed back to the medical plaza parking lot.

She studied his profile as he drove. She wished she could read his mind. Could see all his secrets.

There was a mystery she doubted could be solved in several lifetimes.

Braddock lived in a condo near Whitesburg Drive's shopping and restaurant district. Like all good Huntsville views, his balcony looked out over the treed mountains that flanked the city. What she'd seen of the condo confirmed what she knew so far about the man. The decorating was nice, probably here when he moved in, but there were no personal touches. Nothing that explained the man beneath the unreadable, however attractive, exterior.

"I don't have any clean glasses." He offered her a cold bottle of beer.

"This is fine." Since he'd already removed the top, she took a long swallow. It felt good. The heat had dampened her skin and the humidity made a deep breath an effort.

He'd said they needed to talk. A crystal ball wasn't required to know the subject matter. He was a cop; it was his job to protect and serve. He wanted her to cease and desist with this little private investigation.

He braced his arms on the balcony railing, his own bottle of beer dangling from one hand. "I've been working on pulling together a case against Nash for almost three years. Every time I take one step forward, I get pushed back two."

That was as good a starting place as any.

"You've been investigating Tyrone that long?" He'd mentioned something to that effect before, but the other distractions had sort of blurred it.

Braddock took a long swallow of his beer, then set those dark eyes on hers. "Unofficially for most of that time."

Confusion drew her brows together. "I don't understand."

"I'm about to tell you something no one else knows. Except my partner and my chief."

Stunned didn't begin to describe the impact of that statement.

"Why would you do that?" Even the few times they had dated, he'd kept his professional life a closed book. Truth was, she hadn't really learned very much about him at all. Except that, like her, he'd been lonely. Had just wanted someone to talk to about nothing in particular.

"Because I'm scared to death you're going to get yourself killed if I don't tell you." He shrugged. "Maybe when you understand what I'm doing and why I'm doing it, you'll back off and let me get the job done without having to worry about your safety."

"Okay." She took a sip of beer. "I'm all ears."

"I know you're trying to help, but what you're doing is too risky. You didn't see what I saw in Banks's house this morning. Trust me, it's not worth the risk."

That was his guilt talking. "Because you feel guilty about Shelley. You think working with you may have gotten her killed, and so you have to protect me. Don't you get it that I feel that way, too? You did what you did. Now I have to do what I have to do. We're both after the same goal."

"I was desperate." He downed another gulp of beer. "Otherwise I might have done things differently when Shelley came to me." He gave her one of those looks. "I'm a cop. Doing this is my job. It wasn't hers and it's not yours."

If he thought that changed how CJ felt, he was wrong. "My sister is dead because of Tyrone Nash." The reality hit like a tidal wave, washing over and over her. Maybe Ricky hadn't killed Shelley. Maybe he was a victim of Tyrone, too. "What makes you more desperate than me?"

He turned his face to hers, held her gaze for a long moment. "Her name was Kimberly. She was nineteen years old. Nash murdered her. Cut her throat. Left me a message written in her blood." He looked away. "She was my niece. She had nothing to do with any of this. Her only mistake was having me for an uncle."

CJ's heart went out to him. "I'm sorry." Jesus Christ. She'd had no idea.

"When Shelley made the offer . . . how could I say no?"

She ached for his loss. "Shelley trusted you." And maybe CJ

should cut him some slack. "She thought you were going to save the village."

"I'm doing a bang-up job so far," he muttered.

"At least you're not giving up." She had to let go of some of this emotion, starting with all her pent-up frustration with Braddock. She just couldn't contain all of it any longer. Not and deal with this insanity. "That's more than I can say for most who try to make a difference."

The silence lagged on.

Finally she couldn't take it anymore. "Where does this leave us? I mean, we have no evidence against Tyrone. Banks is dead. I can't begin to figure out who the father of Shelley's baby was." She heaved a disgusted breath. "It's like a dead end with absolutely nowhere to go."

"I suspected she was seeing someone." Braddock stared out at the city's twinkling lights as he spoke. "When I asked, she played it off. At first I thought it was Banks, but the last couple weeks I was pretty sure it wasn't him."

She hadn't even told CJ. That hurt a lot. There were times when Shelley didn't tell her anything. But on those rare occasions when she wanted to talk, she spilled her guts. Maybe one of those rare occasions would have come along soon if she'd lived. The voice mail she'd left the final night of her life replayed in CJ's mind. She shouldn't have ignored that call.

"Banks swore they hadn't been intimate in more than three months." She turned to Braddock. "He really thought it was you."

"I respected Shelley too much to even go there." Braddock shook his head. "That one crazy moment was the only time . . ." He shrugged. "Our relationship wasn't like that. It was all about getting Nash."

Had he not said the words with such sincerity, CJ might have thought he was telling her what she wanted to hear. But the genuineness in his voice was real. "Thank you."

He looked confused. "For what?"

"Respecting her. She didn't get that often." Maybe CJ was the one who'd overreacted. Maybe it was that whole sibling rivalry thing and Braddock had just gotten caught in the middle.

She didn't know how to explain to him or anyone else that sex, or any part thereof, wasn't just sex to her. She needed to believe it meant something more than what she'd been exposed to growing up. That was why even one kiss with another woman, her sister no less, was a betrayal.

But she wasn't sure she could explain that to him. Not and have it make sense. She vaguely recalled having screamed something along those lines at him.

"She wanted you to be proud of her," Braddock told her.

Emotion swelled in CJ's chest. Had she ever once told her sister she was proud of her? God, she didn't think so. CJ closed her eyes. How could she have let her frustration and impatience come between them?

"She was enormously proud of you."

CJ opened her eyes and looked at the man, some part of her needing to hear exactly that. "I don't know why." She cleared her throat. "I let her down."

"You were always there for her." Braddock smiled sadly. "That's what she said. Whenever she needed you, you were there."

CJ had to be stronger than this. She needed to be there for her sister now. "What're we going to do about this?"

Braddock held her gaze, his wary. "Do you really understand what you're suggesting?"

She nodded. "Without question."

He stared back out at the city lights. "We have to tie Nash to the murders."

CJ knew that wasn't going to be easy. "Tyrone never touches the business. He stays clear, lets his goons do the dirty work. You won't catch him in the act of dealing or pimping. He's too smart for that." Shelley had told her that ages ago, back when her sister had foolishly admired the bastard.

"Even the best make a mistake now and then," he offered but it was no consolation. "We have to find a mistake."

"How do we do that?"

Braddock apparently didn't have a ready answer for that question.

"Look," he finally said, "there's a chance that Nash isn't the one who killed Shelley or Banks. Like I told you before, the MO is a little sophisticated."

He was confusing her. "Then if he didn't do it, why are you focusing completely on him?"

"Because," he explained patiently, "the murders happened in his territory. If Nash didn't order them, he's going to want to know who did. He's not going to stand for someone coming into his territory and whacking his people."

She could see his point. "So if you watch Nash, he could lead you to the killer. Assuming he's not the killer."

"Exactly."

"But," she countered, "you're always going to be one step behind him because none of his people are going to risk giving you the information you need, when you need it."

"There is that."

"Unless . . ." The idea gained momentum so fast CJ could hardly find the proper words to say. "Unless I give him something he's wanted for a very long time."

"What the hell is that?"

"Me."

CHAPTER THIRTY

Edward peered at the dark street beyond the parlor window. CJ had promised to stay at his home for the remainder of her visit. He sincerely hoped she would not be persuaded to do otherwise.

Each day he grew more and more concerned about her ability to make proper decisions. He had thought that she would surely come to terms with her sister's death after the prime suspect's murder. Instead she and that inept detective had found reason to think Banks wasn't Shelley's killer.

This simply wouldn't do.

Pain pierced Edward as he turned away from the window. How could he make her see what a tremendous series of mistakes she stood on the verge of making?

Her residency at Johns Hopkins was at stake.

Her entire future.

Her work at the clinic was nothing but a distraction. Juanita Lusk and that pig Carter Cost would love nothing better than to distract CJ and ruin the future she had worked so hard to attain. That Edward had worked so hard to see that she achieved.

Lusk was insignificant in Edward's opinion, but Cost would need to be watched.

As for the other, if the police had determined that Banks

was not Shelley's murderer, then perhaps their attention had shifted to Nash. Even if Nash's guilt for ending Shelley's life could not be proven, he had been slowly killing her for years. That made him guilty. As did numerous other atrocities. He did not deserve to breathe the same air as CJ.

Though Nash's annoying phone calls were becoming tedious, of the two, Cost concerned Edward the most. He knew all the right buttons to push. He would play upon CJ's sympathies, urge her to continue helping at the clinic. As if he cared. Edward's lips curled in disgust. The man did nothing for anyone but himself.

Edward would need to intercede.

Soon.

For now, he needed to relax. To release the rage and frustration that tormented him. CJ would be here soon and he did not wish to convey his tension to her.

He crossed the grand parlor, the one his mother had so meticulously decorated for entertaining, and lowered himself onto the gleaming bench nestled before the Steinway. A true concert grand, a full nine feet of polished wood, intricate brasswork, and glorious magical strings. Edward closed his eyes and allowed his fingers to caress the pristine keys.

"Für Elise." A simple piece by his favorite composer. The music flowed around him, cloaked him in its beauty. One day he would play for CJ . . . when he'd found the perfect arrangement. One just for her.

Edward Abbott!

His fingers stilled on the sleek keys. Tension rippled through his body. Suddenly he was twelve years old again with his mother standing over him as he rehearsed.

Again! This time play the piece properly. Your timing was off ever so slightly. That won't do. It simply won't do.

He played the piece again.

And again.

Each time his mother's voice rang in his ears.

A Beethoven you will never be! Now, sit up straight. Play it again.

His hands dropped to his lap. Practice truly was the essential element in perfecting any piece. He turned from the piano and stood. He would try again another time. He wasn't himself tonight. Perhaps that was the reason his timing was a bit off.

His mother was always right.

He checked the street once more. Sighed. Where was CJ at such a late hour?

It was best, he supposed, that she had not arrived as of yet. He really did need to see to the mess he'd made in the fireplace. He stirred the ashes, ensuring they had cooled sufficiently.

Making quick work of the task, he scooped the ashes into a container, then meticulously swept the firebox. His housekeeper would happily take care of the cleanup in the morning, but Edward had learned well from his mother. One did not leave such a mess overnight. Pride would not permit such a lackadaisical attitude.

Appearances were, after all, everything.

He surveyed the street once more. Disappointment began to pulse inside him. CJ would be here soon. She had never once let him down.

He carried the container through the kitchen and out the back door. The ashes would combine well with the compost his gardener maintained. Another enormously useful lesson his mother had taught him. Fire cleansed and purified. Many times as a young man he had made poor choices. Her prompt correction of the matter had helped to mold him into the man he was today. No matter how vile or evil, fire rendered any earthly matter impotent . . . harmless.

He poured the impotent ashes into the compost container with the grass and shrub clippings.

There was a use for all things. Some simply did not find their true potential until they were dead.

After putting the container away in the garage, he returned to the kitchen and washed up before taking up his position at the parlor window once more.

He felt great relief at having taken care of that task. His retirement had allowed him to focus more fully on his goals. Every minute of life was precious. He did not want to waste even a second.

A smile touched his lips when CJ's rented car rolled to a stop on the street. She was home.

The smile faded as another car parked close behind hers. Detective Braddock.

Irritation swelled inside him. If the detective spent as much time attempting to solve his cases as he did following CJ around, perhaps he would be a bit more effective.

The two talked for a moment. Edward started to turn away, but then the detective reached out and pulled CJ into an embrace.

Uneasiness settled deep in Edward's bones. This would never do.

You see! One should staunchly avoid the lower class, Edward. They simply cannot rise to our standard. She is beneath you . . . unless, of course, you're like your father. Are you going to fail as he did, Edward? Be like him?

"This time you are wrong, Mother."

CJ pulled away and hurried up the walk to safety.

"You'll see." Edward would not fail.

CJ would not fail him. She was coming along exactly as planned.

Though his innocent CJ truly had no idea how many enemies were closing in on her. Circling like buzzards, threatening her future. He would guide her through this as he always did.

The doorbell chimed and Edward's spirits lifted.

She was here now, and that was all that mattered.

He would keep her safe.

CHAPTER THIRTY-ONE

What the hell had she done with it?

Juanita looked around the office one more time. Every chart she'd viewed in the past six months was piled on her desk. She'd gone through every damned one.

Why the hell hadn't she just shredded the lab results?

No, she'd foolishly thought she might need it in the future. Maybe when Cost forced Shelley to take a home pregnancy test or when her period came. If things had gotten hot enough, she always could have told him it had been a joke to get back at him for being a bastard. Otherwise he might have called the lab and thrown his granddaddy's prestigious name around.

But Juanita had known it would never come to that. A few days would pass and Shelley would get her period. No big deal. Cost would breathe a sigh of relief and Juanita would have gloated about how she'd gotten him good. She'd waited a long time for the opportunity.

But then things had changed. Shelley had gotten murdered before her period came, so Cost had never found out it was all one big fat joke.

Juanita had realized that she could use this situation to her benefit.

Now she couldn't find the real fucking lab sheet so she could shred it!

She slammed the file drawer and took a deep, calming breath.

The autopsy was today, but she shouldn't worry. It wasn't going to be a problem.

Lots of women had spontaneous abortions. The fact that the autopsy wouldn't discover a pregnancy would be insignificant. CJ would question the results and the ME would say as much. It happened all the time. Women conceived and then abruptly aborted for whatever reason and never even knew it.

When CJ came to Juanita with that question, she would repeat what the ME would no doubt say.

All she had to do was calm down and keep her cool. No one could prove anything. Well, maybe they could if CJ pushed the issue and requested a copy of the lab results for closer inspection. But there was no logical or compelling reason for her to do that.

Shelley Patterson was dead. There were no grounds to pursue the issue of who the father was since she hadn't been pregnant at the time of death. The idea that the biological father could have been her killer would be irrelevant since there was no zygote for DNA testing.

Juanita was covered.

She closed her eyes and shook her head.

It wasn't supposed to have gone this far. She'd lied to Shelley about the lab results just to—

"What the hell are you doing here so early?"

Juanita whipped around. Carter Cost stood in the door of her office.

"The better question is," she said as calmly as her nerves would allow, "what're you doing here this early?" Her heart bounced around erratically. She shouldn't have lied to Shelley. But she'd wanted to get back at this son of a bitch so bad she couldn't help herself.

And she'd done it. Juanita pinched her lips together to hold back the smile that came each time she considered how he'd suffered at the idea that the whore he was banging had gotten knocked up by *him*.

"Most likely for the same reason you're here." He stared at the piles of charts on her desk, then moved in on her, trapping her against the file cabinet. "You think this is funny, don't you?"

She couldn't help herself. She smiled. "I think it's fucking hilarious, you egotistical bastard." The last came out in a snarl.

"You breathe one word of what you know to anyone and you'll spend the rest of your life regretting it while I raise that little *bastard* of yours."

Fear snaked its way around Juanita's throat. "You've threatened me with that before." She stared right back into those evil eyes. "I'm not sure I believe you have the balls to tell Mommy and Daddy about your illegitimate son."

"Don't you fuck with me," he warned, "or you'll see just how big my balls are."

"Oh, I know from experience they're not that big."

"If CJ finds out anything about this—"

"That her sister was pregnant?"

"No," he spat, "I know she knows that part. Did she ask you about the father?"

"Of course she did. I told her it was you and she's already planning with that detective how to pin the murder on you."

The fleeting instant of fear she saw in his eyes was worth every second of fury that followed. "You think you've got me right where you want me, don't you?"

She smirked. "I know I do. Shelley Patterson was brutally murdered by someone who had a motive to do it up right. Being the father of her unborn child is motive." Juanita leaned her head toward her shoulder in the hint of a shrug. "A scandal like that could ruin you—or should I say your social status? Not to mention I'm sure Mommy and Daddy would cut you off and send you far away before allowing your unacceptable behavior to reflect badly on them."

"What's it going to take to keep your mouth shut? Permanently."

"Well, let's see." Juanita pretended to think for a bit. "I have to consider how upset CJ would be if she knew you'd been secretly screwing her sister for months. Using her in all kinds of sadistic ways."

"She was a fucking whore. The only difference was she did it with me for free."

He was so angry now his nostrils actually flared. Juanita loved this. "Still, I don't think CJ will take it well. She'll be convinced that her sister had fallen in love with you, which she had, and that you needed rid of her. Voilà—murder motive."

"Get to the point," he warned. "How much?"

Juanita considered all her son had done without the past nine years, not even counting the fact that she'd had to raise him alone because this bastard wouldn't acknowledge his existence except to threaten Juanita.

She worked long hours; most weeks she worked seven days. She'd managed to get a modest house and a decent car. But she and her boy deserved better.

"One million."

"You are out of your mind!" His face reddened, and those blue eyes that had so charmed her as a med school student bulged with fury.

"I know how much you and your family are worth, Cost. That's nothing. *Your* son deserves every penny of it. And"— she folded her arms over her chest—"that's just for starters."

"One hundred thousand," he offered. "Not a penny more."

She scooted away from him, started straightening the charts on her desk. "In that case, I guess you'll learn what it's like to be a murder suspect."

He moved in close again, so close she could feel his hot breath on her cheek. "Watch yourself, Lusk. I'd hate to see that boy of yours end up an orphan."

She turned her face to his, glared into those furious eyes. "You don't have the guts to kill anyone."

He lifted a brow. "Don't I?"

CHAPTER THIRTY-TWO

CJ waited in a small conference room. Braddock had instructed her to wait here while he and his partner reviewed the autopsy findings. Apparently the ME had only just faxed the report to him and he wanted to be prepared before discussing the findings with CJ.

Exhaustion clawed at her. Sleep had been impossible last night. Edward had been the perfect host, as always. Usually that was a relaxing retreat. He catered to her every need. But she'd awakened repeatedly after horrific dreams. Expecting a decent night's sleep under the current circumstances, she supposed, was a little foolish, anyway.

Evidence technicians had scoured for prints yet again or other elements that might lead to the identity of the intruder who had come into her house and doused her bed in blood, but they'd found nothing useful. The blood on the linens had been analyzed and wasn't Ricky's type, but unless they had a comparison specimen, it was of no use to this investigation or any other.

CJ already knew who'd come into her room.

Tyrone Nash. Maybe not Tyrone himself but one of his minions.

While the evidence techs worked in her bedroom, she and

Braddock had changed the locks on the doors. If Edward had his way, she wouldn't be staying the night there again, but the house needed to be secured as well as possible. Truth was, in the village, nothing was secure unless it was nailed down, and sometimes not even then.

When this was done she intended to take the first step in moving forward with her plan. No matter that Braddock had raised almighty hell last night before she'd left his condo and had beaten that same dead horse over and over today. He hadn't let her out of his sight all day. Still, she would not be deterred.

She would get this done one way or another. With or without Braddock's help. And certainly discussing her plan with Edward had been out of the question. He would probably have had her locked away for her own protection.

And maybe that was what she needed.

No. What she needed was to find Shelley's killer. Tyrone had contacts everywhere. He knew every damned body in this town. If he wasn't the one who killed Shelley, he would make it his business to know who had, since, as Braddock said, he considered her his property. He would want to set an example for anyone else who might decide to come into his territory and mess with his people. CJ wanted to be there when that happened.

If along the way she learned enough to put Tyrone away, too, that was all the better. Far too many women had suffered at his hand. It was time someone made it stop.

Braddock could cooperate with her or she would go it on her own.

Shelley had done it.

CJ could, too.

Maybe they had been more alike than CJ had realized.

"Sorry to keep you waiting, Dr. Patterson." Detective Cooper breezed into the room, Braddock close behind her. "Would you like something to drink?"

CJ shook her head. "I'm fine. Thank you."

The two detectives settled into chairs on the opposite side of the table from CJ. Both wore those impassive official faces that gave away nothing of their thoughts.

Braddock opened the file in his hand. "I have the final autopsy report." He scanned the first page. "Cause of death was asphyxiation. But"—his gaze locked with CJ's—"the injuries sustained were not consistent with a hanging scenario. This was a far more intimate act. The perp used, according to the ligature marks, his gloved hands. She was already dead when he suspended her body in the woods. The pattern left by the rope wasn't a deep enough imprint in the skin to have been used in her death."

CJ was thankful for that. A hundred times she'd imagined Shelley fighting her attacker, clawing at the rope to get free those final moments before . . . CJ shuddered and pushed the thoughts and images away.

"No additional trace evidence was discovered. Her skin and fingernails had been thoroughly cleaned. The perp took no chances. Finally, the ME concluded that the staging was completed postmortem."

CJ thanked God her sister hadn't suffered those atrocities as well. The bastard had wanted to humiliate her in death. All of it pointed to her drug use and her sexual promiscuity. Had he known about the pregnancy, too? CJ rubbed her eyes with her thumb and forefinger. *Keep it together.* "How far along was the pregnancy?"

Braddock and his partner shared a look.

Didn't they know she could see them? They were sitting right in front of her.

"Shelley was not pregnant at the time of her murder." Braddock made the statement as if he were making it for the record.

"But her lab results at the clinic . . ." CJ tried to reconcile this new information. Shelley had just gotten the word shortly before she was murdered. Lab results were often a false negative, but false positives rarely occurred.

"The ME," Cooper spoke up, "suggested that it was possible she had been pregnant and the pregnancy was spontaneously—"

CJ held up a hand. "Yes, I know all about how that works. But this would have been recent. Unless she'd had a full menstrual cycle, there would have been evidence that she had recently lost a pregnancy." Shelley hadn't had a period, otherwise she wouldn't have called CJ the night before she died and left that elated message. If she'd gotten her period, she would have been depressed. Or maybe the opposite was true. Maybe she'd had the pregnancy scare, gotten her period, and been thrilled not to have to face that.

CJ didn't know. She was guessing. But if the ME didn't find any indications a pregnancy had existed since the last menstrual cycle, then it didn't exist. Shelley had obviously gotten her period since taking the pregnancy test at the clinic. There had been no reason for her to call Lusk and tell her.

But why keep the evidence she had been pregnant hidden? Had she forgotten? This didn't make sense.

"Where does this leave us?" CJ's voice was thin. She was tired. Most of this news she had known was coming. Still, it drained her emotionally, frazzling already raw nerves.

"Since there was no pregnancy issue," Braddock offered, "her murder likely wasn't related to an angry lover who didn't want the child."

CJ agreed.

"Banks is dead," Cooper put in. "We can assume that rules him out as a suspect, or we can presume that he was the killer and Nash took him out as payback. He doesn't like any of his people making decisions or taking action without his approval."

CJ didn't like where this was headed. "If Tyrone settled the score by killing Ricky, then that's the end of it. The only way we can hope to know for sure is to watch him and see what he does next."

"With no evidence or other leads," Cooper concluded, "the end game comes down to Nash. Preliminary tox screen results showed Banks had not been drugged, but his alcohol levels were off the charts. He appeared to have been repeatedly disabled with the Taser. That's why his body showed no signs of resistance to his attack." Cooper leaned back in her chair and pursed her lips a moment. "The whole excessive force thing is definitely Nash's MO. He enjoys the struggle. Wants the victim to experience every moment of the pain. Yet the scene had that complicated feel the same way Shelley's did, and something about that doesn't feel right."

"The investigation still boils down to Nash," Braddock countered.

"Which brings us to the plan you proposed to my partner," Cooper said. She turned to Braddock. "For the record, I think this is the stupidest idea yet."

"I said the same thing." Braddock looked to CJ. "About how many times?"

"Several. Nothing you say is going to change my mind. I'm doing this with or without the two of you."

Cooper pushed back her chair and got up. She started pacing the small room. "Do you have any idea how dangerous this plan you're suggesting is? Nash will kill you without so much as a blink if he figures out you're up to something. And he's going to be suspicious."

Braddock had been over all this with her last night. "Yes. I understand the risk."

Cooper wheeled on her, braced her hands on the table, and glared at CJ. "Are you stupid? Or does mental instability run in the family? Getting yourself killed isn't going to bring your sister back."

CJ stood, the legs of her chair scraping across the tile floor. "I could say the same thing to you, Detective. You put your life on the line every day for people who aren't related to you by blood. Does that make you any different from me?"

Cooper held her gaze a moment, then shook her head. "The chief won't allow this."

"The chief won't know," Braddock clarified.

"Maybe you don't mind losing your shield," Cooper argued, "but I got a major problem with that." She let out a big sigh. "The chief's already got his eye on this investigation. What if she gets herself killed?" Cooper leveled a look at Braddock. "Can you live with that?"

CJ didn't wait for Braddock's answer. She'd heard enough. "Like I said, I'm doing this with or without your cooperation."

She walked out. She didn't care if Jenkins or even Braddock himself followed her.

There were things she had to do. Talk to Lusk about those lab results. And make a plan for taking the first step toward getting in with Tyrone.

She had to be on her toes for this. Tyrone had been doing this for years. He wouldn't be easy to fool. CJ had to come up with a strategy clever enough to beat him, and she had to do it as quickly as possible.

The sooner he was behind bars, the sooner she could lay her sister to rest in peace.

CHAPTER THIRTY-THREE

CJ accepted the glass of wine. "Thank you." It felt good to sit down and just relax. Edward's home was like a refuge. One far away from the madness that had plagued most of her life. As soon as she had arrived, he'd served a decadent dinner and then ushered her here to the parlor for wine.

After what she'd been through today, it felt particularly good to be here with him. She'd tried to track down Juanita Lusk after going over the autopsy findings with Braddock and his partner. No luck. She would be at the North Huntsville clinic tomorrow morning, CJ had learned. She would catch her there.

A false positive on a pregnancy test was possible, but not nearly as likely as a false negative. The confusion only added to the complicated layers surrounding Shelley's death.

Uncovering the real story was paramount if she was going to find Shelley's killer.

Tonight CJ needed this time to relax in a safe place. Tomorrow she would need all the strength and courage she could summon to carry out her plan. Though a bit sketchy, it was the best she could come up with. Ricky was dead. The idea of using his murder to her advantage wasn't something she was totally comfortable with, but the bastard owed her sister. If his murder could help her solve Shelley's, then at least he would have been good for something.

The thought had guilt bearing down on her, but she refused to be swayed. She would tell Tyrone that Ricky had given her evidence against him, evidence she would exchange for the truth about Shelley's murder.

If that didn't get a reaction, she wasn't sure what would.

Braddock wouldn't like it and Edward surely wouldn't.

That was exactly why neither one could know.

"I've been thinking about the memorial service," Edward said, drawing her attention back to the here and now. "Would you like to host it here? I'm certain you'll only wish to invite close friends. My staff is at your disposal."

He'd already offered to take care of all the arrangements. And CJ appreciated that more than he could know, but Shelley had lived in the village. Those who knew her were there.

Tyrone Nash was there.

As much as it grieved CJ to admit the fact, having the people in the village attend the memorial service would allow her to ask more questions. Perhaps learn something new. That had to be her priority.

"Whenever I come back . . . for anything . . ." She swallowed back the emotion crowding into her throat. "You take care of me. Of everything. This is something I need to do myself." That hadn't come out right. "It's not that I don't appreciate your offer, but you've done far too much for me already."

He cradled his elegant stemmed glass, the red wine an exquisite merlot, as he digested her words. She had been so lucky to find a good friend like him. He'd taught her so much. Set her life on a course far different from that of what she'd come from. Turning down his generous offer felt like a betrayal.

"The decision is yours to make, CJ." Patience warmed his eyes. "The offer is merely that, an offer. It's not necessary to explain your reasoning."

But it was. She owed him too much to pretend otherwise. "I think it would be best to have a very informal gathering at the house in the village. Shelley had friends there." And the truth was, CJ had no friends here or in the village other than Edward.

And maybe Braddock, though she wasn't convinced he counted. "I still have questions. The people there may have the answers I'm seeking."

"Why don't we discuss the questions you have?"

He would attempt to talk her out of pursuing the issue. She knew him too well. Though she was a grown woman, he still treated her like a little girl sometimes. She should appreciate that he cared so much, and she did, most of the time.

"You said the police believe Banks may have been responsible for Shelley's death."

"That's one scenario. But there are questions," CJ reminded him. "Neither Shelley's nor Ricky's murder was Tyrone's usual MO." They'd been over all this. Edward simply didn't want her to keep digging. "I don't want to risk that whoever did this to her will get away with it." She needed him to understand that. "I need to know for sure."

He didn't respond right away. His words and logic would be carefully chosen. "I do understand. But what you're doing is very dangerous, CJ." He stroked his chin thoughtfully. "And distracting. You've been here almost a week now. You must know that your attending is going to be anxious as to when you plan to return to Baltimore. No matter that he's agreed to this arrangement; it simply won't do to push his patience."

All true. "I am keeping those points firmly in mind. I don't want this to drag out any longer than necessary. I am fully aware that could prove detrimental to my future in Baltimore." She took a deep, bolstering breath before sharing what she could with him. "So, I have a plan. First, I have to talk to Lusk and find out about the lab test." She shook her head. "I know it really doesn't make sense. Shelley's dead. What difference does it make, right?"

Edward understood that the question was rhetorical.

CJ stood, stretched her back, and walked over to the grand fireplace. She sat down on the hearth, her favorite place whenever she visited in the winter. "I need to understand what Shelley was feeling . . ." She shrugged. "What was going on in her life those last few days? Maybe it's irrelevant, but I *need* to know. I want the police to determine who killed her and arrest that person. I don't think any of that is unreasonable."

"Practical questions. Rational reasoning." His voice sounded somewhat distracted. "Do what you must. But please be careful."

"Of course."

He stared into his glass of wine a moment. Maybe she'd said something that had upset him. "I will be careful, Edward. I hope you won't worry too much."

He lifted his gaze to hers, offered a pleasant smile that didn't reach his eyes. "I hope you won't forget that you may call upon me for help . . . as long as it's legal."

She laughed. Couldn't help herself. The idea of Edward doing something illegal was preposterous. "I'll be sure not to call you for the illegal parts." Her cell vibrated. "Excuse me." CJ straightened, slid the phone from her pocket to check the screen.

Carter Cost.

She didn't want to talk to him right now. He could leave a voice mail. She tucked the phone away and smiled for her host. "I know it's still early, but I'm exhausted."

"Of course you are." Edward stood. "Have some more wine and retire to your room. I have reading to catch up on. I'll see you in the morning. Sleep well." He hesitated. "I took the liberty of picking up a few things you might need. I hope you don't mind."

"You do too much for me, Edward, but thank you." CJ pushed to her feet. She felt achy and wholly spent. "Goodnight."

He placed a chaste kiss on her cheek and said his goodnight. She watched him leave before going to the sideboard he used as a liquor cabinet. The bottle of wine waited on the counter. Another glass was a very good idea. Maybe she would manage a few hours' sleep without waking.

When she'd filled her glass, she wandered into the entry hall. Each time she visited his home she was astonished all over again. The magnificent house had been built in the early eighteen hundreds, one of the first true mansions in the Huntsville area. No expense had been spared in designing and decorating the twelve-thousand-square-foot home. Marble and limestone floors were interspersed with gleaming hardwoods. The opulent Persian rugs alone were masterpieces. Soaring coffered ceilings and massive fireplaces were in most every room. And the staircase.

She paused at the newel post, surveying the sweeping stairs

as if for the first time. Imported, piece by piece, from Italy. Every brick, every stone, every timber and finish piece of the prestigious residence was a work of art.

But her favorite room was the library. Wall-to-wall, floor-to-ceiling books. Decorated and furnished like a den or study, complete with fireplace. It was amazing. She and Edward shared the love of books.

She climbed the stairs and found the guest room she always used when visiting Edward. She set her glass on the bedside table and ventured to the chair by the window where three—no, four—bags waited. Slacks, blouses, sandals, even underthings. All in her size and in her preferred colors. The price tags had been removed, but the designer labels told her he had spared no expense. She fingered the delicate lacy panties. Exactly the styles she loved. She would have to thank him again in the morning.

For now, the wine was calling. She climbed amid the mountain of pillows on the massive four-poster bed. It felt so good. Safe and quiet. She didn't realize how much she'd needed the silence until just now.

Her phone vibrated, reminding her that she had a voice mail. She should see what Cost wanted. Not that he likely had anything important to say. There was always the possibility that he'd remembered or heard something about Shelley. Only one way to find out.

He didn't mention what he wanted, only that she should call him. Very clever. Now she had no choice. She couldn't totally ignore contact from anyone who had known her sister.

Her fingers entered the necessary keys, then reached for her wine. He answered on the first ring.

"Carter, it's CJ." He asked about the autopsy. She filled him in on what she had learned from the autopsy report. He, too, was puzzled by the lab results versus what the ME had found. He agreed with CJ that labs made mistakes at times.

Then the real motive behind his call became apparent. He wanted CJ to have dinner with him tomorrow night. This was the third time he'd asked. Maybe he was hoping it would be the charm. He claimed this would be a business dinner to discuss her continued work at the clinic. She knew better.

Same old Carter.

"As much as I appreciate the invitation, I already have plans." With Tyrone Nash, if she was lucky. "Of course I'm committed to helping at the clinic for a while longer." Why was he suddenly worried about her rushing back to Baltimore? "Don't worry," she reassured him, "I won't leave you or Juanita high and dry." He made one last attempt to entice her into saying yes to dinner. She declined once more and ended the call. She stared at the phone and shook her head.

Funny, she never would have imagined that she would be working with those two *ever*, in any capacity.

Then again, she wouldn't have imagined her sister being murdered, either.

Pain tightened her chest.

Damn it. She missed that crazy girl.

As long as she was involved in the investigation, she didn't dwell on her sister's death.

Maybe that was the reason she couldn't let it go.

To put it behind her meant that Shelley would no longer be a part of her life. She sipped her wine, considered that thought.

She would go back to Baltimore and there would be no reason to come back here. To be a part of her past.

Not once in her life had she ever missed this life or her past. Now it felt as if leaving it behind would close the book on her sister.

And Braddock.

She hugged her knees to her chest. She'd had one lover before now. That jerk Carter Cost back in college. That was the only time she'd let herself have a physical relationship. Between what she'd witnessed growing up with her mother and all that Shelley had gone through, CJ hadn't wanted a physical relationship. She'd steered clear of men beyond the platonic level. Beyond that one dumb slip in college, Braddock was the first man she'd wanted to know . . . to be with.

Maybe that was part of the reason that thing between him and Shelley had thrown her for such a loop. She understood that she had possibly overreacted. But he had to understand that the kind of trust it took to give her body to a man was difficult for her. She was damaged goods. Who wouldn't be after what she'd lived through?

But she'd had no trouble the other night. She downed the last of her wine, savored the exquisite flavor.

She shivered when she thought of how it had felt to have him inside her. Her eyes closed and she let the sensations flow over her. She loved touching him. His skin was so hot, his muscles so lean and firm. She'd definitely never experienced an orgasm like the ones he'd given her.

Okay. She had to stop. She set the empty glass on the table and burrowed into those fabulous pillows. What she needed was sleep.

Her brain refused to cooperate. She couldn't stop thinking about Braddock. What he'd gone through losing his niece.

He and CJ were both pretty much in the same boat.

Some foolish part of her still wanted to be angry with him for allowing that single moment with Shelley. But she was learning damned fast that life was too short.

There was no promise of tomorrow. A smart woman would start living today.

She had learned a lot these past few days. As a kid, things had been different. Life in the village had been about staying out of her parents' way and playing games in the street. She was only just beginning to understand the intensity of that life as an adult. Of being a part of the village the way Shelley had been. Of investigating heinous crimes day in and day out the way Braddock did. Getting caught up in a moment—in the struggle for survival—wasn't so hard to understand.

She needed to put the past behind her. Whatever happened between her and Braddock from this point forward didn't need to be about the past.

CJ had to remember that when this was over, she still had a future. So did Braddock.

Whether the two would intersect was yet to be seen.

Her eyes drifted shut with the wine's coaxing.

Tomorrow maybe she would figure this all out.

She really didn't want to die trying.

CHAPTER THIRTY-FOUR

Carter watched the headlights go black.

His heart rate bumped up a notch.

He surveyed the dark, wooded park around him. As he'd turned from the parkway onto Hobbs Road, he'd been nearly certain he was being followed. But when he'd taken the first entrance into the park, the other car had continued on.

This whole cloak-and-dagger shit was just too fucking much.

Carter stared at the Escalade a few yards in front of him. No one had gotten out. Carter damned sure wasn't getting out first.

What the hell did this scumbag want now?

Carter needed that video. He didn't have to ask what was on it. He remembered every goddamned detail of that night in gut-wrenching detail.

The argument he'd had with Shelley, the things he'd said . . . they were motive. He didn't need a lawyer or a cop to tell him; he knew perfectly well. According to CJ, the police didn't have a damned clue who had killed Shelley.

If Carter was lucky, it would stay that way.

The whore was dead.

End of story.

And Lusk. When he found that bitch he was going to get the truth out of her one way or another.

The autopsy had determined that Shelley had not been pregnant. He had agreed with CJ that labs did occasionally make mistakes.

But not with his goddamned life!

Someone was going to pay for that mistake.

Starting with Lusk.

If he found out she'd had anything to do with this screw-up, she would so regret it.

His hands shook. He reached for another Vicodin. Swallowed it dry. This was bullshit.

One of Nash's bodyguards approached Carter's car.

Stay cool.

He powered the window down and looked up at the man.

"The King says join him in his car."

The King. Carter gritted his teeth. "Fine." Deep breath and he climbed out. He followed the goon to Nash's car. The rear passenger door opened and Carter peered inside.

"Get in. Close the door." Tyrone Nash reclined in the leather seat, a Black & Mild in his right hand contaminating the air inside the SUV.

"What do you want, Nash?"

The goon who'd knocked on his window moved in behind Carter. "He said get in."

Fury broiling, Carter climbed into the seat and closed the door. A front interior light remained lit, preventing total darkness.

"Did you decide what your future is worth?" Nash asked.

Carter thought about the question. His fury dissolved into amusement. He was going to enjoy this. "Funny thing about that, Nash." He turned to the black bastard. Lowlifes like Nash made him long for the days of slavery again. "According to the autopsy report, Shelley wasn't pregnant." He let the amusement slide across his lips. "So, you see, that video you have is no longer relevant."

Nash took a long drag from his Black & Mild. "When did you get this news flash?"

"Just a few hours ago." Carter relaxed, enjoying the upper

hand Nash couldn't possibly deny. "I considered calling you, but I didn't want to waste my time."

Nash chuckled. "You hear that, boys? The man didn't want to waste his time."

The two goons seated up front burst into laughter.

The laughter abruptly stopped and dead silence reigned for about ten seconds.

"What you fail to comprehend, *Dr.* Cost," Nash countered, "is that at the time the video was made you thought Shelley was pregnant. You reacted based on that concept. Just because you found out she wasn't pregnant after you killed her—"

Carter tensed. "Who said I killed her?"

"Don't matter who said what." Nash shook his head. "Uh-uh. That don't matter one bit. What matters is what you thought the night she was murdered. What you think or know now don't mean shit."

Carter couldn't breathe. His heart rammed mercilessly against his sternum. "What do you want, Nash?" He'd asked him that twice already. Why didn't the son of a bitch just answer the fucking question?

"What I want is simple," Nash said. "About a quarter mil ought to convince me to part with that video." He took another puff of his cigar. "Maybe we better add another fifty thou for the sentimental value. Shelley was my favorite ho, you know."

"Three hundred thousand." Carter felt his insides twisting into screaming knots. "I . . . I can do that." His mind raced with the hoops he'd have to jump through to pull together that kind of cash. But he had to do it. He couldn't risk that video getting out.

"Why don't I give you a couple days to come up with the money," Nash offered, "then we'll talk again? Course, unless you think it might be a waste of your valuable time."

"How . . ." Carter scrambled to think clearly. "How can I be sure you won't make a copy of the video? You could keep blackmailing me—"

"Blackmail?" Nash reared his head back and guffawed. "This is a business transaction. What you talking about *blackmail*?"

Carter blinked. What the hell was he supposed to say to that?

"You pay me," Nash said, "I give you the only copy of the video. A simple business transaction." Nash leaned in close. "Then you never have to see my pretty face again."

Carter couldn't help himself. He stared at the scar on the man's cheek, flinched when Nash reached up and traced the scar.

"You see, if you're smart, you can learn something from our business relationship. Never, ever let a bitch get you in a vulnerable position." Nash turned his attention forward. "You'll get fucked every time."

CHAPTER THIRTY-FIVE

Monte Sano
Saturday, August 7, 9:00 AM

"Why did you bring me here?"

Braddock surveyed the rustic setting, then looked across the top of his G6 at his passenger. "I rented this cabin so we could talk without any distractions." The state park's campgrounds and cabins were no more than half an hour from Huntsville proper, but there was nothing else this deep in the woods atop Monte Sano.

He'd rented a cabin here a couple of times. Once just to get away for the weekend; the other time so that he and Cooper could escape to brainstorm on a particularly puzzling case.

Escape was the other reason Braddock had made the decision to come here. He had allowed his need for vengeance to override his logic twice now. Shelley Patterson was dead for that reason. Now CJ was going down that same path. Both had made that decision of their own accord. He'd gone along with Shelley out of sheer desperation. But he couldn't let CJ do this.

He'd suspected she wasn't going to wait for him. If she'd gotten away before he'd arrived at Abbott's this morning . . .

He couldn't let that happen.

"Is this about yesterday's meeting?" she asked as she followed him to the cabin.

"It's about the investigation in general." He unlocked the cabin's front door and pushed it open.

She considered the open door before swinging a guarded gaze toward him. "You're not changing my mind. In fact"—she hitched her purse strap higher up her shoulder—"the only thing you're doing is wasting my time."

He didn't doubt that for a moment. "I'm not going to waste *my* time trying to change your mind. What I am going to do," he said, stepping across the threshold, then turning back to face her, "is make you an offer Nash won't be able to refuse."

Unconvinced, she stared at him a moment.

"Trust me, CJ." He moved back to give her room to enter.

The stare-off lasted another few seconds. Then she brushed past him on her way inside.

He closed the door and moved around the cabin to open the shades, letting in the morning sun. The place was primitive, but it did offer a small basic kitchen and bath beyond the one main room. A bed, a couch, and a fireplace—not that they would be needing a fire. Noon was hours away and the temperature had already climbed into the low nineties. The altitude and the cloak of thick woods kept the cabin's interior reasonably cool.

She tossed her bag onto the plaid couch and moved to a window with a view of the valley below. "I lived here most of my life and I've never once had the luxury of staying in a place like this."

He glanced around. "I wouldn't exactly call it luxurious."

"You know what I mean."

"Your folks weren't into weekend getaways with the kids, huh?" He braced one shoulder against the window frame and studied her profile. He loved looking at her. That delicate jawline and nose. The blond hair she usually kept up out of the way. There was a strength about her that amazed him.

"My folks were into drinking and partying." She didn't look at him, but continued to stare out the window. "And God only knows what else. The village was all Shelley and I had. We talked about vacations in what we considered faraway places, like Florida or even Tennessee. But we never had a vacation. Not even once. The only getaway we enjoyed was the occasional sleepover at Widow Daniels's house across the street." She did glance at Braddock then. "She died last year."

He could imagine the blond-haired sisters playing in the street. Skipping along the sidewalk, waiting for the ice cream truck to come around the neighborhood. From what Shelley had told him, that had been the highlight of their summers. "You never stayed with friends?"

She laughed. "The parents of the nice kids at school didn't invite kids from the village to stay at their homes. The other kids in the village had it as bad as we did, so that wasn't an option." She turned away from the window. "Besides, I couldn't risk staying away from home overnight unless it was absolutely necessary."

"Why is that?"

"Because my mother might pass out with a cigarette in her hand. Or leave something burning on the stove." CJ plopped down on the sofa. "Or pass out in the bathtub." She pulled out her cell phone, checked the screen. "The only time we stayed away from home was when my mother and father got into a major war, which made staying at home hazardous to our health, or after my father's murder, when my mother brought in a drunk-ass slob who leered at us."

"So you'd take your sister someplace safe." What kind of childhood was that? There were people who didn't deserve to be parents. CJ's fell smack into that category.

"Look, I have questions for Lusk. Can we get on with this?" She cleared her face of the emotions he'd watched play out as she spoke of her childhood. Gone was the vulnerable little girl she'd dared to allow to surface, and back was the hard-edged doctor who wasn't taking any grief from anyone.

"I told you that Shelley wanted Nash to pay for what he's gotten away with all these years. Besides the murders he's suspected of being responsible for, he's the major contributor to the prostitution and drug markets in Madison County. Basically he's a low-life scumbag who doesn't deserve to live. But then, you know all that."

"Better than I would like." She pulled her knees to her chest and wrapped her arms around her legs.

She looked so painfully young when she did that. Made him want to protect her—the way he hadn't protected Shelley. He couldn't imagine living the way she and her sister had as children. His childhood had been pretty much ideal. Loving, doting parents. He'd never had to worry about what he would eat or wear . . . or if it was safe to go to sleep at night.

His protective instincts surged. The need to show her that it was possible to depend upon another human being and not be disappointed. Would she ever really trust anyone? Well, he supposed she trusted Edward Abbott.

But would her past allow her to trust anyone enough to make a deep, unconditional commitment? The memory of sinking inside her tight, hot body abruptly took his breath. He'd wanted to make love to her practically since the day he'd laid eyes on her. But not like that.

He'd wanted to do it right.

"Earth to Braddock."

He snapped back to attention. "I . . . I was thinking." *Focus.* "There was one thing Shelley knew for certain." He settled on the arm of the couch, opposite CJ. "Nash wants me as bad as I want him. In order to keep him off guard, Shelley went along with his idea of luring me into a compromising position. Whenever she was around, he would get so preoccupied talking about planning my fall that he would let things slip, allow her to see things he wouldn't have under any other circumstances."

"For example?"

"Nash has six men, five now that Banks is dead, who oversee his prostitution business. The city is divided into territories. Banks had the village and a number of streets beyond. One of those men is on the verge of talking. Cooper and I have him primed to spill the beans on everything he knows about that aspect of Nash's business."

"What's keeping him from talking now?"

"He wants to keep breathing. He won't talk unless Nash is already on his way down. No one wants to take the risk unless we have something big enough on Nash to start the ball rolling. Besides, I want that bastard to go away for the rest of his life. I need more than the prostitution."

"You have no evidence tying him to any of the disappearances or the murders," she reminded.

Braddock hated that feeling of helplessness. To know a man is guilty of so much and to be unable to prove one fucking thing . . . "Not yet. But if we bring charges of any kind that will stick, our man will talk. To be honest, I have a feeling lots of witnesses will be coming forward. I've made a number of contacts in the village. There are plenty who would like to see Nash brought to justice, but they're afraid."

"What about his bodyguards and the others who protect him? Won't those same witnesses fear repercussions from his chain of command?"

"That's true," Braddock agreed. "Some will still be afraid to talk, but it only takes two or three to get the job done."

She dropped one foot to the floor, pulled the other beneath her as she shifted to face him. "So, what exactly is it I'm to offer Tyrone?"

Braddock's attention stalled for a moment on her breasts. The blouse she wore was one of her conservative ones, but she hadn't buttoned it to the throat today. Just enough cleavage showed to make him sweat. He licked his lips, could still taste those taut nipples.

She was staring at him, waiting for him to go on. He blinked, cleared his mind yet again. What the hell was wrong with him? This was far too important for him to get distracted. "Nash has had his way with law enforcement for a long time. Those who try to levy justice can't get anything on him."

"He's too slippery for them," she suggested. "He doesn't do the dirty work himself. His underlings take the risks. And the falls."

"Exactly. He pays them well for the gamble." Disgust consumed him when he considered what he had to say next. "There are those on the force who look the other way because it's more lucrative to do that than to do their jobs."

She exhaled a big breath, drawing his attention to her chest once more. He had to stop that.

"This is Huntsville, Alabama," CJ complained. "How can a man like Nash have gotten away with this crap for so long? It's not like this is Baltimore or Atlanta. There can't be that many dirty cops around here."

"It only takes a few. Evidence can disappear. Information leaked. Two or three sellouts can do a lot of damage. Nash always seems to be one step ahead of us. This might not be Baltimore, but you'd be surprised at how much of what goes on in towns just like Huntsville feeds what happens in the bigger cities and vice versa."

"You mean like a network?"

"Nash has suppliers in Mobile, Memphis, Atlanta, even as far away as Mexico. What he does here fuels the business in those places."

She shook her head, chewed on her lower lip.

His throat ached to lick those full lips. *Get a grip, buddy.*

"Explain to me how this ties in to why Nash will want to negotiate for you."

Braddock had to stop getting off track. "Because of what he did to my niece, he knows I won't stop until I nail him. He can't buy me off. Or scare me off. He tried that. I don't get frustrated and walk away. I keep pounding at his people. I was so close with Shelley."

CJ looked away.

Yeah. So close. Close enough to get her killed.

"Nash wants me off his back," Braddock went on. "He made big promises to Shelley if she could make it happen. But she didn't care about his promises. She just wanted free of him."

CJ's eyes glistened with emotion when her gaze met his once more. "Will taking Nash down do it? I mean, won't someone else just step up to the plate and take his place in the village?"

"They'll try. And people like me and my partner will just have to see that it doesn't take root. Nash's power has built over time. He's like those annoying little weeds that crop up in a nice lawn. If you ignore them, they'll take over. You have to wipe them out as soon as they crop up. The new chief is working hard to clean up a mess that accumulated over two decades, but we have to be able to tie Nash to the murders to take him out."

"If Nash wants you out of his way, why doesn't he just do it?"

You know," she said with a shrug, "pop a cap in your ass or whatever it is guys like him do?"

He smiled. Fair question. "I'm a cop. There are those at HPD who will look the other way for a few extra bucks, but most aren't willing to pretend they don't see when one of their own is murdered. Nash isn't going to risk having his resources dry up on him or, worse, turn on him. He has to find a way to get rid of me that doesn't include blatantly killing me. Plus, I can be slippery, too. I'm not going to make whatever he decides to do easy for him. He already knows that."

"Are you saying he's tried?"

He lifted one shoulder and let it fall. "I've had the usual tactics attempted. My car's brakes were tampered with more than once. The first apartment I lived in got a sudden gas leak. One or all may have been coincidental, but I don't take the risk. I pay attention. Don't let him catch me by surprise. He'd like nothing better than to see me suffer a little *accident*."

She shuddered, got up, started to pace. "So, what was it Shelley was supposed to give him? Some sort of evidence?"

"Nash wanted her to video me in a compromising position. You know, drugs, sex. She was supposed to slip me a mickey, so to speak, and then she and some of her friends were going to make it look as if we were—"

"I don't need to hear the dirty details."

Braddock heaved a sigh and went on. He hated like hell to tell her this part. "We had planned to . . . last weekend."

She sat in silence a long moment, absorbing the impact of his statement. Stewing, probably, over the pain he'd already caused her without adding this insult to the injury.

"Okay." She seemed to gather her strength around her. "Why didn't you . . . do this thing the two of you had planned?"

He tamped back the emotions that accompanied the answer. "She was supposed to call me when she had it set up, but she didn't call. When I tried to call her, I got her voice mail."

CJ blinked, her face a visible stage for the emotions playing out inside her. "I can see how what Shelly was supposed to give him would make you look bad, but how was that supposed to stop you?"

"He wanted leverage to be able to use me, I think. At least that was Shelley's impression. Nash figured if he could get me in a malleable spot, he could up his ante of HPD assets."

She thought about that a moment. "So I go in, tell Tyrone I want the truth about what happened to Shelley. He laughs in my face." She sent a knowing look at Braddock. "Then I say that if he'll tell me who killed her, I'll give him something he wants."

Braddock stood. "No. You tell him that and you may get asked for more than you want to give."

Embarrassment darkened her cheeks. "I didn't think of that." She leveled her gaze on his. "So what do I say?"

"You tell him one thing and one thing only."

Her gaze held his.

"That you can deliver me."

CHAPTER THIRTY-SIX

North Huntsville Clinic, 11:00 AM

Fucking bitch.

Carter glowered at the Camry he'd parked next to in the clinic's lot. If he found out she had played him . . .

What the hell was he thinking, *if*?

She would regret this.

He tossed back a couple of Vicodins, shoved out of his BMW, and stalked up to the entrance. He'd tried to find her ass last night. But she'd ignored his calls. She wasn't stupid. She'd likely figured out that he'd heard from CJ about the autopsy report. Well, if she thought she could avoid answering his questions, she was insane.

Despite the lack of vehicles in the parking lot, the waiting room was jam-packed. Pathetic losers. The poor from neighborhoods all around the clinic's Mastin Lake location walked here each Saturday. To see that stupid bitch.

Carter cut through the line at the reception desk and elbowed his way to the front. "Tell Lusk I need to see her outside," he ordered the girl behind the desk. No way was he speaking to her in here.

The harried receptionist stared up at him as if he'd lost his mind. "What?"

Carter glanced at the lengthening line in front of her desk. "Never mind. I'll find her."

When he got his hands on Lusk . . . his body shook with rage. He pushed through the door leading to the exam rooms, came face-to-face with the object of his fury.

Surprise flared in her eyes. "Cost. What're you doing here?" She closed the chart in her hands.

"What the hell did you do?"

She blinked, glanced around the corridor. "What're you talking about?"

He backed her into the closest room. The patient seated on the exam table looked from Cost to Lusk.

"Get out," Carter demanded.

The startled woman hopped off the table, pulled the paper gown around her more tightly, and hurried from the room.

"You can't come in here—" Lusk began.

Carter slammed the door, cutting her off. "She wasn't pregnant!"

A hint of fear flashed in the bitch's eyes. "What?"

Fury exploded inside him. "Don't you try that shit with me," he roared. "Shelley wasn't pregnant. The ME found no evidence whatsoever of a pregnancy."

The fear vanished, replaced by a smug smile. "I guess the lab made a mistake."

Desperation, outrage, too many emotions to label coalesced inside him. He fisted his fingers in her blouse and shoved the bitch against the wall. "You fucking played me! She was never pregnant. You did this to get back at me."

She had the audacity to laugh. "Worked, didn't it?"

The desperation overpowered all else. "Do you have any idea what you put me through? You made me think I'd gotten that whore pregnant!"

"You, of all people, should know how to practice safe sex, *Doctor*."

He shook his head. Wanted to kill her. "You don't know what you've done."

Lusk stared into his eyes, amusement twinkling in hers. "Don't I?"

"I'll get you for this." He released her, turned his back, and hauled the door open.

CJ stood in the corridor, the shock on her face confirming she'd heard the entire conversation.

She stared at him. Just stared.

"If you're finished," Lusk snapped, pushing him aside to get out the door, "I have patients—" She drew up short. "Patterson?"

CJ shifted her furious stare from Carter to Lusk. "My sister trusted you."

Lusk dropped the chart she'd been hanging on to as if it provided some protection. She held up her hands. "Wait. I didn't—"

"Yes," CJ accused, her voice shaking with fury, "you did. I heard every word the two of you said." She moved closer to Carter, looked him dead in the eye. "Shelley was not your entertainment. She was a person." She shook her head, fell back the step she'd taken. "You'll both regret this."

When she rushed out the door, Carter resisted the impulse to go after her.

It was no use.

He was fucked.

CHAPTER THIRTY-SEVEN

Braham Spring Park, 1:15 PM

"We've seen this before."

Braddock crouched next to his partner. "Yep." He shook his head, surveyed the young woman's body. Partially nude and sprawled on her back in the grass near the picnic tables, she'd been found around noon by the lawn service personnel.

Cooper set the purse on the grass between her feet. "Wallet, including ten bucks, is still here. Tube of lip gloss, mascara, and her driver's license. Couldn't have been here too long or the ten bucks would have been long gone."

The ME wasn't here yet, but Celeste Martin had been dead long enough to be in full rigor. Her skin had that gray death cast. What was visible of the torso was badly bruised. Her face was bruised, both eyes blackened. A fly lit on her cheek, crawled toward her open mouth. Braddock waved it away. Someone had beat the crap out of her before killing her. His gut clenched.

"No blood on the ground," he noted. "No way she bled out here." He cocked his head to study her left side. "Looks like she lay on her side for several hours after death." He pointed to the darkened area along the length of the left side of her body where the blood had pooled initially after death. Once the heart stopped beating, gravity ensured the blood settled in the lowest point of the victim's positioning. "Probably dumped here sometime this morning before daylight."

"Whoever sliced her throat was clean and efficient. One stroke." Cooper leaned closer to the vic's face. "Most of the tongue is missing. The removal not quite so clean. She must have moved around some." Cooper sat back on her heels. "Just like the Hispanic girl from six months ago."

"That one worked for Nash, too." And he just kept getting away with it.

Cooper nodded, then set her gaze on his. "She's the one who talked the most to Patterson."

"She's the one." The outrage was stoked into a full burn. "Tests will probably confirm the blood found on CJ's bed came from this woman." The ME would estimate time of death, but he was reasonably sure she hadn't been dead much more than a day. He needed to break this news to CJ before she heard it some other way.

"We got company."

Braddock looked up expecting to see the meat wagon. Not so lucky. The chief. Perfect. He and his partner stood, walked beyond the cordoned-off crime scene perimeter to meet the boss.

"Prostitute?" Chief Burton Spencer asked.

"Looks that way, sir," Cooper answered. "We'll need to confirm it, but we believe she's one of Nash's."

Spencer planted his hands on his hips and shook his head. "God almighty, we got to find a way to nail that slippery bastard." He glanced at Braddock, making no attempt to disguise the sympathy in his eyes. "You holding up all right on this? I don't want any mistakes."

"Yes, sir." Braddock gritted his teeth. He could not allow his emotions to show. If Spencer thought for a second he wasn't handling this objectively, he'd be off this case. "We'll get him."

Spencer had been chief of police in Birmingham for twenty years. He'd come here a year ago with a special agenda: to turn HPD back into what it once had been, particularly the west precinct. He wanted Nash, and those like him, cleaned up.

Quickly but legally. The only thing he hated more than scumbags like Nash were dirty cops.

"That's three west-side murders in the space of one week," he reminded. "We're going to take some heat on this."

By heat he meant bad publicity. Since arriving on the scene Braddock had already gotten a couple of calls from local reporters who wanted to know what the hell was going on.

He glanced back at the sheet now draped over Celeste Martin's body. It felt like a war. Nash was fighting to keep his people in line and the cops out of his business.

The only way to end this was to cross the line.

That was something he would have to do alone. CJ would give Nash the message, then Braddock would take it from there.

Before someone else died—images from his niece's murder and half a dozen others flashed in his mind—like this.

CHAPTER THIRTY-EIGHT

Mr. O'Neal no doubt thought CJ was crazy, but she didn't care. She'd knocked on his door and borrowed a number of tools, more than a hammer and nails this time. Though he hadn't been able to go to the garage with her, he'd told her where to find what she needed.

Hammer, small crowbar, screwdrivers, and flashlight.

Her neighbor hadn't always been wheelchair-bound. He'd once been quite the handyman around the house as well as a shade-tree mechanic. And he still had the tools to prove it.

Tools in hand, she'd begun her mission.

That had been a full hour ago.

And she still hadn't found anything other than dust and the occasional earring along with a few nickels, dimes, and pennies. Not even a quarter for her trouble.

"Shit." She surveyed the mess she'd made in Shelley's room. She'd pulled up several loose floorboards and turned a small hole in the wall behind an old junk sale painting into a new entry into the next room.

Braddock had said that her sister was planning to video an encounter that would get him busted. To do that she would have needed equipment. A setup. The way people who videoed their sex activities did. But there was no equipment anywhere in the house that she'd found. Nothing.

And yet it had to be here.

She had practically torn apart the sparse furnishings. Two windows, walls, floor, and a dinky closet were all that remained. She'd explored every crack in the wall in addition to all the loose floorboards. She'd torn the closet apart.

Think! CJ looked at the bed. If she were going to video a sexual encounter, the most logical place to set up the camera would be aimed at the bed. The only thing on the wall across from the bed was the closet.

Just get it over with and look again.

The closet door stood open already; all the clothes and shoes it had held were now piled on the bed. CJ stepped into the small rectangle and slowly checked the wall. No cracks. No holes. She looked up at the shelf overhead. Nothing there, either. But the ceiling . . .

CJ grabbed the one chair in the room and dragged it to the closet. She climbed onto the seat and poked her arms above the narrow shelf. The ceiling seemed awfully close to the shelf . . .

The boards moved. Her breath stalled in her lungs. The ceilings in this old house had once been old-fashioned beadboard, the kind that came in four-inch strips. Most of the rooms had been plastered at some point. But not inside the closets.

She pushed until the boards were out of the way.

It was nothing. Dammit! Just the small square hole that provided entrance to the attic.

Frustrated, CJ stepped off the chair and considered whether she should clean up the mess now or later.

Later, she decided. She should check the other two bedrooms. Just in case. She'd checked this one from top to bottom already.

Wait. She looked up. She hadn't checked the ceiling. Hadn't even thought about anyone trying to go up in the attic. Truth was, she hadn't even known where the attic access was.

There was a small round hole on the ceiling above the center of the bed and right next to the light picture. The hole was s small she almost missed it. It didn't really appear big enough to provide camera access, but it was worth a look.

She climbed back onto that chair, considered her options, and then just went for it. It took a bit of pulling and swearing, but she finally levered herself into the attic.

On her hands and knees, CJ surveyed the rafters and uneven boards that made up the floor. The steep pitch of the roof made the attic large enough for another floor. Light from the small windows on each end kept the darkness at bay to some extent. She'd had no idea it was so large. And dusty. She sat back on her heels and swiped her palms together to dispel the black dust. Years of burning coal in these old houses had left its mark.

Between the dust and the smothering heat, it was difficult to pull in a decent breath. Boxes were scattered about. Medium to large boxes with product imprints boasting the contents. A part of her wondered what was inside. Remnants of her and Shelley's childhood?

No time to get lost on memory lane. She pushed up to her feet and moved carefully between and around the boxes. Years of dust covered everything. She tried to estimate where the center of the room below would be.

Right here. She stopped, stared down at the box at her feet. Now that she really looked, it was the only one not layered in dust.

Anticipation detonated in her veins.

A hand on each side of the box, she lifted.

It felt empty.

When she tossed it aside, her heart stumbled into a frantic pace. A video camera, the kind used for security purposes, and accompanying VCR sat on the old wide plank floor where the box had been.

She dropped to her knees. An electrical outlet had been wired directly into some of the light fixture's wiring. The red light on the VCR glowed, indicating there was power. Hands trembling, she reached for the eject button. A grinding sound, then nothing.

No tape popped out.

Dammit. She bent down, pushed back the door on the VCR, and tried to see inside. Black hole, but no tape. The camera had no storage tape or disk.

But the VCR remained powered on.

Someone had gotten here before her.

That had to be the case.

Unless Shelley had had the tape with her the night she was murdered.

But Braddock said they'd never hooked up to follow through on the faked tape for Nash.

It didn't make sense that the equipment was turned on but there was nothing inside.

No dust on the equipment, which meant it hadn't been up here long.

Could there be other tapes hidden up here somewhere?

CJ looked around the attic, at all the boxes. Only one way to find out.

She searched the first box, then the next and the next. Old toys. Mostly junk.

As she scooted across the old boards she noticed that wherever she stepped, the dust was, of course, disturbed, leaving an easy-to-follow trail of where she'd been.

Digging the flashlight from her waistband, she scanned the floor carefully. Other trails where the dust had been disturbed jumped out at her. There had definitely been some serious traffic up here.

As she followed each trail of disturbed dust, she found another spot, still over Shelley's room—the one they had always shared. A perfect square of the wood floor, approximately twelve by fifteen inches, was relatively dust free. A small hole, this one about the size of a dime, was nearby.

Had Shelley changed the placement of the equipment?

CJ moved back to the VCR and camera she'd found beneath the box. The hole for the camera was so close to the light fixture it wouldn't be easy to see from below. The camera was one of the high-tech kinds, a long snakelike projectile that would curl or twist into most any position. Similar to the kind used for performing exploratory surgery.

Wait. CJ stared at the small hole. *Wait. Wait.* This wasn't the hole she'd seen from the bedroom. The one she'd noticed was the other one. Her gaze shifted to the second place, where she'd estimated that maybe Shelley had first set up the equipment.

But there was no electrical access there.

CJ looked around the attic again. An outlet had been installed on one of the rafters. She made her way to the outlet. New. Much newer than the ones in the house.

Why hadn't Shelley used an extension cord to access this spot? Why go to the trouble to tie one into the light fixture's hot wire? Then she got it. The VCR and camera had been hidden beneath a box. An extension cord running to the overhead outlet would have given away what was hidden under the box.

What had her sister been up to? Had she been making videos and blackmailing her johns, those who were married or held prestigious positions in the community? Those who would do anything to prevent being exposed?

What the hell were you doing, Shelley?

1407 Dubose, 3:30 PM

CJ parked her car in front of Tyrone's house and got out. She was covered in soot and dust. Her clothes were wringing wet with sweat.

But she'd found a tape in one of the boxes.

"Dr. Patterson?"

She glanced back at the car that had pulled up behind hers. Jenkins was climbing out.

She wheeled on him. "You listen to me, Detective," she snarled, surprised herself with the ferocity. "This won't take long. You stay in your fucking car, do you understand me? If I need you, you'll hear me scream."

He blinked. "Ah . . . okay. Yes, ma'am." He climbed back into his car.

CJ turned back to Tyrone's house. Took a breath and pushed

the hair out of her face as she hustled up the sidewalk. Like her clothes, her ponytail had wilted. But she didn't care how she looked or how she smelled.

"Better turn your nasty ass right back around," one of Tyrone's goons advised. He lounged in a generic plastic chair on the end of the porch where the overgrown trees provided the most shade.

"I need to see Tyrone," she said, not slowing down. She stopped on the porch and glared at the man. "Now."

He pushed out of his chair and started in her direction. "You think he ain't got nothing better to do than sit round here waiting on you to pay him a visit?"

"Actually"—she folded her arms over her chest since he appeared to prefer staring at her breasts—"I don't care. Tell him I'm here."

"Who the fuck you think you are, bitch?" He halted two paces away. Glared down at her.

Fear tap-danced up her spine. "The bitch who has what he wants." That her voice remained steady startled her.

He stared at her, apparently searching that fat head of his for some sort of comeback.

Rap music blasted the air. The goon reached for the cell phone clipped to his waist. "Yo."

CJ resisted the impulse to make a go for the door. She didn't have her pepper spray and this guy was big.

He closed the phone without further conversation and sent her another of those lethal glares. "The King says you can come in."

Deep breath. *Be calm.*

She paused, one hand on the door.

No.

Not calm.

She squeezed her eyes shut, summoned the necessary attitude, then gave the doorknob a twist. She stamped inside and searched the living from for the man she'd come to see.

Where the hell was he?

"I thought we was done talking, Doc."

She turned in time to watch him descend the stairs.

He took the final step. "Maybe you didn't get the message the first or the second time." He stared straight into her eyes with his bottomless dark pits. "Do I need to send it again?"

The blood on the bedroom wall . . . on the sheets . . . the bruises on poor Celeste's slim body floated in front of her eyes. "I got the message, Tyrone." She reached for all the anger, all the fury she could muster. This son of a bitch might have killed her sister and Celeste. He'd killed others . . . mistreated all within his realm of power.

She hated him.

Wished that the knife she'd wielded all those years ago had hit its mark—his no-good throat instead of his face.

"I have an offer for you." Fear tried to usurp her bravado. She tamped it back. "One I don't think you'll be able to refuse."

He reared his head back and laughed. "You stupid bitch." He shook his head. "What the hell you think you got that I'd be interested in? It sure ain't that frigid pussy."

Contempt so strong that she could scarcely speak coursed through her. She thought of what Lusk and Carter had done to Shelley. They would pay, too. But first Tyrone would get his. "That makes it easier, doesn't it?"

His own contempt for her flared in those evil eyes. "What the hell is that supposed to mean?"

"You couldn't have me then, you know damned well you can't now. So you pretend you don't want me. Makes it easier."

He rushed into her personal space. "You listen to me, CJ Patterson." He put his nose tip to tip with hers. "I will cut that sharp tongue outta your mouth if you keep getting in my shit. They like doctors who can't talk up there in Baltimore?"

Fear thumped against her chest walls. *Don't let him see it! Stay strong. Pissed off! This motherfucker abused and murdered women!* "I guess you don't want to know what I have to offer."

He drew back just far enough to look her up and down. "Speak. Fast. You smellin' up my house."

Here goes. "I will gladly bury my sister and go back to Baltimore. On one condition."

He snickered. "Ho, you ain't got no leverage here. Don't be telling me you got *one* condition. I don't give a flying fuck what you got."

"You tell me," she pressed on, "who killed my sister. And I'll give you what my sister made for you."

Those evil eyes narrowed. "What the fuck you talking 'bout?"

"You had a deal with Shelley. There was something you wanted her to *make* for you."

Anticipation flickered in his eyes, but he held it at bay, kept the suspicion firmly rooted. "You gonna have to be more specific before this goes any further."

"It's like a movie," she offered. "You know, a videotape."

He shook his head. "Uh-uh. You ain't got no shit like that."

"I found the video equipment in the attic," she argued. "The tape was missing from the VCR, but there were lots of boxes up there. I just started looking, and what do you know. My worst nightmares all on one vile tape."

Still suspicious, he ventured, "What kind of nightmares?"

"That's for me to know and you to find out." She lifted her chin and called upon every ounce of fury she could dredge up. "Suffice it to say that Braddock is going down for this. He will not get away with what he did to my sister. He used her." She leaned toward Tyrone. "That bastard did things to her . . ." She shuddered. "There were other girls, too. It's sick. He's just like all the other cops around here. And I'm going to see that he goes to jail."

"No. No. No, chickee." Tyrone held his hands palms out and waved them back and forth. "You don't want to do that. You know they'll just cover that shit up. You let me take care of Braddock." He pushed back his shoulders and puffed out his chest. "Why you think I had Shelley working on him? I knew what he was; I just needed evidence."

"I don't think so." She shook her head. "I want him to go to jail. What could you do with the tape?"

Tyrone smirked. "I could make him pay in ways you can't even imagine."

"Whatever." Anticipation had her nerves jangling. "You tell

me who killed my sister and we'll make a trade. I give you the tape and then you can do whatever you want to Braddock."

"Doesn't work that way." He walked over to the coffee table, got a cigarette from the pack lying there, and lit it. "You show me a preview of what you got, I'll give you the name. No negotiations." He blew out a plume of nasty smoke.

Don't let him see any hesitation. Counter him! Think! "Fine. But I have to warn you, those girls spent a lot of time talking about you while they were doing Braddock."

His eyes narrowed again as he moved back to where she stood. "What kind of talk?"

CJ shrugged. "Oh, nothing that would interest anyone but the police."

He shoved his face in hers. "What fucking kind of talk?"

"The names of people you've had murdered. The reasons you had them murdered." *What else? What else?* "Dates, locations. You know, stuff like that."

He searched her eyes, looking for the lie.

"So, do we have a deal or what?"

"How 'bout you show me the tape right now?" He reached for her.

She stepped back. *Shit!* "Do you think I'm stupid? I didn't bring the tape with me. I pick the place where the trade goes down."

He still wasn't completely convinced. "As long as it's neutral territory."

Relief burned in her chest. "Fine." She moistened her lips, needed water badly. Her throat was utterly parched and full of coal dust. "How about—"

"I pick the time," he countered.

"All right, all right. My house."

He made that annoying sound that indicated a wrong answer on game shows. "Neutral territory. That ain't neutral."

Well, she'd tried. "The village clinic. It won't be open again until Wednesday. I have access to a key." Not that she would need it. She wouldn't help Lusk or Carter again if her life depended upon it, but she would get the key back from Lusk for this.

Then again, she hadn't been helping them. She'd been helping herself and the people of this village.

"Tomorrow morning, ten sharp," he told her. "After all them Jesus-loving niggers get out of their houses and off to the church of their choice."

Would that give her time to pull together a plan? She had to talk to Braddock first. *Damn! Say something!* "Okay, but . . . you . . . you bring proof," she said, only just thinking of that. "Otherwise you could just toss out some random name. I want proof that the person you say killed her actually did it."

He laughed. "You learning, Doc. You always got to hedge your bets." All signs of amusement vanished and he pointed a deadly glare at her. "But you better not be fucking with me."

She started to go, but hesitated. "What if it's you?"

He made a face like he didn't understand what she meant.

"What if you're the one who killed her?"

Tension thickened in the room. He didn't move. Didn't toss out one of those witty remarks right away.

"Then you better call your preacher, Doc."

"Why is that?"

" 'Cause you dead, baby." Their gazes locked. "I have to kill you then."

The door opened, breaking the stare-off.

The goon from the porch stuck his head inside. "You got company, Ty."

"What the fuck," Tyrone muttered. "Grand fucking Central Station 'round here."

CJ pushed past the goon. She was out of here. She came to an abrupt halt at the steps.

Braddock and Cooper did the same on the sidewalk.

"CJ." Braddock's face was pinched in frustration. "What're you doing without Jenkins?"

Cooper looked from CJ to Braddock and back, obviously confused as well.

The goon moved up behind her. "The King said he ain't taking no more visitors."

CJ, taking advantage of the interruption, stamped down the steps and right past Braddock.

"CJ." He came after her.

She wheeled on him. "Stay away from me." She held up her hands when that didn't slow him. "Just stay away."

Don't look back. Just move. She hurried to her car, got inside, and drove away.

Jenkins followed her.

She didn't breathe again until she'd reached her house.

Pressing her forehead against the steering wheel, she fought to catch her breath. She'd done it. Propositioned Tyrone and managed to make her fury at Braddock look real.

Right in front of Tyrone.

Was that luck or what?

But why had Braddock arrived? Had he been looking for her? What was he thinking? Jenkins had probably called him. But he would have had to be close by to get there so quickly. She dug the cell phone from her jeans pocket. Three missed calls from him. She'd been so caught up in the confrontation with Tyrone she hadn't realized her cell had vibrated.

Just as well. She had accomplished her mission.

Now she needed a shower. She pulled the damp T-shirt from her chest. Tyrone was right. She smelled.

CJ felt human again after a cool shower. She wiggled into a pair of Shelley's jeans and pulled on a blouse. Unfortunately she'd ruined the nice outfit Edward had bought her. It would never come clean.

She frowned when, even after tugging at the blouse, it didn't cover her stomach. "You had that whole I'm-hot-look-at-me thing going on, didn't you, sis?"

CJ pulled the blouse away from her skin and sniffed it. Smelled like her sister. God, she missed her.

Those painful thoughts tried to resurface, attempted to undermine her courage. CJ pushed them away. She couldn't go there and get this done. She had a meeting with Tyrone tomorrow morning. Between now and then she had to decide what she was going to do about a tape. She hadn't exactly lied to him. She had found a tape.

But it was blank.

Somehow she had to finagle a way to get him to tell her the name before she showed him the tape. There was an old television and VCR in the clinic lobby. If she was lucky, it wouldn't work. She could tell him to just take the tape . . . as soon as he told her the killer's name.

Surely her little performance outside his house was proof enough that she was upset with Braddock.

Maybe.

One step at a time. She should call Braddock and explain what she'd done.

Strike that. She wouldn't have to call him. He was likely waiting outside her house right now.

She clipped her wet hair up and opened the door. She should eat. Braddock had insisted she have breakfast this morning, but she hadn't thought about food since.

Right now she was starved.

She drifted down the stairs, tried to think what she'd noticed that was edible when she'd torn the kitchen apart.

"What the hell was that all about?"

CJ's heart lunged into her throat. "Braddock." He was standing in the middle of the living room.

"What," he reiterated as he moved toward her, "was that little show in Nash's yard all about?"

She opened her mouth to tell him, but there was too much to say. "Come on." She grabbed his hand. "I'll show you."

Not about to climb into that dusty attic again, she sent him up there to see for himself.

When he climbed back through the narrow access, he dusted off his hands. "Looks like she was all set to go."

"But she got interrupted." CJ glanced around at the mess she'd made. Shelley had been doing exactly what she'd said she was doing. Getting her life together for real this time.

And CJ hadn't given her the chance to explain.

Misery swelled inside her.

"What did you say to Nash?"

CJ lifted her gaze to Braddock's. "I . . ." The smudge of coal soot on his jaw distracted her. Probably because she needed an excuse to touch him, she reached up and swiped the black smudge from his jaw. He tensed at her touch. "Sorry. You had soot on your face."

His gaze dropped to her exposed belly. She blushed but didn't move to try to tug the blouse down. Wouldn't have done any good, anyway. She let him look. Needed to feel something besides the pain of loss.

When he lifted his gaze to hers once more, there was no way to miss the desire there. It startled her a little. She didn't see herself that way. Another reason she'd been so jealous of Shelley with Braddock. Shelley had been the sexy, flirtatious one. CJ had always been the bookworm.

"Nash," he said, his voice a little thick. "What did you say to Nash?"

She gave herself a mental shake, ordered her heart to slow. "I told him I had you on video doing all sorts of bad things." Then she told him about the other part she'd added, the talk of Nash's activities. And about the meeting tomorrow morning.

"He won't wait until morning."

Fear trickled into her veins. "You think he'll come after me tonight?"

Braddock nodded. "We were supposed to plan your meeting with him."

She shrugged. "I found the video equipment and I got fired up. You weren't here, so . . ."

"He could have forced you to tell him the truth right there in his house." Braddock's jaw started that flexing that meant he was pissed. "You went in his house and basically threatened him. You ordered my detective to stay in his car. If I hadn't showed up—"

"I was already out the door when you showed up," she argued. He wasn't going to make her feel like a fool. She'd gotten a reaction out of the man. "It's like you said, he'll be on the move tonight. Attempting to find that tape. If he comes in here, that's breaking and entering."

Braddock shook his head. "It won't be him. It'll be some of his men. Like always."

Had she done nothing right? "So what do I do? You're the fucking detective."

"You come home with me, where you'll be safe."

"Braddock, I can—"

"Don't argue." He exhaled a weary breath. Pain flashed across his face. "Celeste Martin's body was found today."

CJ's heart sank into her stomach. "He killed her because of me."

"No," Braddock said firmly. "He killed her because he's a low-life scumbag."

She wrapped her arms around her middle. She'd known Celeste was probably dead, but hearing it . . . *Dear God*.

"Pack for an overnight stay," he ordered. "I'm not letting you out of my sight."

Wait. She pushed away the misery. His suggestion would ruin everything. "What if Nash sees me leave with you? I didn't put on that performance for nothing."

"You leave in your car. Then I'll leave. We'll rendezvous at the cabin. I'll keep you in sight to make sure you don't have a tail. I'll give Jenkins the night off."

She nodded. "I can be ready in five minutes."

She turned her back on him and bounded up the stairs.

As she shoved her nightshirt and a change of clothes into a bag, she paused. What if this didn't work? What if Tyrone didn't show in the morning?

Would she ever know who killed her sister?

She stared up at the small hole in the ceiling over the bed. Why couldn't there have been a tape in there?

Someone had to know what happened.

Who had taken the tape out of that VCR?

Had Shelley hidden it? Taken it with her to blackmail the person she'd left with that night?

How the hell was she ever going to find out?

CHAPTER THIRTY-NINE

It was cooler on the mountain.

Once she and Braddock had rendezvoused at the cabin, he drove her to Hampton Cove to pick up dinner at Mikato's. It wasn't like there would be any delivery service deep in the woods of the state park.

And for the first time since she'd gotten Braddock's phone call, she was hungry. Really hungry.

She'd eaten her fill of steamed vegetables and fried rice. Now she felt tired and satisfied to some degree. She had called Lusk about the key. She hadn't answered so CJ had left a voicemail. One way or another she was getting in that clinic tomorrow.

There were many things about her sister's life that she now understood. Like the deceit and the inability to depend upon those who were supposed to provide protection. Like law enforcement officers . . . and medical personnel.

Lusk and Cost had taken advantage of Shelley. Had used her like she was some disposable product manufactured for their entertainment.

The idea made CJ sick. They wouldn't get away with this. That was one thing she could ensure.

And Celeste. Poor Celeste. Nash couldn't keep getting away with what he was doing to those women.

Braddock joined her on the couch. "You okay?"

CJ closed her eyes, drew in a deep, deep breath. "The one thing I'm certain of right now is that I'm not okay."

"What those two did is criminal."

Over dinner she had filled Braddock in on the confrontation between Lusk and Cost.

"I suppose"—CJ opened her eyes—"Carter Cost was the secret man in Shelley's life." It killed CJ to think that Shelley had been so happy. She'd thought she finally had a good guy. A guy who was somebody. And he'd only been using her.

Braddock nodded. "You know that makes him a suspect."

He was right. "Oh, my God." The words he'd screamed at Lusk finally made sense. "He said something like, 'You don't know what you've done.'" Her gaze lifted to Braddock's. "Do you think he could have killed her because he thought she was pregnant?"

"Before Banks was murdered, I would have said that was very possible. But the MO used to murder Shelley was the same one used on Banks. I can't see any reason Cost would have killed Banks."

"True." CJ made a disparaging sound. "I can guarantee he isn't man enough to get close to that dog, much less use it as a murder weapon."

"Sounds like you and Cost have a history."

"Believe it or not"—CJ hated how this was going to sound—"back in college, Cost dropped Lusk and went after me for a while. Trust me, his motives were only related to nailing a virgin. He dropped me soon after he had attained his goal. I guess Lusk still carries a grudge." Poor Shelley. How was she ever supposed to have gotten life back with odds like this?

But she had been doing exactly that. There was no way to know if her determination would have withstood the pain of learning Cost had used her, had she lived.

CJ dropped her head on the sofa back. How could so many people associated with the village be so crazy? Evil?

Maybe it wasn't all of them, just the ones she knew.

What did that say about her?

That she'd grown up in a dysfunctional, drug-abusing household.

Sad.

"I'll have Cooper haul Cost in tomorrow just to rattle his cage." Braddock smiled. "When she gets through with him, he'll be a far humbler man."

CJ touched his arm. "Only if I can watch."

Braddock looked down at her hand on his arm, then lifted his eyes back to hers. That desire was there again. She should have moved her hand. Shouldn't have just sat there staring at him. But somehow she couldn't. He felt warm and strong. And she needed to feel those two things right now.

He took her hand in his, gently explored it. "So, you made it to college still a virgin?"

The rush of sensations, the pad of his thumb caressing her palm, those long fingers cradling the back of her hand, made a coherent thought impossible. "It's weird, I know." Flashes of him caressing her in other places, his hands all over her body, kept rushing through her head.

His fingers stilled and his eyes met hers once more. "Not weird at all. You were trying to do better for yourself."

"As you say, I did a bang-up job. Carter was a colossal mistake. But I learned my lesson, I never let it happen again."

"Meaning?"

The way he was looking at her . . . like he already knew the answer but wanted to hear her say it. "There wasn't anyone else until you." Memories of the other night, of him filling her so completely, set every single nerve ending in her body ablaze.

He leaned toward her, brushed his lips across hers. She eased forward, met his kiss. He tasted like coffee and Braddock, strong and caring.

Banging on the door had CJ jumping back.

Another round of pounding echoed through the small cabin.

Braddock released her hand and went to the front window. He took a look, then opened the door.

Detective Cooper waltzed in, her arms loaded with bags. "I came bearing gifts."

CJ felt her cheeks redden. Talk about bad timing. If Detective Cooper suspected anything was going on between CJ and Braddock, that could make them both look bad.

Braddock took the Wal-Mart bags from his partner. "What's that?" He nodded to the big Priority Mail envelope beneath her arm.

"Evidence." She shot a look across the room at CJ. "I don't know about you, but I could use some coffee."

CJ ordered herself to relax. "Sounds good to me." Even though they'd had coffee from the restaurant, she could use more.

"I know what that means." Braddock set the bags aside and headed for the tiny kitchen.

CJ moved to the table and watched as Cooper opened the envelope and pulled out a manila file folder.

By the time Braddock returned with the coffeepot and three mugs hooked on his fingers, Cooper had a number of photos and reports spread across the table.

"Thanks, partner," she said as he set the cups and the pot on the rustic table amid her display.

CJ leaned down, took a closer look. "Crime scene photos?"

"That's right." Cooper poured herself a cup of coffee. "All believed to be Nash's work."

CJ shuddered, drew back. She noticed that there wasn't one of Shelley. She was glad.

"Did you drive through the village before coming here?" Braddock wanted to know.

"I did. Chief Spencer gave us the two cops you asked for. Metcalf is watching the alley behind the Patterson house and Wallace has the front." She reached into her back pocket and pulled out a folded-up envelope. "By the way, Lusk stopped by and stuck this on your door."

"Why are they watching the house?" CJ had just assumed that since she wasn't there, the surveillance wouldn't be necessary. She accepted the envelope and opened it. "The key to the clinic." Good. Part of her was glad she hadn't had to face Lusk to get it.

Braddock passed CJ a cup of coffee, then poured one for

himself. "If Nash gets any ideas about checking out your story, he won't have any luck getting into the house."

"Good point." CJ hadn't thought of that. Good thing she wasn't a cop. She placed the key on the table. Braddock picked it up and tucked it into his pocket. "That's one obstacle out of the way."

"Okay." Cooper gestured to her display of photos and reports. "All of the murders, including Shelley's and Banks's, have similarities. The murderer took a souvenir of sorts. Tongue, ear, foot, hand, et cetera. With Kimberly's murder, he did the same, but he also left a written message—like the E. Noon or No One messages that have been left this time." Cooper shrugged. "Sort of, anyway." She picked up the evidence photo of the note Braddock had gotten when his niece went missing and placed it atop the others. "The one thing that these two recent murders have in common that none of the others do is the staging. That's the part that doesn't add up to me."

"Maybe he's trying to be clever," CJ suggested. "He gets off on making other people look stupid. Maybe he thinks this is like an in-your-face thing directed at Braddock and you."

Cooper downed a slug of coffee. "That's a definite possibility. He likes kicking us in the teeth. There is also the possibility that it isn't Nash."

"But when you consider the most recent victims," Braddock offered, "the one thing all three have in common is Tyrone Nash."

"And living in the village," CJ added. "Each was involved in drugs and prostitution." She steeled herself against the emotions that tried to pound her composure. "Shelley was turning her life around, but . . ." She licked her lips. "Those activities were still a part of her recent history."

Braddock tapped one of the photos. "The other sticking point is there was no signature at the scene where Celeste's body was discovered."

"Tyrone definitely killed her," CJ protested. "He as much as said he did when he threatened me. Carter Cost had a motive for wanting Shelley out of his way, but even if he had killed her, he'd had no reason to kill Ricky or Celeste."

"Just because we haven't found the signature yet doesn't mean it isn't there," Cooper argued. "The ME may find something on or in the body that we missed."

"True," Braddock allowed. "What we need now is to make Tyrone believe that CJ has something real on him. Maybe get him in a negotiating posture."

CJ was counting the hours until her meeting with Tyrone. She tried not to be nervous, but her efforts were failing miserably. "He'll want at least a glimpse of the tape as proof."

"Exactly." Cooper walked over to the bags she'd brought with her. "On my way here I stopped at Wal-Mart." She looked from CJ to Braddock. "We're going to make some porn."

"Okay." Cooper sat back on the wood beam. "Hand the camera up to me."

Braddock stood on the bed and extended the handheld video camera to his partner. "You need anything else up there?"

"That'll do it." Cooper flashed one of those cheeky grins of hers. "Everything else is up to you two."

CJ felt her pulse skip. This had seemed like a really good idea when Cooper had come up with it. But now CJ wasn't so sure.

"You're still okay with this?"

CJ met the question in Braddock's eyes. Why was she second-guessing herself? It was the right thing to do.

"I'm good. Let's do it."

"You're going to have to look naked," Cooper reminded from her position on the ceiling beam.

Yeah . . . that was the problem.

Just stop. Do it and stop thinking. CJ peeled off her tee. Thankfully her bra was a nude color. Once she was standing there with nothing but the bra and her jeans, she didn't give herself time to think. She climbed beneath the quilt on the bed and pulled it up to her chin.

"You'll need to keep your face over hers," Cooper said to Braddock. "The hair color is the same, but we don't want him to get a glimpse of the face."

"Uh-huh." Braddock started unbuttoning his shirt.

CJ stared at the ceiling, just past where Cooper sat on the beam. She could do this. They had kissed just a little while ago. Only a few days ago they'd had sex. It wasn't a big deal. Cooper would be watching. The video camera would be rolling.

It wouldn't be real.

Maybe that was the problem. Maybe she wanted it to be real.

The bed shifted. Her breath evacuated her lungs.

He slid beneath the quilt. His leg brushed against hers and heat shot through her veins.

She blinked. His trousers were still on. They weren't naked. It wasn't a big deal.

"Jesus, Braddock," Cooper said, "you're going to have to get on top of her so her face doesn't show."

His dark gaze collided with CJ's. "Yeah, yeah. I got it."

He sounded as nervous as she felt. This was ridiculous. They'd had sex, for Christ's sake. *They were adults.*

CJ thrust her arms around his neck and, deciding there was no turning back now, pulled his face closer. "We have to make this look real," she muttered.

"That would be nice," Cooper shouted down.

CJ felt her face flush. She hadn't meant her to hear the comment.

"Real," Braddock echoed. "Yeah."

He dipped his head, brushed his lips across hers. She didn't mean to, but she made a little sound . . . just a soft sigh. And she shivered.

He drew back, stared down at her.

She blinked.

God, this was so awkward!

He stared at her mouth a moment, then dove back in with his.

The kiss went on and on. Deeper. Soft at first, then harder. CJ forgot about Cooper up on the ceiling beam. Her entire focus was on his mouth . . . the feel of his muscled body pressing into hers. Her fingers threaded into his hair. His chest flattened against her breasts. Her nipples tightened and tingled.

Her heart started to beat faster and faster. She didn't want this amazing sensation to stop. The firm ridge pressing into her pelvis had her tilting that part of her body into his. Couldn't help herself. It was sheer instinct. And sheer pleasure.

"I'm sorry, guys," Cooper announced.

CJ's eyes flew open. Braddock's lips drew away from hers. He turned his head. "What?" The single word was rough, thick.

CJ wasn't the only one feeling the tension.

"The kissing is great," Cooper explained, "but you're going to have to move around some if you expect this to look realistic."

Braddock turned his face back to CJ's. He stared a long moment. The desire in his eyes made her heart thump harder.

"Gotcha," he mumbled.

And then his mouth came down on hers. His body started to move, mimicking that up-and-down, grinding motion of lovemaking.

CJ lost herself to the rising sensations. She didn't even want to think how long she'd been without sex until a few days ago. His back . . . his torso . . . she loved to touch him. Perfectly sculpted muscles . . . so warm. So strong. She imagined having him inside her now. Hard and thick. As if he'd imagined the same, his tongue thrust inside her mouth. Her legs wrapped around his and she lifted to meet his movements.

Waves of pleasure washed over her, started her toward that plunge of release. She tried to hold it back . . . couldn't. Braddock's breathing was heavy between kisses. His body tense. His movements grew more frantic, harder. The urge to rip off her jeans and take him was overwhelming.

"That should do it."

Braddock froze.

CJ bit her lip to hold back a whimper. She blinked. Tried to catch her breath. Her entire body pulsed.

"Help me out here," Cooper called down to Braddock.

He scrambled from under the quilt, climbed up to take the camera.

CJ scooted off the mattress. Grabbed her blouse and pulled it back on. Her body was still strumming with pleasure. She was so close to . . .

"I need some air." Braddock stormed out of the cabin.

Cooper dropped down onto the bed. She shook her head. "Men. They just can't take the heat."

CJ managed a shaky smile. At the moment, she wasn't exactly taking it too well either.

She rammed her fingers through her hair. Straightened her clothes.

Cooper prepared to copy her camera work onto a videotape and ensure it was good to go.

As soon as the images flashed on the small television screen, CJ was out of there.

"I'll make a fresh pot of coffee," she mumbled.

"You might want to put some ice in that," Cooper called behind her. "I think you both need to cool off."

CHAPTER FORTY

Cooper took her equipment and files and left.

Braddock stared out the window long after she'd driven away in the Monster.

He was avoiding eye contact and conversation with CJ.

If he looked at her now, even exchanged a single word with her, he wasn't sure he could control his baser urges.

"Hello?"

He flinched at the sound of her voice. Soft, tentative. He glanced over his shoulder to confirm that she'd gotten a call on her cell.

Most likely Abbott.

Braddock needed a walk.

The last one hadn't been nearly long enough.

He stormed out the door. Walked to the narrow road that cut through the trees past the tiny cabins, making a long circle through the park. He didn't go far enough to lose a visual on the cabin, kept his pace brisk and steady. Still, the walk, the night air did nothing to calm him down.

The idea that CJ had only had one lover before him made his skin tighten and his lower anatomy harden. She'd waited years . . . and he'd ravaged her on that couch like . . .

"Jesus Christ." He blew out a halting breath. "So much for finesse."

He turned to the cabin. Knew he couldn't stay out here too long. She would sense that something was wrong. Sure enough, she peered out the window as if he'd telegraphed that last thought straight through the walls.

Just get it over with. Go inside and be cool.

When he opened the door she was waiting for him.

"That was Edward calling. He was worried."

Of course he was. "You told him you were okay?"

She nodded. "He couldn't believe what Lusk and Carter had done to Shelley." She shivered, hugged her arms around herself. "I still can't believe it."

He couldn't do this. "We should get some sleep."

"Okay." She tucked a handful of hair behind her ear. "You want me to take the couch?"

"I can take the couch."

She moistened her lips. His gaze tracked the move.

"Okay." She walked to the bed, straightened the covers they had tousled.

He looked around. Decided he'd grab one of the pillows from the bed.

She turned at that same moment and they ran smack into each other.

"Sorry," she muttered.

He gestured at the bed. "I just need—"

Her. He needed her.

She looked up at him with those blue eyes and he was lost.

He grabbed her. Kissed her hard.

Her arms went around him and she leaned into his chest.

His fingers found the hem of her blouse, peeled it up and off. She struggled with the buttons of his shirt.

"Forget the buttons." He whipped the shirt up over his head and tossed it to the floor.

She splayed her hands on his chest, smoothed them over his skin. He wanted to touch her that way. Pulling her bra loose, he dipped his head down, tasted one of those high, firm breasts. His body shuddered with need, as did hers.

Her fingers tackled his fly. She dropped to her knees as she dragged his trousers and boxers down his legs. He stepped out of one shoe at a time, allowing her to drag his trousers free, first one leg, then the other. She sat back and studied him. All of him. His heart bolted into a gallop.

Then she touched him, traced his fully aroused length, her expression filled with wonder. When she leaned forward and tasted him, he lost complete control. He grabbed her up and carried her to the bed. Pitched aside her sandals and peeled off her jeans and panties.

He slid into bed next to her, skin to skin.

It felt so good. She was soft and hot and he couldn't wait to be inside her.

Slow down. He had to do it right this time.

He started at her throat, careful of the healing nick that could have been so much worse. His chest squeezed at the thought. Kissing his way down her chest, he traced her body with his hands. Learned all her curves and valleys and those lush, firm mounds. She whimpered, undulated her hips in anticipation.

Not certain how much experimenting she'd done in the past, he decided to show her how delicious sex could be. He pushed her thighs apart, admired her sweet pink sex. Then he dipped down for a taste.

She cried out, tilted her pelvis for more.

He traced her labia with his tongue. Sucked and nibbled her clit until she came right in front of him. He sat back, watched her body quiver with the waves of pleasure. Then he kissed his way back up her torso. Licked and sucked until she begged for more.

"Hurry," she pleaded, wrapping her legs around his and urging his hips to hers.

He guided his cock to her wet opening. Nudged inside. God, she was tight. He pushed all the way in. Her fingers fisted in the sheets as her body arched upward to meet him.

Braddock braced his hands on the mattress on either side of

her head and leaned down to kiss those lush lips. She opened for him, his tongue swept inside her hungry mouth. He wanted to know all of her. Every inch. Every strand of hair. *All of her.*

When she came a second time, he let go, drove hard and fast until he roared into his own climax. He collapsed on the bed next to her, pulled her close.

Long minutes passed before their breathing slowed and the quiet crept in.

He wanted to hold her close like this, protect her, for as long as she would let him.

How could he let her go into that meeting with Nash tomorrow morning?

So damned dangerous.

She snuggled against his chest. Sighed softly.

Whatever it took, he would keep her safe.

He couldn't lose her.

She'd managed something no one else had ever been able to do. CJ Patterson made him want something more than to catch the bad guy.

CHAPTER FORTY-ONE

"I can't get in the house."

Tyrone turned to his most trusted eyes. What the hell did he mean, he couldn't get in the house? That was unacceptable. When the King gave an order, it was to be carried out. "You breathing, ain't you?"

"But the police." His loyal soldier looked ready to cut and run. "They watching the house. Front and back. No way I can get in."

Rage erupted in Tyrone's gut. "The po-po is guarding that fucking house?" His soldier nodded. "Get out!"

The man 'bout broke his fool neck getting out of the room. What the hell?

Tyrone paced the length of his prison. That's what his house had become. He couldn't leave without the trinity. The house had to be watched twenty-four/seven. There was no peace to be found no more. His foot soldiers couldn't stay in line. Run their fucking mouths more and more. His eyes and ears were falling down on the job.

Some fucking body shoulda noticed that doctor bitch digging around in Shelley's goddamned house!

Nobody knowed nothing till it was too late.

Fuck. If there was one video, there might have been more. Then he coulda cut CJ out of the equation.

"Goddammit!"

Now he had no choice. If he wanted Braddock, he'd have to deal with CJ. She was pissed bad at Braddock. She wanted the name of her sister's killer. Tyrone could give her what she wanted. Then, by God, he was gonna see to it that bitch had herself an accident.

His fingers traced the scar on his jaw. She'd had it coming a long fucking time.

Tomorrow he would deal with CJ.

He took a breath, cleared his head. He had other business to attend to. Cost better get his ass on the fucking ball. Tyrone wanted that goddamned money. Just in case this shit went south. His liquid assets were a little low right now. Cash was necessary if worse came to worst.

Braddock wouldn't fucking back off.

If CJ had something on him, Tyrone might just finally be free of that asshole. His face twisted with the rage busting inside him. If he had his way, he would kill that mofo today. Cut off his fucking nuts and shove 'em down his throat.

None of this was necessary. Shelley and Ricky both would still be alive if they hadn't stepped out of line. What did Braddock care if two pieces of shit got what was coming to them?

No. Tyrone shook his head. This wasn't about Shelley or Ricky. It was 'bout that fucking niece of his.

Tyrone had thought the niece would teach the scum cop a lesson. But it hadn't. Just made him more determined to come after Tyrone.

Well, his days were fucking numbered.

All Tyrone had to do was give CJ what she wanted, and that motherfucker was going down. Tyrone wanted him on his knees so bad he could taste it. If the tape had everything Shelley had promised to deliver on it, Tyrone would own Braddock.

Right now, he better hear from Cost.

The other bastard was avoiding his phone calls.

Tyrone would give him a couple more chances. If he didn't take his call, he would wish he had.

Tyrone knew where he lived.

He was through playing with these people.

An example had to be set.

The King don't tolerate this shit.

Braddock had better brace himself. The killing wasn't over yet . . . not by a long shot.

The King was about to give them something they wouldn't forget.

CHAPTER FORTY-TWO

Village Clinic, 11:50 PM

Juanita hurried down the dark alley. As hot as it was, she shivered. She hated this fucking village. It was creepy. Every lowlife in the city appeared to live here.

Not wanting anyone to see her car at the clinic, she'd parked in the alley. CJ had demanded the key back. She had to be planning something. Probably to look for those damed lab results.

As soon as Juanita made it to the clinic's rear entrance, she pulled the ring of keys from her pocket. Her hand was shaking. The keys hit the ground. "Dammit." She picked them up and rammed the key into the lock. As soon as she had the door open, she hurried inside. Cost wasn't supposed to be here for another hour, but he could come earlier. She had to be prepared.

The bastard might think he was going to give her a hard time, but that wasn't going to happen.

She wasn't going down without taking him with her.

CJ Patterson could threaten all she wanted. Cost would simply have to deal with her. If it put a big-ass debit in his bank account, well, that was just too bad.

Juanita didn't have any savings. No 401(k). Nothing. She'd finally managed to buy a decent home for her son. Just last year she'd purchased the first new car she'd owned in her whole life. She wasn't going to be the one losing here.

Cost should have kept his dick in his pants. The bastard.

She had documented everything. The whole sordid history since he'd become preceptor of the clinics where she worked. The STD he'd given Shelley three months ago. The stupid bastard had been whoring around with the prostitutes on this side of the parkway for years. Too fucking egotistical to use a condom every time. He had access to the clinic records, knew who was clean and who wasn't. But that little strategy had failed him. Still, he'd thought he wouldn't get caught if he kept his nasty business in the ghetto. Why would he worry? He'd had Juanita to cover his back.

And the Vicodin. She knew all about that. He thought he was so smart. He'd kept that part hidden from her. But she'd figured it out. Did he think she was stupid? Please. The stuff the pathetic tramps asked for was usually for him. He paid them big bucks to get prescriptions filled and then give the painkillers to him. Shelley had never ratted him out, but several others had. Juanita had gained their confidence. They'd gotten tired of being abused by Cost. Juanita had lent a sympathetic ear.

She had it all documented. Every fucking part of it.

He'd called and demanded this meeting, and she was going to show him just how much trouble he was in. CJ Patterson was the least of his worries. If he gave Juanita any grief, he would be sorry as hell. She would go straight to his big-shot grandfather, and his life, as he knew it, would be over.

She knew exactly how afraid he was of his grandfather.

Switching on the lights as she went, she tossed her purse onto her desk and flipped through the pages of the file she'd brought along with her.

A smile tugged at her lips. Boy, was he going to be surprised. He would wish he hadn't made this appointment with destiny.

A distinct click told her he'd come through the rear exit. *Shit.* She'd forgotten to lock the door. The bastard was early. As she listened, she heard the deadbolt turn. He'd locked the door behind him.

She smiled. *That's right. Take those precautions now.* He should have been doing that way before now.

Her smile slid into a grin. She couldn't wait to hear him beg. The mere idea was more than enough to make coming to this appointment at this hour worth the trouble of finding a sitter.

She sat down on the edge of her desk and reached into her purse for the gun she'd bought a couple of months ago. Her neighbor had thought it was a stupid idea. *Never carry a weapon and definitely never pull a weapon on someone unless you plan to use it.* She didn't know if she could really use it on someone, but she felt safer having it with her.

Feeling pretty damned cocky, she waited for Cost to reach her office. Boy, was he going to get the shock of his life. The whisper of rubber soles on the tiled corridor floor fueled her anticipation.

Carter Cost was about to have his first real wake-up call. An appointment with the destiny he'd been avoiding for a whole goddamned decade.

And no amount of threatening to take her son was going to get him out of this one. That threat had always been an empty one, anyway. He wouldn't have dared let his father and grandfather learn of that little indiscretion.

Her appointment paused before he reached the door. Bracing for the battle, she supposed.

"Come on, you wimp," she baited. "It'll only hurt for a minute."

"Actually . . ."

Her eyes widened as her own appointment with destiny appeared in the door.

"It's going to hurt a lot longer than that."

CHAPTER FORTY-THREE

"Remember," Braddock warned, "only let him watch thirty seconds. Any more than that and you're in trouble."

CJ nodded. "I understand." Her body had only just now stopped humming with desire after waking up in Braddock's arms and making love this morning.

Her breath hitched a little even as she recalled those incredible minutes.

If CJ closed her eyes, she could still feel his weight on her body . . . his mouth on her skin.

"CJ?"

She hauled her attention back to the present. "I'm sorry. What did you say?"

"Cooper is already in position. I'll be in the Comcast van across the street. Once you get inside, stay in the lobby, since that's where the TV and VCR are located. Place the listening device I gave you on the receptionist's desk. Cooper and I will both be able to hear whatever is going on in the room."

He'd told her that it would be too dangerous for her to wear the device on her person. Nash would likely want to make sure she wasn't wearing a wire.

"I understand." She glanced at the clock. "I should go."

"All right. Remember." He waited until she met his eyes to

continue. "If at any time you feel physically threatened, you say 'I've had enough' and we'll be in there in seconds."

"Okay."

He stared at her, but he didn't get out of the car as she'd expected he would. Instead he grabbed her face in his hands and kissed her. Soft at first, then harder, desperately. Her heart reacted.

"Be careful," he murmured against her lips.

She nodded. "I will."

He got out of her car and headed toward the Comcast van one of his friends had lent him for this impromptu sting.

Sting. CJ had never been involved in a sting. She closed her eyes a moment to clear her head. She couldn't screw it up.

"You can do this," she mumbled as she cranked her car. She drove the short distance to the clinic and parked. No other vehicles were in the parking area or on the street near the clinic. Relief washed over her. The point of arriving early was to ensure Nash didn't get here first. The listening device and the videotape were in her bag. She grabbed the bag and headed for the front entrance.

Stay in the lobby, she reminded herself. Hand shaking, she unlocked the door and went inside. She left the door unlocked. She wanted Tyrone to enter that door as well.

After a quick survey of the lobby, she placed the listening device on the reception desk. It was no larger than a credit card. With the calendar and sign-in board on the desk, the device wasn't even noticeable.

She thought about taking the video out of her bag but decided to wait until Tyrone demanded to see it before doing that. On second thought, she figured she'd better take a look at the VCR control. Maybe even turn it on. The last thing she wanted to do was stick that tape in there and press the wrong button.

Her nose wiggled. What was that smell?

As if all other thought had vanished and her cognitive powers had zeroed in on the smell, her brain instantly analyzed the scent.

Blood.

She moved toward the door that separated the lobby from

the corridor dividing the exam rooms. Braddock had told her to stay in the lobby, but this was . . . weird.

Once beyond the door, the smell was overpowering. A dim light glowed from the last exam room on the right, the one where the X-ray machine was.

She flipped on the corridor's overhead light. Her heart jolted hard. Bloody shoeprints led from that exam room to the back door.

"Oh, God."

She was moving, walking toward that end of the corridor before her brain kicked into gear. This couldn't be happening. Not again. Tyrone wasn't here yet. There were no cars in the parking lot. No one else was supposed to be here.

She stopped at the door to that final room on the right. A bloody handprint on the door frame at her eye level caused her to blink. Her heart stumbled. Then she looked into the room, toward the exam table in the corner.

"Jesus Christ." The floor shifted beneath her feet. She grabbed the door frame.

Juanita Lusk, her body stripped naked, lay on the exam table. A lateral incision had been made across the lower part of her abdomen.

CJ rushed to the exam table. Slipped. Almost fell. Blood was all over the floor, had dripped down the end and sides of the exam table to create a wide pool. It was thick. Coagulated. Had been there a while. More of those shoeprints.

Lusk's body was cool to the touch. Grayish pale. Her arms were restrained above her head with layers and layers of gauze. Her feet were stationed in the stirrups and restrained in the same manner.

CJ knew she should call Braddock, but she couldn't move. Couldn't respond. A section of lower intestine drooped between the poor woman's spread legs. *Dear God, who would have done this?*

As if the talons of fear had suddenly released her, CJ started to move, backing away from the horror in front of her. She lost her balance. Fell backward, hitting the tile floor on her hands and butt. "Braddock," she whispered.

Scream.

She couldn't.

Her hands and feet scrambled for purchase on the blood-slickened floor.

Get up! Get out of here!

Her gaze locked on the underside of Lusk's left thigh.

Written in blood was . . . *E. Noon.*

CHAPTER FORTY-FOUR

"That's his attorney, Suzanne Parker," Cooper told Braddock. "She's one of several local attorneys on retainer for his family."

CJ stared through the one-way mirror at Carter Cost. He sat at a table, his attorney whispering to him.

Could he have killed Shelley because he thought she was pregnant? Would he have gone that far? A file had been scattered all over the office floor at the clinic, statements Lusk had taken from several young women who lived in the village. Most of whom had been picked up and questioned in the past three hours. Every single one a foot soldier for Nash. More than half of those had confirmed Lusk's allegations against Carter. He had used the women to satisfy his sexual perversions and to get massive quantities of Vicodin.

CJ closed her eyes and banished the images of Lusk. A wad of gauze had been stuffed into her mouth to stifle her screams. The ME had suggested that the surgery had been performed prior to death.

How that woman must have suffered.

Opening her eyes, CJ stared at the man on the other side of the glass. How could he have done such a thing? She wouldn't have thought him capable. But those were his shoeprints all over the floor. His bloody handprint on the door frame.

Were the E. Noon references his perverted way of showing that those he had murdered were nothing, no one? But CJ still couldn't get right with the idea that it was Cost. This felt more like Tyrone's work. The fact that Tyrone had used "no one" in his note to Braddock when his niece had been murdered could be coincidence and totally unrelated to the murders that had taken place in the village and signed E. Noon. Braddock had confirmed with Dobbins, the ME, that she had found no trace of such a signature on or in—CJ shuddered—Celeste's body.

Did that mean that the only recent murder Tyrone was responsible for was Celeste's?

It just didn't feel possible that a man like Carter Cost, a man she'd known on some level for more than a decade, who had so very much to lose, could actually be capable of murders this horrific.

Nash hadn't showed for their meeting, which looked suspicious. He hadn't been at home when two HPD officers had gone to his house to round him up for questioning.

His absence didn't make him guilty. Nash hadn't known the details of what Lusk had done to Shelley and Carter. He hadn't known the lab results were fixed. That Lusk had been playing this sick, twisted game. CJ supposed he could have heard through the grapevine after yesterday's confrontation between Lusk and Carter at the North Huntsville Clinic, but even if he had, why would he have cared?

And if he hadn't cared, why would he murder Lusk in such a manner? Braddock had said this kind of mutilation took one of two things: extreme evil, like a psychopath's, or intense rage, the kind that comes with a revenge motive.

Then again, Lusk's murderer had known something about the human body and how to access what was inside. The scalpel had been wielded with precision. A lateral incision had been made on her lower abdomen to access her uterus—which had been severed from her body. The organ hadn't been found at the scene. Apparently the killer had taken it, the same way he did Shelley's missing body part. Considering the dog had eaten portions of Ricky, it was impossible to tell if the killer had taken anything from him. But it was entirely plausible to believe that was the case.

Cost certainly possessed the skill to perform the unspeakable act. But so could pretty much anyone else with the aid of the Internet and a steady hand.

Shaking off the horrifying thoughts, she forced herself to pay attention to what Braddock and Cooper were discussing.

"Let's get this party started," Braddock said to his partner before turning to CJ. "You're sure you want to watch this?"

She nodded. "I have to." She doubted anything she would hear would prove more horrifying than what she'd already observed at the scene.

He squeezed her arm. Heat slid through her. Felt soothing. She was so cold inside.

"Okay," he relented. "The chief and the deputy district attorney will be joining you."

"I'll be fine."

"Braddock," Cooper called from the door. "Let's get this done."

His hand fell away from CJ's arm, but he hesitated another moment before turning away.

CJ watched him until the door had closed behind him. She thought of the way he'd made love to her this morning. They'd both needed to feel something besides this horror.

As Braddock and Cooper introduced themselves to the attorney, the door to the viewing room opened and two men entered, nodded to CJ, and took up positions next to her.

One she recognized at the chief of police. The other she presumed to be the deputy district attorney Braddock had mentioned.

"My client," Parker began, drawing CJ's attention to the interview room beyond the one-way mirror, "is prepared to make a statement. You may question him, as long as I approve of the questions, but only after he has made his statement."

"Makes our job easier," Cooper said as she dragged out a chair and sat down. "But keep in mind that we have his shoeprints and a perfect handprint in the victim's blood."

Braddock adjusted the tape recorder positioned on the center of the table. For the record he stated the date and time and named those present. When he'd taken a seat, he said, "Dr. Cost, you may begin the statement you, of your own accord, have prepared. Start by stating your name and address for the record."

Carter glanced at his attorney then cleared his throat. "My name is Carter Cost. Dr. Carter Cost. I live at eight-oh-one Governor's Bend. On July thirtieth I was approached by Shelley Patterson and informed that she was pregnant."

CJ's insides tied into knots. She ordered herself to stay calm and pay attention. She needed to hear what he had to say. She could deal with the emotions later.

"Do you recall—"

"No questions, Detective," Parker warned. "Not until he's finished."

Braddock yielded to her demand.

"I have an addiction to Vicodin," Cost confessed, "and Shelley and a number of her . . . colleagues had been helping me by obtaining prescriptions for the Vicodin I required. I paid them well and participated in sexual activities, particularly with Shelley, on several occasions."

Cost stared at the table for a long moment.

The district attorney standing next to CJ whispered something to the chief, but she couldn't make out his words. She wanted to believe this would finally be over. That Cost had done these horrible things and that now she could finally start to put this nightmare behind her. But she couldn't get right with the idea. She just didn't believe he was capable of these kinds of gruesome murders.

"A few days ago," Cost continued, lifting his gaze to the detectives across the table, "I was contacted by Tyrone Nash. He claimed to have a video recording of the events that transpired in Shelley's house the night she was murdered. He said that if I didn't give him three hundred thousand dollars, he would ruin me with the video."

There *was* a video! CJ rode out the wave of anticipation that urged her to go in there and shake the whole truth out of the man.

Another drawn-out silence from Cost. CJ was on the verge

of shouting at him through the glass when he finally continued. "I visited Shelley that night." He blinked repeatedly, as if holding back the emotion. "We argued. I told her that she should get an abortion . . . or else. She threw the television remote at me. And a bottle of water. She didn't hit me and I didn't hit her. We yelled at each other a lot, made stupid threats, but then I left. When Nash approached me, I was scared. I knew how the argument between Shelley and me would look, and I didn't want anyone to see the video. Nash said if I gave him the money, he would give me the video. But I didn't trust him to stick to his word."

He took a long, deep breath. "Then I learned that Lusk had tampered with the lab results and that the pregnancy was a hoax. I confronted Lusk at the North Huntsville Clinic yesterday. Anyone present can certainly tell you that the confrontation was quite ugly." He looked from Braddock to Cooper and back. "But I did not kill anyone. I couldn't kill anyone. I took a solemn oath to help others, I couldn't possibly kill another human being."

"Really?" Cooper countered. "And yet you just stated that you ordered Shelley to have an abortion. You don't feel that to terminate a pregnancy is taking a life?"

"Detective Cooper," Parker charged, "this is not a debate about Dr. Cost's stand on the issue of abortion. Your question is irrelevant."

"I'll answer the question," Cost countered. His attorney sent him a look that let him know she wasn't pleased. "An abortion is a medical procedure decided upon by a woman who has the right to exercise her civil rights, Detective Cooper. That's not murder in my opinion."

"What about," Cooper returned, "the medical procedure that killed Juanita Lusk? Would that, in your opinion, be murder?" She pulled an eight-by-ten photo from the file in front of her and tossed it at Cost. "What would you call that? A hysterectomy? That one was performed while she was still alive."

"Oh, my God." Cost covered his face with his hands. "I didn't do this." He dropped his hands away. "I didn't do any of this. You have to believe me. All I did was ask her to meet me at the clinic at midnight so we could talk. I couldn't have—"

"Why don't you tell us where you were last evening after eight PM?"

Cost looked to his attorney. She nodded. Cost turned to Braddock. "Between eight and midnight I was at home walking the floors, trying to figure out how I was going to fix all this. Suzi and I had several discussions on my home phone."

"That's correct," the attorney confirmed. "We spoke four different times, each time on the landline at his home. I recommended that my client attempt to provide Ms. Lusk with a monetary gift for her son's future as a way of putting this painful business to bed. I further advised my client to do the same with Dr. Patterson, in hopes of avoiding legal action."

"Shortly before midnight I drove to the clinic to meet Lusk," Cost continued. "We were going to have it out. She claimed to have something more I needed to see before I started laying all the blame on her. When I got there, the rear entrance was open and I found . . . her." He let go a big breath. "I was terrified. I ran. Later, I hired three . . . prostitutes to help me get my mind off what I'd seen and Nash's relentless demands. They were with me the rest of the night. I can give you their names."

"How convenient," Cooper offered. "And how much did you pay them, Dr. Cost?"

"Five hundred dollars each, for the night."

"That's a lot of money to a hooker," Braddock commented. "Enough to ensure they said whatever you needed them to."

"Braddock," Parker warned, "the three women were still with Dr. Cost when two HPD officers busted into his home and dragged him out of bed. I would think that confirms his statement."

"That still doesn't put him in the clear," Cooper argued. "He admits to being at the scene. Evidence confirms it. We know he had motive for wanting Shelley out of the way and for revenge on Lusk. The bottom line is, we've got him. I'm reasonably sure a jury would see things our way, given the evidence and his own statement of motive."

Cost swallowed hard. "Give me a polygraph. I'm telling the truth."

"Have you seen this video Nash claims to have?" Braddock asked, moving on.

Cost shook his head. "No, but he repeated a number of phrases I distinctly recalled saying to Shelley, so I'm sure it exists."

"You want us to believe you're innocent," Cooper suggested. "If that's true, an innocent man would be more than happy to help the police solve a multiple-homicide case if he had the means at his disposal."

"Are you making my client an offer?" the attorney asked.

Cooper and Braddock exchanged a look before Braddock said, "If Dr. Cost is willing to help us gain access to the videotape in Nash's possession, we would certainly be willing to forgo the solicitation charges as well as the drug possession charges. However, he will remain a suspect in all three homicides until we can eliminate him from that list with evidence."

"What drug possession charges?" Parker demanded.

"For the Vicodin we found in his home as well as in his car," Cooper explained. "Since he doesn't have a legal prescription, that makes his possession illegal."

"I'll help you," Cost volunteered. "Whatever you need me to do, I'll do it. I didn't kill anybody."

"Carter," his attorney argued, "we should hear the plan first."

He shook his head. "Doesn't matter. I'll do whatever I have to."

As the interrogation continued, CJ couldn't focus on the discussion. Cost's words kept replaying in her head. *A video recording of the events that transpired in Shelley's house the night she was murdered . . . She threw the television remote at me.*

Since there was no television in Shelley's bedroom, that meant just one thing to CJ.

There was another video camera setup in the house.

Which could mean there were more videos . . . somewhere.

All she had to do was find them.

CHAPTER FORTY-FIVE

Tyrone pulled back the drapes and let the light flood the suite. He needed the sun to go down. He needed out of here. He'd been hiding out since before noon.

This shit was getting too crazy.

That bitch CJ had called his cell phone four or five times. Did she think he was stupid? His ears at HPD had warned him that Cost had rolled over on him. Fucking pussy bastard. Tyrone should have gotten that 300K from that weasel motherfucker days ago.

Now that shit wasn't happening. And he wasn't going nowhere near that doctor bitch. She wasn't setting him up. No way. Hell no.

He needed to start liquidating some assets just in case the shit went any further south.

Cost was gonna pay for this shit.

He would wish he'd kept his ass on the east side of the parkway when Tyrone got through with him.

But first he had one more business matter to attend to. And that old motherfucker better answer his goddamned phone this time. Tyrone was getting sick of his shit.

"You coming back to bed?"

Anticipation pushed a smile across Tyrone's lips even when

he had not a fucking thing to smile about. He turned back to the king-sized bed. Admired the beauty of his lover sprawled naked across those crisp linens. Long, lean legs. Sculpted torso. His cock hardened just looking at all that smooth white flesh wrapped around such perfectly toned muscles.

Widow's black lace and silk dress, along with stilettos and stockings, were scattered across the floor. When they'd first checked into the room, Tyrone had stripped Widow naked and fucked him against the door. But that had been hours ago. They'd had drinks, ordered room service, then slept like the dead.

"Definitely." Tyrone crossed to the bed. As he did, he watched his reflection in the big-ass mirror on the other side of the bed. He was black as night, every bit as lean and muscled as his lover. His cock was large. He fondled it proudly. Wasn't nothing more natural than a man having pride in his personal assets.

He crawled onto the bed like a sleek tiger.

Might as well enjoy himself.

He had some time before it got dark.

"You're the King," his lover crooned. "I'm your humble servant. Punish me."

Tyrone slid his hands around that long silky neck. "I'll punish you." He leaned down, put his mouth close to Widow's ear. "Then I'll make you come so hard you'll beg me to do it again."

If he was forced to relocate from the 256, this might be the last time he saw Widow . . . that would be the hardest part of all.

No one else understood him the way Widow did.

CHAPTER FORTY-SIX

CJ scanned the living room ceiling again. She'd done this about ten times already. She'd pulled the kitchen table in here and stood on it to inspect the light fixture in case Shelley had gotten more high-tech equipment. She'd checked the smoke detector.

Nothing.

Dammit.

There had to be a camera for the living room. If Shelley and Carter had argued in here, where the TV was, there had to be a camera. Maybe they had been in the bedroom and the television remote just happened to be in there, too, but that didn't make sense.

It had to have happened here.

She bounded up the stairs again and checked the floor over the living room. Nothing, except a small section of wood floor that had once been removed and then put back into place to add the wiring for the living room light. She'd taken the crowbar and pulled those boards up. Nothing but dust and the wiring for the light fixture.

Slowly, inch by inch, foot by foot, she checked what had once been her parents' bedroom floor.

This was ridiculous. She had to hurry. When Braddock got out of that meeting with the chief, he would come looking for her. He'd told her to stay put at the precinct, but she couldn't. She had to know if there was another camera and VCR.

Jenkins had followed her here. He'd probably already informed Braddock what she was up to. Time was likely shorter than she knew.

She trudged back downstairs. Checked the doors again, since dusk was falling. Front and back were locked. She'd shoved a piece of furniture in front of each to give her warning if anyone tried to break in.

Cost had probably been released by now. Tyrone, to her knowledge, had not been found. He was wanted for questioning. Braddock told her that Tyrone had his sources within HPD. Someone had no doubt given him a heads-up hours ago.

As bad as she felt for Lusk, CJ couldn't help regretting that she hadn't been able to go through with her meeting with Tyrone. She'd called his cell half a dozen times. The idea of going over to his house had even crossed her mind. But he wasn't there. The King was in hiding. But if this was ever going to be over, CJ needed whatever information he had.

She dropped on the sofa and heaved a disgusted sigh. She was getting nowhere here.

Cost's attorney had scheduled a polygraph to back up her client's statement. CJ didn't need a polygraph to know Cost hadn't killed anyone. Carter didn't have it in him. Of course, drug abuse could make a person do things he or she wouldn't ordinarily do. Still, she couldn't get right with that scenario.

Tyrone was her prime suspect. He would kill his own mother if she got in his way. The whole E. Noon/No One theory was in all probability his way of casting doubt on his guilt. To the powers that be, killing on the west side of the parkway was one thing. But to kill a member of the medical community was another. Lusk's murder would receive far more media attention.

But why had he killed Lusk? All the evidence discovered so far had nothing to do with Tyrone and everything to do with Cost. Maybe, considering he'd known about Carter and Shelley, he'd intended to make Cost look like the killer all along. Braddock had suggested that scenario. Cooper wasn't buying it.

She felt there was something more going on. Something that hadn't been revealed just yet.

Braddock just wanted it to be Tyrone.

Maybe CJ did, too.

Two more weeks and she had to be back in Baltimore. Shelley's memorial service needed to be arranged. It would seriously help if people would stop dying.

A rap on the door jerked her attention in that direction. She pushed up, walked soundlessly to the window to see who was at the door. No one knew she was here. She'd hidden her rental in the alley.

Edward.

Relief sagged her shoulders. She really did need to get a handle on her nerves. She was a mess.

She pushed the chair out of the way and opened the door. "Edward, how did you know I was here?" He stood on her porch looking regal as ever and sporting a brown shopping bag, the kind with handles.

"Certainly not because you're answering your cell phone," he chastised gently.

She patted her pockets. Where was her phone? "I'm sorry. It's around here somewhere. Probably still on silent." She'd had to silence it at the precinct. "Come in." She ushered him inside. "What's in the bag?"

"Dinner." He turned the bag so she could see the Panera Bread logo. "Since you forget to eat far too often, I felt confident that it was a safe wager you hadn't eaten this evening."

The relief she'd felt at seeing Edward at her door flooded her twofold. "You always take such good care of me." She glanced around the room. She'd made quite the mess. "Sorry for the disorder."

"You're looking for another camera?"

She'd told him already about Cost's interrogation. "It's probably a waste of time, but I had to try."

"Of course you did." He set the bag on the coffee table, and this time he did the ushering. "Eat. The summer salad is your favorite." He smiled as he settled next to her. "Strawberries and pecans included."

"You'd make the perfect husband," she teased. "Thoughtful." He blushed. "Always ready to defend my honor. And even though you didn't prepare this yourself"—she dug into the bag—"you're an amazing cook."

"Chef," he reminded.

"Sorry." She sent him a sidelong glance. "Chef."

The dressing was light yet creamy. Had her taste buds exploding. "Hmmm."

"Indeed," he agreed.

"Edward." She turned to him. "Do you remember the first day we met?"

He thought a half a second, smiled. "I do. You were trying to drag Shelley into the children's section of the library. She clearly was not pleased."

Fragments of the memory whispered through CJ's mind and she smiled. "She wanted to . . ." She frowned. "I can't remember. But she wanted to be someplace else . . ."

"*The park.*"

"That's it." She shook her head. "How can you remember that? I think maybe I blocked it from my mind because she pitched such a fit. Everyone in the library was staring."

"When I promised to buy the two of you ice cream, Shelley had a change of heart."

Now she remembered. "You walked with us to the ice cream shop where the Medical Plaza is now."

"I did. You interrogated me the entire distance."

Another smile tugged at her lips. "You were a stranger. A girl couldn't be too careful."

"Yes, we discussed that issue over scoops of triple chocolate chip."

"Whenever we needed anything, you were there." CJ let the flood of memories she'd been holding back wash over her. "Every August before school started, packages of clothes would be delivered to our door. You always swore you weren't the one who sent them, but I knew better."

"Then you grew up and I had to resort to gift cards."

There was a question she'd thought of asking him many

times, but she'd never worked up the nerve, or maybe the time had never been right.

"Edward, are Shelley and I the reason you never married? I'd hate to think we prevented you from having a full life of your own." God knows they'd kept him busy fixing their problems.

He set his salad bowl and fork aside. "CJ." He touched her cheek so very gently. She leaned into the touch. "You and Shelley were and still are my family. You, in particular, have made my life abundantly full. Don't ever think for a moment that you and your sister have been anything but a treasured part of my existence."

CJ reached over, hugged him. She didn't care that her salad bowl tilted precariously in her lap.

They finished their dinner in silence. The blissful feeling faded and her thoughts returned to the investigation. She needed to find any other tapes that might be here. If Nash disappeared or destroyed the tape he had in his possession, they might never know the truth. But then, maybe the tape showed nothing relevant except the confrontation with Cost.

Edward set his bowl aside once more; this time it was empty. She placed hers beside his. She'd devoured every crisp, tart bite.

"I have no plans this evening," he announced as he stood. "I'd like very much to help you search."

She started to say no, but a fresh set of eyes could prove useful. "That would be great." She hesitated. "If you're sure." She pushed her weary body off the sofa.

"I'm absolutely positive."

"I've basically torn the upstairs apart," she confessed. "Including any suspicious-looking spots in the floor. If there's another camera, it has to be somewhere down here."

"You said Dr. Cost mentioned the television remote," Edward noted. "That would mean the most likely place was in this room."

"True." CJ propped her hands on her hips. "But I've searched every square inch of the walls and there are no holes that would provide the necessary view for the camera lens."

He surveyed the room. "What about the bookshelves?" He nodded toward the pair of bookshelves that flanked the century-old coal fireplace.

"I pulled everything off the shelves. Didn't find anything."

He walked the length of the room. Considered the options. "What about the furniture? The television?"

"I checked the television." It was one of the old floor models from the seventies. It was a miracle it still worked. "I even removed the back panel." Probably didn't work anymore.

He carefully surveyed the sofa. She tried not to look guilty considering what she'd done on that sofa. Edward moved to the chairs in the room, checked those as well.

Then he took a moment, turning around slowly to consider the room. "Perhaps the VCR is in the crawl space under the floor."

"Already thought of that. It's not."

"What about the fireplace?" He started in that direction. "Did you inspect it closely?"

"I looked, but it's a disaster. I don't see how an electronic device could survive in there."

"Well." He crouched down. "We'll see."

CJ was reasonably sure the fallen bricks and mortar piled atop the coal basket had been there a few decades. "I'll get a trash bag."

Edward started to pick through the rubble. "That would be a good idea."

When she returned from the kitchen with a trash bag he was inspecting a black box.

"You found it!" She dropped to her knees next to him. The VCR was dusty as hell.

"It was under that plastic container." He nodded to the pile of discarded rubble.

Shelley had taken a plastic storage container, cut out a portion of one long side, and used the container to protect the VCR from debris. She'd had it well camouflaged.

"How was it plugged in?" She wouldn't have thought to look there for another obvious reason: no power supply.

Edward pointed to an extension cord amid the remainder of

the rubble. "It was hidden behind the screen, looped into the bookcase." He bent down, peered into the bottom shelf. "There has to be an access to power there."

CJ lifted up on the bottom shelf. It moved. "What the . . . ?" She'd missed that, too. A hole had been drilled in the floor beneath that shelf and an extension cord run through the hole from the crawl space.

"It's probably plugged into an exterior outlet."

CJ wasn't aware they even had an exterior outlet. "This is crazy." How had she missed that extension cord? Probably because it had been dark and damp under the floor. She'd scurried around like a mole and then gotten the hell out.

She inspected the VCR. "Will it turn on? Is there a tape inside?" Her heart started that frantic pounding.

He pushed the power button. A red light blinked to life. Then he pressed the eject button. Her chest constricted as the grinding sound echoed in the silence. The door opened, but there was no tape.

"Damn." She sat back on the floor. "All this searching." She glanced around the room. "And nothing."

"At least you know Cost was telling the truth." He settled on the floor near her feet. "There's no wire leading to the camera." He turned the VCR over and inspected the back. "Ah. Wireless."

"But the camera is in here somewhere." She scrambled up and started her search again. Finding the camera likely wouldn't help, but it was something she needed to do. She hadn't worked this hard to settle for half what she'd been looking for.

"There's likely a distance limitation," Edward offered. "So it would probably be close by."

Then she knew. Her gaze locked onto the flue cover about four feet above the fireplace opening. The decorative metal cover had been there for as long as she could remember. She dragged a chair over and climbed up to get a closer look. The flowers on the pressed metal disk were faded. The center of one was missing. A hole had been drilled in its place.

Using her short nails, she tugged until the cover came free. In the circular opening was the small camera. State of the art, just like the one she'd found upstairs.

And Edward was right. No wires.

"Damn."

"It's not a total loss," he offered gently. "You know there was a second camera. Perhaps you'll find more tapes hidden somewhere in the house."

But not *the* tape.

She admitted defeat. She was exhausted. "I think I'll just clean up this mess and call it a night."

"I'll help."

She started to argue, but when she looked around the room, she surrendered to another glaring fact: this was too much for her to do alone.

An hour later, less than half the time it would have taken her alone, the house was set back to rights.

"Thank you so much." She swiped her forehead. "I'm not sure I would have made it without your help."

He dusted his hands together. "That's what families do. They help each other."

She hugged him tight. He was the one part of her life that hadn't let her down. "Okay." She drew back. "I've successfully ruined your clothes." She gestured to his soiled shirt and trousers. "It's a good thing it's dark. I'm certain no one has ever seen Professor Edward Abbott looking quite like this."

He chuckled. "My gardener, perhaps."

That was right. Edward was an avid gardener in addition to his many other talents. "Come. I'll walk you to your car."

"You're not staying here, are you?"

"Probably not. I just need a shower and then—"

"You'll come to my home." He paused at the door, faced her. "CJ, it's not safe for you to stay here. That awful Nash is still out there. He could show up here, and with you alone . . ."

"All right." She was no fool. He was right. "Will you stay while I take a shower? Then I'll check in with Braddock and we'll go."

"Hurry along, then. I'll see to the dishes in the meanwhile."

She started to argue but knew it wouldn't do any good. She backed toward the stairs. "I can't thank you enough."

CJ bounded up the stairs, picked an outfit from Shelley's closet, and hurried to the bathroom. She twisted the knobs to start the water running. It always took the water forever to get warm.

Catching a glimpse of her reflection, she made a sound of disbelief. And she'd thought Edward looked a fright. She could easily have been mistaken for one of the poor homeless folks who lived under the Governor's Drive bridge.

She stripped off her clothes and stepped into the tub. The water felt amazing. The scent of Shelley's preferred shampoo filled her senses as she washed the grime from her hair.

No! It stings my eyes!

Memories of attempting to wash Shelley's hair when she was a kid bombarded CJ. Their mother had always bought the cheapest shampoo available. Never the good stuff that promised no more tears. Shelly rarely stayed still enough to prevent getting shampoo in her eyes. But CJ tried.

Tears filled her eyes and slid down her cheeks as if she'd gotten shampoo in her eyes. Her sister was gone. All CJ had left were the memories, and far too many of those were painful.

She washed her skin and rinsed her hair one last time. A quick shave and she felt tremendously better.

As soon as she'd dried her body, she wiggled into Shelley's tight jeans. Tugged the tee over her head and pitched the dirty clothes and wet towels into the tub. She'd have to deal with that later.

She hesitated at the door. Sniffed. Smelled like . . .

Smoke.

"Oh, God!" She twisted the knob, flung the door open. Smoke greeted her in the hall. "Edward!"

No answer. Just the distinct crackle of wood burning.

She dropped to her hands and knees and crawled along the hall and down the stairs. The smoke was thicker there. The flames leaped and clawed at the kitchen walls. "Edward!" She coughed. Pulled her T-shirt up over her mouth and nose.

Go! You have to find him!

The living room was thick with smoke.

Sirens blared in the distance. Someone had already called 911. Good, because her cell phone was God only knew where.

"Dr. Patterson!"

Jenkins.

"Edward!" She tried to see. It was impossible. "He's in here somewhere! Help me!"

She coughed. Crawled deeper into the room.

"I've got him!" Jenkins shouted.

Through the haze she caught a glimpse of blue—Edward's shirt. Jenkins was dragging him from between the coffee table and the sofa.

CJ scrambled to her feet. "Is he okay?" A coughing jag followed the words.

"Let's just get out of here."

CJ grabbed Edward's legs, helped Jenkins haul him onto the porch. She paused long enough to get a breath while Jenkins dragged him away from the house.

CJ rushed past him and opened the gate.

By the time they reached the sidewalk, the fire truck, sirens screaming, was skidding to a stop on the street. Then another and another.

"Anyone else in the house?" a firefighter shouted.

Jenkins explained there was no one else in the house as far as he knew.

A paramedic pushed CJ out of the way to get to Edward.

"Wait," she argued. "I'm a doctor."

"You're also a victim," the paramedic said as he examined Edward.

Victim.

CJ looked back at her house. The century-old wood fed the fire as if it had been soaked in gasoline.

The firefighters rushed past her, hoses in tow.

But nothing they could do would save the house or any of the memories . . .

Or any possible evidence left inside.

CHAPTER FORTY-SEVEN

Carter had turned out all the lights hours ago. He'd turned off every phone in the house as well as his cell.

He couldn't talk to anyone.

Suzi had threatened to go to his parents if this went any further.

And it would go further.

Much further.

Nash had called. From one of those disposable phones he likely bought at Wal-Mart. Carter had done exactly as Braddock ordered. He'd told Nash he was ready to give him the money as long as he got the video. Nash hadn't seemed as overjoyed as Carter had hoped. In fact, he'd made some ridiculous statement about being able to smell Carter's fear. Then he'd said he would call back and promptly hung up.

Carter was a dead man.

Nash was suspicious.

No matter that Braddock had posted surveillance on Carter's house. Nash was too good. Too sneaky. Too crazy.

He would find a way in if he wanted in.

Nash would kill him.

The police wouldn't be able to stop him any more than they had all the other times.

Carter pressed his hands on either side of his throbbing skull.

He was so fucked.

There had to be a way to get out of this. All that money and he was afraid to leave his house. Afraid for anyone to know he was here.

What the hell was he going to do?

His father had called twice before Carter had turned off the phones. He hadn't left a message, which was not a good thing. His father always left messages.

If that bitch attorney had told him a single word about what had happened . . .

He'd do what?

He was fucked.

So, so fucked.

He needed a drink. The police had confiscated all of his Vicodin.

A drink would help dull the anxiety.

He made his way to the great room. His mother had been so proud when he'd bought this house.

His first mansion.

Now he was a damned prisoner inside it.

He didn't bother with a glass. Opened the bottle of Scotch and downed a long gulp. Then another. And another.

He coughed. Heaved.

Had to keep it down. He needed some relief.

A few more swallows and the burn faded into that relaxed sensation he'd longed for.

He moved to the leather sofa his decorator had so painstakingly selected, and plopped down. Maybe if he drank the whole bottle he would pass out and wake up tomorrow to find that this had just been a bad dream.

"Yeah, right." He swallowed another mouthful.

A creak jerked his attention toward the entry hall.

He'd locked the doors. He was sure of it. Had he set the alarm?

Fuck! No, he hadn't. Fuck!

Calm down and go set it now. His imagination was running away with him.

He pushed up from the sofa, swayed a moment before he captured his equilibrium. Damn, that Scotch had done the trick. He walked unsteadily into the entry hall. The cool marble floor beneath his feet made him laugh.

How could he have heard the floor creak when the entry hall was marble? Yeah, yeah, he was scared shitless and hearing shit.

He reached the keypad. The buttons gleamed in the darkness. What the hell was his code? Maybe he should have done this before he drank the Scotch.

Who cared about the alarm? He should just open his front door and wave to the officers in the squad car parked in his driveway. They were supposed to be his security system.

He heard that sound again. Not a creak this time . . . a soft whisper of leather against stone.

He turned around too fast, swayed, dropped the bottle of Scotch. It crashed against the marble.

"Tsk, tsk, Doctor. Such a waste of good Scotch."

Carter peered through the darkness. Tried to make out the face of the form. There was someone there. This was not his imagination. He analyzed the voice, but it was too soft, too low.

"What do you want? How did you get in here?"

"Carter, Carter," the voice whispered. "You've been a very bad boy."

Fury whipped through him, making him sway again. "Did my father send you?" That would be just like the old man. Send someone to shake him up, teach him a lesson. "The police are right outside."

"No, I'm afraid your father didn't send me. And your policemen are too busy discussing how it sucks to work so hard for so little while jerk-offs like you are born into money."

"Who the hell are you? And why are you here?" His tongue was thick now. He had a hard time getting the words out. Wait . . . he knew. "Nash? Did that bastard send you?" Carter should push those two buttons. The two that summoned emergency services. He tried to focus on the keypad. Couldn't.

His visitor said something he didn't understand. Carter didn't care. He tried to see the keypad again. His vision blurred. He couldn't see which buttons to push.

"Come, Carter," the voice said.

He shuddered. It was right behind him now. He needed to run. Before he could make his legs react, something hit him in the back. Something small. He yelped.

"You're going to do us all a very big favor, Carter."

He tried to reach behind him, tried to pull it off.

A jolt went through him. His muscles convulsed. His face was suddenly lying against the cool marble.

What the fuck?

He told himself to move. Couldn't.

Something moved beside him.

He tried to turn his head . . . couldn't.

"You're going to die, Doctor. Any last requests?"

CHAPTER FORTY-EIGHT

Braddock skidded to a stop in front of Abbott's home and jumped out of the car before it stopped rocking at the curb.

Both CJ and Abbott had been treated and released from Crestwood Medical Center's ER. CJ still wasn't answering her cell. She'd called from Abbott's home number and left him a message saying she was here.

Braddock rushed up the steps and pounded on the massive door. His gut had been in knots since he'd gotten the call about the fire. He'd still been stuck in the meeting with the chief and the DDA going over evidence they didn't have. A strict no-interruptions decree had kept anyone from informing him about the fire until nearly an hour after the fact.

He'd thought CJ was still at the precinct. No one had bothered to let him know she'd left, including her.

His pulse jumping erratically, he pounded again. Where the hell was she?

The door opened and she stood there, staring up at him like a lost child.

He grabbed her, held her as tight as his arms would allow.

She melted against his chest.

When he'd conquered his emotions enough, he murmured, "You sure you're okay?" He drew back then to look at her.

She nodded. "I'm fine. A little shaken, but that's to be expected."

"How about Abbott?" According to the ER, both were fine.

"He's sporting a few butterfly bandages, but otherwise he's fine." She tugged Braddock inside and closed the door. "He retired to his room as soon as we got here." She shrugged. "Couple hours ago. I think he was pretty shaken as well. But I couldn't sleep. I wanted to hear from you."

"We're still trying to locate Nash. He's supposed to call Cost back to set up a meeting." Braddock shook his head. "But I have a feeling the only thing Nash is going to do is attempt to get the hell out of town."

Worry cluttered her blue eyes. "I need a drink."

He wasn't surprised. He could use one himself, but he didn't dare.

She led the way into an enormous parlor. Went straight to the bar and poured herself a shot of bourbon. After she'd downed it, she looked him in the eye. "Someone burned down my house with me in it." She poured another shot.

The police who'd responded to the call had already given Braddock the facts. CJ had been in the shower. Abbott had taken a blow to the side of his head and when he woke up he was in an ambulance. "Had to be Nash. Jenkins claims the only time he wasn't looking right at your house was when he got a call from dispatch saying the meeting I was in would be prolonged. He hung up and the next thing he knew there was smoke seeping from a cracked window."

"It was Nash," CJ agreed. "He wouldn't have wanted me to find anything in the house. The fact that I told him I'd found a video most likely rattled him. Now that we know he has a video, he was likely pissed at the possibility that I might cut into his deal with Cost."

Braddock nodded. "I should have had Jenkins inside the house instead of outside." Jesus Christ. CJ could have been killed. She wasn't supposed to have left the precinct, but he knew her well enough not to depend on her following orders. He should have been thinking ahead. But with Lusk's murder and with questioning Cost and then the meeting called by the brass, he'd fallen down on the job. There was no excuse.

"I found the other camera."

He hadn't heard about that. "Tape?"

She shook her head. "This one was in the fireplace. The last place I would have thought to look."

"Nash probably set up the cameras for Shelley. Don't forget, the whole video idea was his plan. But after you told him you'd found that tape, he got nervous." Braddock resisted the impulse to reach out and sweep the hair from her face. She looked so tired. "With what Cost told us, we have to assume that Nash was the last person to see Shelley alive. He was the one to take the tape from the VCR."

"That just confirms the theory that he's most likely the one who killed her."

"That's the presumption we're working under. Nash is going down, one way or another."

She leaned against the bar. "I'll be very glad to see this finished. I am so tired."

"Why don't you go to bed? I'll be here." She looked ready to drop. "I'm not letting you out of my sight again."

She stood there a moment, undecided. "I do need sleep."

He didn't respond; he understood that she was attempting to convince herself.

"Yeah. Okay." She looked up at him, the vulnerability showing in her eyes. "Will you stay with me? In my room? I don't want to be alone."

"I'll be wherever you want me to be."

"Thank you."

Their gazes held a few seconds longer as if she wanted to say more, but she didn't. She gestured for him to follow as she led the way up the grand staircase and along the upstairs corridor to the left.

"Wait." She turned in the other direction. "I should check on Edward before I call it a night. I've been pacing the floor downstairs waiting for you. I haven't checked on him since he went to bed."

Braddock waited while CJ walked quietly to the double doors leading to what was obviously the master suite. She pressed her ear to the door and listened.

"He's up," she said, moving away from the doors. "In the shower. I could hear the water running." She hesitated. "You think I should go in there? Make sure he's okay?"

"Is there reason to be concerned that he might black out?"

She shook her head. "The blow stunned him but he didn't black out. No concussion, just a nasty contusion and a laceration. Probably just rattled him and then he was overcome by the smoke."

"In that case, I'm sure he's fine. You should get some sleep. I'll keep my ears open. If I hear him up during the night, I'll check to see if he needs anything."

"Okay." Moving more slowly than before, she wandered along the corridor until she reached the guest room. From the size of the place, there were probably several guest rooms.

He settled into a comfortably upholstered chair while she went into the en suite bath and changed. When she'd climbed into the big four-poster bed, he tried to close his eyes to prevent staring at her.

The task proved impossible. He surrendered and allowed himself to stare. She lay on her side facing him, her blond hair splayed across the pale blue pillow. Beautiful. She really was beautiful. His body tightened at the memory of how it felt to kiss those full lips. Of how it had felt making love with her. He was relatively certain the memories would be with him for the rest of his life. He'd never felt with anyone the way he did with CJ.

As if reading his mind, she rolled over.

He wished she would turn off the bedside lamp, leaving the room in darkness so he wouldn't be tempted to continue staring. But she didn't.

He dropped his head back on the chair and closed his eyes. *Focus on the case. Go over the details.*

"Braddock?"

His head came up. "Yeah?"

"I can't sleep."

He sat up straighter. "Do you want the television on? That usually puts me to sleep."

She sat up. "Can we just talk?"

He shrugged. "Sure."

To his surprise, she climbed out of the bed and came over to sit on the footstool in front of him. The nightshirt hit midthigh, but when she sat down, it slid higher. His throat went bone dry.

"If I have to go back to Baltimore before this case is completely wrapped up"—she stared straight into his eyes—"will you promise me that you won't give up until you finish it?"

"You have my word." The thought of her going back to Baltimore sat like a stone in his gut. He'd known, of course, that she would be going back. It shouldn't matter. But somehow it did. "When are you going back?"

"I have about two more weeks. Then I won't have any choice without creating major complications." She sighed. "I wanted to make sure Shelley's killer was brought to justice. But it seems like the more bodies that pile up, the less evidence we have. Unless this thing with Nash pans out, we're basically back at square one."

"Like I said before, even the most brilliant killers make mistakes," he reminded her. "We just have to find the one he's made. It's there . . . we just don't see it yet."

She met his eyes again. "Will you hold me?"

"Definitely." He opened his arms as she climbed into his lap, then closed them around her. It felt natural holding her this way. Touched him deeply that she trusted him so completely. That had been a long time coming.

"I just need . . . you to hold me."

She snuggled against his chest, and something inside him shifted. He wanted to keep her safe, to hold her this way until he took his last breath.

Eventually she lifted her face to his in invitation.

He lowered his head, let his lips rest against hers. She took charge from there. The kiss was soft, sweet, and incredibly innocent for a woman who'd seen and endured all that she had.

The kiss went on and on, but he knew it would never be enough. Just like last night. Touching her, kissing her, wasn't nearly enough. But after what she'd been through, he didn't want to push. When her warm fingers started to unbutton his shirt, he knew she wanted more, too.

He held her tight against his chest, pushed out of the chair, and moved to the bed. When he'd laid her gently in the center of the tousled sheets, he toed off his shoes and climbed in next to her.

CJ peeled his shirt off his shoulders; he assisted by pulling his arms free. The shirt landed on the floor. Her fingers busied with the task of releasing his belt and the fly of his trousers. He lifted his hips as she tugged the trousers down and off. His boxers followed the same route. She sat on her knees and regarded him a moment.

He was hard as a rock.

She pulled the nightshirt up and off, tossed it to the floor. His attention settled on her breasts, then lowered to her slim waist and lower still to the tuft of blond hair between her thighs.

God, she was so beautiful. He could have her every night and it would never be enough.

She crawled up his body on all fours. Settled her bottom on his waist. "You make me want to do things," she murmured as she traced a line down his chest with trembling fingers, "I've never wanted to do before."

CJ's breath caught when he wrapped his arms around her and rolled, putting her beneath him. He kissed her lips, slowly, slowly, slowly. She melted. Then he gave the rest of her body the same treatment. She shivered and sighed. Made those soft sounds to let him know he was doing something so very right.

Finally he nestled between her thighs and slowly, inch by inch, thrust inside. Still a little sore from last night, she bit her lip, clawed his back as he settled in, pelvis to pelvis.

She wrapped her legs around his and rocked her hips ever so slightly. He started that rhythm that quickly sent them both to the edge.

The quiet sounds of their lovemaking filled the air. Quick breaths, soft sighs, urgent moans, and the raw, primal glide of their bodies connecting in the most organic behavior of their species.

CJ lay in his arms afterward, the sweet scent of their lovemaking enfolding them. Her body felt right snuggled against his that way. He reached up and turned off the bedside lamp, cloaking them in the darkness. It felt good. Felt right.

She slowly drifted to sleep.

Something brushed against her senses, dragged her from that warm place.

Her eyes snapped open.

The room was dark.

The hair on the back of her neck stood on end.

Braddock's body was still nestled against hers. He slept soundly, his respiration slow and steady.

A dream must have awakened her.

She was safe with Braddock.

Nothing could touch her in his arms.

CHAPTER FORTY-NINE

Carter Cost had lived in a mansion on a hill. He'd driven a BMW, the high-end model that cost more than most folks made in three years.

He'd died the way he lived . . . in excess.

The ME hadn't arrived yet. Evidence techs were doing their thing. Cooper was interviewing neighbors. Braddock studied the staging of the victim.

Seated in a recliner in front of the massive flat-panel television in his living room, Cost's body was nude. One of hundreds of homemade porn videos showcased his lack of skill with a video camera on the widescreen hanging on the wall. One would think he'd simply sat down to relax and watch his cinematography were it not for the empty Vicodin prescription bottle glued into his left hand and the way his right hand was similarly glued to his penis.

His throat had been slit, and blood had leaked down his torso to pool in his lap. The lack of arterial spray indicated that final travesty had taken place during the last moments of his life, after his heart rate had slowed to a near stop.

E. Noon was written in blood across his forehead.

The cops sitting in the cruiser out front hadn't heard or seen a thing. The house, and Cost, had been quiet all night.

Braddock moved his head side to side. They were turning Huntsville upside down in an attempt to find Nash. Not surprisingly, he'd disappeared. Four victims, not counting Celeste Martin, whose body hadn't been staged like the others, and not a single fucking piece of evidence to go on.

This one would be just like the rest. There would be no fingerprints other than those of the victim and his guests and family. No trace evidence. No witness accounts of seeing anyone arrive or depart from the residence. Braddock didn't have to hear the confirmation from Cooper's interviews with the neighbors.

He knew.

This killer was not just good, he was brilliant.

Tyrone Nash wasn't that fucking smart.

At that moment the reality of the situation crystallized for Braddock.

This was not about Nash . . . not about the village or Shelley Patterson.

This was about CJ. Somehow those murders were about *her*.

Cooper burst into the room. "The chief's here. And he doesn't look happy." She jerked her head toward the body. "The father's here, too."

Carter Cost's family was one of the most prominent in Huntsville.

This was going to get ugly.

CHAPTER FIFTY

CJ stared at what used to be her childhood home. Mostly it was a pile of charred remains now. The smells of smoke and damp charred wood filled her nostrils. Yellow tape surrounded the house as a warning that it was an official crime scene.

The fire marshal's investigation had discovered an accelerant. The fire had been started in the kitchen.

How was that possible?

She'd been in the frigging shower, for Christ's sake.

Edward had been in the living room tidying up. He'd stated that someone had come into the house. He'd heard a sound and was attacked before he could turn around.

The house was a total loss.

Everything inside was gone.

All the photos of her and Shelley as children. The boxes in the attic that contained relics from their past. That tattered old sofa.

Everything representing CJ's life . . . gone.

Her sister was gone.

Ricky was dead. Juanita and Carter were dead. It was hard as hell for CJ to feel sorry for Ricky and Carter. But she did somewhat understand Juanita's motives, her bitterness.

They were all dead—murdered.

There was no one left to blame except Tyrone.

He was the only person who had motives for every single murder committed. Including Celeste's.

How could it not be him?

CJ had tried to call him a dozen times since yesterday. He wasn't taking or returning her calls.

Did that mean he was scared? Or just didn't trust her to go through with the exchange now?

What did he have to offer?

Whom could he possibly name as Shelley's killer? Anyone who could have wanted her dead was dead.

"I've contacted a service," Edward said as he moved to her side, "to go through the rubble. Perhaps they will find some mementos salvageable."

Did it really matter? "Thank you." Was there really anything about her childhood worth salvaging?

Just the few photos of her and Shelley that hadn't been stolen. And none of those likely survived. But she appreciated the thought. As always, Edward came through for her.

Misery settled heavily onto her shoulders.

Where would she hold Shelley's memorial service now? There was a church on Triana that most of the older village residents attended. She supposed that would be okay.

"CJ."

She blinked, looked up at Edward. He nodded toward the south end of the street. "Do you know those people?"

CJ turned to see whom he meant. Eight . . . no, nine young women, miniskirts or short shorts showcasing their long thin legs, marched in their direction. As they neared, CJ recognized a couple from the clinic.

Tyrone's foot soldiers.

"Yes," she said to Edward. "They live around here."

The leader of the pack was one of the women she'd treated at the clinic. For the life of her, CJ couldn't remember her name. She only remembered the miniskirt she'd been wearing. Today she wore pink short shorts.

Pink Shorts Girl walked up to CJ. "We heard about your house." She jerked her head toward the remnants left by the fire. "We wanted you to know that we sorry as hell about everything. Shelley . . . the house."

CJ swallowed back the emotion that crowded into her throat. Hearing those words from these women meant more than anyone else could possibly understand. "Thank you."

"You being a fancy doctor and all," the woman said, "we figure you prob'ly don't need no help from us. Don't think you'd want to wear none of our clothes."

CJ smiled. "It's the thought that counts." Keeping the tears from brimming past her lashes wasn't easy. "I appreciate it so much."

"Yeah. Well," the woman went on, "we wanted to tell you that we're holding a little something for Shelley and Celeste tonight. You white folks prob'ly call it a wake or something, we call it a party. Anyways, you come on by twenty-eight-oh-five Dubose Street about nine, Doc." She glanced at Edward. "Bring your friends. We got plenty a room in the yard. We'll throw back a few beers and talk about the good times with them two."

CJ smiled, feeling a kinship she hadn't felt for anyone in this village for a long time. "I'd like that. Thank you."

Pink Shorts Girl shrugged. "Shelley'd like it. She liked music and dancing. Like the rest of us."

CJ nodded. "That's a wonderful idea."

Each of the women made eye contact with CJ before turning and marching away.

There were a lot of things CJ had been wrong about in her life, but at that moment she realized for the first time that she truly had been wrong to some degree about life in this village.

Yes, it was hard. Yes, it was not always nice. The people here stuck their heads in the ground too often . . . but they were a family of sorts. They were there for each other to the best of their ability.

"Are you sure coming here at night is a good idea?"

CJ turned to Edward. Of course he would be terrified and more than a little mortified on her behalf. Her safety and happiness were always paramount to him. She was very lucky to have someone who cared so much. The way Braddock had made love to her last night filtered through her senses. He cared about her, too. What they'd shared had been far more than a physical coupling. There was something there . . . something more than just good sex.

"It's more than a good idea, Edward." She turned and watched the women disappear from sight. "It's the right thing to do."

Shelley's life needed to be celebrated. What better place to do it than here, with the people who'd shared that life with her?

CHAPTER FIFTY-ONE

815 Wheeler Avenue, HPD, 2:00 PM

Huntsville's almighty were all present: the chief, the mayor, the district attorney himself, and select members of the city council.

All wanted the same thing.

"I don't care what it takes," Mayor Newman reiterated, "you find Tyrone Nash and you arrest him. No one sleeps until he's in custody. I want him charged with five counts of murder."

The chief said nothing, nor did the DA.

Great. "Sir," Braddock broached, "with all due respect, we have no evidence connecting Nash with a single one of these murders."

Beside him, Cooper shifted. Braddock didn't look at her. He knew she would have kicked him had they not been standing at attention before the conference table lined with the city's gods.

The chief cleared his throat, which meant he would be talking to Braddock later. "I feel confident Detectives Braddock and Cooper can find the necessary evidence to obtain a warrant for his arrest."

"It won't take that much," District Attorney James Ayers suggested. "All we need is enough to charge him; the jury will take care of the rest. Folks are sick to death of men like Tyrone Nash. Dr. Cost's father and grandfather have learned of the fiasco involving the questioning of Carter Cost. They're out for blood."

Translation: they'd heard about Braddock's coercion. If Cost wanted to avoid charges, he would help reel Nash in. Braddock had badgered him into going for the deal.

"So, finding the real killer isn't the goal here."

Cooper inched her sneakered foot onto the toes of Braddock's loafers and pushed hard.

The fury that blazed across the faces lining that conference table would have melted steel.

"Do your job, Braddock," the chief warned, "or find another one. This case will be closed with the arrest and prosecution of Tyrone Nash. The *Huntsville Times* raked this department over the coals this morning. Tomorrow's headlines will read entirely differently. Do you understand me?"

"Yes, sir." That certainly didn't give them a lot of time.

"Detectives," the chief said, looking from Braddock to Cooper and back, "you are dismissed. I don't want to see your faces again until Nash is in a holding cell."

Braddock executed an about-face and walked out of the room. Cooper followed. Neither spoke until they were outside headed across the parking lot.

He stopped at his car, glared at Cooper across the top. "Thanks for the support, *partner.*"

She scoffed. "Like there was any point arguing with those assholes."

Braddock shook his head. This investigation could not turn into a political circus. And yet that was exactly where it was headed. The mayor would not allow the city's reputation to be tarnished with these murders. It might affect tourism or the government's consideration of Huntsville as a prime location for military and space research facilities.

"You heard the order the same as I did," Cooper reminded. "So, what do you say?"

"I say fuck 'em. Nash needs to be found and questioned." He sent a look at Cooper that warned there would be no negotiations. "But he isn't our killer."

"When did you decide that?"

"When I got a long, hard look at Cost's puny penis," he tossed back. "Nash doesn't think that way. All this staging is far too sophisticated and time-consuming for his methods. Look at the vics we know belong to him. Like Celeste Martin. Simple, straightforward. Make the mark, do the kill. No games, no fucking this-is-your-life venue."

She shrugged. "I guess we look for a different killer. God knows we have loads of suspects and evidence."

Braddock slid behind the wheel of his G6. "That's why we need Nash."

Cooper fastened her seatbelt and sent him a sidelong look. "You just said Nash isn't our guy."

"Nash makes it his business to know what's going on in *his* village. He knows something. That's most likely why he's gone into hiding. We have nothing on him. He's not afraid of us. But he is afraid of whoever is behind these murders."

"You got a point, partner."

"All we have to do is find him and that video."

"Easier said than done."

No shit.

But first Braddock needed to talk to CJ. She needed to stay off the streets.

This, whatever *this* was, was about her. She was either the next victim or the trophy the winner expected to take home.

CHAPTER FIFTY-TWO

904 Williams Street, 3:05 PM

"Detective Braddock is here."

CJ looked up from her work. Edward waited near the French doors. Her heart thumped at hearing Braddock's name. "Okay. Thanks." She set her notes aside and stood. She'd escaped to the sun porch to think. To try to make sense of all this tragedy. She'd made a list of all the victims and how they were tied to Nash as well as what he might have hoped to gain by eliminating each of those victims.

As she entered the long hall leading to the front of the house with Edward, he hesitated. "Will you be all right?"

She couldn't help smiling at the worry etched across his face. He was still fretting about her going to the party on Dubose Street tonight. He insisted he would have gone with her had he not already been obligated to attend the library's board meeting. He didn't want her out of his sight. He was as bad as Braddock.

"I'll be fine. Detective Braddock may have news about the investigation. Hopefully this will all be over soon."

"Very well. I'll be in my library."

CJ hurried through the den and entry hall. Braddock waited in the parlor. The urge to run into his arms was nearly overwhelming. "You have news?" Maybe the killer had finally screwed up and left evidence at the scene of his latest murder.

"Unfortunately not." Braddock shoved his hands into the pockets of his trousers. "I just came by to check on you."

Beyond the floor-to-ceiling windows she noticed that Cooper waited in Braddock's car. "You're on your way somewhere?"

"We're working on rounding up Nash for questioning."

CJ moved a few steps closer to the man whose mere presence took her breath. "You still believe Tyrone is the killer?" She knew he'd killed Celeste. But the others . . . she wasn't so sure. She kept trying to connect the dots, but the puzzle wasn't coming together.

"I don't think he is." Braddock shook his head. "But the chief and the mayor are determined to nail someone for these murders, particularly since the Cost family is . . ." He shrugged. "Well, the Cost family. He wants this wrapped up. If Cooper and I don't find Nash first, he may end up dead no matter who finds him."

"Oh." CJ knew all too well how the politics of any organized situation worked. She dealt with that in the hospital. The first cop to spot Nash the suspect was either going in or going down. She understood that as well. Without Nash to question, they might never know the truth. "You'll keep me up to speed on what's going on?"

"I will. That's part of the reason I stopped by."

Her heart sank a little. She'd hoped he had stopped by just because he wanted to see her. *Foolish, CJ. Truly foolish.*

"I need you to promise me that you'll stay right here. No going out for anything. You're safe here. Abbott has a state-of-the-art security system and I doubt that he'll take his eyes off you for more than an instant at any given time."

A frown furrowed its way across her forehead. "You think I have reason to be afraid? I mean, if it's not Nash, why would I be in danger?"

He closed the final steps between them, took her by the arms, and peered down at her with such earnestness that her chest constricted. "I don't believe these murders are about the victims or anything they did or didn't do. I think this whole thing is about you . . . somehow. I need you to promise me you won't do anything foolhardy."

"I'll stay here." She braced for his reaction. "Except the women on Dubose Street are having a celebration for Shelley and Celeste tonight. I promised I would stop by." Before he could argue, she offered, "I thought maybe Jenkins could go with me. He can come inside and stay right next to me if that will make you more comfortable."

Braddock shook his head. "I don't think it's safe for you to be outside this house at all."

CJ rested her hands on his arms. "If this is about me, as you suggest, the killer will try to get to me no matter where I am. Look at Carter. He was locked away inside his home and the killer still got to him. I have to do this, Braddock. It's important to me."

He exhaled a heavy breath. "All right. But Jenkins will be armed and you aren't to leave his sight. We've got two uniforms watching Nash's house, so they'll be close by as well."

CJ nodded. "Thank you."

Braddock hugged her, held her close to his chest. She felt his heart beating. Wished she could stay in his arms like this forever. But he couldn't do his job with her in the way.

He kissed her forehead. "I'll check in with you every couple of hours. There will be a cruiser out front. And Jenkins is on the porch."

She nodded.

Then he kissed her lips. One of those slow, sweet kisses he was so good at.

She wanted this investigation over.

For the first time in her life, she wanted something more than her career.

She wanted a real life. And she wanted this man to be a part of it. On what level she didn't know just yet. But she wasn't letting go of what felt like a good thing.

One her sister had recognized way before CJ had.

Maybe there were a few things CJ could learn from her sister's life.

Live for the present . . . not the future.

CHAPTER FIFTY-THREE

Dallas Mill, 7:08 PM

Where the hell was that motherfucker at?

Tyrone paced back and forth in the warehouse.

He'd come in alone, just like he'd been told. Well, he appeared to be alone. That would have to be enough.

Tyrone wasn't no fool. He never went anywhere alone. He'd sent his two most trusted men, two-thirds of his trinity, here to take up positions an hour before his scheduled arrival. His driver waited in the Escalade.

Wasn't nobody pulling no shit over on him. Too many dead bodies piling up lately.

"What the hell?" he muttered as he checked his Rolex. That motherfucker was supposed to have been here at seven sharp. It was ten after.

Too fucking dark in here. Couldn't hardly see shit. He'd left the loading dock doors open wide enough to let some light from the street filter in, but it was still too fucking dark.

A rusty creak echoed in the darkness.

Tyrone turned toward the sound, tried to see through the dark.

"That you, motherfucker?" He wasn't playing no games with this asshole.

A rolling sound told him the dock doors behind him was

being pushed closed. He whipped around. The narrow beam of light from the street disappeared as the door slammed shut.

He snatched the 9 millimeter outta his waistband. "You don't want to pull no shit on me," he warned. "I got the video. You fucked if you mess with me."

A footstep, then another . . . coming closer.

Shit. What the fuck? "You better talk to me 'fore I start shooting."

A click echoed and a blinding light hit him square in the eyes. Tyrone tried to shield his face with his hand.

"Where's the video?"

"You got the money?" Tyrone demanded.

"The tape," the voice pressed. "It wasn't in your SUV."

What the hell was he talking about? "Ain't no way you been in my Escalade." Bullshit.

"You mean because of the ape behind the wheel?"

The beam of light circled around Tyrone's face. He backed up a few steps. "That's right. My man woulda killed your ass if you'd come near my Escalade."

"That would have been very difficult for him to do, considering he's dead."

Fear slammed into Tyrone's chest. "Antoine! Jerome!"

"They're dead, too," the voice warned. "It's quite thrilling how quickly a man bleeds out if you open up the proper artery."

"You dead, motherfucker."

Something hit him in the chest. Tyrone hesitated. Tried to see what the hell it was.

The jolt of electricity loosened his fingers on the gun. It clattered to the floor. Tyrone tried to speak but his mouth wouldn't work.

Another jolt hit him.

He crumpled to the floor.

The footsteps came closer and closer. The beam of light shone straight down in his eyes, but he couldn't close them. Couldn't even blink.

"What a pity."

Hands groped his body, searching for the videotape. Tyrone

would have smiled if he could have. That motherfucker wasn't never gonna find that tape. Fuck him.

Strong hands dragged him across the floor, then lifted him into a chair.

Tyrone tried to make his body move . . . couldn't.

Piece after piece of duct tape was ripped from a roll and wrapped around and around his arms and legs, securing him to the chair. The light was in his face, leaving the bastard in darkness. Tyrone wanted to close his eyes against the light but couldn't. That Taser had fucked him up. But it wouldn't last much longer . . . he could feel his strength coming back.

When the motherfucker had finished, he stood back, the light still shining in Tyrone's face. "Tyrone Nash. The King. You are so full of yourself. It's time the world saw you for what you really are.

"No one."

CHAPTER FIFTY-FOUR

CJ sipped a Pepsi as she listened to the women of Dubose Street regale her with tales of life in the village. It wasn't always pretty, but they made the best of it.

The music was loud in the living room, where those who preferred to dance were bumping and grinding to their favorite rappers. She didn't even want to think what was going on upstairs. Didn't matter. Here, in the kitchen, it was just girl talk.

The foot soldiers she'd met at the clinic puffed on their Newports and sucked on Grey Goose and Patrón. Most were inebriated, but CJ didn't mind. They talked about Shelley and how she had rescued each of them at one time or another.

All this time CJ had considered her sister so helpless. But the truth was, she'd been far stronger than CJ could have imagined. Strong enough to survive this life. To help those around her and to stand up for what she believed in.

"That's what got her kilt," the girl with the seventies' fro confirmed. "She wasn't taking no more of Ty's shit."

Pink Shorts Girl, who now wore a skimpy striped sundress, shot 'Fro Girl a look. "I know you drunk, but you better be careful what you say. You know Ty has ears all over the village." She looked to one of the others. "Could be you." Her attention shifted to another. "Could be you."

"It's okay," CJ said with a wave of her hand. "I've come to terms with my sister's life and her death." Emotion tightened her throat. "It's not how I would have liked it to be, but who am I to judge her?" She met each gaze in turn. "Or any of you. You're just trying to survive."

"That's what I'm talking 'bout," Super-tight Jeans Girl said. "I ain't ashamed of how I make my living." She shrugged. "Hell, somebody's gotta do it or all these old rich freaks would go psycho or some shit."

"Poor ones, too," Tube Top Girl added. "They worse than them old rich dudes. 'Here baby,' " she mocked, " 'I got ten dollars. What that git me?' "

Laughter teetered around the table.

"I got a good answer for that," 'Fro Girl said. "He can lick my ass for ten dollars. Most nights I could use a cleanup anyways."

More of that belly-busting laughter.

"Cleanup on aisle brown!" someone shouted.

CJ's escort shifted in the doorway. She smiled at him, was relatively certain he would prefer to make an early exit. CJ wouldn't prolong his misery. She lifted her Pepsi can. "To Shelley and Celeste." CJ surveyed those gathered around the table. "And all of you lovely ladies of Dubose Street."

Glasses clinked with her can amid the chiming toasts.

CJ pushed back her chair and stood.

"So you leaving us, Doc?" Striped Sundress Girl asked.

"Well . . ." CJ gestured to the handsome young detective waiting at the door. "I'm sure my escort is feeling the effects of all the estrogen. I really shouldn't drag out his misery."

Jenkins held up both hands in surrender. "Just doing my duty, ma'am."

"You mighty cute for a cop," Tube Top Girl teased. She stood and twisted right up to Jenkins. "I might've seen you around, sweet thang."

"I . . . don't think so, ma'am." Jenkins managed a nervous smile.

More of that earthy laughter erupted.

"You on to something, girl." Super-tight Jeans Girl slinked

over to join the other two. "This cutie pie does look a little like somebody I've seen before." She looked him up and down. "You got a thing for black, Mr. Detective?"

CJ slid her chair in. She was pretty sure if she didn't get Jenkins out of here, these ladies were going to eat him alive. "Thank you, ladies. This was the most unique memorial service I've ever attended."

"Course it was," Striped Sundress Girl said. "You on Dubose Street, girl. We all unique."

Hugs were exchanged. CJ didn't miss the relief on Jenkins's face. He was definitely ready to get out of here.

Once they were out the door, the detective took a look around, checking the street, before escorting her to his car. He unlocked the passenger-side door and opened it for CJ. "Thank you," she said.

He gave her one of those shy smiles and hurried around to the driver's side. Once they were out of the village he appeared to relax.

"I really appreciate you coming with me tonight, Detective Jenkins."

"Not a problem, ma'am."

Such a nice guy. She'd certainly unfairly judged HPD cops by the ones she'd known in the village as a kid.

More of that unsettling silence. Jenkins was likely tired. Braddock had kept him on surveillance duty extra-long hours.

"Do you think Nash will be found?"

"I doubt it." Jenkins slowed for a traffic signal. "He's not going to go down easy for murders he didn't commit."

Surprise jarred CJ. The light changed to green and he rolled through the intersection. "You don't think Tyrone committed these murders?" Braddock had suggested he was leaning that way as well.

The dash lights allowed CJ to see the flush of embarrassment that climbed the detective's neck. "I . . . I'm just saying that it's possible he isn't the one."

For a moment CJ considered all that she knew. "I'm beginning to think you're right."

Jenkins glanced at her, his expression startled. He quickly set his attention back on the street and maneuvering through traffic.

Another space of silence elapsed before he spoke again. "He's not really the way you think he is. I mean, if you consider his history and all that, like a profiler would. A lot of what's going on doesn't add up."

CJ started to ask what he meant, but he rolled to a stop in front of Edward's house.

"Here you go, ma'am." Jenkins hopped out and rushed around to CJ's door.

She'd scarcely emerged when he offered, "I'll walk you to the door."

"That's not necessary." He could see the door from here.

"I have my orders, ma'am."

He was right. He climbed the steps next to her, waited as she unlocked the door. Edward had given her a key.

"Thank you again, Detective."

He nodded and double-timed it back toward his car. He pulled out his cell phone as he went. CJ wondered vaguely if it would be Braddock calling with news.

Not another murder, she hoped.

CJ went inside and closed the door behind her. A few taps of the keys and the warning tone of the security system was silenced.

After checking the door to see that she'd locked it, she wandered through the house. Surely Edward was home by now, but it was awfully quiet if he was. He'd left well before she and Jenkins had.

Wine would ensure she slept well. She'd abstained from alcohol at the party, mainly because she'd wanted to be fully alert for anything the girls getting loose might have said. But now she could relax.

She stepped into the kitchen. Froze. Her heart rocketed into her throat.

The man turned from the sink and relief flooded her. *Edward.* "Whew." She pressed her hand to her chest. "You scared me. I didn't think you were home yet." She couldn't help staring at his choice in attire. She'd never seen him wearing a T-shirt. Black tee, black trousers. Different. He was generally dressed as if he were headed to the university to teach. She'd never known him to wear anything less than a crisply starched button-down shirt and elegant trousers.

"Sorry for the fright." He smiled. "I just returned." He finished drying his arms with a hand towel.

That was another thing. His shirtsleeves, even in hot weather, were always long, never short.

She shook her head. She was obsessing. "Don't mind me. With all that's happened, I'm a little skittish." She moved to the massive double refrigerator. "Would you like to have wine with me?" When she closed the fridge door to look to him for his answer, he was mopping his face with the towel. Now that really was bizarre. Not like him at all.

"That would be quite refreshing."

She carried the bottle to the generous island. Told herself not to stare at him, but simply couldn't help it. She blinked, looked again.

"You have . . ." She rounded the corner of the island, took the towel from his hand, and dabbed at his forehead. "There was blood on your forehead." Had his wound from the knock on the head been oozing? "Are you all right?"

He stared at her a moment, then seemed to snap to attention. "I'm fine, really. I came home to quite a mess. That's all."

"What happened?" Her pulse jumped.

He took the towel from her hand. It was then that she noticed it was quite bloody. Far more so than simply wiping that few drops from his forehead would have made it.

"A neighbor's cat had been hit by a car." He sighed, the sound weary. "I picked it up from the street, tried to do what I could." He shook his head. "But it was too late."

"It's a wonder it hadn't scratched you." Instinctively, she surveyed his arms and hands. The vision of those words scrawled on the bedroom wall in cat's blood flashed across her retinas. "Are you sure you're all right?"

"Yes, yes, I'm fine. The poor thing was a bit far gone to give me any trouble. It died soon after I came to its rescue. I wrapped it in a plastic bag until morning. I didn't see any point in upsetting the neighbors at this hour."

She couldn't help herself. She had to hug him. "You're too kind for your own good, Edward Abbott."

"Did you have a nice evening?" He opened a cabinet door and tossed the badly soiled hand towel into the trash.

"I did." She smiled, relaxing again. "It was nice. Exactly what I needed to feel as if I'd done right by Shelley's memory."

A shadow passed over Edward's face, something akin to irritation or frustration. "I'm glad you have that behind you."

His comment seemed strange. Maybe he was still annoyed that she hadn't allowed him to host a memorial service for Shelley. "Did your meeting go well?" She was beginning to think it hadn't. Edward rarely showed such a moody side.

"Not as well as I'd hoped." He gathered two stemmed glasses. "If I hadn't made an appearance, I'm quite certain the funding for many important programs would have been slashed."

Edward donated much of his time and his money to see that all of Huntsville's children had the opportunity of books. "I'm glad you went."

She poured the wine. "To the library." She lifted her glass. "And the man who gave me the opportunity of books and so much more." It pained her to see that small wound on his forehead. Reminded her of what he'd risked for her.

He touched her glass gently with his own, his face a study in perplexity. "Does this mean you're thinking of returning to Baltimore soon?"

She nodded. The decision had only just solidified. "Yes. I need to ensure that someone takes over the clinics here, but yes. I'm going back as soon as possible." She met his eyes, hoping her determination showed in her own. "I don't want to miss a minute of my future. The one you helped me attain."

The relief that showed in his face, his posture, made her heart hurt. She'd put him through the wringer. He knew what was best for her and she'd skated very close to letting him down.

A wave of exhaustion washed over CJ. She was spent. It was all catching up to her now. Somehow tonight had felt like the final hurdle. All that was left to do now, beyond ensuring that the clinics were covered, was to bury her sister at Maple Hill Cemetery. As girls they'd often played there. It was a lovely, historic cemetery. Shelley would be pleased.

Braddock had promised to take care of the investigation. She trusted him to do that. He wouldn't let her down.

She gave Edward another hug and headed upstairs. Maybe a long bath and then a good night's sleep. She didn't really expect to hear from Braddock. He had his hands full with this investigation. She would talk to him tomorrow.

Maybe they would get through one night without a murder.

CHAPTER FIFTY-FIVE

"No, man," Buddy Henagar said, "I didn't touch nothing."

Braddock knew better than that shit. The guy had probably gone through the Escalade looking for money or anything he might be able to pawn.

"You just happened to walk through the area and see the vehicle sitting here?"

"Yeah." The guy nodded over and over. Had the shakes. Bad teeth. Stringy hair.

Meth addict.

"I saw it sitting here and I thought, what the hell is a fancy car like that doing sitting here? I wandered over." He shrugged. "Took a look through the window and saw the big nig—big *guy* with his throat slashed." He shuddered. "I run all the way back over to my cousin's and called y'all."

Bullshit. "See that uniform right there?" Braddock pointed to the cop guarding the perimeter. "You give him your statement. Don't go anywhere until he's taken your statement. He'll need a statement from your cousin as well."

"Don't worry, man. I ain't going nowhere till y'all say so. This is some shit. I ain't never seen no one murdered before."

Braddock rested his attention on the vehicle once more. Tyrone Nash's vehicle. A member of his unholy trinity behind the wheel with a permanent grin beneath his chin. He and Cooper had gotten here maybe five minutes ago. Jenkins had arrived a couple of minutes later. Officer Larry Metcalf and his partner were watching Abbott's house. Metcalf was the best of the best on HPD's beat force. Braddock had known when he got the call with Nash's license plate number that he was going to need both Cooper and Jenkins on the scene.

"Braddock!"

He turned to the warehouse. It was condemned. Part of the property had burned a few years ago. But that didn't keep the homeless and kids from prowling around in it. Cooper and Jenkins had gone in to start the search inside while he'd gotten the sketchy guy's story. "Yeah."

"You're gonna want to come in here," Cooper shouted at him.

Jesus Christ. Just what they needed. Another fucking body. He didn't need a crystal ball to know who it would be.

Dammit all to hell.

He crossed the crumbling pavement. Weeds had grown up through the cracks. The city should have torn this damned thing down ages ago. Cooper waited for him at the door. "We got another body?"

She shook her head. "Three more."

Son of a bitch.

"Is Nash one of them?"

She nodded. "Our killer got him good."

Jenkins stood thirty feet from the entrance, his flashlight spotlighting Tyrone Nash. As Braddock neared, his eyes took in the killer's latest work.

Nash had been secured to an old chair with duct tape. His nose and ears had been removed. Blood had run down his chest, over his shoulders. His fingers had been severed from his hands; same with the toes, which had been whacked off, leaving stumpy feet. Nash's head was tilted back, his mouth wide open.

"Check it out." Cooper shone her flashlight into his mouth.

Braddock swallowed. Leaned down to look. All those missing body parts, or at least a finger and a toe and maybe part of an ear, had been shoved into his throat.

"People always said he was full of himself," Cooper murmured. She flicked her light toward an upper-level storage area. "The other two bodyguards are up there. Throats slashed just like the one outside."

"No sign of the videotape?"

"Not yet, but it's dark as hell in here. We need a generator and some lights."

Fuck. "Yeah. I'll call for support."

Jenkins dropped his flashlight, staggered a few feet away and started puking his guts out.

Braddock and Cooper shared a look. *What the hell?* Jenkins had seen bodies before without losing it.

"Try not to contaminate the crime scene," Cooper cautioned. She made a face at the violent heaves coming from their colleague.

"What about the ME?" Braddock asked her.

"Evidence techs and the ME are on their way."

Perfect. Just fucking perfect. Not only did they not have any evidence in this case so far, the last official suspect had just become a victim. The chief and the mayor were going to be seriously PO'ed when they heard this.

Fuck.

Jenkins suddenly rushed out of the building.

Cooper stared after him, shaking her head. "Maybe he had something bad to eat at that party on Dubose."

"Maybe." Braddock caught up with the younger detective outside. He was braced on the side of the building, struggling to regain his composure. "You okay, Jenkins?" They all lost it at homicide scenes from time to time. But there wasn't a cop at HPD who, for whatever reason, hadn't been looking forward to this one.

Jenkins shook his head, didn't make eye contact.

The fact that he was shaking like a leaf in a windstorm struck Braddock as damned wrong. "What's going on, Jenkins?"

Jenkins turned to Braddock. "I want immunity."

"Come again?" He couldn't have heard what he thought he heard.

"I can give you the killer." Jenkins wiped his mouth with the back of his hand. "But I want full immunity."

Braddock went stone cold. For more than two years he had been battling Nash. Trying to get one step ahead of him, and he could never make it happen.

Now he knew why.

"You have the right to remain silent." Braddock grabbed Jenkins's left arm, wheeled him around to cuff him. "Anything you say—"

"I want a lawyer," Jenkins demanded.

Part of him felt victorious that Tyrone Nash had gotten what he'd had coming for a long time. For Kimberly. For the dozens of other victims he'd abused and murdered.

But there was something incredibly wrong here.

And it was way bigger than Tyrone Nash.

CHAPTER FIFTY-SIX

904 Williams Street
Tuesday, August 10, 1:59 AM

CJ jerked awake.

She rolled onto her back. Blinked. Had to gain her bearings. Edward's home. She glanced at the clock.

She listened. Something had awakened her. A sound. She shivered, chafed her arms. Goose bumps covered her skin. She sat up and listened. All quiet.

But she was awake now. Throwing back the covers, she dropped her feet to the floor. She could eat. She'd scarcely touched a bite at the party tonight.

Party. She smiled. Shelley would have loved that. A party instead of a wake. That was definitely a first for CJ.

She stopped midway across the room. Why was the door to her room open? She'd closed it when she came in to go to bed. She was sure of it. Maybe Edward had peeked in on her.

Braddock had called to check on her before midnight. He'd told her about Nash. As much as she was relieved that the village residents would no longer be held hostage by him, the news hadn't given her the solace she'd hoped it would. Shelley's murder, Ricky's, Lusk's, and Cost's were still unresolved on some level. Unless Braddock could find evidence linking those murders to Nash, would they ever know what really happened?

The idea that they might not twisted inside her as she padded along the wide upstairs corridor.

At the top of the stairs she paused. Was that music she heard coming from Edward's wing? She wasn't sure that side of the house was actually a wing, but if it was as large as the opposite side, it was certainly big enough to be one in her opinion.

Maybe he couldn't sleep, either.

Just in case he was sleeping, she moved as quietly as possible down the stairs and toward the kitchen.

She paused at the entrance to the parlor. Sniffed. What was that smell? Moving with caution, she entered the parlor. It was dark, but the smell was much stronger. She switched on a table lamp and glanced around.

Recognition startled her. It smelled like the rubble of her burned-out home.

Had something been burning?

No alarms had gone off.

She walked over to the massive fireplace and squatted to get a look. Frowning at the dust—Edward's house was always immaculate—she reached down and touched it. The bricks still felt warm. Had he burned something? It was as hot as Hades outside. That didn't make sense. She sniffed her fingers. Not dust. The soot left behind by ashes.

Something snagged her attention. She reached deep into the fireplace, beyond the grates. She picked up the object. Black. A scrap of fabric. She'd have to ask him. Strange.

Who knew? Maybe he burned any personal papers he didn't want to throw in the trash. With the rampant identity theft, she couldn't blame him for that. But what about the piece of fabric? That he had been wearing a black tee tonight entered her mind.

Whatever, CJ. She was being ridiculous. It was his house; he could burn whatever he wanted. Maybe he'd gotten blood on his T-shirt and had decided not to try to wash it out. Big deal. Weird. But then, he could have simply tossed it in the trash. Weird.

She left the scrap of fabric on the brick hearth, dusted her palms together, and pushed to her feet. She resumed her trek to the kitchen, washed her hands, then opened the fridge and considered the contents. A sandwich didn't really appeal to her. She checked the freezer. Smiled. Ice cream would definitely hit the spot.

Chocolate. Edward always stocked her favorite snacks whenever she was in town. She set the container on the counter and searched for a bowl and scoop. When she'd found what she needed, she heaped a generous portion into her bowl.

She grabbed a spoon and started out of the room but noticed she had dribbled ice cream on the granite counter.

"Paper towel," she mumbled as she scanned the kitchen counters. By the sink, of course. She wet the paper towel and cleaned up her mess.

Munching on her ice cream, she padded back to the entry hall. Some reading might help her get back to sleep. Something mundane and clinical.

She shuffled to the library and switched on the light. A smile touched her lips. Books, books, and more books. All around the room. Still nibbling on her ice cream, she drifted around the room, scanning titles.

Electric Wiring for Dummies. She laughed, shook her head. Not quite that mundane. *Compost Gardening*. "I don't think so," she mumbled.

By the time she'd made it around the room, she'd decided that she was too tired to read. She reached for the switch at the door, but then wandered back to Edward's chair to look at the selections he had set aside.

Climbing into his chair, she pulled her feet under her and set her bowl in her lap. She picked up the first book. *Self-Defense*. She made a face. Was Edward brushing up on self-defense because of what had happened to Shelley? She thumbed through the book. A chapter on handguns and Tasers caught her eye. Then there was another on disabling an attacker. Maybe she should study this book.

She set the book aside and picked up her bowl of ice cream. As she savored the delicious dessert she considered the titles of the other two books. *Surgical Procedures* and *Police Procedures*.

Odd. Edward had always been well read, but those two were a little strange considering what had been going on. Maybe he'd looked into the subjects after all she'd told him. She supposed the horrific goings-on in her life at the moment were plenty enough to stir anyone's curiosity.

That could very well be the reason he had chosen to read them. Edward made it a point to keep up with basically any subject that concerned her.

The fact that she'd never had a decent father had not once bothered her because she'd had Edward.

Go to bed, CJ. She placed the books back in the order Edward had left them and turned out the light. In the entry hall she peeked out a window to ensure her surveillance was still on duty. Now that Nash was dead, that might no longer be necessary.

Braddock wasn't taking any chances. The car was there.

As she reached the second-story landing she heard the music again. Was Edward still awake? He'd never played music at night before. Okay, she was being beyond ridiculous here. Just because she'd spent a few nights here and hadn't heard music didn't mean he didn't ever play music.

She needed to stop second-guessing and analyzing everything. Maybe hearing about yet another murder had her nerves on edge. *Just stop, CJ.*

Edward was fine. She was fine. The decision to go back to Baltimore was a good thing. As much as she felt compelled to help here, for now her future was in Baltimore.

But that meant leaving Braddock. For the first time in her life she really wanted to be with someone, to see where it went. To try out the whole relationship thing.

A thump slowed her progress.

She turned back to the double doors leading to his suite. Was Edward ill? Maybe they'd missed something in the CT scan.

He hadn't been himself tonight.

She walked straight up to those double doors.

CJ bit down on her bottom lip and held her breath. She leaned close to the door and listened.

She could hear nothing but the music. She was being foolish. Going back to bed was by far the best idea.

The knob turned.

Her eyes widened and she stumbled back. As the door started to open she flatted herself against the wall behind the decorative column that stood on that side of the double doors.

Edward stormed to the stairs. His movements as he descended were stilted, angry.

She'd never seen him angry. Certainly not like this.

Just go back to your room, CJ. This is none of your business. She was being ridiculous. Hiding like this was childish. What would Edward think if he saw her?

Obviously he was all right. There could be something going on in his life that she didn't know about. He had been terribly upset by the meeting he'd attended.

She inched around the column, keeping an eye out for Edward to come stamping back up the stairs. As she stepped past the open doorway, a glimpse of Edward's suite snagged her attention. The walls were pink—soft, soft pink.

He liked pink? It was her favorite color, but she'd never known he cared for it. He was far too traditional for that.

She took a step into his private domain. Then another. The more she saw the more she had to keep looking.

The room was enormous. A massive canopy bed with sleek linens. More pastel colors. Fresh flowers all around the room. Four . . . five . . . six vases. The room was beautiful, but extraordinarily feminine.

So maybe Edward had a feminine side. A lot of men did.

Or maybe . . .

Oh, God.

This could be his mother's room. The flowers could be some sort of tribute to her. He rarely spoke of his mother, but when he did there was such reverence . . .

CJ shouldn't be in here.

She wheeled around, put one foot forward, and halted.

Edward stood in the doorway.

"I'm sorry." She glanced around the room. "It's a beautiful

room, but I shouldn't have come in here uninvited. I am so, so sorry."

He stared at her. Just stared. The tiny healing wound from the bump on the head he'd gotten in the fire reminded her he'd almost lost his life helping her.

She swallowed. The chocolate suddenly tasted bitter in her mouth. She shouldn't have spied on him like this. "Is everything okay?" Like her, he had no family left. That he still paid such tribute to his mother was likely a very private matter to him. He wouldn't want CJ intruding like this.

"I'm glad you like it." He slid his hands into the pockets of his trousers. He no longer wore the black tee and jeans. He'd changed into the usual gray trousers and a crisp white shirt.

She nodded. Looked around again. "And the flowers are gorgeous."

"They came from my garden."

"Wow."

He stepped into the room, surveying it himself as if for the first time. "I hoped you would like all the little touches. I took great pains in selecting each one."

She gripped the bowl of ice cream, nodded. She could not recall a time when she'd ever been this embarrassed or felt this awkward in his presence.

"Seeing you here," he said, "completes the room. Makes everything perfect."

She tried to force her lips into a smile, but what he said made no sense. "Thank you." Okay, it wasn't the right thing to say, but it seemed like what he expected.

"I've waited a very long time, CJ."

He came closer as he spoke.

Now she didn't know what to say. This felt wrong.

"I've watched you since you were just a girl. Waited. No matter the stumbling blocks thrown in our path, I never gave up."

Now she was seriously worried. He wasn't himself. The things he was saying were out of character. Maybe that knock on his head had shaken him more than either of them realized.

"Are you sure you're all right, Edward?" She tried to think how to explain her worry, but no words came.

"As you can see, there's no reason for you to be sad about having lost everything when the house burned," he went on as if she'd said nothing. "I had already taken the things you cherished the most for safekeeping."

As if his words had provided the necessary coordinates, she turned to the shelves that lined one wall, zeroed in on the framed photographs there.

The bowl in her hand hit the floor and bounced quietly on the carpet, sending chocolate drops splattering over her feet and the carpet.

She was moving toward the shelves, her movements on automatic pilot. She picked up first one, then another. Her and Shelley as kids. Teenagers. Even the one recent photo they had taken last Christmas.

"How . . . ?" She turned to Edward, the precious photo in her hand. "I don't understand."

"I knew you would want those near you."

But . . . how would he think she needed them *here*? And when had he taken them? The house had burned yesterday—day before yesterday.

"The house was falling apart. You no longer needed that burden."

"You . . ." He couldn't have set the fire—they were both inside. He wouldn't have taken that risk . . . would he?

"Our time has finally come, CJ." He reached out, caressed her cheek. "Nothing stands in our way now."

"I don't understand." Warning bells were going off inside her head. "In our way of what?"

"Of spending the rest of our lives together," he explained. "I've waited. Groomed you. Prepared you to be the perfect bride. You've almost completed your residency." He smiled. "Close enough. There's no need to wait any longer."

"I'm sorry." She backed away from his touch. "I don't understand what's going on here. This isn't your mother's room?" Her instincts were screaming at her to run. His words kep echoing in her head. Denial had swaddled her instincts. She couldn't think how to react. This couldn't be.

He laughed softly. "Of course not. This is *our* room."

All the times he'd been there for her, encouraged her, helped her to attain a goal, she'd counted herself lucky to have such a wonderful friend.

He hadn't wanted her to be his friend . . . ?

"Edward, I admire and respect you." She eased back another step. "I adore you. But like a father. Not like . . . that."

"I'm prepared to wait. You'll come to feel a physical attraction for me in time. I understand that you have needs. I overheard you and . . . Detective Braddock. But he is not the one for you. I am."

He'd heard them making love? Okay, this was way, way crazy. What he was proposing was surreal. "Edward—"

He held up a hand. "You don't have to say anything now. I know this is all a bit of a shock for you. But you'll see. Everything I've done has been for the best. I've always known what was best for you."

Fear, slithering and threatening, snaked its way up her spine. "What do you mean, *everything you've done*?"

"Sometimes the people we love hold us back. Sacrifices have to be made."

She stared at him, her heart refusing to believe what her brain was telling her. "What sacrifices?"

CHAPTER FIFTY-SEVEN

"I'm not talking until my attorney is present."

Braddock stalked back and forth in front of the interview table.

Cooper leaned across the table, glaring at Jenkins. "Listen, you little piece of shit, if you know what's good for you, you'll start talking now."

Jenkins moved his head side to side. "No way."

They'd put off allowing his call to an attorney in hopes of getting the truth out of him. The little bastard wasn't budging. Considering he didn't have a fucking clue what was happening, Braddock couldn't waste any more time. Every minute that passed allowed for the unexpected. He couldn't risk waiting this bastard out.

Braddock glanced at Cooper. "Go have a smoke."

She straightened, looked at her partner. "I quit smoking."

"Then go take a piss," he growled.

"Look." She turned to him. "This is one of those moments, Braddock. I'm your partner—you can't go doing stupid shit without me."

"Out," he ordered.

She looked from him to Jenkins, heaved a frustrated sigh, and walked out. Slammed the door.

Jenkins licked his lips, shifted as best he could considering his skinny ass was shackled to the chair. "You fucking touch me and I'll file charges, Braddock. The chief, the mayor . . . they're all watching this case. You can't fuck this up."

Braddock walked around behind him. He no longer felt angry or frustrated. He just wanted to tear this little fucker's head off. He grabbed a handful of his hair and yanked his head back. "Don't worry, the only thing I'm going to fuck up is you." Then he rammed the muzzle of his service revolver against Jenkins's temple. "Now talk."

Jenkins screamed.

Braddock released the safety on his weapon. The click resonated in the room.

"Okay! Okay!" Jenkins wailed. "It wasn't Nash. He killed Celeste, but he didn't kill the others."

"And how would you know this?" Fury pounded once more in Braddock's temples.

"Because . . ." Jenkins's eyes were wild with fear and something else Braddock couldn't label. "Because I was his lover. He confided in me!" Jenkins sobbed. "Told me everything."

"And you"—Braddock twisted his hair, garnering a yelp—"were his snitch."

"Yes! Yes! Please . . . please don't kill me."

"Is there a video?"

"Yes." Jenkins dragged in a quavering breath. "Yes," he whimpered. "I know where it's at. I can take you to it."

4:50 AM

The screen flickered and images came into view.

Braddock had accompanied Jenkins to where Nash's SUV had been towed by the forensic folks and retrieved the video from its hiding place. By the time they got back to the station the whole fucking world was standing by, casting accusatory looks at Braddock.

Like he gave a shit. He'd done what he had to do.

He and Cooper sat up straighter as images came into focus on the screen.

"You will do it!" Cost screamed at Shelley.

"Rewind it," Braddock ordered. His body literally shook with the anticipation now.

"Rewind." Cooper pressed the necessary button and the whir of the tape sounded. A click indicated it was back at the beginning. Cooper pressed play.

Shelley opened the front door and Cost stormed in.

"Fast-forward," Braddock ordered. "Do it slow, where we can see what's happening."

"Forward search," Cooper said as she pressed another button.

Braddock's heart threatened to burst out of his chest as he watched the altercation between Cost and Shelley play out without the sound effects. Finally the bastard stormed out the door. Shelley leaned against it and cried.

His heart ached for what this would do to CJ if she saw it.

The images faded to black. *What the hell?* There had to be more than that.

The screen flickered and Shelley was opening the door again. "Hit play," Braddock ordered.

Cooper hit play.

"What do you want?"

Edward Abbott stepped into view.

"What the fuck?" Braddock muttered.

"You made the first move, Shelley," Abbott said. "This is your game. What do *you* want?"

Shelley went toe-to-toe with the man and stuck her finger in his face. "I want you to stay away from my sister. I know what you're up to, and if you don't back off, I'm going to tell her about the cameras . . . about everything! Then she won't ever have anything to do with you again."

Abbott stared at her a moment. "Your whole life you've done nothing but try to hurt your sister. You're the one who needs to stay away from her."

"Who do you think you are?" she demanded. "You're nothing but a pervert. CJ's never going to love you. When I tell her, she'll see the truth. You're crazy."

Abbott grabbed her by the throat. "You will not"—he shook

her harder, squeezed her throat harder with every word—"tell her. If you do—"

Shelley ripped away from him, raced out the still-open door.

Abbott went after her.

A half minute turned to one and no one reappeared on the screen. The house remained empty. No sound. No nothing.

"Forward search again." Braddock couldn't breathe. This couldn't be what he thought.

He didn't know how many minutes elapsed. Suddenly Abbott appeared. Alone. He looked around the living room, then walked out of the house and closed the door.

Cooper turned to Braddock. "It was Abbott."

Braddock grabbed his keys from his desk and ran for the exit. He'd failed again.

He'd ordered CJ to stay put . . . with the killer.

CHAPTER FIFTY-EIGHT

"I only did what was necessary," Edward assured CJ.

This couldn't be happening.

Couldn't be real.

He couldn't have . . .

Wait. Stay calm.

CJ had to remember that she was alone with him in his home. The cops outside couldn't help her if they didn't know she was in danger. She had to play this out. Stay calm. Try to survive.

She forced air into her lungs. "Sometimes that's what we have to do." The words came out far steadier than she'd expected. Images of her sister running through those woods kept flashing in front of her eyes. He couldn't be saying that he'd killed Shelley.

That wasn't possible.

"That's so true." He smiled. "Unpleasant, but true."

Think! She needed an excuse to get out of this room.

She glanced at the melting ice cream on the pristine white carpet. "I'm sorry. I've made a mess. I should clean it up."

He caught her by the arm when she tried to move past him. "Don't trouble yourself. I'll have it cleaned."

"All right." She pushed a smile into place, felt her lips tremble despite her best efforts. "Wine would be good. We can toast the future. And closure on the past."

He stared into her eyes for a long moment. She prayed with all her heart that he wouldn't see the fear . . . the lie.

"That's a marvelous idea."

He kept his fingers wrapped around her arm and led the way to the stairs and then down. Each step sent her heart into a faster, more panicked rhythm. When they reached the entry hall, all she had to do was get away from him and run out the front door.

The police were right outside.

As if he'd sensed her thought, his grip tightened when they reached the entry hall. He held on so tight it hurt. She kept her mouth shut, pretended not to notice.

There was a rear entrance in the kitchen.

There were knives in the kitchen.

She would find a way to escape. She could do it.

The silence boomed in her ears. Should she say something? Anything?

When they reached the kitchen, he loosened his grip but didn't let go. He paused in front of the wine fridge. "How about that Saracco you love so much?"

"That would be wonderful." She swallowed back the panic. "I love the bubbles." What should she do? Panic swam in her veins.

He pulled a bottle from the fridge. His gaze settled on CJ once more. "I'm so glad we've gotten the ugliness out of the way. I don't want anything standing between us." He stared at the label on the bottle of wine. "Shelley made your life so unhappy. She made her own life equally miserable. She's at rest now. It's for the best."

Emotion rammed against CJ's sternum. She fought the rising sobs. Couldn't let herself break down. But she couldn't believe he would kill Shelley. It just didn't seem possible. "Edward . . ." She moistened her trembling lips. "Surely it was an accident. You didn't mean to—"

He slammed the bottle on the counter and glared at her. "Shelley was a sniveling whore. I could not let her ruin all that I'd worked for."

CJ's entire body shook. She tried to stop it. Couldn't. "But she was my sister." Blackness threatened. This was too much. It couldn't be . . .

His fingers dug into her flesh where he held her arm. "Are you questioning my decision?" His eyes were wild with fury. "After all I've done?"

CJ forced her head to move side to side. "I just . . ." *Think! Don't push him too far!*

"You just what?" he demanded.

"You killed her." She searched the cold eyes—the face—she didn't recognize. "Ricky? Juanita? Cost? I just don't understand how you could have done this."

"Mother warned me that you weren't suitable." The icy fury in his voice sent a new rush of fear crowding into her chest. "But I refused to listen. I knew." His expression turned wistful. "I knew without a doubt that I could nurture you, mold you into perfection. She tried to stop me, but I defied her every challenge. Ignored her every warning. You were worth any sacrifice."

"Edward." She had to make him see this was insane. "You're . . . you're not well. This isn't rational."

He grabbed her with both hands. Shook her hard. "Are you questioning my judgment?"

Heart pounding in her ears, she mentally scrambled for the right answer. She had to get the situation back under control. Had to escape. Arguing with him would only push him further over the edge. "I—I didn't mean to question—"

"Do you have any idea what I gave up for you?" he roared. "I struggled my entire life to live up to *her* standards. To prove I was worthy. Not like my father. But then I found you, and she . . ." Fury flashed in his eyes, flared his nostrils. "She tried to stop me. But I loved you more than her. I would not be stopped. Not by anyone."

Dear God.

"I'm sorry." CJ forced her lips to stretch into a wobbly smile. "Of course. You're right. I don't know what I was thinking. You did exactly what needed to be done. They . . . they were in the way of our future. How could I possibly be upset by all your hard work? You saved me." Tentatively, she reached up as if to hug him. He resisted at first. "Forgive me, Edward. I was a fool not to recognize immediately the brilliance in what you'd done."

For one endless moment he hesitated.

Please let him believe me.

Then he surrendered and she put her arms around his neck. She tiptoed, pressed her cheek to his. "Thank you," she murmured. "For loving me enough to sacrifice so much."

He embraced her tightly, his own body trembling now. "CJ, my sweet, sweet CJ."

She drew back only far enough to meet his eyes. "Let's have that wine now. We won't talk of those unpleasant things ever again. The future is all that matters now."

He smiled, relaxed his hold on her. "I knew Mother was wrong."

CJ reached for the bottle of wine. "We need the corkscrew and glasses?"

"We do." He smiled at her once more before reaching toward the drawer next to the wine fridge.

CJ's fingers tightened on the neck of the bottle. She hesitated a fraction of a second. He'd been her and Shelley's savior so many times.

Her hero.

More of a father than her biological father had ever dreamed of being.

And then she stopped thinking at all.

She drew back and swung the bottle with all her might. She slammed it into the side of his head.

He staggered back.

The bottle crashed on the marble floor.

And then she ran like hell.

She'd almost made it to the front door when she heard him crying her name.

Hurry!

She fumbled with the locks. Wrenched the door open and burst out onto the porch. She opened her mouth to scream—

Strong arms caught her.

Braddock.

"You okay?"

"Edward!" She turned to see if he was coming. "He killed Shelley! And the others."

Braddock pulled her to the side of the open door. Cops rushed up the steps, poured through the entry.

She swayed. Braddock steadied her.

How could this be real?

"He can't hurt you anymore."

She turned to Braddock. Fell into his arms and closed her eyes against the reality.

It seemed there was nothing but lies and betrayals and pain everywhere she turned.

Except here . . . right here . . . in this man's arms.

CHAPTER FIFTY-NINE

"Are you sure you have to do this?"

CJ looked into Braddock's worried eyes. He didn't want her to talk to Edward. But she had to. She had to ask him why.

All the books necessary to research electrical wiring, police procedures, surgical procedures—every detail essential to carrying out the murders—were in his personal library. Between the room he'd prepared for her, which was way, way over the line, deep into the obsession zone, and the items they'd discovered in his home, like the Taser and Shelley's cell phone, as well as cameras he'd obviously at one time had in her attic, and dozens of videos of her all through the years, they had sufficient evidence to go forward with charges for all the murders.

Possibly even his mother's. Considering all that he'd said to CJ, an order had been issued to exhume his mother's body and take a closer look at cause of death.

But Edward refused to talk. He hadn't uttered a single word since CJ had run out of his house.

She, Braddock, and Cooper had pieced together a theory. Edward had intended to make her his wife—the one he'd deemed his perfect mate. Shelley had interfered once too often for his liking and he'd gotten her out of the way.

The pain of it lunged deep into her heart like a knife.

He'd been so obsessed with the idea that CJ couldn't fail, had to accomplish all these goals. He must have been afraid Shelley would keep getting in the way. It seemed from the videotape that she had figured out he was basically insane and she'd confronted him. She'd obviously found his video equipment in the attic when she'd gone up there to set up her own.

And all this time CJ had thought she was the one doing the protecting. She'd had no idea what her sister had done in an effort to help her.

The Taser found in Edward's home was the kind used on Ricky, Lusk, Cost, and Tyrone.

CJ could only assume that Edward had killed Ricky because of something he knew. Maybe Shelley had told him what Edward was up to. Or perhaps he'd killed Ricky in hopes of putting an end to the investigation into Shelley's murder. Lusk and Cost because of what they had done to Shelley and how their actions hurt CJ. Or maybe because he feared her relationship with them would prevent her from going back to Baltimore. CJ couldn't be sure. She'd gone over and over everything she'd said to Edward about the victims. It seemed every one she'd complained about had ended up dead.

He'd killed Tyrone for obvious reasons. Tyrone had probably tried to blackmail him just as he had Cost.

Five murders. Five people had lost their lives. CJ just couldn't come to terms with all this.

"Whatever he says to you won't change anything," Braddock offered in a last-ditch effort to change her mind about talking to Edward again.

She pushed all the questions aside. "I know. But I have to have closure. I need to speak to him alone."

"All right. If that's what you really want."

A psychiatrist was scheduled to start an evaluation tomorrow morning. Edward likely wouldn't talk to him either.

"Don't worry," CJ assured Braddock. "He can't hurt me any more than he already has."

Braddock walked her to the holding area. "He's in a private cell. Don't get too close to the bars, okay?"

She nodded.

He gestured to the guard who opened the door. "I'll be right here," Braddock reminded her.

She nodded, then walked through the door that separated the common area from the individual holding cells.

"Last cell on your right, ma'am," the guard told her.

Her shoes creaked on the slick tile floor. She reached the last cell and turned to face the man who had betrayed her and her sister.

He sat on the bench staring at the wall.

"Edward."

He turned to her. Stared. Didn't speak.

"I need to know the truth."

He blinked.

"Did you kill Shelley because she discovered your video equipment? I just need to know what happened to . . . to trigger all this." CJ's heart wrenched with the misery that accompanied the words.

Edward said nothing.

She shook her head. Braddock was right. This wasn't going to help. He wasn't going to give her the answers she sought. And if he did, what difference would it make? Shelley was dead. They were all dead. Anything Edward said at this point might be some twisted, surreal version of the truth.

She took a breath, squared her shoulders. "I'm going back to Baltimore and finish my residency."

Another of those empty blinks.

"I'll be back to visit." Maybe if she goaded him . . . "Braddock and I are together now. When I return I'll be moving in with him."

Nothing. Not even a blink.

"I've never been in love before, but I think he's a man who'll be easy to love."

Still nothing.

CJ stared at Edward for a while. She wanted to remember every detail of this moment. The moment she realized that she was finished with allowing anyone else to run her life.

She was starting over. From now on her every choice would be her own.

"Goodbye, Edward."

She turned and walked away.

She didn't slow until she was on the other side of that big steel door and looking into the eyes of the future.

"You were right," she confessed. "Talking to him didn't change a thing." She reached up, put her arms around Braddock's neck. "I'm never looking back again. Only forward."

He kissed her.

And the hurt dissolved a little.

This wasn't the end . . . it was the beginning.

CHAPTER SIXTY

Edward stared at the place where she had stood.

His heart had already shattered into a million screaming pieces.

She was gone.

Nothing else mattered.

He had lost her.

Whatever the authorities did to him, he did not care.

His life was over.

His precious CJ was lost to him.

He closed his eyes and wrapped the agony into a small mental box and stored it away.

Edward!

His eyes opened.

Edward Abbott!

Did you really believe you could do such a thing? You possess neither the brilliance nor the courage to attain such a lofty goal.

You are just like your father and you always will be.

Edward nodded. "Yes, Mother." His mother was always right. "It's just as you say. I'm a failure, just as Father was. I'm nothing . . . *no one.*"

That was as it had always been and always would be.

But Edward had shown her—for his long-deceased father's sake as well as for his own—when he'd placed that feather-soft pillow over her sleeping face.

Edward had felt that same curious anticipation as he had when he'd watched her do the same to his drunken father.

Edward smiled. He might be no one, but she was the one rotting in the ground.

Bitch.

Sunday, December 17, 8:42 PM
Laurel, Mississippi

Jingle bell . . . jingle bell . . . jingle bell rock.

Danny Benson lay in bed and hummed the Christmas song. He didn't know all the words, but he liked this one a lot.

His mommy had told him at breakfast this morning that in just eight more days it would be Christmas. Another good thing about today was that it was the last day of school for two whole weeks. The paper ornament he had been working on at school was on the Christmas tree. Pretty soon his mom would put some presents with his name on them under the tree so he could try and guess what was inside.

But the bestest part of all was the stories she told him every night. Some of the stories were about the elves and the reindeers. His favorite one was about how good little boys always got what they wished the hardest for at Christmas.

But she hadn't come to his room to tell him a story tonight.

His dad was in one of his moods.

More of the yelling made Danny put his hands over his ears. He didn't like when his mommy and daddy had fights. Tonight was scarier than ever before. His daddy was screaming real loud. Saying the meanest things. Meaner than the other times when he'd yelled.

"I told you not to let this happen! Goddamn you!"

Danny pressed his hands harder against his ears, but he could still hear his mommy crying and his daddy yelling.

"Now look what you've done! You've ruined everything!"

Danny tried to block the bad words his dad kept yelling by singing along with the Christmas music. "Jingle bell . . . jingle bell . . ."

His mommy screamed. Danny burrowed deeper under the covers, but he could still hear her crying . . . crying and begging for his dad to please stop.

"There will be no princess in this house!" his dad shouted.

Something crashed. Sounded like glass. It was the same sound the kitchen window made when his baseball went through it last summer. His dad had been real mad about that, too.

The screaming and the crying stopped.

Danny dragged his hands from his ears. He lay still for a moment and listened to make sure it was really over.

No more screaming. No more crying. Just the Christmas music.

Jingle bell time is a swell time . . .

Maybe his mommy would come tell him a story now.

. . . to rock the night away . . .

His bedroom door flew open, banged against the wall.

"Danny!"

Danny bit his lips together to keep from crying out as his daddy jerked the covers off him.

"You should be asleep by now, son."

His daddy sat down on the side of the bed. Danny tried not to shake or to cry for his mommy. That would only make his daddy mad. He told his mouth to smile, but his lips just kept shaking like he was cold.

"Don't be afraid, son."

His daddy smiled at him, but the smile looked funny with all that red stuff smeared on his face. Why would his daddy have ketchup on his face?

"You don't have to worry about anything, son," his daddy promised. "No princess will ever take your place."

Friday, December 23, 10:30 AM
Huntsville, Alabama

The Christmas tinsel tickled her breast.

She shivered.

The shiny silver strands slid down her sweat-dampened torso. Over her belly button. Along her inner thigh. The tip of a deliciously wicked tongue followed that same path.

A sigh whispered from her lips. *God, that felt good.* But she was so ready to get on with it. This guy was evidently going for a foreplay record.

Adeline Cooper propped up on her elbows and peered down her nude body at the red and white hat. She couldn't believe she was about to say this. "Look, Santa, patience has never been one of my virtues."

Her lover lifted his attentive face from the task of tugging down her skimpy panties with his teeth. His brown eyes were glazed with the same anticipation currently throbbing through her veins.

"I'd like my present now." She crooked her finger. "Come on up here and show me what you've got besides that nifty hat."

His well-shaped mouth split into a grin as he crawled his way up her tingling body, all those gorgeous male muscles rippling with the effort. "Baby," he nipped her lips with his teeth, "I got the package you've been waiting for all year."

"Oh, yeah?" Adeline lifted her pelvis into that impressive package.

"Yeah," he growled as he nibbled her chin.

Pounding on the front door dragged her attention from his hungry mouth. *Damn.* "I should get that."

"It's your day off," he muttered between kisses.

"Yeah, well," she reached for the cuffs on the table next to the bed. "That's the thing about being a cop, there's no such thing as a real day off." She fastened one cuff around his wrist with a titillating click. "Now, don't move, because I'll be right back to interrogate you, mister." While she plundered his mouth with her own, she attached the other bracelet to the iron headboard.

Adeline scooted off the bed and grabbed his shirt. She poked her arms into the long sleeves and hugged the warm flannel around her. At her bedroom door, she paused, surveyed his long, lean frame stretched out on her bed, and made a sound of approval deep in her throat. *Merry Christmas to me.*

He plucked the Santa hat from his head and settled it over his erect penis. "Hurry on back, now," he teased, "and you can unwrap your present."

She would definitely hurry back.

Another round of pounding echoed from the front door. "Hold your horses," she shouted as she padded through the house. "I'm coming." Or she would be if whoever was doing all the banging hadn't interrupted.

She yanked open the door. "What?"

"Morning, Cooper." The man in the FedEx uniform, Wesley McElroy, nudged his Ray-Bans down his nose and surveyed her from head to toe. "You look all relaxed this morning."

"It's my day off," she said. She sent a pointed look at the large padded envelope in his arm. "That for me?"

"Yes, ma'am." He held out his electronic clipboard. "You need to sign for it."

She put her signature where he indicated. McElroy passed the large padded envelope to her. "You have a nice day now."

"You, too." Distracted by the sender's address, she pushed the door closed and leaned against it. Though she didn't recognize the specific return address, the location surprised her. Besides her mother, there wasn't a soul in Mississippi who would contact her. Not by mail anyway.

Both Christmas and her birthday were coming up . . . maybe her scumbag uncle had finally decided to forgive her for doing her job nine years ago.

"Yeah, right. And hell just froze over." She stalked into the kitchen and placed the envelope on the counter.

"Santa's waiting!" her cuffed lover shouted from the bedroom.

She ignored him. Her well-honed cop instincts were revving up, overriding all else. Getting anything from anywhere in

Mississippi was too bizarre to ignore—even for great sex. She dug up a pair of latex gloves and scissors. Pulled on the gloves and then slowly cut the envelope's flap free. Parting the severed edges carefully, she bent her head down and peeked inside.

Adeline jerked back. Her heart bumped her sternum.

"What the hell?" She tucked two fingers inside and pulled the item from the envelope. A white sheet of copy or printer paper.

More of that pulse-pounding adrenaline seared through her as she read the cut and pasted words.

Pretty, pretty princess. See her smile . . . see her die.

"Shit. Shit. Shit." Adeline dashed back to the living room and searched through the stack of old mail on the table by the door. In her haste, she sent junk mail and monthly statements fluttering to the floor.

Where the hell was that other letter? Unlike this one, the first letter had been hand-delivered to her mailbox. No return address, no postage. And no fucking prints.

She'd nagged the guys at work, thinking one of them had been playing a joke on her related to her birthday. She'd brought the letter back home that same day. It had to be here.

"Addy! What the hell are you doing?"

"Gimme a minute." She shoved a handful of hair behind her ear. The letter wasn't in the stack. What about . . . ? Hand shaking, she yanked open the drawer.

There it was.

She picked up the single sheet of plain white printer paper. Stared at the words that now carried entirely new significance.

She was born a princess for all to see. Her light was so bright that they could no longer see me.

Adeline returned to the kitchen to compare the two notes. Paper looked to be the same weight and shade of white. The way the words were pasted on the page, right side angled slightly upward, was the same.

She pushed the two letters to the side and looked in the envelope to see what else it contained. A newspaper clipping. Big article. Front page. She pulled it out. *Hattiesburg Press.* She read the headline.

City Attorney Cherry Prescott Missing.

Adeline skimmed the article. Prescott served as City Attorney to Hattiesburg. Four years older than Adeline, Prescott was married with two kids. A photo accompanying the article was in black and white, but the woman's smile was nothing less than dazzling—oozing self-confidence. Blond hair, pretty lady. According to the article, she was a brilliant attorney with a great future in politics. Prescott had gone missing three days ago.

Adeline braced her hands on the counter, analyzed the details a second time. The woman was presumed to have disappeared in the Three Rivers area . . . only a few miles from where Adeline had grown up.

There were no suspects as of yet. No ransom demand. Just the woman's abandoned vehicle. Her family was offering a sizeable reward for any information that helped to find her and the person responsible for her abduction.

Adeline threw her hands up. "What the fuck is this?" Why would some perv send her these stupid princess letters and an article about a woman who'd gone missing near her hometown? A woman she didn't know . . . had never even met? Adeline shook her head. Didn't make any kind of sense.

And yet, there had to be a reason.

Instinct nudged her.

There was some kind of connection here that she just couldn't see. This was no joke about her thirty-first birthday.

This was . . . a piece of some kind of creepy puzzle.

Setting the newspaper clipping next to the letters, Adeline opened the envelope wider to see if there was anything else she had missed.

A photograph. She frowned, then shook the envelope and allowed the photo to fall onto the counter.

The old Polaroid type snapshot.

Same woman, Cherry Prescott, pictured in the article. Only in this color snapshot her eyes were closed and she definitely wasn't smiling. No way to tell if she was dead or alive. No apparent injuries. Since only her upper torso and face were visible in the photo, there was no way to be certain of anything. Her makeup job was overdone, clownish; she wore a crown and nothing else as far as Adeline could see.

But it was the words scrawled across the image that sent tension roaring through her veins.

One dead princess, two to go.